Library of Congress Number: 2023943127

ISBN (paperback): 978-1-956450-76-7

ISBN (eBook): 978-1-956450-77-4

For further information, contact:

Thousand Acres Press

825 Wildlife

Estes Park, CO 80517

FAYTTE

Tim Rayborn

Praise for *Faytte*:

"Highly recommended... Tim Rayborn excels in crafting a fitting conclusion to his series. The action is fun and unpredictable, the characters multifaceted, and the plot evolves some satisfyingly unexpected twists that will keep prior fans and newcomers engrossed."

~ D. Donovan, Midwest Book Review

Praise for *Chantz*:

"There's never a dull moment when it comes to the lives of Qwyrk and Jilly, and Chantz continues to perform and enchant in new ways as we discover more about them and their friends. Readers will dive into another page-turning adventure full of not only myth and magic, but whole cauldrons full of wit and heart!"

~ Laura Tempest Zakroff, author of *Visual Alchemy* and *Weave the Liminal*

"*Chantz* neatly juxtaposes real-world concerns with the concurrent presence of magical forces underlying them for a rich read in fantasy and social ideals alike."

~ Donovan's Literary Services / Midwest Book Review

Praise for Lluck:

"Wacky... twisty... the dialogue is a demented fruitcake of British humor, and you won't be able to stop turning the pages."

~ Diana Paxson, author of *Sword of Avalon*

"Qwyrk is back along with Jilly, Blip (pardon me, Mr. Blippingstone) and friends for another adventure! In this tale, we get a deeper glimpse into Qwyrk's world, discover a boy of unusual circumstance and talent, and there's even a fabulous queer love interest, all tied into a race against the clock to save the world from a nefarious being. Tim serves up another fun romp through a well-built world, full of wit, mystery, and magic!"

~ LAURA TEMPEST ZAKROFF, author of *Anatomy of a Witch*

Praise for *Qwyrk*:

"Charming and funny, the characters are delightful. I wouldn't have missed it for anything."

~ PETER S. BEAGLE, author of *The Last Unicorn*

"In times when we all need distraction, here is a tale to take your mind off your troubles for a while."

~ DIANA L. PAXSON, author of *Sword of Avalon*

"Fans of Pratchett, Gaiman, Beagle, and de Lint will absolutely feel at home in this story! Such a fun read."

~ LAURA TEMPEST ZAKROFF, author of *Sigil Witchery* and *Weave the Liminal*

CHAPTER ONE

The whole peculiar business started with a key.

Winston Croaf enjoyed his daily without-fail stroll. He never took a set route, mind you, but preferred more of a meander. Each afternoon brought new possibilities, depending on his mood and the weather, inclement or otherwise. Today presented a mixed bag: clouds and rain and occasional sunny spells. And yet, he'd felt almost compelled to be outside and had chosen a route that took him to the very edge of Knettles.

He happened to pass by a rather large and long hedge at the town's northern end, with green fields beyond as the countryside beckoned. Not being in the mood for a more ambitious ramble, he opted to wander down a narrow dirt lane with hedge and country-side on his right and an array of houses in the distance to his left. Nothing seemed out of the ordinary at all.

Except for the key.

In fact, he mightn't have seen it at all, had it not been for a glint of sunlight illuminating its silvery shimmer at just the right moment. He stopped with a start, surprised by the antique, ornate object that hung by a maroon silk cord on one of the thorny, brambly branches of said hedge, set in a fair bit.

"How remarkable!" he said, looking about to see if anyone else was nearby. Satisfied that he was quite alone, he retrieved it. It seemed oddly warm for a metal object that had been outside in the autumn elements. As he closed his fingers about it, he felt as if it somehow called to him, almost as if it were trying to communicate. That was a rather strange, even ridiculous, notion. Keys open things; they don't speak, after all. In a moment, the sensation faded away until the mysterious object became merely a key again.

"Just my imagination, surely," he said, placing the unusual implement in his coat pocket and taking up his stroll again. "I'll have a closer look when I get home. It could be quite the find! Imagine, just hanging out here. What luck!"

Glancing up, he noticed that a dark cloud hovered over him and even seemed to follow behind as he made his way back to his neighborhood, but he put that notion down to nothing more than the changeable weather during this most changeable of seasons.

* * *

Qwyrk hit the ground hard.

Damn it! That hurt. She spun around to get back up as fast as possible. Her opponent wouldn't give her any time to recover. *Not that I'd expect it.* That thought only made her more determined.

She was on her feet again, arms up, fists clenched, fighting stance assumed. But her foe was gone. She looked around in confusion.

"What the hell? Where did you—"

A whack on her back sent her stumbling forward and another hit to the side of one foot tripped her and sent her crashing to the ground, flat on her face.

"Oh, you sneaky little—" She rolled over and jumped to her feet. "You're not catching me out again."

She lunged and tried to get ahold of her adversary's legs, but mistimed her jump and fell into empty air, and shortly thereafter, ended her flight with a third embarrassing collision with the ground. Her antagonist stepped to one side and brought another blow down on her back.

"Ow!" Qwyrk swore. "Right, that's it. I've had it!"

Waving her arm in a circle, she opened a portal of sparkling purple lights in front of her and rolled through, closing it so she couldn't be followed. A moment later, she reemerged directly behind her nemesis, whom she caught off-guard and trapped in a full headlock.

"Ha! Got you now... what?"

She wasn't quite sure what happened next, but it involved her being flipped over the head of her opponent, sailing through the air in a spiral and landing on the ground—yet again—with a spectacular thud. She lay still on her back, though everything was spinning.

"Bloody hell, where did you learn how to do that?"

She looked up to see Holly come into view, grinning from ear to ear. Holly, her girlfriend. Holly, the remarkable Indian Yakshi who was elegant, posh, and refined, but who could be utterly and brilliantly dangerous in a fight, which just made her all the more fanciable in Qwyrk's eyes. This well-equipped training room in Holly's home made Qwyrk appreciate her even more. Even if she did just get her arse kicked.

"Well," Holly answered as she knelt next to her defeated opponent, "I admit it was a rather cheap shot, but you did agree to no teleporting for this training session, so you cheated. Therefore, I was fully entitled to use everything I have at my disposal to teach you a lesson. Always ask yourself: what would you do if you couldn't teleport?"

"Call it a day and go home?"

"Qwyrk."

Qwyrk pulled herself up. "I know, I *know*. Look for the opponent's biggest weakness, exploit it."

"Exactly."

"And clock them in the sensitive bits, if they have them."

"I mean, I suppose?" Holly sat down on the floor.

"Yeah, all right, but look, in a real combat situation, I wouldn't be limiting myself."

"In a real combat situation, we wouldn't be sparring on soft mats."

"Um, excuse me, these are not 'soft'!" Qwyrk swatted the mat with one hand. "They hurt when you crash-land on them."

"Well, I wouldn't know," Holly teased. "It's not like you've ever knocked me down."

Qwyrk sat up and glared at her. "You are so going to get it!"

"I'm counting on it, but before that, should we train a bit more?" She grinned that vexatious yet adorable grin.

Qwyrk shook her head. "I'd love to go a few extra rounds, but I have a lookout in Pateley Bridge to get to in a bit. I'm still trying to make nice with the council after that whole buggane incident in Richmond."

"Too bad," Holly quipped. "I was so looking forward to throwing you around a little more." She retracted her Silambam stick and took it in one hand, balancing it on two fingers.

"Oh, you'll get what's coming to you, missy," Qwyrk mock threatened.

"Now you're just tempting me." Holly stood and offered Qwyrk a hand up at the same time. "So, my turn: can I possibly tempt you with a shower before you go? A lovely, outdoor magical cascade of water amongst the trees?"

"You can indeed, and normally I'd jump at the chance, but I can't right now. Sorry, love. I've been trying to make sure I'm on site early for every assignment these days, just so I don't have to listen to those council twats yap at me again. But," she wrapped her arms around Holly's waist, "maybe a bath later? At my place? Candles? Some sort of adult beverage that will have no effect on us whatsoever?"

Holly smiled a dreamy smile. "Mmm, sounds lovely. Wait a minute." She took a step back. "Is this just an excuse to try out more of those ridiculous bath bombs of yours?"

"No!" Qwyrk answered, stepping back and crossing her arms in a defensive posture. "Well, I mean, it's not the main reason—that would be *you*, obviously—but I like to have a go with new ones. You know, just to try them out?"

Holly raised a skeptical eyebrow.

"What? They're really nice, I'll have you know. I have a new thematic collection..."

"Mmm hmm."

"...based on classic works of human literature."

"Oh, really?" Holly's eyebrow raised even higher.

"Yeah, they've all got witty and clever names, like—"

"Like what?" Holly crossed her arms, too.

Qwyrk looked down. *The Sud Also Rises.*

"That's appalling."

"And, *The Way We Lave Now.*"

"Oh, Goddess."

"*Great Exfoliations?*"

"Why?"

"How about, *Macbath: Bubbles for Your Toils and Troubles?*"

Holly put a hand to her face. "These are even worse than those dreadful film titles from last week."

"Hey! *Hell Bent for Lather* is quite amusing, thank you very much!" Qwyrk declared, uncrossing her arms just to cross them again.

"Let's agree to disagree, shall we?"

"What's wrong with *The Seven-Per-Cent Ablution?*"

"How long do you have for an answer? I thought you needed to go."

"*Gel or High Water?*"

"You're not helping your case here, I should just like to point out."

"Come on, *Episode IV: A New Soap*... you have to admit that's pretty clever!"

"I don't have to admit anything."

"You're no fun. Like, not at all."

"I'm cracking good fun, thank you very much."

Qwyrk smiled. Holly smiled. The smiles turned into laughter.

"Yeah, you really are." Qwyrk leaned in and kissed her. "But I do have to go. We can discuss the merits of bath bomb wordplay later."

"I'm not sure there are any, but I look forward to your attempt to convince me."

Qwyrk gave her a wink and blew her a kiss before circling her arm in the air and conjuring up the ancient magic that whisked her away to places and tasks decidedly less soapy and appealing.

*   *   *

"This time of year is quite appealing, it must be said!" Blip declared, gazing out the window of Jilly's living room at the autumnal foliage and the varying types of seasonal weather blowing across the sky. "Shorter days, a chill and chimney smoke in the air, a brandy to keep away said chill, a good bit of spookery from the old Irish traditions, it's all rather grand. I can almost see why those goth bohemians you are so enamored of try to keep the spirit going all year. Good heavens, the 'spirit.' Ha! A fine one, even if I didn't intend it."

"It's very funny sir," Jilly answered, trying not to encourage him too much; Blip puns were the worst. She looked down at her laptop and tried to seem busy, hoping he wouldn't launch into either a lecture on some philosophical topic, or a lesson on the history of Halloween.

"So, will you be celebrating this Samhain?" he asked instead. "I can hardly imagine a witch of your talents allowing such a prime holiday to go to waste without some ritual or other to mark the changing of the days."

She looked up at him and shrugged. "I hadn't really given it too much thought, to be honest. I suppose I should do something, but with Granny always in and out whenever she pleases, I've no idea if she has anything planned, or if she'll even be here. I suppose it's odd that she hasn't said anything yet. Halloween seems like something we should be marking, somehow."

"And you are too old for tricks and treats, I presume?"

"Yeah, it's been a while since I've done that. You asked me that last year, and I told you the same thing then, remember?"

"Did you? Oh, well, I suppose I'd forgotten. I am rather busy, you know."

"With what?" She'd been asking him since last spring why he'd been so preoccupied, and each time, he'd evaded her and given less than satisfying answers.

"Oh, you know, this and that. There are boring administrative chores, filings, reports, and so on."

"Reports? Like, about me? I can't imagine I'm that interesting!"

"Oh no, not about you, my dear. It's more, how shall one say, in the manner of routine observations of the magical realms, you see, and how they intertwine and interact, that sort of thing. I don't just provide intellectual companionship, you know. We jirry-jirries have several appointed tasks, and our keen observations help to keep the magic machine running smoothly, if I may use an Industrial Revolution metaphor."

"It sounds terribly exciting," she said without any conviction.

"Oh, I admit that it might not seem scintillating, but there is much satisfaction to be drawn from the mystical surveying that we do, studying the enchanted landscape, making note of the magical patterns, and so on and so forth. It's rather like weather forecasting. In fact, I'm reminded of a passage from Aristotle's *Meteorologica*, wherein he states—"

"Excuse me sir, I have a bit of a headache, I think I'm going to go upstairs and take something for it, and then lie down for a while." It wasn't the most elegant of fibs, but she improvised. And she was a bit tired, so that much was true, at least.

"Of course, my dear, do what you need to do. You've seemed rather distracted this afternoon, anyway. We shall leave the discussion of the *Meteorologica* for another time."

"Thank you, sir. I just want to have a lie-down for a bit. I might even take a short nap."

"If you must, but do try not to be overly idle."

"I'll keep that in mind." She closed her laptop, grabbed her sketch book, and ascended the stairs, though not quickly, lest she look overly eager to avoid his latest lecture. It was a rather desperate little plan, but it worked, and in fact, a nap sounded like a very good thing right about now, come to think of it.

*   *   *

Holly busied herself with putting away the training mats she'd just happily dumped Qwyrk on to, musing on besting her worthy opponent, and just how deliriously happy she'd been these past six months. A memory flashed into her mind about something strange that had happened one night around Beltane, but it faded almost as soon as it appeared.

"Nothing important, I suppose," she said as she tidied up. "Even the trees outside Qwyrk's home stopped wandering around right about then. I'm sure it was all just some residual magic from some inept spell-caster. Maybe I dreamed it—"

A wave of pain rushed into her head. She cried out and fell

to her knees, clutching at her temples. Surge after terrible surge pounded through her and she feared she might pass out. She saw herself in a dark area. In the distance, a shadowy, robed figure seemed to be waiting, arms folded and hands hidden in its sleeves. There was something familiar about it, as if she'd seen it before. Did it say something to her? She thought words formed in her head, but the figure faded back into the dark before she could make them out.

"Beti?" she heard a voice say, and she was back in the training room, crouching on the mat. Through the agony, she looked up to see her mother, Vishala, running to her and kneeling, reaching out to comfort her. "Beti, what is wrong? What is happening?"

At once, the pain passed. Holly lurched forward, feeling sick to her stomach. That sensation soon faded, though her face felt hot and flushed and she breathed in gasps, each intake of air bringing her back to her senses. She looked up at Vishala.

"Mother? What happened?"

"I do not know. Tell me, Beti, tell me what you felt."

"It was horrid. Qwyrk just left. We'd been training. One moment, I was fine, and then I was in agony. It was like a hammer was striking at my head, but now it's passed. I closed my eyes and saw... something? I can't remember what. I've had several of those kinds of experiences recently, at least I think I have."

"Since when? For how long?"

"I don't know, maybe since spring? It's like I'm in one place and then somewhere else, and then I'm back, but I never remember what I saw, or if I saw anything at all, or if it was just my imagination. Sometimes I think they're just bad dreams or that I'm tired. It hasn't happened for a while I don't think, but this one was vivid.

And it hurt. There's always someone there, wherever it is I go, or whatever I see."

"Someone? What someone? What do you see? Who is there?" Vishala held her by the shoulders in a firm grip and looked at her with a worried expression.

"I don't know." Holly shook her head. "I feel like I should, but I can never remember. I think it might be a woman? In a robe? A red robe? But that may just be me making things up. Oh, maybe I'm just going mad!"

Vishala gazed at her with concern and perhaps a hint of fear, shaking her head a little.

"What is it, mother? What's happening?"

"I'm not sure, my child. But we will find out, I promise you."

Holly gave her a weak nod, but she thought her mother knew more than she was saying.

* * *

Qwyrk settled into an alleyway in Pateley Bridge, keeping out of view to avoid being seen by humans, which would just cause a panic and make everything so much bloody worse. No one in this small and charming Dales town would expect to run into a shadow with glowing red eyes, and she wanted to keep it that way. This particular excursion seemed like a rather stupid assignment, anyway: a Nighttime Nasty break-in at a local bakery.

"Way more than rather stupid. Probably trying to steal food for Bogtrotter. I swear if I didn't need those pillocks for information now and then—"

She heard voices and melded into the shadows of a nearby

corner. It wasn't dark enough yet to truly hide, but the clearing skies afforded some nice lighting contrasts.

"What're we doin' tonight, then?" one squeaky voice asked.

"We're making some foods for a banquet hosted by his eminence," a squeakier voice answered.

Those bastards, I knew it! Qwyrk thought. She saw two small creatures, no more than two feet tall each, saunter into view. They wore ill-fitting clothes that looked like rejects from an amateur Shakespeare production. One seemed to be a tiny version of a bulbous-nosed goblin or troll, while the other resembled a bipedal honey badger.

"Yeah? What's gonna be on the menu, then?" the goblin asked.

"Rat pasties and beetle butties. Got the bag of beetles right here!" The diminutive honey badger produced a burlap sack.

Qwyrk shuddered, being quite happy that she didn't need to eat, Holly's mum's excellent food notwithstanding.

"Ooh, I do love a good rat pasty!" the goblin cooed. "Especially all smothered in gravy with a side of moldy carrots and grubs."

"Yeah, that's the delicacy, and the master specifically requested we make it."

"How many do we need to do?"

"About a hundred or so."

"And why're we makin' them here, then?"

"Don't know. We was just told to use the facilities at this 'ere bakery in this 'ere town, and someone else would join us in a bit. I does not ask questions. I just does the work."

Yeah, that's odd, Qwyrk pondered. *Why here?*

"We should get on inside," the badger continued. "The owner

closed up shop early today, so we'll have the run of the place. Since the kitchen's in the back, no one will even know we was there."

"Yeah, until they come in next morning and see our rubbish and smell the rat pasty!"

"But that ain't our problem, is it? We'll be long gone by then, ha ha!"

"Actually, lads," Qwyrk announced, stepping out from her hiding place, "I'm pretty sure you're going to have to make other arrangements for your Nasty nosh, since I'm shutting down this little culinary operation now. Oh, and kicking your tiny arses all the way to the end of Nidderdale and back. That'll be happening, too, just so you know."

"Aw, shite!" The badgerling dropped his bag brimming with beetles.

"Yeah, that's usually what you lot say when one of us shows up. I never get tired of hearing it, to be honest." Qwyrk made threatening fists. "So, who's first?"

"We don't want no trouble, Qwyrk," the goblin pleaded, hands held out in supplication. "We just wanna make food for the boss, meet our third, and go."

"Yeah, see, there's a slight problem with that. You'll foul up everything in there and leave a big mess behind for the owners to have to clean up and wonder where the hell it came from."

"True," the goblin conceded. "But it'll be right funny!"

Qwyrk took a menacing step toward him, and he flinched, holding his gnarled hands up over his face. "All right, all right! I was just havin' a laugh!"

"I'm not laughing."

"That's 'cause you're a pretentious, humorless, grumpy, walkin' snooze-fest, ain't ya? I mean, that's what everyone says."

"W-wait, what?" Qwyrk sputtered, momentarily forgetting the thrill of the arse-kicking she was about to administer. "Who says that?"

"You know."

"No, I damned well don't! Who the bloody hell is calling me all that?"

"Well, the boss, for one."

"Oh, he does, does he? Maybe it's time for me to pay him another visit."

"Yeah, but let's be honest, he ain't the only one."

"Snickle!" the honey badger belted out, "shut it!"

"No, please, do tell." Qwyrk folded her arms and glared.

"I mean, it's not something *I* personally believe..."

"But?" She glared harder.

"But I've heard, ya know, a number of NNs—just here and there mind you—say that you're, um, boring and always angry."

"For Goddess' sake, I am not always angry! Why would anyone think that?" Her eyes started to glow red.

"You're uh, you're threatenin' to thump us right now, yeah? All the way up Nidderdale and back, you said?"

"That's because you're about to use a human kitchen to make some absolutely revolting food for your complete wanker of a boss and his stupid ego bash. It's my bloody job!"

"Yeah, but you do kind of enjoy it a bit too much."

She threw out her hands. "Well, you lot make it easy to enjoy! Look, to show you I'm not perpetually livid and just taking it out on you, go on: turn around and walk away right now, and I won't thump you. We'll pretend this whole thing never happened and you can go prepare your—whatever the hell those things are—over an open fire somewhere far from human view. Fair enough?"

"Fine!" Snickle snorted. "But if the rat pasties are undercooked and the banquet is thus sullied, it'll be on your conscience!"

"I'm pretty sure I can live with that."

"Hmph!"

The two little creatures turned and stomped off, bags and bushels in hand, huffing and puffing, but no doubt glad to have avoided the arse-kicking into scenic parts of the Dales that Qwyrk had promised. She waited and watched until they were well out of sight, then waited a little while longer to make sure they didn't try to sneak back and just do it anyway.

"Right, that was the most ridiculous assignment I've had in a long while," she sighed. "And how dare they? Boring and angry... really? I'm not! I'm so not!"

But the more she thought about it, the more it bothered her. If the Nasties had that opinion of her, what did others think?

"Oh, why should I care? They're just a bunch of tossers, anyway. It's not like... whoa!"

A wave of dizziness washed over her, enough to make her stumble and have to steady herself with one hand on the closest wall.

"What the hell?" she said, putting a palm to the side of her head. "That was crazy! That was—"

Another spate of spinning slammed her, and she nearly fell over. She dropped to one knee, clutching her head.

"All right, this is not good at all! What is going on?"

The second spell ended as abruptly as it had begun, and everything returned to normal. Whatever that meant these days.

"I need to get out of here. Maybe it's some Nasty magic, revenge from those two for chucking them out."

She looked at the little gold ring in her right hand, set with a small green gemstone.

"Holly? It's me. Um, I don't feel so good, and I want to stop by."

She waited, but there was no answer.

"Holly?"

Nothing.

"Damn it, where is she? What's going on?"

She stood up, relieved that no more dizzy spells descended on her, and resolved to go Holly's home at once. As her head cleared and the spinning stopped, she had a vague memory pop into her mind of something that might have occurred months ago, something disturbing and worrying, but she couldn't recall the details.

Shaking her head, she swirled one hand in a circular fashion, drawing a halo of violet, sparkling lights in the air. She stepped into them and vanished from this place, focused only on finding her girlfriend and figuring out what the blazes was going on.

*　　*　　*

Jilly opened her eyes. She was lying on her bed, her laptop and sketchbook right next to her where she'd left them after escaping another Blip lecture from Hades.

"So, I did nap!" She looked at the clock. "But only for about twenty minutes."

She flipped open her laptop and checked her email.

"Oh brilliant!" She was thrilled to see a new message from Moirin Moeran, the fabulous young singer of the Mystic Wedding

Weasels whom she'd helped out of a predicament last spring, or rather, whom she'd helped to escape the clutches of an ancient and evil banshee who just happened to be her great-great-one-hundred-times-grandmother, or some such. Moirin had promised to stay in touch, though she hadn't always been so good about it. Jilly expected as much from a rock star, but when Moirin did write to her, it was always the highlight of her day.

She opened the email and read it aloud: "Hi Jilly, Moirin here. So sorry not to write sooner. It's been a strange time, these last few months. Anyway, I wish I could say all's well, but it's not. I think I'm trouble again. And I need your help. Let me know if I can phone you. Luv, Moirin."

Jilly read it again, and a third time. Something dawned on her. "Last time she was here was right at Beltane, and now Samhain's coming up. Pretty sure that's not a coincidence."

She scooped up her laptop and left her room, bounding down the stairs to see that Blip was still there sitting on her sofa, ensconced in another of his philosophical tomes.

"Ah, Ms. Pleeth, I trust you've fully recovered? If so, I am glad to hear it, so that we can revisit our study of—"

"Sir? I've got some news."

"News?" He set down the book.

She nodded. "And it might not be good."

CHAPTER TWO

"It's rather extraordinary, wouldn't you say?" Winston held up the hedgerow key admiringly. He let the last of the afternoon light reflect off it through the large window of his sitting room, a charming, if cluttered makeshift study comprised of a large, antique desk, a few chairs, and walls lined with dark, old bookcases filled with more books than could probably be counted with any accuracy. More piles of reading material were stacked in even (and not-so-even) manners at various places on the hard wood floor, several of them threatening to topple over without warning, which would cause quite the calamitous nuisance.

"It is quite unusual, Winston," Penelope Weatherwick said, smiling and trying to be attentive. She had a terrible fondness for him, this odd but charming professor who'd taken early retirement for reasons he'd never made quite clear, and now liked to fuss over the most unusual things. "And it was just hanging in the hedge, you say?"

"Quite! I've never seen anything like it."

"I can't imagine why such a lovely thing would just be left outside like that."

"Nor I, especially since it bears all the hallmarks of an antique. I'd hazard a guess that, based on the style alone, it must be at least twenty-five hundred years old—possibly older—but it looks as if it were made yesterday. I simply cannot fathom that discrepancy. Absurd as it sounds, it's almost as if it were thrust through time from that long-gone age to now, with no intervening centuries at all. Most peculiar!"

"And you've never seen one like it before, out on your walks, I mean?"

Winston shrugged. "I've been by that very place a dozen times this year, and there was nothing there. It must have been placed by someone, and rather recently."

"Do you think it was stolen? Perhaps from a museum, or some such?"

"It's certainly possible. But why would someone simply leave it there?"

Penelope entertained a disturbing thought. "Unless they were planning for someone else to come along and take it first. Oh, Winston, what if you've gotten yourself entangled in some sort of crime? Should we alert the police? What if someone saw you and comes looking for it?" Penelope found herself now panicking over worst-case scenarios involving criminal masterminds doing nefarious things. She was well aware that she watched too many police procedurals on television.

"I find it highly unlikely, my dear."

She always blushed with delight when he used words like that. If only she could tell him how she really felt...

"It would be a damned foolish way to commit a crime," he went on. "Leaving the artifact out in the open, risking someone else coming along and taking it first, like me? No, I suspect there is something deeper happening here, a genuine mystery as odd as the history of this old town. And I intend to get to the bottom of it!"

"I'd be delighted to help you, Winston!" She regretted looking over eager.

"And I should be most grateful for your assistance, Ms. Weatherwick," he answered.

Relief flooded through her. At last, a project to work on, together! "Where do we begin?"

"At the beginning, I suspect, which means looking at the town records to see if there is anything out of sorts about the area in which I found it. From there, we will attempt to see if we can date the key and learn a bit more about who might have made it. From there..."

Penelope smiled. She loved watching him immerse himself in a new academic undertaking. If only she could shake the feeling that something seemed off about this situation, and that they wouldn't like what they would find.

*   *   *

"So, Ms. Moeran has reached out to you, apparently in some distress," Blip pondered.

"Looks that way," Jilly said, trying not to sound sarcastic.

"And she's been in touch at other intervals in the past, I presume?"

"Not a lot, but now and then. Things seemed all right before, but maybe she wasn't telling the truth."

"It is a possibility, though we must presume that her current situation is indeed dire. You've not spoken on the telephone yet?"

"No, I thought I should tell you first, and maybe Qwyrk. I figured you might want to listen in, though that's a bit deceptive. I think she only wants to talk to me."

"Underhanded it may be, but it could also be a wise strategy. I should like to be privy to this conversation, and I suppose Qwyrk and Vishala the Younger should probably attend as well." He gave the slightest sneer that suggested he'd be quite happy to leave them out of it.

"I feel a bit guilty about you all being there," she said to deflect the idea of excluding them.

"You have a means of contacting Qwyrk then?"

"Uh, a few actually, but they're not always reliable."

"Color me surprised. Why hasn't her sweetheart given you one of those rings of hers, the ones that let you talk like some kind of trans-dimensional Forkbeard device?"

"You know about Forkbeards?"

"Very little, I am happy to declare. Mainly from the fact that Ms. Holly pretended to be using one that evening when we waited in the queue to see Ms. Moeran and her ensemble in York. Since I could not be seen, she thought it wise to appear to be talking to someone via one of those damnable contraptions, so as not to appear mad. A sensible precaution that deflected any curious onlookers, even from among that rabble of oddities. In any event, you don't have one of those trinkets, then?"

"I never really thought about it," Jilly said, realizing he had a good point. "I guess I never figured I'd need to speak just to her, since she and Qwyrk are always together."

"They are individuals, Ms. Pleeth. Do not view Ms. Holly as a mere appendage of Qwyrk. She's quite remarkable in her own right."

"Oh, I know that," Jilly said. "I'm the one that nudged Qwyrk to ask her out, remember?"

"I do. And a good thing that you did. Ms. Holly has been quite the maturing influence on Qwyrk, who is now the better for it, irritating though she remains. A few more years in her gentlewoman's company, and she may yet be tolerable."

"That's one of the nicest things you've ever said about Qwyrk," Jilly joked.

"I think you should contact Ms. Moeran and cease trying to be funny," Blip retorted. "Do that thing you do, what is it? Scribing? Quilling?"

"Texting. On my phone. The one my parents got me. I think as an apology for always ignoring me?"

"Yes, that. Do that, and arrange a time when we can all be a hidden audience."

"It still seems dishonest."

"My dear, a bit of skullduggery may be called for in this situation. I for one, am fairly bursting to know more of the issue at hand!"

Jilly nodded, though she found it rather odd that he seemed so eager to eavesdrop, something decidedly un-Bliplike. But she let it pass and texted Moirin.

"What happens now?" Blip asked.

"Now we wait until she gets back to me. Could be a few minutes, could be a few hours."

"Excellent! Time enough to delve into Aristotle, then!"

Knowing she had no escape, Jilly resigned herself to her fate.

* * *

In a flash, Qwyrk blinked back to Holly's training room, where everything had been put away nice and proper, nothing out of order. But Holly was gone, even though she'd seemed quite set on training a bit more on her own. Forcing herself not to be too worried—and failing rather spectacularly at it—Qwyrk left for the main portion of the house, where an eerie silence seemed to have settled.

"Um, hello? Anyone home? Holly? Srimati Vishala? Mango? Minty? Anyone?"

Met with no response, she checked the kitchen and the main sitting room, both empty. With trepidation, she made her way up the stairs to Holly's bedroom, tried the door, and found it to be unlocked. Opening it, she beheld a sight both relieving and unsettling: Holly lying in her bed, being attended by her mother and the family cats, who sat next to her, presumably prepared to administer their own special form of feline pharmaceuticals.

"Oh, Goddess! Holly, what happened?" Qwyrk rushed in, scarcely acknowledging the others, before realizing her rudeness and stopping to bow her head to Vishala.

"After you departed, my Beti was taken ill, with a terrible pain to the head, Shadow Qwyrk," Holly's mother answered before she could. "I insisted that she retire to her chamber and lie down."

"I'm fine now, mother, honest," Holly said, clearly exasperated. "Hello again, darling. I hope you didn't interrupt your assignment just for me?"

"Just for you? Are you kidding me? A herd of pissed manticores wouldn't keep me away!" She turned to Vishala. "Srimati, may I speak with her alone?"

Vishala nodded. "But do not tire her out." Vishala stood up and made for the door in her most elegant manner. "I will be in the kitchen if you need me. Food is a remedy for everything, and later on, we will dine well."

"Thank you, mother," Holly said, with a genuine look of gratitude.

Qwyrk eyed the finicky felines still flopped by her. "Um, alone?"

"What?" Minty said, looking up, as if in shock. "We weren't doing anything, we were just sitting here."

"Yes, exactly. Sitting. *Here.* I want you to be sitting outside the door, *there.*" Qwyrk pointed. "Get it?"

"Fine!" Minty grumbled, rousing himself as if with great effort, stretching and leaping off the bed, trotting away to find something to complain about.

"You too." Qwyrk looked at Mango.

Mango opened his eyes and yawned. "I was sleeping. I wasn't paying attention to anything you said about wanting to be left alone... damn it!"

"Off you go then, dear," Holly said with a scritch on his head. "I'm sure mother will find something tasty for you to eat if you go and bother her a little."

"Well, I am rather starving," the cat admitted, and with that, he followed his brother out the door.

Once everyone was well out of the way, Qwyrk leaned in for a kiss and an embrace. "For the record, I'd swim across the great ocean and wander through every domain of the World Tree 'just for you.' So, what happened?" She stroked Holly's hair, fearing the worst, despite all assurances to the contrary.

Holly replied in kind, running her hands through Qwyrk's short hair. "You're a treasure. It's nothing much, really. After you left, as I was putting away the mats. I had a series of headaches, surges of pain. They came about suddenly and made me feel quite ill for a short time. Then mother found me on the floor, but soon, the pain vanished."

"Oh, Goddess! Holly, I'm so sorry!" Qwyrk took her hands and held them with a firm grip.

"I'm fine now, I promise," Holly protested.

"But, do you know that? I mean, really? That's not something that should happen to you."

"No, but honestly, I feel perfectly well. I'm just sitting here because mother insisted. If it were up to me, I'd go downstairs and start training again."

"Well, good thing it's not up to you," Qwyrk said.

"Oh, please don't start sounding like her," Holly said with a pout. "Between her and the cats, I'm quite put out by the overprotective parenting at the moment."

"I just want to make sure you're all right."

"I know, and you're a love for doing so." She squeezed Qwyrk's hands and smiled.

"The thing is," Qwyrk said, "something happened to me, too, out in Pateley Bridge." She scrunched her nose in confusion. "Something really odd."

"What was it?"

Qwyrk relayed the strange events of her encounter with the Nasties and their proposed culinary adventure (which Holly thought was as revolting as she did), and the sudden onset of spinning and dizziness that followed from it.

"Oh, darling, I'm so sorry. Are you well, now?"

"Like you, I feel just fine. It was there one moment, and gone the next, like someone had flipped off a switch."

"Exactly! Only..." Holly frowned.

"Only what?"

"It's very odd, but at the same time, I had a flash of a memory of something happening to us, I think. Do you remember a strange event occurring right around Beltane? It would have been after we sent off Aeval and Aileen at Moirin's show in Newcastle, I think. Something that night, or maybe a day or two later?"

Qwyrk felt a tingle in her belly and had a sense of something creaking open. "Yeah, I *do* remember something. But I don't know what it was. Something bizarre definitely happened then, but for the life of me, I can't recall exactly. It seems like it was—"

"Dangerous?"

"Yes! Even threatening, like we had to fight something that wasn't the banshee. But what was it?"

"I don't know." Holly sat back. "The pain seems connected to it somehow. I remembered more when the headaches hit, but now it's all obscure again."

Qwyrk nodded. "I felt the same when those dizzy spells came on. It was like a few moments of clarity—"

"And then the door shut again."

"Exactly!" Qwyrk snapped a finger. "It's like a door." Like a long-shut door to a dark, upstairs room that she wasn't allowed to enter.

"What do you think it is? Do you suppose this has something to do with that war that Aeval told you about at Castlerigg, the whole secret Darkfae conflict thing? She did say it was going to get worse."

"I'm not sure," Qwyrk said with a shake of her head, "but you might well be right. It'd be just like them to rope us into that bloody nonsense, somehow. I think someone's been using magic to mess with our memories, and when I find out who it is, I'm going to knock their damned head so far into the ground, they'll be looking for fossils."

"You and me both, you mean," Holly said.

"Yes, yes, of course. Uh, I did it again, didn't I? That whole 'speaking for you' thing?"

"A little, but under the circumstances, I understand. It sounds like we need to pay a visit to Qwyzz about this. If our memories have been altered by magic, maybe he can recover them. Perhaps we'll even learn who did it."

"You read my mind, darling. I'll check. If he's free, we can go on over there tonight. I don't want to wait on this."

"Assuming my overprotective mother even lets me get out of bed," Holly said, folding her arms, and Qwyrk knew she was only half-joking.

"I would say leave that to me," Qwyrk said, "but honestly, she still sort of terrifies me, six months on. How long before she finally accepts me?"

"I'm quite sure she already does."

"Well, she has an odd way of showing it." Qwyrk gestured toward the door and the kitchen.

"That's just how she conducts herself," Holly assured her. "But I've seen how impressed she looks when you're around. She's grown very fond of you, even if she's a bit uptight about admitting it."

"Uptight? I've seen statues with more emotion!"

"I know, I know, but after fifteen hundred years, I've quite the good sense of her moods, and I'd be willing to bet she's firmly on team Qwyrk by now. Speaking of statues, we *will* have to get past the fearsome gargoyle guard, I presume?"

Qwyrk groaned. "He was kind of amusing in a perverse sort of way. For a while. Now he's just bloody irritating."

"Well, I still want to see him dance someday."

"Oh Goddess, no." Qwyrk tensed up.

"And you, for that matter! You still owe me a performance of Bogtrotter's turgid Terpsichore."

"Yeah, don't hold your breath, love."

"I'll get it out of you eventually."

"Forever is a long time, and we've got forever," Qwyrk taunted.

Holly shrugged. "I'm patient."

"Just not *a* patient."

"Not at the moment, despite the best efforts of everyone else in this house to turn me into one, present company excepted."

"Well, just in case you're prescribed bedrest, be prepared to sneak out later."

"Ooh, I love it. Creeping out of the house undercover to go get into trouble. It'll be like being seventy-five years old again!"

"Yeah, that's us. Bloody juvenile delinquents."

"I'll get into trouble with you any time." Holly nudged her.

"I know. What worries me is that we may have gotten into trouble last spring and for some reason, we can't remember it." Qwyrk didn't mean to quash Holly's affectionate joke, but the more she thought about it all, the more uneasy she became.

* * *

"We have already discussed the first causes of nature, and all natural motion, also the stars ordered in the motion of the heavens, and the physical element-enumerating and specifying them—"

"Sir! She just texted me back!" Jilly was much relieved at

Moirin's quick response, even if it meant her friend was probably in trouble.

"Well, what does she say?"

"She wants to chat on the phone a bit later, say at seven?"

"That seems perfectly reasonable. Will your parents be home?"

"They were going to be, but some work thing came up, and now they'll be out late again. Big surprise. But that's fine. We can all be here when I talk to her. I won't have to hide in my room or whisper."

"Hmph, well, I suppose you should attempt to contact Qwyrk, then, and make sure she and her lady can be present."

"Yeah, I'll text Lluck and have him contact his mum. Then she can tell Qwyrk."

"It seems as if you're taking the long way around with that method."

"I know, I've got to do something about that. We'll have to pause the lesson, sorry to say." Pleased about that bit, she sent Lluck a message to reach out to Holly. Less than a minute later, she was pleased to receive his response, but not happy with the message itself.

"He says he reached out to her with his ring," Jilly explained, "but she didn't answer. That's odd. She's always there for him. It's something she's really strict about with herself. She'd never not get back to him unless something was wrong. I'm going to phone him."

She dialed and sure enough, he answered right away. She set her mobile to speaker phone for Blip's convenience, knowing he detested the things. That made it all the more amusing, she decided.

"Hiya," she started.

"All right?"

"So, what's up with your mum? That's so not like her."

"Yeah, don't know, really. I mean, I know sometimes she gets busy, has things with her mum, but maybe she's just out with Qwyrk on a date, or something."

"But she'd still answer you, right?"

"I guess. But if they're like, you know, *busy*, I wouldn't want her to answer, anyway. That'd be right awkward."

"I hadn't thought of that." Jilly blushed at the suggestion. "Fair enough, I suppose that makes sense. Maybe try again in a bit and let me know how you get on?"

"Yeah, no worries. What's this for, anyway?"

"I need her and Qwyrk to stop by my house when they can; there's a phone conversation with a friend of ours they need to hear. Remember when I told you about Moirin last spring? She's in trouble, I think."

"So, you phoned me, to have me reach out to mum, to have her tell Qwyrk to come to you, so she can listen to a call on your phone? Yeah, that's not sounding like much of a straightforward plan, to be honest."

"Exactly my thought," Blip interjected.

"Honestly, Qwyrk needs a mobile," Lluck said.

"Yeah, no chance of that ever happening. She hates them," Jilly answered.

"Well, at least she's doing one thing right," Blip interrupted again.

"Whatever." Lluck sounded not bothered. "I could ask mum to give you one of her rings. You know, cut out a few middlemen."

"Precisely my suggestion!" Blip announced triumphantly with a wave of his hands.

Jilly shot him an annoyed look. "Yeah, that'd be brilliant, but that's not going to help us now. Right, phone back if you hear anything?"

"No worries. Bye for now."

"Yeah, bye." She looked back over to Blip. "I'm worried about Holly."

"I wouldn't fret overly, my dear," Blip said. "Either she is occupied with whatever concerns the Yakshi, or, as our young friend suggested, she and Qwyrk are engaged in amorous pursuits of which we do not need to be privy. I am sure she will return his message in due course."

"I guess, but I really want them to be here."

"It may be up to us in this instance, I'm afraid. Set up the telephone meeting with Ms. Moeran, and converse with her regardless. Let the chips fall as they may, and if our colleagues are present, all the better. But if not, know that we are most capable of extending an initial helping hand. Keep calm, my dear and all will be well."

Jilly appreciated Blip's optimism, but the situation seemed to be growing more complicated and concerning with each new development, and she wasn't at all sure that everything would be as simple as he suggested.

* * *

In a flash, Qwyrk materialized in Holly's bedroom. Holly was delighted to see her, even as she sat on the side of her bed, grappling with anxiousness.

She stood as soon as Qwyrk arrived. "Well?"

"He's home and is happy to see us now."

"That was quick. You didn't have trouble with the usual security protocols then?"

"I did an end-run around Gargula this time. I tossed a handful of stones behind the mansion to distract him, and then just barged right inside. It was a bit rude, but I took the chance that Qwyzz would be more interested in what's going on with us than worrying about a lapse in courtesy. And I was right."

"Bold and smart of you."

"So, are you ready? I mean, you're dressed and all, but are you feeling up to it?"

"I'm fine, darling." She gently touched Qwyrk's arm. "You worry too much. And I have a plan." She lowered her voice to a whisper. "Minty!"

The door pushed open, and a slender and pointy feline tabby face peered around. Holly motioned toward herself, and in slinked the smaller of the two cats.

"Do you remember what I told you?" Holly asked, not convinced he was capable of holding up his portion of her plan.

"Oh yes." Minty nodded. "I am to tell the lady of the house that you're asleep, that you decided to turn in early, and don't want to be disturbed for the rest of the evening."

"Exactly!"

"I don't like this," he complained, having a quick groom of his left arm.

"Oh, come on," Holly grumped, "it's not like you haven't done it for me before!"

"Maybe when you were an adolescent, like, ten thousand years ago."

"Oh, thank you very much. I'm not that old, you know."

"I'm exaggerating for dramatic purposes."

"Of course you are. So, will you help?"

"On one condition."

Holly raised an eyebrow, annoyed.

Qwyrk watched the whole exchange with seeming amusement, or bemusement, or perhaps confusement.

"You must listen to my musical," Minty declared. "It's very nearly finished, and I want to sing all the numbers to an appreciative audience to make sure I've put it together correctly."

Holly shook her head. "Fine, all right, but it might have to wait for a while. We're very busy at the moment."

"Agreed. Oh, and she has to listen, too." He motioned with one paw toward Qwyrk.

"Wait, what?" Qwyrk blurted.

"Come on darling, it'll be ever so entertaining," Holly teased. "I'm sure you'll be utterly enchanted. Perhaps we can program it together with a ballet recital from Gargula. Oh, and you can be the encore: dance, dramatic sonnet readings, whatever you fancy!"

"I don't, wait, hold on! I mean—"

"Glad to see you agree," Holly said with satisfaction. "Very well, we accept. Now, go and keep watch, and be sure to tell mother exactly what I told you."

Minty nodded with a smug smile. "Done!" And off he trotted.

"What... just happened?" Qwyrk looked back and forth between Holly and the now-closed door, ever more confused.

"I've signed you up for an evening of culture. It should be grand!"

"How did that even... what? A cat yowling a bloody musical, a gargoyle dancing to a violin with no player. What the hell?"

"And don't forget," Holly said, nudging her, "you dancing and reciting poetry! Sounds rather enchanting, doesn't it?"

"No! It doesn't. Really!"

"Oh don't be so uncharitable. Where's your sense of adventure?"

"I put it away for the winter?"

"It's still autumn."

"Might as well be prepared."

"Tosh! It'll be fun." Holly leaned in to kiss Qwyrk on the lips. At once, a violent and painful shock surged through her. Both of them flew backwards in opposite directions, landing on the floor some distance from each other, both with an inelegant thud. "What the blue, bloody hell?" Qwyrk swore, one hand over her mouth. "Are you all right?"

"Yes, I think so," Holly answered, rousing herself from her prone position. "That was not good."

"No, it damned well wasn't!" Qwyrk sat up.

"That happened last spring, remember?" Holly stood up, shaking it off. "We put it down to some kind of residual magic, the same sort that was making trees and rocks wander about near your home?"

"Yeah, I was pretty sure that's all it was. But this is bad. Far worse than before. It was almost like—"

"Something forced us apart?"

"Exactly!"

Holly moved over to Qwyrk and took her hands. Nothing happened. She leaned down, and though nervous, they kissed again.

Nothing at all. A perfectly normal, lovely kiss.

"It's so odd," Holly said in frustration as she drew back. "One moment, pandemonium is breaking loose, and the next, it's like it never happened."

"Same as with your headaches and my dizziness," Qwyrk said. "Something's messing with us, love, and I've about had it. We have to go see Qwyzz, now. We need answers."

Holly nodded and stood. "Let me put my ring back on, just in case." She slid the slender band on to her finger. "Oh, oh no."

"What? What is it?"

"It's Lluck. He tried to reach me earlier. I shouldn't have taken it off, but I didn't want to be contacted in case the pain came back. I have to answer him, it won't take long."

"Of course, whatever you need to do," Qwyrk said, dragging herself up from her undignified sprawl on the floor.

Holly closed her eyes and focused for a few moments. "Lluck? Yes, darling I'm here. I'm terribly sorry not to have heard you before. Something came up and I couldn't answer, but I'm here now and... oh? Oh. Yes, yes, of course. I'll let her know. Right now? Of course. Thank you, dear. We'll talk more soon. I love you."

She opened her eyes and glanced at Qwyrk with a concerned expression.

"That look," Qwyrk said with trepidation, pointing a finger at her. "That's not a great look. That's not even a good look. That's the kind of look that means some shite has hit some fan somewhere. Tell me that look isn't the look I think it is."

"I wish I could. He said Jilly needs to get in touch with you. Apparently, Moirin reached out to her today."

"Moirin? Oh, crap."

Holly nodded. "She's in trouble, and Jilly needs us to come to her house, right away."

"Of course she does," Qwyrk said. "Bloody hell, and on top of this other crap. It doesn't rain but it pours, eh?"

"Well, things were starting to get a bit dull," Holly jested. "What with us having a whole peaceful and lovely summer together with nothing untoward happening? It's about time something went to blazes again, so we can be terribly inconvenienced, stressed and panicked, have all of our plans upended, and have to go save the world and whatnot. It's becoming an annual tradition!"

"I wish I shared your sunny outlook, love," Qwyrk said, "but I've a feeling everything really *is* going south again." She sighed a sigh she was already tired of sighing. "Right, Qwyzz will have to wait until later. Let's go find out what's up with our human friends, or banshee friends, and just how much of a bloody apocalypse we're dealing with this time."

"I wouldn't miss it," Holly smiled, taking and squeezing Qwyrk's hand, this time without a shock.

"The thing is, love, you don't really have a choice."

CHAPTER THREE

Winston sat reading in his favorite armchair. He'd enjoyed an early supper with Penelope, who'd since gone home. Though always grateful for her company, he never quite understood why she gave it to him. In any case, he couldn't look into any town records until tomorrow, so he sipped sherry and read up on the history and lore of the area by consulting his 1910 printing of *Birdwhistle's Annotated Gallimaufry of Nearly Every Odd Thing, Yorkshire Edition*. Alas, so far, nothing of any great interest popped out at him, beyond an entry about a mysterious woman in a red robe said to haunt the region around Gaping Gap cavern in the Western Dales. She could see the future, or some such, and people feared to meet her, much less consult with her.

"So frustrating," he sighed, enjoying his sherry and turning the page. "Nothing about ornate keys at all. Beyond the obvious use for doors and locks and whatnot."

Though the evening was still young, he felt rather weary. Perhaps it was the season. Or the meal. Or the sherry. But he found himself nodding off at regular intervals as he browsed for answers, so he set his glass aside and closed the book. Within moments, he'd closed his eyes and drifted off into a peaceful doze.

Except that it wasn't. Peaceful, that is. It was anything but.

In his mind, he opened his eyes, though he realized at once how strange that very notion seemed. He couldn't be sure if he was dreaming or hallucinating, but he had the sensation of being somewhere else, a place of rocks, mists, and shadows. He perceived dark, rather like twilight, though he could see no visible source of illumination. If the sun were present, it was quite obscured.

"Hello?" he called out. "Is anyone there? Where am I? Hello?"

His voice echoed off the rocks, but he received only silence in response, save for the sound of a slight breeze whistling back and forth.

"Right, I don't know what's going on, but this is decidedly not funny. As in, I am not amused. If someone is trying to unnerve me, then they're doing a damned good job of it, but I fail to see what that will achieve. I mean, none of this can possibly be real, so I don't believe in it to begin with, but that doesn't change the fact that this is simply not on. So, either tell me what's happening, or I shall have to lodge a particularly stern protest with whoever is behind this nonsense! Even though it's not real, I mean."

A sense of something "other" came to him; not so much of being watched, but rather that the space around him seemed inhabited. No, that made no sense at all, and yet, there it was.

"Little fleshly vessel," he heard, or rather, sensed as more of a feeling than a sound, though if he had to put an audible quality to it, it would have seemed like a whispery growl. "Rejoice and be thankful. You have been chosen."

"Chosen? Chosen for what? What are you talking about? I didn't volunteer for anything, I'll have you know. Therefore, I cannot be chosen. And I've not entered any contests, so I'm not expecting to be picked for anything."

"Yes," the sensation answered. "You will do. You will be appropriate when the time comes."

"What do you mean? What time? Appropriate for what? I'm not about to be ready for anything if I don't know the details. And furthermore, this is all merely the product of the sherry or the Yorkshire pudding, or some such, so you'll excuse me for not taking it seriously."

He heard no reply, but something lingered, almost like mocking laughter, there one moment and gone the next. The wind around him became stronger, whipping up into a furious bluster that soon battered him about on all sides. He raised his hands and swatted in every direction in a desperate and futile attempt to fend it off, squinting as the force of the elements overtook him. He had the terrible and unnerving sensation of a singular, glowing, red eye staring at him, probing, searching, as if peering into his very being. He wanted to run away, to do something, but was trapped in the furious flurry flapping around him.

He yelled and opened his eyes, his real ones. And there he sat, in his chair, in his study, *Birdwhistle's Annotated Gallimaufry* having fallen to the floor, though his sherry glass remained on the small table next to him, undisturbed.

"How odd! Oh decidedly that, how jolly horrifying!" He felt for his reading glasses, relieved to find them still firmly on his face.

"There must have been something very off in the pudding. I've a good mind to write a sternly-worded letter. No more of those frozen foods for me. From now on, I shall only purchase my puddings from a proper pudding and pie purveyor."

Reaching for his book, and now quite awake, he settled back into his chair, took a nice gulp of sherry, and delved into reading about the antiquated curiosities of the region once more, but something lingered in his thoughts, the memory of a voice that menaced and portended something terrible.

*   *   *

In the now-familiar dazzling display of violet lights, Qwyrk and Holly stepped through a tele-portal and into Jilly's living room. After the usual exchange of hugs and greetings (Blip refrained from the hugs, as he was wont to do in all but the most extraordinary of circumstances), Qwyrk pressed Jilly for more details, only to find that Jilly herself knew very little.

"So, Moirin didn't tell you what's going on, then?"

Jilly shook her head. "No, but I think she needs our help. She wants to talk right away. I mean, she wants to talk to *me*, but I figure, rather than chatting with her on my own and trying to remember everything and tell you later, you could listen in while I pretend to be alone. It's kind of dishonest, but just in case it's something serious? I don't want to upset her."

Qwyrk put a hand on Jilly's shoulder. "It's a really smart idea. I know it's a bit underhanded, but whatever happens to her concerns all of us, and if Aeval is back, or if your spell is wearing off, it's better that we all know about it, sooner rather than later. If we can help her, I'm pretty sure she'll forgive you if she finds out."

"But she doesn't have to find out, as long as you're all quiet," Jilly answered, casting a quick glance at Blip. Qwyrk followed her lead and set her eyes on him. Holly did the same.

"What?" Blip said, looking back and forth between them as if offended. "Why is everyone looking at me? What are you implying?"

"Just that you're well known for your prolix verbosity and lack of restraint, that's all," Qwyrk teased. She knew it was what they were all thinking, anyway.

"My tendency to speak at length on subjects of which I have great knowledge has no bearing on my ability to hold my tongue in the middle of a covert fact-finding mission, I should like to point out. Since I know nothing of what she will reveal, I shall have nothing to contribute to the conversation in the short term!"

"I'm sorry, did you just say what I think you said?" Qwyrk squinted and drew back in mock astonishment. "That you actually don't know something, and therefore you'll keep quiet until you learn more? I think we've reached the bloody apocalypse for real this time."

"As usual, your attempts at humor are ill-conceived and mirthless. I am perfectly capable of absorbing information without commentary, especially when skillful spy-craft is called for."

"You're serious?" Qwyrk threw open her arms. "Really? I bet you can't even remotely do that."

"Oh, you do, do you?" Blip folded his arms.

"I do! In fact, I'm so sure, I'll bet that you can't listen to Jilly's conversation without butting in with some asinine comment before it's over, blowing our cover and screwing up things."

"And what shall I gain when I win this bet?"

"I'll apologize profusely and defer to your decisions for a whole day. Oh, and I'll do that bloody Nighttime Nasty dance that Holly's been wanting to see since last winter, not just for her, but for all of you." She motioned a hand to everyone present.

"Oh, I like the sound of this!" Holly flashed a huge smile. "Please don't let us down, Mr. Blippingstone?"

"I'm not normally one to gamble, my dear. It's a foolish waste of one's time and resources." Blip stroked his froggy chin as he addressed Holly. "However," he turned back to Qwyrk, "given the immense satisfaction that I shall obtain from—how should one say—rubbing your nose in it for twenty-four hours, as well as seeing you humiliate yourself with some preposterous gyration, I shall happily accept your challenge!"

"Ah, but you haven't heard what I get, if I win," Qwyrk said with a smug expression.

"Oh? And what do you propose, pray tell?"

"If I win—and I will—you'll have to sing karaoke to cheesy pop songs of our choosing from the 1980s, while drinking an American lite beer, from the can. No brandy or Bach for twenty-four hours!"

"Oh!" Jilly interjected with a mischievous smile, "and you have to tell us why you and Father Christmas don't like each other."

Blip looked back and forth between Qwyrk and Jilly with a sour and defensive expression, before settling into a more contented countenance. "Very well, since I've no intention of losing, I accept."

"Oh, this is going to be splendid," Holly chortled. "No matter who loses, we win!"

"Thanks for the support, love," Qwyrk snipped.

"I'm terribly determined to see that dance, darling. Otherwise, I'd be all in for you, you know that."

"Yeah, yeah." She turned her attention to the whole group. "Right, let's get on with this."

CHAPTER THREE

*   *   *

Winston now found himself completely absorbed in his venerable *Birdwhistle's* guidebook, even if he wasn't finding any answers. A veritable cornucopia of curiosities jumped out at him, from legends of ghostly hounds to stories of nasty plagues, Viking raids, and assorted medieval machinations. There was the account of Grandmother Boatford, of course, who was said to have lived in this very town in that cave down by the river, but he knew it was really just a collection of folk tales and whimsies, if she'd even existed at all. The tale of William de Soulis was quite unnerving, he conceded, even if most of the story took place in Scotland, rather than Yorkshire. And who wouldn't feel a chill down their spine reading about the Wild Hunt, which roamed over the moors and forests of medieval England, its master the Erlking ever on the search for human souls?

"Splendid stuff, all of it," he muttered, "but nothing about a blasted key... just a moment—"

His eyes happened to fall on an entry concerning the region's metalwork in pre-Roman times, which would have been something of an atypical bore in a book such as this, but...

"The Brigantes, the Celtic peoples of the region," he read aloud, "may have engaged in the practice of forging elegant and elaborate tools for magical purposes. That is, they believed in a kind of sympathetic magic; a special ornate plow might be created to ensure a fruitful harvest, a ritual spear would be crafted to assist in winning battles, and a decorative key might have been fashioned to symbolically keep something in or lock it out."

There was an engraving of a key next to the text, and it looked suspiciously like his.

"Good heavens! Can it be?"

He retrieved the item from his pocket and looked it over again. It didn't appear especially ornate, but something about its shape, its very existence, spoke to him, suggesting that it had an importance all out of proportion to its size. And though it wasn't exactly like the book's illustration, he couldn't deny the similarity. Was this in fact, against all odds, some kind of magical key, used by an ancient Celtic tribe that once lived here?

"Maybe Penelope was right, maybe you were stolen from a museum or some such. No, that's absurd. I rather think you were left there by some foolish person who didn't know your value. To think you might have been sitting in someone's attic, or in a charity shop, and then discarded, only for me to come along and rescue you? What a good bit of fortune for both of us, eh?"

He reached for his glass of sherry and took a nice, satisfying sip, confident that he was getting somewhere at last.

"So," he said, turning the mysterious object over in his hand and letting his lamp illuminate its angles and facets. "If you're an ancient key, what are you for, then? Are you meant to keep something locked up? Or perhaps to keep it locked out? And where do you fit, hm? Every key needs a keyhole, after all, even a metaphoric one. So, the next step is to go about finding it."

Setting the implement aside, he closed the book and stood up, deciding that he might just retire early. He had a sudden but vague sensation of being watched, though a quick peering out the window from behind the curtain showed nothing of the sort, just an empty street on a quiet October evening. He shook his head and put it down once more to the ill effects of a poorly-made pudding that most definitely demanded a stern letter of reproval.

CHAPTER THREE

The phone rang. Jilly pressed the speaker option on her phone and set it down on the coffee table so everyone could hear. She worried about what Moirin might have to say, and about Blip screwing up, not necessarily in that order.

"Jilly?" A familiar Irish-accented voice said.

"Moirin?" Jilly asked.

"Hey there, hiya," Moirin said. "Sorry to be out of touch. I'm a bit rubbish with things like that."

"Aw, no worries, I figured you were pretty busy."

"Well, it's still no excuse. It's not like I've been on tour with the band. But anyway."

"Yeah, it's fine. You, um, you said you needed to talk to me. Is, is everything all right?"

Morin paused. "Uh, not really, no. I mean, it's not all gone to shite, but well, it could, I guess?"

"What is it? Is Aeval back in your head? Is the spell wearing off?" Jilly's nerves rattled at the thought.

"No, not exactly."

"What do you mean?"

"I mean, I'm not hearin' her voice in my head again, so that's all good. But there's somethin' else."

"Something else?"

"Yeah, it's not like she's there, but I think she's still there, if that makes any sense."

"Not really?"

"I mean, she's not tellin' me what to do like before, but I feel like over the past few weeks, something's been nudging me, pokin' at me, trying to get me to do something, but I don't really know what it is, not yet. I think it's getting stronger."

"How do you know it's her?"

"I don't. Not exactly, but it feels like her, I guess? I don't know. I'm probably just talkin' bollocks at this point and I'm actually goin' mad or something. Maybe it was a mistake for me to bother you."

"No! It's no trouble. I'm glad you did." Jilly looked back at the others, who motioned to her to keep the conversation going. Blip in particular seemed to be struggling not to contribute, looking about in darting glances. "If you think something's wrong, then it's good that you reached out to me, really. Um, where are you now?"

"I'd rather not say, if that's all right."

"Sure, of course. Are you, are you in danger now?"

"No, I don't think so. I mean, not as far as I know."

Blip raised one finger, ready to comment, but put his hand down again in frustration. Qwyrk glared at him

"All right, that's good," Jilly said, trying to sound encouraging. "So, what can I do?"

"I don't know, it's just, with your magic and all that, I figured you'd be the best person to reach out to. And you have all those friends of yours. I mean, they're cool and all, but still: elves, fairies, and a talking frog? It's bloody mental!"

Her friends scowled, and she stifled a giggle.

"You haven't found Aileen, have you?"

"No," Moirin's voice was wistful and deflated. "I've tried, but it's like she's just disappeared. I hoped maybe she'd want to get in touch with me again, but I guess I'm no use to her without that banshee bitch attached to my brain."

"Maybe she's just scared. Maybe she feels bad about it all."

"I don't know. Anyway, could we, maybe, you know, meet up? Like soon?"

Blip opened his mouth, clearly struggling to stay quiet.

"You're in the area?" Jilly asked eagerly.

"Maybe. Is there like a forest we could meet in, later tonight, or something? Some dark place without people? That's what witches like, right? For covens and sabbats, and all that?"

"Yeah, that's a bit of a dumb stereotype, honestly. But sure, if you want to meet some place secret, I can do that."

"Great, brilliant. So where would it be? If we were going to, I mean?"

"I'm not sure." She happened to look over to see Blip open his mouth again and almost say something but clamp a hand over it instead. He looked decidedly uncomfortable, which she found quite amusing, despite the seriousness of her conversation. "I mean, there's some places around here, little forests and such, but some of them aren't much more than clumps of trees. We might need to go out to the Dales or something."

"Yeah, that could be a bit of a problem. Kind of hard to get to, and all that."

Blip wrestled with himself to keep quiet. Qwyrk and Holly watched him with eagle eyes, and were both smirking, only just controlling themselves.

"Um, all right, what about Nicewood Park in Leeds?" Jilly suggested, trying not to be distracted by the increasing chaos of the struggle for silence. "You could get to it pretty easily by bus or taxi, and there won't be anyone there after dark. Lots of trees and places to hide in. Kind of a neutral ground, too, so you don't have to come all the way up here. Qwyrk and Holly could be there, if you like. I mean, I'd need Qwyrk to take me there, anyway."

"Yeah, I like that. That could work. So, tonight? At midnight?"

"Tonight?" Jilly looked at the others for confirmation. Qwyrk hemmed at Holly, and Holly hawed at Qwyrk. Blip shook his head rather vehemently. "Um, yeah, I think that'd be fine. Maybe Mr. Blip can come, too?" she asked. "We can meet you at the edge of the forest. It's dark out there, so you'll need a torch or something, but if you get a taxi to drop you off at the houses nearby, you'd be fine, and the driver wouldn't ask any questions."

"Brilliant! Oh, thanks loads, Jilly. This makes me feel so much better, you've no idea. I feel like a weight's been taken off my shoulders, just bein' able to talk to you and all. I can fill you in more later, but yeah, this is really good. Thanks again."

"No problem. I'm glad we can help. We'll all be there at midnight."

"Confound it girl!" Blip blurted out. "I cannot make it tonight! I'm needed elsewhere, and I would have greatly appreciated you not volunteering me for this proverbial wild goose chase without first checking with me!"

"Who's that?" Moirin asked. "Is that Blip?"

Crap! "Yeah, um, he just walked in right now, actually, and he says he can't make it, but I'm pretty sure Qwyrk and Holly can be there, so is that still good?"

"Yeah, yeah. Fine. He uh, he didn't hear much, did he?" Moirin lowered her voice.

"I don't think so." Jilly felt awful about lying to Moirin of all people.

"Good. I don't want this getting around, at least not until we can talk."

"No worries. See you there, then?"

"Absolutely!"

"Great. It was really good talking to you, Moirin, and nice to hear your voice. I mean, I hear you on your recording, but just your... regular voice? The one you speak with? That one?" She cringed. *That sounded really stupid.*

"Yeah, you too. Thanks again. I'll see you tonight."

"We'll be there. Bye then."

She ended the call and glanced back at the others. Blip was fuming, Qwyrk had a particularly smug expression on her face, and Holly looked torn.

"So, Mr. 'I can control myself,'" Qwyrk smirked. "How'd that all work out for you?"

"It was the heat of the moment. I needed to inform Jilly that I am not available at the last minute for an emergency meeting, regardless of its nature. That cannot possibly count against me in terms of our wager!"

"Oh, but it can, and it does," Qwyrk said. "The bet was that you had to say nothing. Zip. Nil. Not a word, to make sure that Moirin didn't think anyone was spying on her."

"And she still doesn't," Blip protested, "thanks to the quick thinking of Ms. Pleeth, whose clever fib made it sound as if I'd only just arrived. Well done, my dear, incidentally."

"Um, thanks?" Jilly shrugged. Blip compliments were always rather odd.

"Doesn't matter," Qwyrk dismissed. "A bet's a bet, and the bet was not a word from you. And you lost, and good Goddess, am I going to look forward to the consequences."

"And I can't wait to hear the Father Christmas story," Jilly added with glee.

"I'm just sad that I've missed yet another opportunity to see the dance," Holly sulked.

"Yes, how terrible for you." Blip sneered at her. "In any case," he said as he turned his attention back to Qwyrk, "I do not have time for this nonsense now. I must attend to a number of other tasks. That much is true."

"Fine," Qwyrk countered, "but don't think you'll just get to disappear and get out of it. If you can't be here right now, then the punishment for losing doesn't start until you can."

"And who inserted this particular codicil into the agreement?" Blip sniffed.

"Simple fairness," Qwyrk said.

"If we were going by simple fairness, my protest at my unavailability would not count as a loss of the wager."

"I'm sorry to interrupt this very entertaining exchange," Holly said, looking at Qwyrk, "but don't we also have an appointment that we need to get to?"

"You're right," Qwyrk nodded. "Look," she turned to Jilly, "I'll come back for you tonight, say at about half past eleven? And then the three of us can head on down to the park?"

Jilly nodded. "Sure. Where are you off to now?"

"Oh, it's just a trip over to Qwyzz's. We, um, we need to ask him about some things. Residual magic that's been left behind and what to do about it."

"Anything I can help with? I've got Granny's library and all."

"Thanks, but we've got this one for now. It's pretty minor, really. But if that, um, changes, we'll let you know, yeah?"

"Sure," Jilly conceded. "Whatever works for you."

"Good. We should be getting off, then?" She looked at Holly.

"Yes, yes, the sooner the better," Holly answered. She glanced at Jilly. "But we will be back later tonight. Ta for now, darling."

Qwyrk and Holly stood, and taking hands—with what almost looked like some hesitancy—they vanished into a circle of light.

"I must go, as well," Blip declared as he hopped down from the sofa in rather a hurry. "I'll be in touch soon, most likely tomorrow. Have a good evening and all that. Give my regards to young Ms. Moeran. I, um, I hope whatever ails her is nothing too serious. Cheerio!"

And just like that, Jilly found herself alone in the living room, save for her dog, Odin, who was sleeping, as usual, in his beloved bed in the corner, having long since learned not to be bothered by the strange comings-and-goings of her magical friends. Friends that Jilly now had the distinct impression were not telling her the truth about several things.

CHAPTER FOUR

Winston wrestled with restlessness. Whether plagued by the surreal, pudding-induced hypnagogia, or the revelation that the key he'd found might well be a priceless Brigantes relic, or the unsettling sense that someone was spying on his home, he couldn't relax. Even listening to the music of his beloved Ralph Vaughan Williams wasn't doing the trick. The Lark most decidedly was not Ascending, and sleep was out of the question.

Also, he kept having the urge to go on another walk.

"That's absurd!" he insisted. "It's after dark, and it'd be terribly irresponsible, to say nothing of the fact that some hooligan might be lying in wait for me in the shadows. I can't possibly risk something so foolish."

So, he paced. And he continued to listen to music. And he sat. And he stood. And he paced some more. He noticed that, while he was positively exhausted only an hour earlier, he was now fairly zinging with energy. He wanted to jump, to skip, to play football (he'd never played in his life), something, anything...

"Sitting about is doing my head in!" he complained aloud after another few minutes, ready to throw something in frustration.

The urge to leave the house became even stronger, despite his reservations.

"I mean, perhaps I could take a short stroll around the block, just to clear my mind?"

And that was all he needed to talk himself into going outside.

"It's more than a tad chilly tonight. I suppose the fresh air might do me some good. Yes, indeed it might just well."

He bundled up in his favorite long wool coat, threw on a scarf and hat, and made for the front door, but he stopped for a moment and looked back. Without knowing why, he went and retrieved the key and stuffed it securely into his inside coat pocket.

"Best to keep it near me, just in case."

In case what? He had no answer. He stepped out into the cold, closed the door behind him, locked it, and checked it thrice to be sure. Not knowing which direction he should take, he decided to let his intuition guide him. That was an odd idea, but a rather liberating one. And so he set off into the dark, feeling a bit of a tingle of anticipation as to what he might encounter.

* * *

"Right," Qwyrk sighed, anticipating what she might encounter as she looked at the odd home—part Tudor manor and part medieval castle—in the forest clearing ahead of them. "It's time for one of *my* absolute favorite things to do: getting interrogated by a statue and accused of being a spy for Vlad the Impaler, or whoever."

"Oh, come on, he's quite sweet in his own way," Holly objected. "And if he's the worst we have to deal with, I can think of far more terrible fates."

"Always looking on the bright side, eh love?" Qwyrk leaned in to kiss her but hesitated. "Um, maybe we should wait on that until we've, you know, spoken to Qwyzz?"

Holly nodded, now looking less amused and more concerned. But just for a moment. "Come on," she said. "I've an idea about how to avoid the interrogation."

"You're welcome to try, but I haven't figured anything out yet, short of throwing rocks."

Holly strode up to the ornate front door of Qwyzz's magnificent, ramshackle mansion, while Qwyrk marveled at her eagerness to go through with this pointless portion of the salutation. Holly rang the bell and stepped back to gaze up at the roof.

"One... two... three..." Qwyrk counted with dread.

"Allooooooooooo!" a scratchy, stony little voice sounded amid a light shower of pebbles and dust that cascaded down on them.

"Gargula, darling," Holly called up. "It's me, Holly. I'm here with Qwyrk, you know, my gorgeous girlfriend? I've just called by because I'd love to know how your ballet dancing is coming along. Did you decide on which work you're going to focus on? Also, do let me know when you plan to give a proper recital with that magical violin. I should like to see it ever so much!" She turned and winked at Qwyrk, who was rather astonished.

"I, uh, I mean... well, yes, oui, merci," Gargula called down in his phony, out-of-era French accent. "I have decided, indeed! I am devoting my efforts to a portion of *Giselle*, you know, zee famous ghost story? I like how it unfolds with such majesty, such mystery, such tragedy. I feel I can best express myself in trying to present zee drama, romance, and horror of it all."

"It sounds utterly enthralling!" Holly encouraged him. "You simply must tell me all about your progress. From what little I've seen, you're doing very well."

"Well, um, but of course. I would be happy to! Uh, merci for showing such a keen interest."

"Not at all. I told you I've danced ballet myself off and on over the years, though I'm sure I've not reached your level of accomplishment."

Qwyrk watched this exchange—a faery and a gargoyle discussing human ballet—in veritable disbelief, now quite certain she could see the little creature blushing. How such a thing could even be possible, she had no clue.

"Wellll," Gargula countered, "I'm not so good. Not yet, anyway."

"Oh, pay no mind to him. He's doing very well!" a second little stony voice sounded behind him, as Babewin, his partner gargoyle, came into view. "He's been practicing and shows real promise." She rested one wing on his back and gave him a little pat with it.

"Bah! You are all too kind," Gargula protested with embarrassment. "I've simply laid a good foundation for myself. Oh, ha ha! Zat's a good one!"

Qwyrk winced.

"Well, I look forward to hearing more about your artistic journey," Holly smiled. "In the meantime, if it's not too much trouble, could you let the master of the house know we're here? He's expecting us, I think."

"Of course, mademoiselle!" Gargula said. "Avec plaisir!" And off he went in a shuffle of gravel. Babewin remained behind, smiling at them.

Qwyrk looked up at the roof and back at her girlfriend, and back up, and back down again. "Um, what just happened?" she said in a lowered voice.

"You see?" Holly smiled. "You just have to speak to him in his own language."

"What? Pigeon medieval Anglo-Norman babbling?"

"Silly. No, just a bit of flattery and genuine interest in his passion, and see? We've disarmed him of his other obsession with historical military threats to the house. And he and Babewin didn't even get into a fight."

Qwyrk observed her with some disbelief. "I'm pretty sure you could charm an ogre into giving up his favorite war club."

The door opened, and Qwyzz stood before them in all of his dazzling, semi-comical majesty. He looked the same as always, a dapper gentleman with long white hair and a well-trimmed white beard, wearing one of his resplendent robes, in this case, a green velvet affair with images of golden grotesques embroidered onto it, various of which seemed to be carrying on conversations with each other in several languages. Some of these were cordial, but a few seemed to be on the verge of arguments. A disembodied face jested with an ape holding a fiddle, while a cloven-hoofed creature with legs and a human head—but nothing in between—seemed to be in a standoff with a rabbit armed with a sword, who confronted its adversary with a sneer. Other creatures pavaned and galiarded to the back side of the robe, but they didn't make a return journey to the front side. Maybe they were taking a quick rest, Qwyrk thought.

"Qwyrk and Holly! Splendid!" Qwyzz clapped his hands

together. "Come in, please come in. I've just decanted a superb new port, which I think you'll be most appreciative of—"

"That sounds lovely, really, but we have a big problem." Qwyrk couldn't believe she was about to turn down the offer of his magnificent drink, especially an untasted vintage.

"Oh? Do tell."

Qwyrk glanced at Holly and then back at him. "Something's up, I mean, something magical. We should have mentioned it to you six months ago when it first happened, but it just kind of... went away? Now it's back, and it's really worrying."

"Worrying how?"

"Let's go in," Qwyrk motioned. "We may all want that port after all."

*   *   *

Jilly was skeptical. And grumpy. Skrumpy? In any case, having watched her friends abscond to various places without giving her any details was more than just annoying; it felt rather like a betrayal.

"It's like they don't even trust me. Now that I'm learning all about witchery and can finally hold my own, they don't even want me around anymore. Yeah, really nice, thanks everyone." She brooded. "Oh, calm down, Jilly, it's not like they haven't done rubbish like this before, and there's always been a good reason for it. And they've let you know when the time was right. It's probably just that again."

But something about Blip's behavior in particular bothered her, nagged at her. It had been going on for too long, and he was not one to be secretive. As she sat stewing over it, a thought came to her.

"What if I could spy on him? Check out where he's going without him realizing? I wonder." She peered out the living room window across the street. Granny wasn't home as usual, but Jilly had complete run of her house while she was away. She checked the time: 8:00 pm.

"Mum and dad aren't going to be home until at least ten, so that only gives me a couple of hours to go on over and poke around. Unless, what if..."

She went back upstairs to her room and found a small book she'd been reading recently: *Fludd's Phenomenal Grimoire of Useful and Slightly Annoying Enchanted Distractions*. Leafing through it, she found the page she'd recalled, in a section about how to divert attention from oneself.

"Here it is, brilliant!"

She noted a simple little apotropaism to buy her some more time away at Granny's. Speaking the two-line spell, she waited just a short while, and sure enough, the sound of mild snoring began to drift through the bedroom. She smiled, satisfied.

"With the light off, they'll never even think to check in on me! Still, better pile up a few pillows under the duvet, just to be sure."

Once she'd created a convincing snoring dummy of cushions, she turned out the light and shut the door. Going back downstairs, she grabbed her coat, and hopped off to Granny's for a good evening's snooping.

❊   ❊   ❊

Winston had second thoughts about his impulsive evening stroll. The colder-than-usual weather, and the fact that he had no idea where to go after the first couple of blocks only made it worse. Being spontaneous was assuredly not his thing, unless he'd planned it out well in advance. Now, he found himself heading out to the hedge.

"I am most certainly not going all the way out there again," he commanded to himself, and yet, on he trudged, despite his sincere desire to return to the warmth and safety of his house.

"No, this is foolish, this is... well, it's almost unsafe. Who knows what manner of ruffians might lie in wait out there? Or perhaps someone is looking for the key, and you've foolishly got it with you and are bringing it right back to them! Turn around! Stop this, you clodpate! At once!"

But by now, something seemed to be drawing him back, and he couldn't resist. Against his better judgement and his wishes, he realized he stood on the dirt path which led to the hedge, which led back to the resting place of the little implement in his pocket. The whole experience would have been quite fascinating if he were less apprehensive.

"Whatever's happening here," he whispered in protest, watching the steam of his breath rise in front of him, "I want you to know that I am extremely unhappy with it. I don't know who you are, but you can't simply go around invading people's heads and making them do what you want. It isn't proper or civilized. Whatever you think you're doing by forcing me out here against my will cannot be any good whatsoever, so I demand that you release me at once, that you—"

He stopped with a sudden lurch finding himself at the same place where he'd spied the key. And he wasn't alone.

*　*　*

Jilly sat in one corner of Granny's impressive library, which was actually a few rooms wherein books lined all the shelves and trailed down the hall in stacks to connect to the nearest adjacent chamber.

She drew the curtains and kept the light low, so as not to attract any unwanted attention.

"Not that my parents would ever think to look over here, even accidentally," she sighed as she flipped through page after page of book after book on all manner of enchantments.

"Ceraunomancy? No, there's no thunder tonight, not even any clouds. Capnomancy? Unlikely, I'd have to light a fire in the fireplace. The last thing I want to do is draw attention to myself." She turned to another page at random. "Moon Glamoury? Hmmm. 'On clear nights, the moon's reflection in a mirror may give the viewer a glimpse at another's actions and whereabouts, by use of these arcane words and the focus of one's intention.'"

"That'd work, tonight's perfect for it!" She paused, feeling a twinge of guilt. "Maybe I shouldn't. It doesn't seem right. Oh, sod it. I'm sure he's lying to me! And it's not like I'm going to watch him for long. I just want to see what he gets on with when he's not here. That's not so bad, is it? No, it bloody well isn't. If he's not telling me the truth, I have a right to know why!"

And with that, she'd convinced herself and set about preparing to do the spell.

* * *

"Hmm," Qwyzz said after listening to their concerning news, the three of them sipping port (they'd given in to temptation, after all). "This is odd. Very odd, indeed."

"Do you have any idea what's happening?" Holly reached for Qwyrk's hand but pulled back before touching it, which only made Qwyrk feel even worse about their plight.

"Not the specifics, I'm afraid," Qwyzz answered, "but this sort of interference has the signs of some kind of reactive magic."

"Reactive magic?" Qwyrk asked. "What does that mean?"

"That some kind of spell is set up to cause a negative reaction when something happens that the caster does not wish to happen, in this case, when you two express affection for one another. At the moment, it appears to occur on random occasions, but there does seem to be intent behind it."

"Hold on," Holly said, "so this isn't just residual magic from some other enchantment? Sort of hanging about in the air, or some such?"

"It's rather unlikely, I should think." Qwyzz shook his head. "You said it's happened both at your home and at Qwyrk's?"

Holly nodded.

"Hm. It's taking effect in more than one world, then. That's a clear sign of calculated intent."

"So, someone deliberately did this to Holly and me? Put some kind of hex on us?" Qwyrk struggled to contain her anger. "Why? What possible reason could they have? And how could they even manage to do it?"

"I cannot say, I'm afraid, unless..." He looked at Qwyrk. "You did say that Qworum took you aside in private last spring and advised you to end your relationship, yes? Or at least keep your distance from each other? But he didn't insist on it, or give you any further reason?"

"None." Qwyrk shrugged. "I just assumed it was because he was unhappy that Holly had joined me on an assignment, so he was trying to make a show of authority, or something. Since nothing else came of it, I just put it down to him bluffing, and I ignored him. I'd pretty much forgotten about it, to be honest."

"Hm, I wonder," Qwyzz said, stroking his beard. "A Shadow and a Yakshi. Different worlds. Different orders. Excuse me for a moment, will you? I'm going to look up something."

"Of course," Qwyrk said. She now took Holly's hand and squeezed it in defiance of any potential for a painful outcome. Nothing happened, so she continued to hold it, taking some comfort in that simple pleasure, at least.

"What do you suppose is going on?" Holly asked, a distressed look on her face.

"I don't know." Qwyrk shook her head. "But I've seen that look, and it's not a good one. He's worried about something, and if he's gone to that library of his, he must have some inkling of what's happening."

"Who would want to hurt us?" Holly asked. "I mean, all right, undoubtedly we both have enemies, but who could even do this? Who could get to you here, or me in my own home?"

"No one I can think of off the top of my head, but given all the crap we've gone up against, I wouldn't rule anything out. Everything's been kind of mental for the last year and a half, and we still don't know why. Maybe there really *is* something to what Aeval told me at Castlerigg, Maybe there is some kind of secret Darkfae war going on, and somehow we've gotten ourselves caught up in it?"

"But why would it affect us?"

"Well, we have a bit of a reputation for screwing up the plans of the heinous and the nefarious, haven't we? And if there *is* some hidden battle royale going on, maybe the good are getting pulled into the feud between the bad and the ugly."

Holly gave Qwyrk a puzzled look. "That was an old movie reference, wasn't it?"

"Sort of. Sorry."

Holly shrugged. "At least it wasn't more bath bomb humor."

"There is nothing wrong with a bit of clever balneological wordplay."

"Except, that it really does need to be clever."

Qwyrk gave her a mock sneer. "You're cute."

Holly tossed her hair and beamed. "I think so."

They lapsed into silence for a while. Despite Holly's attempt to lift the mood, Qwyrk's gnawing unease grew. What did it all mean? Could Qwyzz help them? He had to, she told herself. He always knew what to do; everything would be fine. They'd get this solved in no time, and then...

"Terribly sorry to interrupt your deep thought," Qwyzz said, announcing his return. Qwyrk snapped back to attention and saw that he held a very old book with a crumbling cover.

"Did you find something?" Holly asked, her hand still grasping Qwyrk's, fingers intertwined.

"Well, perhaps. Please understand that I'm not absolutely certain, and I should like to undertake some follow-up research to confirm or discard it as a theory."

"But?" Qwyrk pressed.

"But if what I've read here is true, this could be a serious problem, I'm afraid to say. Very serious, indeed."

*　　*　　*

Jilly sat in Granny's backyard garden, a small mirror in one hand, an open spell book in the other, with a small book light clipped to the pages to illuminate the necessary "arcane words," which she was

CHAPTER FOUR

certain were really just modern words spelled as if they were old, plus a few peculiar ones thrown in, but never mind.

"Right, so now, all I have to do is catch the moon's reflection in the mirror, say the words, concentrate on Blip, and try to catch sight of him. Should be easy enough."

She looked again at the text, not at all confident that she was going to say the words properly, but hopeful that her intent was the more important component. She gave it a go:

"Waxyng Moone, waynyng Moone
Bryng my sighte, and bryng it soone,
Shew me nowe the one I seeke
Yet hyde me styll, whenn I do sneeke... um, all right.
Wayning Moone, waxing Moone
Nowe I aske thee for thys boone
Shew at once whatt I maye fynde
So I canne kyck somone's behynde... this is a very strange spell!"

She gazed into the mirror, hoping to catch a glimpse of something, anything, even if it was just Blip lecturing on Descartes to a group of bored brownies. Nothing. No sights. No sounds, just a hint of the moon shining back at her. She tried tilting the mirror both toward her face and away from it. She squinted. She rotated the mirror. She stood up, hoping to get it that much closer to the moon, which she realized was a silly notion. She sat back down in frustration.

"Damn it! Magic is always so much harder than it should be! Why can't these things just work the first time? Why do I always have to try and re-try just to get anything to happen? Hello?" She shook the mirror. "Any magic in there? Hiya, moon? Reflection? Anything you want to show me? I'm here, and it's getting quite chilly out. I'd like to go inside soon and have some hot cocoa, thank you very much."

Just as she was about to give up, she saw a brief flash in the mirror. Excited, she held it up to her face to get a better look.

"What?" It wasn't what she expected at all.

The mirror showed a long stone corridor, lit by flickering torches in wall sconces. It was a dark, unpleasant place, and in the midst of it, a small figure in a tattered black robe strode forth, its face obscured by a large hood.

Jilly didn't understand what she was looking at, but she had a sense that it seemed clearer than what the spell should have been able to show her. Worse, she guessed it might be something she wasn't supposed to see. She bit her lip, even if somewhat certain that she couldn't be seen or heard.

Is that Blip?

The little figure proceeded down the hallway.

Wherever this place is, it's big. She tried to take in as much as she could while the magic held out. The dark silhouette paused, as if sensing something; it started to turn its head in her direction.

Come on, turn around! she insisted. *Is it you?*

But it turned away and started moving again.

Bollocks!

To make matters worse, the vision started to fade around the edges of the mirror.

"Oh, come on, I'm not done yet! I didn't even see if it was him."

The mirror, however, remained oblivious to her pleas, and the whole scene faded away, leaving only the reflection of the moon once more.

"You stupid spell! What good are you if 1 can't even get what 1 wanted?"

She sighed and set the mirror aside, looking at the open book again.

"Maybe 1 didn't do it quite right. Maybe there's another part to it?"

A quick perusal of the next page revealed no such lucky break. She decided to try again later, as the night was too cold to stay outside for much longer.

She packed up her things, crept out of the garden, and started to walk toward her own home across the street. There was just one problem: her parents were now home, sitting in the living room. Even if she entered by the back door, she had no way of getting into the house, much less upstairs, without them seeing or hearing her. Which, of course, would make the snoring coming from her bedroom seem very strange. Which would mean questions, and more questions, and suspicions, and maybe accusations, and probably punishments.

"Well, this night just keeps getting better," she grumbled.

CHAPTER FIVE

"Define 'very serious,'" Qwyrk said, her irritation mounting.

Qwyzz cleared his throat. "Magic, you see, has different uses and permutations, some for good, some for ill. It is spread across multiple worlds and serves different orders of beings in different ways. And that's part of the issue, of course: the different orders react to magic and its effects differently, precisely because of their divergences, which can be traced back to the very earliest times when the strands of enchantment first emerged from the primal cosmos as a force that could be manipulated either for—"

"Qwyzz, I don't mean to be rude, but you're rambling," Qwyrk said. "I appreciate your dedication to research, really, but now isn't the time."

"Yes, yes, quite! My apologies. So then, how can I summarize this? You and Ms. Vishala are of two different orders of magical beings, Fae and Shadow."

"Yeah, so?"

"The different orders dwell in different realms, and though they relate to one another all the time, up to and including intimate interactions, it's relatively rare for them to bond deeply as lasting companions over the centuries, or produce children, and so on."

"Rare, but not unheard of, surely?" Holly asked.

"No, not unheard of, but if what I'm reading is correct, such parings are apparently, um, discouraged by the Shadows. Rather strongly, I'm afraid."

"What do you mean, 'discouraged'?" Qwyrk's irritation began to turn again to anger.

"Well, it seems that—again, if what I'm reading is correct— in the dark days of the Fomóraiġ's rule in Ireland, certain diverse orders of beings, well, paired with one another frequently enough to produce offspring who took to their overlords' service. Some Shadows were among this renegade group, and the children of those inter-order matings proved to be most troublesome. Indeed, they were some of the very worst creatures to be found among the Fomorian allies and armies. The differing effects of magic caused strange and unexpected mutations and changes, you see, which manifested in those offspring in very unpredictable ways. Some of them were quite grotesque and horrific. Monsters, you might call them. All of which only added to the reputation for Fomorian terror. And so, when the Fomóraiġ were finally banished to the twilight realm of the half-dead, the Shadow council decided to place powerful wards in place. In effect, they aimed to prevent any Shadow from coupling with and reproducing with beings of the other magical orders, as a precaution against such creatures being inadvertently created again."

"Hang on just a damned minute," Qwyrk said, shaking her head and trying to process what he'd said. "Are you telling me that these jolts we've been getting are because of some magical law put in place thousands of years ago? That it's some kind of enforced segregation? Is that really what we're talking about here?"

"I'm afraid it does seem that way," Qwyzz conceded, "though I assure you that I've never heard of this particular prohibition before. If this edict and these wards exist, great effort has been made to keep them unknown. I only discovered it by examining this ancient law book, which I'm fairly certain I've never even opened before. And it wasn't the explanation I was looking for, anyway."

"But this makes no sense," Holly said. "It first happened to us back around Beltane. But it was nothing, really. It went on for a few days, and then stopped. It hasn't happened again until today. If it's some sort of magical ward to keep us apart, why was there such a gap in time between then and now?"

Qwyzz shook his head. "I don't have an answer to that, my dear, not at the moment. But I agree, it's very odd."

Qwyrk gripped Holly's hand tighter, despite this news. "So, somehow, after all these centuries, I'm just now learning that my people have some kind of selective law in place to keep us from 'mingling' with anyone outside of our own kind? A law that determines when we've gotten 'too close' to another magical being and will just step in and stop it by force. And I've never heard of this before because the council keeps it secret?"

Qwyzz nodded. "It would seem."

"But," Holly said, clearly trying to keep calm, "how could this law exist at all without someone noticing it before now? Surely there must have been any number of times when a Shadow was drawn to a being of another order. Even another realm? We can't possibly be the first."

"Oh, I don't think it's some all-encompassing spell set up to stop us from having a snog or a shag," Qwyrk said. "I have a feeling it's a law that's enforced pretty selectively, probably whenever the council wants to send a message. And believe me, they're sending us one, right now. I'd bet that's why Qworum pulled me aside last spring. He was trying to warn me without saying why. He was probably looking out for us in his own, odd way. Maybe he was even able to keep it at bay for a while. He's always been on my side, even if he doesn't like to admit it."

"He might have been able to mitigate the effects," Qwyzz agreed. "It's also possible that with the approach of Samhain, the magic is asserting itself and is more powerful now. But it's equally possible that this prohibition isn't universal and is only used against those the council thinks pose a real risk."

"Or in our case, against someone who's pissing them off," Qwyrk growled.

"It's horrid, it's utterly appalling," Holly said, squeezing Qwyrk's hand. "I can't believe what I'm hearing. What's the outcome, then? What will happen if we defy it?"

"I don't know," Qwyzz said, "but in similar kinds of magics, such wards are able to create permanent barriers, say between two criminals, or some such. If you two continue with your romantic relationship, it's possible that you'll be separated permanently, forced apart and unable even to touch one another. And such separations are very difficult to undo, if it all. I'm so sorry, my dears, this is dreadful news. I wish it weren't the case."

Qwyrk's fury evaporated into a feeling of despair, light-headedness, and disbelief. "This can't be happening. It just can't." She glanced at Holly, who placed her other hand over Qwyrk's, and seemed as if she were about to cry. Qwyrk reeled at the thought that everything was falling away from her, that she had no control over anything, and for the first time in a long time, she had no idea how to react, what to think, or what to do.

*   *   *

Winston wandered in a field some distance from the hedgerow, feeling as if he'd just woken up, only now aware of his surroundings. The chilly night air smelled of damp earth, and he shivered a bit as he came to his senses.

"What? How on Earth did I get out here?" He turned about in all directions to get his bearings. "What's going on?"

He had a vague memory of approaching the spot where he'd found the key.

"The key!"

He reached in panic to his left coat pocket.

"No! Where is it? Where—"

He clutched at the right pocket in desperation. And there it was. Relief flooded though him.

"But how can that be? I'm quite sure I put it in the left pocket. When did I move it? Why don't I remember doing it?"

He recalled seeing someone, or rather several someones, lurking by the hedge.

"Who were they? What were they wearing? I'd almost say they were monks." He shuddered. "Or perhaps black magic cultists, or some such appalling thing. They must have been looking for the key. But if they were, how do I still have it? Unless, what if it's not the same key? Oh no, what if they took it and replaced it with another before knocking me out and leaving me in this field to die? That would explain why it's in my other pocket."

He pulled out the key and tried to examine it in the light of the waxing moon, turning it over and over, but alas, Luna's luminosity was too dim. Cursing, he put it away and stomped across the field back toward the hedge.

"I am *not* wearing appropriate footwear for this kind of jaunt," he grumped, noting the unpleasant feeling of his walking shoes getting sucked down by the muddy ground with each step. "If I find out who those hooligans are, I'll be sending them the bill for any needed shoe repairs!"

Soon, he found himself back on the drier main path, facing the hedge. Looking it up and down, he spied the nook where the key had hung.

"Here!"

He peered in, but the dark kept him from seeing much. He felt around, and a twist and tangle of fall foliage greeted his unprotected hand. But nothing else.

"No other keys, anyway." He sighed. "Oh, I don't know what happened. Maybe I imagined it all. Maybe that damned pudding is still playing tricks on me. I'll go home, look it over in better light, and put this wretched evening behind me. I think another spot of sherry might even be in order. What was I thinking, going for a walk at this hour, anyway?"

He set off home, quite convinced that warm, dry feet and a bit more alcoholic fortification would be just the trick to put things to right. Nothing seemed out of sorts on his return. Other than muddy shoes and an unsettling incident, all seemed well enough. He arrived back at his home feeling quite worn out.

As he stepped into his cozy and inviting house and took off his muddy shoes, he wondered how long he'd been outside. It hadn't occurred to him before now, but a quick check of the wall clock in the kitchen made his jaw drop.

"Two hours? That can't be! Twenty minutes or so out there, and twenty back. I was in that wretched field for over an hour? What was I doing? Oh dear, what if I was actually somewhere else? What if those hoodlums kidnapped me and took me away, and dropped me back there only minutes before I recovered? Oh, it doesn't bear thinking about!"

But he did. Think about it, that is. He stewed and pondered. He poured himself more sherry and examined the key again, which, for all intents and purposes, seemed to be the same. Unless…

"What if it's a clever copy? What if they stole the real one and replaced it with a fake and drugged me so I wouldn't remember? What a ghastly thought! No, that's absurd. There must be some other explanation. I wonder if I should ring Penelope and tell her about this? No, no. It's getting a bit late, and I don't want to be rude. I'll wait until morning. Maybe by then, I'll be free of the after-effects of that damned pudding!"

Swallowing the last gulp of his second sherry, he got up, turned out the appropriate lights, intending to go upstairs for a much-needed sleep. But in the darkness, he sensed something, a presence nearby, somehow both there but not there. And the voice he'd heard in that dream-like state earlier, in that land of rocks and twilight: it was there, too, speaking words into his mind, humming like a low-level static. They were words that he couldn't understand, but that filled him with fear, yet also a longing for something, something that would change the world. Something that needed him to accomplish a task.

He shook out his head, as if trying to clear cobwebs, and the sensation vanished. There was nothing now but silence, and the stairs creaking beneath his feet. He sighed.

"Definitely the pudding."

*　　*　　*

Qwyrk and Holly stood next to each other at the lake near Qwyrk's house, the waxing moon reflecting off the gentle ripples of the water. Qwyrk didn't know how long they'd been there, but she realized that neither had spoken during that time, and they hadn't even looked at each other, much less touched. Qwyrk was still trying to process it all, and she imagined Holly was doing the same. Any words she might say about it would just come across as pointless, anyway.

She turned over events in her mind, trying to remember what had occurred at Beltane, and wondering why she couldn't recall it. *Something* had happened in her home then, something very upsetting. Her mind wandered trying to piece everything together. She lost track of her surroundings.

"I know what we should do tomorrow," Holly said at some point, startling Qwyrk and breaking her train of thought.

Qwyrk looked at Holly as her attention returned to the moment. She couldn't think of anything to say, so she just raised her eyebrows.

"We should go to the Shadow council, level with them," Holly continued. "Tell them we know what's happening, tell them we understand why the wards were put in place, but make it clear in no uncertain terms that we will not stand for it, we won't be kept apart for no reason, and we will bring them down if they try to enforce it."

"Uh, yeah, that might not go over so well."

Holly shot her a glance of annoyance mixed with fierce determination. "I'm utterly serious, Qwyrk. There is no way that some fossilized council is going to tell me how to live my life, or who I can live it with. I'm Yakshi. I'm not beholden to them, and I won't be dictated to in that way."

"Unfortunately, I am. Beholden to them, I mean. All Shadows are, in one way or another. The council's had Goddess-knows-how-many members over the centuries, but it's always been there, and even though they can be a bunch of pretentious pillocks, it serves a purpose."

"And what purpose is that?"

"It protects, it actually does do good. There's a lot of evil shite out there that wants to get a toehold in the mortal world, into our world, yours even, and we're the first—sometimes only—line of defense. I know I complain a lot about stupid assignments that turn out to be nothing and waste my time, but I've got all the time in the world, don't I? And it was precisely one of those assignments that led me to bump into Jilly and uncover what de Soulis was doing. And that led to a hunt for his supporters that brought me back north six months later and right into your arms, almost literally."

"A lot of good that all was if now we can't, can't even..." Holly eyes started to tear up.

"Hey," Qwyrk said, drawing her into a hug, oblivious to what might happen; on this occasion, nothing did. "We're not going to let this thing win. It's not going to keep us apart." She stepped back and wiped a tear from Holly's cheek. "And I agree. We should go to the council tomorrow. I'll give them a chance to explain themselves and this appalling law, and I'll ask them to set it aside in our case. Maybe we can appeal to their sense of fairness and decency."

"Do you honestly think they even have those qualities?"

"Not really, but we have to try. Then we can at least justify kicking their arses, if we need to."

Holly chuckled and Qwyrk joined her. They hugged again and held each other for a while, and all was well for the moment.

"There does seem to be a ridiculous number of misfortunes happening all at once." Holly took a step back to gaze at her.

"I agree. Looking back over the past six months, maybe more, there's been a whole lot of bizarre happenings, coincidences, things we can't remember: my dizziness, your headaches, this separation ward, walking trees and boulders, us trying to remember some kind of incident at my home, but we can't."

"Then there's what Aeval told you about a hidden war among the Darkfae and who-knows-what, and the whole business with Moirin and Aileen and the invasion at the night club."

"Bogtrotter telling me about rumors that some bigger bad is lurking out there."

"My dreams, and hazy memories about meeting someone, maybe in a cave? But I can never remember who it is."

"It's a pretty big pile of crap to be happening all at once." Qwyrk nodded, looking up to the moon. "I don't think it's just random. And I think the banshee must be a big part of it. She told me that something really powerful is lurking, hidden, but almost ready to do... something. She even tried to get me to join her side, which goes along with what Boggie said. It's like something, or a group of somethings, is waiting out there to strike, and this nonsense going on all around us is pointing to that, or maybe it's all side effects of it, I don't know."

"If that's true, then the last thing we want to do is let on to the council about what we know or suspect."

"Exactly. I'm all for going there and giving them a good bollocking about this ward crap, but beyond that, Qwyzz and you are the only ones I trust. And Jilly. And Blip, Goddess help me. Whatever else happens, we have to stick together, which is why we need this damned spell removed, neutralized, deleted."

"That's not the only reason we need it removed..." Holly gave Qwyrk a playful look of innocence.

"Oh, there's lots of reasons," Qwyrk assured her with a smile and a kiss.

At once, both were stung with an electric shock and flung away from each other, landing a good ten feet apart in undignified thuds.

"Damn it!" Qwyrk shouted, pounding the ground as she sat up. "Are you all right?"

"No, I'm bloody well not." Holly also pulled herself up to a sitting position. "Are you sure we don't just want to go to the council punching first and asking questions later?"

"I'm starting to think that's a good idea," Qwyrk muttered.

*   *   *

Jilly sat drinking tea in Granny's living room, trying to read, quite annoyed at not being able to go home. It wasn't her parents' fault for being home. But really? This would be the one night they were actually home early and sitting downstairs instead of going right to bed. Jilly needed to be back before half past eleven, and it would be just like them to decide to stay up late for once so she couldn't even get into her own bedroom.

She pondered ways of sneaking in, like a forgetful spell (if she could remember it), or some means of teleportation, but without Qwyrk around, she was very reluctant to try it. Even if such a thing existed. She thought of texting Lluck—again—and having him contact Holly, so she could tell Qwyrk to come and get her.

But she'd left her phone in her room.

"I can't believe Qwyrk and I have never come up with a better way to stay in touch before now," she muttered to herself. "It's not like we ever have to do anything important, like, you know, save the world, or anything."

She stood up, went to the window and peered out from behind the curtains, just as she'd seen Granny do on numerous occasions. Nothing had changed.

"I may as well have another go at trying to see what Blip's up to. That should kill a little time."

She gathered the necessary components, bundled up, and trudged back out to the backyard, where to her annoyance, it was colder than before.

She prepared the spell and recited the poem again (it sounded even sillier the second time), holding up the mirror to reflect the moon and trying to get a fix on her mysterious imaginary friend. At first, as before, nothing came of it, but soon, an image formed in the glass, cloudy but clearing.

"Come on!" she whispered. "Show me something!"

The view came into focus, and she saw the little figure again, now treading with care through another stone hallway, this one less dank and dungeon-like than the previous one, but still dark and lit only by the occasional set of candles set in wall sconces.

The figure moved with surprising swiftness through the gloom, until it came to a large wooden door, lit by torches set on either side. He knocked and was received at once as it swung open. Jilly started to feel afraid and a bit sick, but she couldn't look away, as her viewpoint followed along behind her little robed guide, like a hand-held camera.

She watched as the figure entered a chamber and approached a large, circular, wooden table. Around the table sat several taller figures, also robed in garments of an inky darkness that blended in with the shadows all around them. One stood and said something, but she couldn't make out the words. She concentrated and the sound started to come through better; or perhaps she only heard it in her mind.

"Everything is on order?" the standing figure asked in a raspy voice that sounded as if he were trying to conceal his actual tone, and maybe his true identity.

The little figure nodded. "Indeed. After all this time, the arrival is at hand, and none know of it, save us," it answered in a voice that was little more than a whisper. "It will take everyone by surprise, which is to our great advantage."

The taller one nodded. "Excellent. Preparations are nearly complete on our part. Nothing can stop us now. No one can prevent it. With the coming of Samhain, the world shall be remade. The barriers will fall from the mortal earth, and the Fomóraiġ will seize it once more. The realm of the Shadows will submit to us soon after, and all of Faerie shall then be claimed by his most tenebrous majesty. The worthy will rule again, and the weak shall kneel or fall."

The smaller figure drew back his hood, revealing the froggy shape of the back of his head. Jilly had no doubt who it was. Her heart pounded, and her stomach twisted.

"Hail to the Deathly Eye," Blip proclaimed, raising both hands upward, fists clenched.

"Hail to the Deathly Eye," a chorus of robed figures echoed.

Jilly was gripped by a cold that had nothing to do with her surroundings. A numbing terror befell her, and with it, a sense of awful foreboding, and even worse, the realization of betrayal. Her lower lip trembled, and her eyes begin to water. She shook her head in denial, but the mirror's image did not fade, did not lie. Blip was there among these people, whoever they were, plotting something with them, something terrible, and all this time he'd pretended to be her friend and Qwyrk's ally. It was unbelievable, impossible, yet right in front of her. In her anguish, a choked sob escaped from her and on instinct, she slapped a hand over her mouth, dropping the spell book to the ground. The book light shattered and went out.

Blip and the robed figure both seemed to be startled by this, and he turned to look in the direction of her mirror. He frowned and squinted.

Oh no! Jilly's eyes widened. She wanted to drop the mirror, to run, but her gaze was fixed on the mirror.

"What's happening? Who's there?" Blip demanded. "Who's there?"

CHAPTER SIX

"I've had enough of this crap," Qwyrk fumed, standing but not willing to offer a helping hand to Holly, lest they be shocked again. "We're not waiting till tomorrow. I'm going to send a Faegram to Qworum right now and tell him to assemble the council, because it's an emergency."

"They're not going to be happy when they hear what we're there for," Holly said, dusting herself off and standing.

"And I don't bloody care."

"Nor do I, but if we were going to try to appeal to them with tact and reason, that plan may have just gone out the window."

"Plans get defenestrated all the time. In fact, I'd like to defenestrate a few of the council members while I'm at it." Qwyrk made fists, frustrated at not having anything or anyone to hit.

Holly shrugged "I'll gladly open any windows you might have in mind. So, a Faegram?"

"Yeah. Uh, do you know any couriers who are about at this time of night?"

Holly nodded. "There should be a few. Pop-pluck is quite reliable."

"Pop-pluck?"

"He's a Brownie, the best at what he does, and very trustworthy with confidential messages. He's helped me out on a number of occasions. He charges a premium, but he's well worth it."

"And you're sure this... Pop-pluck is all right with contacting Qworum? The grand poohbah of the council might be just a bit grumpy being interrupted from whatever the hell it is he does when he's not sitting in the council room acting important. Or warning me to stay away from you."

"I think Pop would relish the chance to tweak the nose of the senior Shadow council member. I'll reach out to him on my ring."

Holly seemed confident in her choice. She wandered off a bit, and Qwyrk heard her conversing. After a minute or so, she returned.

"He says he'd be happy to help us out and will be on his way in about a quarter of an hour."

Qwyrk felt a sense of relief. "Fantastic! Uh, what did you tell him to say?"

"Only what you said: that you need to see the council and that it's an emergency. He's not mentioning me at all."

Qwyrk nodded in satisfaction. "Good. Right, this is going to shake things up a bit."

"For better or worse?"

"Well, how much worse can it get?"

Holly frowned. "Over the years, darling, I've learned at least two important things: never ask what else can go wrong, because you'll always find out, and never say that at least things can't get any worse, because they most assuredly can."

"You're just a shining light of optimism tonight." Qwyrk winked at her.

But Holly wasn't amused. "When I can't even kiss my girlfriend without the risk of being hurled through the air, I do tend to get a bit testy!"

"Me too, love. I'm not particularly interested in their excuses, and if they won't help us out, at least we know where we stand. We'll have to find some other way to fix this."

"I have faith in us."

I'm glad one of us does, Qwyrk almost said out loud, but held her tongue. She also held her head as another surge of dizziness overtook her.

"Ugh! Damn it!"

"What is it? Are you all right?" Holly came to her at once, but held back from touching her, which only frustrated Qwyrk even more.

"Yeah, just dizzy again, but it's already passing."

"This isn't good, none of it: your dizzy spells, my headaches, the fact that we can't remember—"

"Wait, hang on," Qwyrk interrupted, an awareness trickling into her mind. "Something just came to me. Maybe it was the jolt, or maybe this spinning is me trying to shake off something."

"What is it?"

"That night last spring, the one that's blocked? I remember something now. I came out of Reverie, but it was, early? Too early. It wasn't even dawn yet. And you, you weren't sleeping next to me. That worried me, so I got up, and I think I found you in the sitting room. Maybe you were asleep there? But there was something else, something bad."

"What was it?" Holly reached out and touched Qwyrk's arm at last, thankfully to no ill effect.

"There was like this, blob of darkness, and it was, I think it was trying to take you, but I wouldn't let it. I struggled with it, like a tug of war, and I almost lost you, but I held on, and it went away. Goddess, I feel sick just thinking about it. That's all I can remember. Does this ring any bells?"

Holly shook her head. "No, sorry, but if I was asleep or unconscious, I wouldn't have seen it, anyway."

"Fair enough. Look, I think someone attacked us, tried to take you, to separate us, but failed. It might be related to this whole stupid ward business. Maybe the council tried to push us apart back then, but we shoved them off, ruined their spell. So, they've had to wait until now."

"Do you think they'd really do something like that?" Holly's worried expression reinforced just how serious this whole intrusion had become.

"Even as long as I've worked for them, I honestly don't know." Qwyrk furrowed her brow, and her anger welled up again. "But we're going to damned well find out!"

*　　*　　*

Jilly sat on Granny's couch, her knees up at her chin, arms wrapped around them, hugging herself, trying to find comfort in something, anything. Her mind reeled at what she'd seen, what she'd discovered.

"What was Blip doing? It felt so icky, so horrible! I'm just glad he couldn't see me. At least, I don't think he could. But he knew something was there. Now he's going to be suspicious. What if he figures out it was me?"

She turned the idea over in her head, which just made her feel worse. She peered out from behind the curtains again. The lights in her house were out at last.

"They've gone to bed, at least. Better wait a while until I go back, though. But what if Blip *does* know it was me spying on him? He might come for me over there. I'd be better off staying here. But then, what if he," she could scarcely bring herself to think it, much less say it, "what if he goes after my parents if he doesn't find me? I have to protect them! Or maybe if he doesn't see me over there, he'll just come over here, anyway, because this is where I'd go, to draw him away from them. Oh, I don't know what to do!"

She started to cry. "I'm hopeless, I'm useless, and I've probably done something really stupid. What if it's not real, or it wasn't him, or I imagined it? Or what if he really is evil, and he's been tricking us all along? I need Qwyrk, I have to tell her. I have to get in touch with her. But what if I'm wrong?"

She buried her face in her hands and curled up even tighter. Everything seemed hopeless and dark.

*   *   *

In the dark, the taxi pulled up to a row of stone cottages at the edge of Nicewood. They were compact, pretty, and well maintained with flower gardens that looked good even at this time of night.

"Here we are, love. You sure this where you want to go?" the driver asked, as he took money for the trip.

"Yeah, this is definitely the place," the passenger answered. "I'm meeting some friends here soon, and then... we're all goin' off for a good long chat. You know, somewhere nice and warm where we can catch up." That was a lie, but it seemed to satisfy him.

"You want me to wait here until they show up, then?"

"That's kind of you, but not necessary. They're good folks, and I'm sure they'll be here on time. We planned it all out earlier."

The driver shrugged. "All right, if you're sure. But don't hesitate to call us back if you need. Me or one of the other drivers can be back in just a few ticks. We pride ourselves on far better service than those plonkers in those rubbishy 'rideshare' companies, like Udder, or whatever."

"I appreciate it, really. I will if I need to, but it'll all be fine. Thanks again."

Moirin Moeran stepped out of the back seat, pulled her long coat about her, wrapped her scarf around her neck, took a deep breath of the chilly but invigorating northern night air, and spied the dark tree line in the distance. She waved at the driver and smiled, waiting until he drove off. No sense in alarming him by not lingering at the houses. With another deep breath, she flipped on her torch and walked out to the green, heading for the trees where her very unusual friends would find her.

"I just hope they can help," she said to herself, doubts about the meet-up already creeping in. "Otherwise, I'm really fecked."

*   *   *

"Pop just got back to me," Holly said, massaging her ring. "Qworum got the message and has agreed to meet you. I don't think he's too happy about being interrupted, though."

"Good, I don't care!" Qwyrk almost yelled. "I'm not happy about this magic crap they've somehow never bothered to tell me about. I'm ready to give them an earful."

"Well, no time like the present. Shall we?"

Holly extended her hand, and Qwyrk took it, relived that nothing happened. With a wave of her free hand, she formed a purple light spiral, and in they stepped, emerging a moment later in front of the council hall. It shone in all white stone and marble, reminiscent of a pseudo-Greek building from the European eighteenth century.

"It's quite impressive, I must admit," Holly said, looking up and down.

"Yeah, I suppose," Qwyrk conceded. "They've remodeled it lots of times over the centuries, but I guess I just see it as kind of pompous. It's more like a monument to the council than something representing the good it's supposed to do. Anyway, in we go."

They walked up a short flight of steps and pushed through a large wooden door, which had just enough creak in its hinges to be befitting of an old, hallowed hall.

"This is rather grand," Holly said, looking around at the neoclassical interior.

"Yeah, they like to lay it on a bit thick. But don't be overly impressed. They really are just a bunch of wankers."

"You have such a way with words, darling!"

Qwyrk led Holly down the main hall to a pair of ornate double doors at the end, which were partially open.

"They're expecting us," Qwyrk whispered, her stomach tightening.

"Here we go," Holly whispered back.

Together, they pushed through the entrance, and Qwyrk strode with all the confidence she could muster into the council room. It looked as it always did: a semi-circular table on a raised platform faced them, at which were seated six council members, dressed in white robes: Qworum, Qwalm, Qwery, Qwote, Qwyll, and Qwire, all looking most unamused.

"Qwyrk," Qworum announced as they approached. He eyed Holly and didn't seem pleased about her being there. "I have received a communication stating that you have an emergency situation requiring our attention. This is highly unusual. Can you explain why we are summoned here in the middle of the night?"

Qwalm sneered. "Some of us were in Reverie and don't appreciate the interruption." Qwyrk ignored him for now, but one day, she was going to haul him off and deck him.

"Why is a Yakshi with you?" Qwyll asked, not in a terribly rude manner, but it still rubbed Qwyrk the wrong way. *She should stick to being a scribe instead of mouthing off*, Qwyrk thought.

"She has a name," Qwyrk answered curtly. "It's Vishala, or Holly, and yes, there is just a bit of an emergency. Or not, depending on your point of view. It is to me, but it might not be to you."

"What is this about, Qwyrk?" a clearly annoyed Qworum pressed.

"Oh, you know, just a little thing about a magical ward being put in place ages ago that effectively segregates us Shadows from prolonged intimate contact with other beings, and which is pretty painful and humiliating. And why the bloody hell have I never heard about this before, and no one else has either, it seems? Care to cough up some explanations about why this awful law is still being enforced?"

There was a moment of silence as the council members looked at each other. They seemed uncomfortable. Good.

"You are no doubt aware of the reasoning behind the creation of this barrier?" Qworum asked, his stare seeming to say to Qwyrk: "I warned you about this months ago."

"Yeah, because of the Fomorians and their weird offspring, and because too much mingling might make monsters. Really? That's why this is still in place? And because Holly and I are from different orders, but we're a 'thing,' we're now being thrown apart by shocks and explosions, because, clearly, we're such a damned threat to your precious barrier."

"The law is the law. You of all people should understand and respect that." Qworum had a coldness to his voice that told her he would not be her ally in this.

"And you really, honestly think that, after all I've done for this bloody council over the centuries, I'm just going to stand here and accept this idiotic ruling by the lot of you?"

"The decision is not ours, Qwyrk," Qworum said. "As you say, this law has been in place for centuries, even before your birth."

"So how the hell is it that I'm just hearing about it now, then, eh?" Qwyrk glared.

"It is revealed on a need-to-know basis, for each individual case, and clearly, it has never been something you needed to know, until now."

"I don't need to know about it now, because it doesn't need to exist! This is complete rubbish, and you all know it!" Qwyrk clenched her fists.

"It may seem harsh, I grant you, but it has served a purpose." Qworum's overall snootiness was infuriating.

"And just what purpose would that be, other than discriminatory nonsense?" Holly interrupted in an icy tone. Her words made it clear that she was also in no mood for this.

"You know why, Fae," Qworum answered bluntly. "To prevent the undesired co-mingling of the different orders, and so prevent the return of Fomorian-like beings, born of unpredictable magical unions. Such offspring present a higher than acceptable risk to peace."

"Um, hello?" Qwyrk nearly yelled. "Two ladies here." She pointed back and forth between herself and Holly. "That means two sets of lady bits, which means, hey, what a shock? No 'undesired co-mingling' and offspring are possible, you pillocks! We might be magic, but we're not bloody miracle workers, so unless you can show me how we're a 'higher than acceptable risk,' I'm calling bollocks on this whole thing!"

"The Yakshi has bred with a human, has she not?" Qwalm sneered. It confirmed to Qwyrk that the council had indeed been checking up on them.

"I *am* standing right here, you know," Holly said. Qwyrk thought she was ready to start throwing punches, as well.

"And she has a name, you bellend," Qwyrk growled.

"That boy is precisely why such mixing is not permitted among us," Qwalm countered, ignoring Qwyrk's insult, which just made her all the angrier. "He is unpredictable, potentially dangerous, living in the care of a fallible human. Frankly, he ought to be removed from that situation."

"Go anywhere near him," Holly declared, "and I promise that it will be the last thing you ever do." Her steely expression told Qwyrk she meant it. Qwyrk smiled with admiration.

"Are you threatening me, Vishala?" Qwalm accused, his voice dripping with mock offense.

Holly flashed an angry and confident smile. "Step down here and find out."

Qworum raised his hand. "Please, all of you, calm down! This is getting out of hand. Qwyrk, Holly: I am sympathetic to your plight, and I understand your anger, but at the moment, there is nothing we can do. This is an ancient law, created for justifiable reasons and bound by powerful magics that cannot just be set aside, as much as I would like to in your case. Believe me, I would do so if I could. I'm afraid that for the time being, you really must stay apart from each other. Your continued... interactions will only cause further chaos. If a suitable solution can be found that allows for you to continue your intimate relationship, we will contact you, but I cannot promise that will be the case."

"So, we just have to stay away from each other, or what?" Qwyrk demanded. "You'll send another bloody black hole into my home, in total violation of my privacy and sovereignty, and try to suck Holly into it? Send her somewhere else to keep us apart?"

"What are you talking about?" Qworum looked confused.

"You know damned well what I'm talking about!" Qwyrk yelled. "That magical void thing that showed up in my home and tried to hoover Holly away last spring. And nearly succeeded. If I hadn't come out of Reverie in time—"

"She's lying, as usual," Qwalm grumped, "making up nonsense to—"

Qworum held up his hand. "When did this happen?"

"Right around Beltane. The damned thing showed up in my

sitting room one night and tried to take Holly somewhere. I don't know where, and I don't want to think about it."

"I was unconscious at the time," Holly added. "I'm starting to recall it now. I felt as if I was drugged, or maybe charmed. I could barely even remember it afterward. It was like a dream."

"Why did you not come to us immediately?" Qwyll asked, setting down her writing implement.

"Honestly, I wasn't even sure if it really happened," Qwyrk said. "The whole thing had faded from my mind by the next morning. It was only when one of these shocks knocked me on my arse earlier that I began to remember it. Since you lot are telling us to stay away from each other, I just assumed you sent it to teach me a lesson. Nothing surprises me anymore."

"It did not come from this council," Qworum answered. "This is serious, Qwyrk. I would guess that something, possibly sent by our enemies, tried to attack you, or rather you, Holly. I do not know why."

"All the more reason you two need to stay away from each other," Qwalm taunted. "You're probably attracting unwanted attention, flaunting yourselves about as you're obviously doing."

"Look mate," Qwyrk said through clenched teeth. "I'm sorry you're not my type, and that I turned you down ages ago, but it's really time to get over the grudge, all right? You're boring, annoying, weak, and pathetic, and literally nothing you've said here has made me change my mind about any of that. Holly's worth a hundred of you, and she has something you'll never have, namely, my heart. So do everyone a favor and go leap off a cliff."

"You dare to insult a council member?" Qwalm stood up.

"Oh, I dare. I double dare." Qwyrk made a threatening fist. "In fact, come here and I'll show you what the hell else I'll do!"

"Stop it at once, both of you!" Qworum admonished. "We're all on edge, and now you tell us of a possible incursion right into the heart of Symphinity? This *is* an emergency, and we must consider how we proceed. Do not test us further, Qwyrk. You have withheld critical information."

"I didn't even know about it! It was erased from my memory."

"Your personal indiscretions have left you open to attack and caused damaging effects to the fabric of magic." Qworum ignored her and stood up. "Some Darkfae may be using that damage as a way of trying to break through to this plane." He pointed at them. "You and Vishala are forbidden to see one another until further notice, and we now must direct our attention to this matter. We will need you to tell us everything you saw, down to the smallest detail."

"You know what?" Qwyrk said. "Sod this. Sod the lot of you. This council created these problems all on its own, so you can bloody well clean them up yourselves. I'm done. I'm done being your patsy, your gofer, your policewoman. I've given up a good portion of my existence for you, and all you do is treat me like crap, so to hell with it. We'll find our own way to fix this disaster, and if any Darkfae do start causing trouble, I'll bloody well beat them to a pulp, too. The lot of you can piss off!"

She whirled around and stormed toward the door. "I'd listen to her, if I were you," Holly said, turning to join her. "This isn't going to go the way you want it to, and in the end, we'll probably just end up remedying it all for you, anyway, since you obviously can't do it yourselves. Think about that the next time you need someone to clean up your atrocious mess."

And with that they strode to the exit.

"Do not defy us!" Qwalm called out. "This is a grave mistake. There will be consequences!"

Without looking back, Qwyrk and Holly gave him and the rest of the council the two-fingered salute and stormed out of the room.

* * *

"Well, this is just lovely." Moirin hugged herself, rubbing her upper arms with her opposite hands to get warm and wanting to give pretty much everyone and everything the two-fingered salute. "Oh sure, Moirin, we'd be glad to meet ya, why not in the woods outside Leeds? It's easy to get to. I guess I'm not worth their time, after all."

She took out her phone and checked the hour. Also, the three texts she'd sent to Jilly were still unanswered.

"Half past midnight, and here I am freezin' me tits off waiting to meet a witch and her magic friends, who clearly aren't comin'. That's my life: askin' for help from people who shouldn't even exist. Brilliant."

"It is time to let them go, to return to your true heritage, and your real family. We are still waiting for you." A familiar voice sounded in her head, fainter than before, but she knew it all too well. It was ancient, powerful, and angry.

"No," Moirin whispered, her heart sinking. "No, not this. Please. I don't want to come back to this. I can't, I won't! Leave me alone!"

But her ancestor's presence seeped into her mind again, like a flooding basement or a creeping tide, and she knew she couldn't long resist it. Jilly's spell faltered, and no one could help.

Aeval's voice turned to a gentle laughter, a glee that declared that Moirin's fate was sealed, and she had no hope of escaping it. She covered her ears and tried to drown out the sound, but it came from inside, as it always did, and nothing could push it away.

"Shut up! Shut up!"

She couldn't fight, she couldn't hope, she couldn't even think. So, she did the only thing she could: she ran, though not for the green of the park and the familiarity of the row cottages, or the safety of a taxi and the well-lit human city beyond. She fled instead into the trees, into the darkness, and into the primal world of her heritage that terrified and beckoned her all at once.

* * *

In an angry flash, Qwyrk and Holly were back where they started.

Without saying a word, they entered Qwyrk's home. Holly kicked off her boots and immediately staggered into Qwyrk's bedroom. Qwyrk followed close behind, as dazed and upset as her girlfriend. Holly collapsed onto Qwyrk's bed and curled up into a ball on her side. Qwyrk laid herself down behind her, wrapping an arm around her, holding her close, not caring if the ward attacked them again.

"What's happening, Qwyrk? How can this horrid, bigoted law even be real? How can they force us apart? We haven't done anything wrong!"

"No, we haven't. And to say I'm livid about it would be the understatement of the damned century. They have no right to make any demands of us at all, but they probably can enforce it, if they really want to. Toss me in prison, or something, or even let the magical barrier go up so we can't actually touch each other at all."

Holly gripped Qwyrk's arm, and her voice shook. "But why? What possible reason? We can't produce any Fomorian children. Why would they be so cruel?"

"Yeah, I don't think logic has a lot to do with it. It's more that if they make an exception for us, then they'll have to start making exceptions for everyone, and instead of revisiting this whole shite legislation and bringing it up to date, they just want to sit on their arses and dictate from on high about who can do what. But I swear to you, I had no idea about this. And honestly, even if I did, it wouldn't have changed anything between you and me. Not at all."

"But what are we going to do?" Holly turned to look at her. "They make it sound like our intimacy is weakening the fabric of Symphinity's protections, like it's our fault that these creatures are trying to get in. That has to be a load of rubbish! It can't be true. Set up this horrid prohibition on beings of different orders from 'mingling,' and then have the outcome for defying it be a depleted magical defense system? It's absurd!"

"You know what?" Qwyrk raised her head. "When you put it that way, it's total bilge. I don't think these two things have anything to do with each other at all. Whatever spell is trying to push us apart, it's completely separate from these probing attacks and random objects getting moved around here like chess pieces. But I think someone wants us to *think* there's a connection as a way of scaring us off from looking into it."

"But why? Who would do that?"

"Maybe someone who wants whatever's out there to break in? Someone who's seen what we did to the Erlking, then saw us get demoralized about the whole banshee thing, and wants to finish us off by keeping us apart long enough to knock down some defenses.

If they can make us scared of some vague consequences, we'll play right into their hands."

"Fair enough, but who?"

"Well, I never did find out who the traitors were behind Qwota and her attempt to unleash chaos on Earth with de Soulis. I wouldn't doubt for one minute that they're connected to this plan."

"But you said de Soulis was favored by the innovators, right? And the Erlking by the ancients, and so were the banshees? Don't they hate each other? Haven't they been fighting some sort of hidden war for centuries to try to take control?"

"According to Aeval, yes. But maybe the traitors want to play both sides against the middle. Maybe they have their own plan that we can't see yet."

Holly sighed and looked away. "That just makes it worse. I'm afraid, Qwyrk. Afraid we'll be forced apart and that we won't be able to stop it. I'm afraid something far more awful than anything we've seen before is going to threaten our world and Earth. I'm afraid for Lluck and Carl. I'm afraid for all of us." She started to cry.

Qwyrk nuzzled her face into the back of Holly's head.

"I wish I could promise that it's all going to be fine," Qwyrk said in as reassuring a tone as she could muster, which wasn't much. "I wish we could just run away together or lock ourselves in here and ride it all out, or hide out at Qwyzz's, or just put it all down to paranoia and forget about it. But none of those things are really options."

"That's not your best pep talk, I have to say," Holly joked with a sniff. "You might want to work on it a bit more. Sprinkle in some kittens and chocolate and roses, or something."

"That's because I wasn't finished, silly! What I mean to say is that we don't have control over outside forces or whatever evil bastard of the month is trying to make us all his slaves, or his personal reality show contestants. But we *do* have control over how we react to whatever gets thrown at us, and that give us an advantage. It used to be that when things seemed hopeless or upsetting, I'd go spoiling for fights, looking to bust some heads to get back my confidence and prove to myself that I could still win."

She hugged Holly closer.

"But there's more to it now. Oh, don't get me wrong. I still love dealing out a good arse-kicking, but just beating the bad guys isn't enough for me, not anymore. I can't only be standing against things, I have to stand *for* things, too."

"But you've always done that! You're caring, kind."

"Maybe, but I forget that part of myself, more often than I should, and it's nice, even necessary, to be reminded of it. Jilly came into my life right when I needed someone like her. Not just a human who required my protection, not just another assignment, but someone that was special, like, *really* special. She has all those artistic and magic gifts, but even beyond that, she's a brilliant girl who's shown me how important being close to others can be, and how good opening myself up to others again is. She's like the little sister I never had, and honestly, if I hadn't met her, I'm not sure I could've been ready to meet you. Mortals have so much to teach us. I feel like they're better at life than we are most of the time, because they don't get a lot of it. Maybe *we* need to learn from them and be more like them. Sorry, I'm rambling. You don't need my musings on the pathetic state of world-weary magical beings. Or even worse, an analysis of Qwyrk's screwed-up mind."

"Your mind and your heart seem to be in the right place to me," Holly said, squeezing Qwyrk's hand.

"Well, that's due in no small part to the amazing folks I have around me these days. And that's what I'm saying. About how it relates to this stupid segregation law, to external threats, or whatever else gets thrown at us. None of that's going to get in our way. I know it. I might still be grumpy and pessimistic and sick of everyone's crap—"

"It's part of your charm."

"...but I also know that the good is here, right beside me. And that good is Jilly, it's you, it's my other mates. With you all being in my long and lonely life, I feel like everything's going to be fine, no matter what happens. Jilly brought me back to a kind of family love again, but you, you've done way more. You're my dawn, the reason I look forward to every day. You're my reason why, and nothing is going to take that away. I won't let it. Ever."

"And you're my evening star," Holly sighed, "the sweetest thought I have as I drift off to sleep every night. You keep the bad dreams away."

"Do you still have bad dreams?"

"Sometimes, but never when I'm here. Being around you makes everything safer and more bearable for me." She caressed Qwyrk's arm. "I've slept better with you next to me than I have in ages.

"I'm glad."

"But... there's one dream that shows up from time to time. Like someone is telling me something. Something awful. I'm only just starting to remember it when I wake."

"Is it the woman you keep seeing? Who is she? Who's speaking to you?"

"I don't know. She wears a dark red robe with a hood, and her skin is grey. I can't see her eyes, I can only hear her voice, and barely. The odd thing is, she's not the threat. She's just telling me something I don't want to hear. Sometimes it feels more like a memory than a dream. Like something that really happened."

"Like she really said something to you, but you don't remember it?"

Holly turned her head "Yes, I think so. Why?"

"I'm not sure," Qwyrk answered. "But obviously, something's making us forget things. Maybe this merits another trip to Qwyzz's tomorrow?"

"Gargoyles and all?"

Qwyrk shook her head. "If we must."

"Oh come on," Holly managed a faint smile. "How often does one get a completely surreal show like that?"

"Um, far too often?"

"Nonsense, you love them!"

"Not the first verb that pops into my mind, to be honest."

Holly's amusement faded. "Will we be safe here tonight?"

"I don't see why not. Like I said, I'm pretty sure those other anomalies don't have anything to do with us being together, and if anything tries to get in here, they'll be right sorry!"

Holly snuggled closer. "You see? You're my evening star, my dame in shining armor. You're my reason why, too." She smiled and turned to kiss Qwyrk who was eager to oblige.

"Oh crap!" Qwyrk gasped, jerking her head up, an awful feeling hitting her all at once.

"What? What is it?"

"It's well after midnight, isn't it? We completely forgot to go get Jilly and meet with Moirin! She needs our help. Damn it!"

"Oh, no!" Holly put a hand over her mouth. "Oh Goddess. Qwyrk, what have we done?"

CHAPTER SEVEN

In a panicked flash, Qwyrk and Holly stepped into the darkness of Jilly's backyard.

"Goddess, it's chilly out tonight!" Holly said, pulling her scarf around her neck. "I wish I'd worn my longer coat."

Qwyrk let go of Holly's hand (no sense in taking extra risks and getting zapped again).

Holly pointed up to the window of Jilly's bedroom. "The light's out, so you were right not to materialize in there."

"Yeah, I didn't want to scare the life out of her. I mean, it's funny when I do it to Blip, but I wouldn't do that to Jilly." She stepped up to the house's back wall and ascended to the level of the window to peer in.

"That's odd," she said to herself. She scanned the room, but it was empty, no sign of anyone, not even Blip seated on the bed poring over some philosophical tome. She decided to venture inside for a closer look, but once in, she found that the room was indeed unoccupied, except for a few pillows piled up under the bed covers, and the sound of snoring. She blinked back out and descended back to the ground outside.

"Jilly's definitely not there," she said.

"Maybe she's down in the living room?"

"I can't imagine that even at her age, her almost non-existent parents would be fine with her being up this late. It's already after one. I'll pop in and check, though, just in case."

A quick reconnaissance of the downstairs of the Pleeth residence revealed only a sleepy bulldog curled up in his favorite bed and all the lights out. Qwyrk blinked back to the garden.

"Not there, which means she's not home."

"Probably over at Granny's," Holly said. "I'll bet she snuck over there at some point while her parents were still out. She's quite the rebel. Good for her!"

Qwyrk nodded. "Let's go on over and see."

They crept out of the garden and across the street, since it would have been rather silly to teleport such a short distance, and risk getting slammed by that accursed ward again.

"See?" Holly pointed. "There's a light on. I'll bet that's exactly where she is."

"Right," Qwyrk said. "I'll pop on in and fetch her and then we can be on our merry way."

She made a circle of purple light and stepped into it... only to re-materialize a few feet farther away and land with an unceremonious splat on the pavement.

"Ow! Bloody hell, what was that?"

Holly tried to suppress a laugh. "I rather suspect Granny has some protective wards of her own set up."

"You're right. It's probably to prevent folks like you or me from barging in unannounced," Qwyrk conceded. "Seems like a sensible precaution."

"Maybe we should try knocking on the front door?"

"Fine," Qwyrk picked herself up. "As long as she doesn't have her own bloody guard gargoyle."

"You must admit, it'd be terribly amusing."

"I don't have to admit anything."

They strode up to the front door. Qwyrk leaned in and tried to knock, only for her and Holly to be thrown back into the street, this time in two unceremonious splats on the pavement.

"Bollocks!" Qwyrk swore in a voice a little too loud for the time of night. "I am getting *really* sick of being tossed around like a rag doll, because of bloody magic! I'm ready to be done with all of it."

"It's quite off-putting, it must be said," Holly agreed.

"Never lose your remarkable ability for understatement, darling," Qwyrk said.

"I'll be sure not to. Short of yelling at the tops of our voices for Jilly to come out and raising quite the ruckus, how can we let her know we're out here? Assuming she's even inside?"

"I'm not sure we can," Qwyrk said with a frustrated sigh. "I think Granny's house is supposed to be kind of a sanctuary for her and whoever she invites in, when she chooses them. I've been inside before, but only because Granny was home and let me enter. And she was expecting me, somehow. She's a bit unnerving that way."

"Well, she *is* a six-hundred-year-old seeress, after all." Holly looked the house up and down. "Maybe we should go up to one of the windows and wave our arms about to get Jilly's attention?"

"But the curtains are all drawn, and we're assuming she's even in there. I hate to say it, love, but we should probably just head on over to Nicewood without her. If Moirin's about, maybe we can even convince her to talk with us in a place that's a bit more hospitable? She can always text Jilly or something, and then we can all come back here and get let in."

"That seems a rather roundabout way of meeting up."

"Indeed. Let's go and see if our wayward Irish singer is still waiting for us. I feel bad enough as it is about forgetting her. She probably hates us now, I mean, more than usual."

Holly nodded, and with some trepidation, they took each other's hands. No violent reaction resulted this time, and in a flash, they left this odd magical building plopped down in the middle of Knettles and made for the dark of Nicewood.

* * *

"Might as well have had a full mug of strong espresso spiked with dark chocolate and cola," Winston grumbled.

All night, he'd tossed and turned, dozing for a bit here and there, but then starting awake again with uncomfortable clarity. Not his sherry, not even a cup of chamomile tea had induced slumber.

He pulled a pillow over his face in a futile attempt to block out what little light and sound were filtering into his bedroom. But his attempt failed.

Slamming the pillow aside, he decided to give up, get up, and read some more.

Only, that's not what happened. Not at all.

He had a sensation of falling, but he was fairly certain he hadn't even stood up. Everything seemed to go dark, and he heard, or rather, perceived the presence in his head again: awful, ancient, alien, and abhorrent.

"Look here," he said out loud, working up a defiant head of steam, "I'm not at all convinced that you're real, and if you are, you've no right to be disturbing me as such. So, I'm telling you for the last time, get out of my head, leave me alone, and stop playing these absurd games! I'm in utterly no mood for it, and you're ruining what could otherwise be a good night's sleep. So—"

His speech was cut short as a freezing, paralyzing sensation, like a winter fog, descended over him. He knew something else now lurked in his mind, and it seemed to somehow shove him aside, as though he were still in his body, but no longer alone in it. He was forced to stand in the proverbial corner and cede control, like letting someone else drive, only far more contentious. And then, the sleep did come. Not the restful kind that he so looked forward to, but a chilly, death-like oblivion, to which he had no choice but to yield. And as he faded away, Winston was no longer defiant.

He was terrified.

∗   ∗   ∗

In a flash that would have stood out with some flair, if anyone had been awake to see it, Qwyrk and Holly stepped out into the green of Nicewood park. All was quiet, cold, and still.

Holly smiled as she looked around. "This is where you asked me out on our first date."

"Yeah, I made a bit of a mess of it, didn't I?"

"I thought it was adorable."

"Well, I'm glad *you* did!"

"What's the problem? You mangle your words when you're nervous, and it's charming!"

"I'm happy you think so. I'd have hated if I'd just looked like a pillock, and you'd said no."

"Why on earth would I have done that?" Holly stopped and stared at her. "I was dying for you to ask me!" She smiled and reached for Qwyrk's arm to take it in hers, but paused and drew back. She sighed. Qwyrk sighed.

"If Moirin's still here, she'll probably be over by the forest." Qwyrk pointed, changing the subject. "Let's go."

They set off in the dark, their magical eyes giving them better views than mere mortals could ever hope for in the moonlight. Which, unfortunately meant...

"I don't see her," Qwyrk said, squinting and scanning.

"Can you track her like you did when Aeval took her from Qwyzz's? Would she have left the same kind of trail?"

"Maybe? If something magical took her away again, then absolutely. Otherwise? I don't know if she leaves any residual signs of her presence. Still, it's worth a try."

With those words, Qwyrk sprinted up to the trees and knelt down, touching the earth. She closed her eyes and tried to tune in.

"Anything at all?" Holly wandered up behind her.

"I feel like something magical was here, not long ago," Qwyrk answered, "but it's hard to tell if it's her. It was a lot easier to track her at Qwyzz's. Aeval's trail was pretty obvious. There are so many other energies about on Earth at any given place and time that the signals get crossed easily. It's like trying to listen to several conversations in a crowded room all at once and keep them straight in your head."

"What? You can't do that?"

Qwyrk shot her an incredulous look. "You can?"

"No, silly, I'm teasing you! But please keep on trying, I'm going to have a quick look about in the trees."

"Don't go too far."

"Yes, mother. I'll stay within shouting distance." She held up her Silambam stick and in a flick of the wrist, it expanded to its full length. She twirled it a few times, leaving trails of light in its wake.

"Do you think you'll need that here?" Qwyrk asked, a bit of worry creeping into her.

"I don't know, but it's probably better to be prepared than not. Ta, darling, I'll be back shortly." And with that, she wandered into the dark woods.

Qwyrk watched her meld into the shadows and then turned her attention back to the ground in front of her. She inhaled the scent of rich, damp earth and moved her hands over the surface, feeling the dirt, the fallen leaves, the rocks, trying to get a fix on her target.

"Come on, Moirin, where are you? I know you were here, like very recently. Where did you go?"

She had an unsettling feeling for the briefest time, no more than a breath. The ancient magic that coursed through Moirin and seemed so foreign, so out of place, flickered into her awareness. But it was just for that breath, before it seemed to dissipate, leaving only Moirin's own faint magical "scent" in its wake.

"What if Aeval *has* found a way back into Moirin's head? What if she's taken her over again?"

She looked up. "Holly? Love? Can you come back here? I've found something, and it isn't good."

The sound of the silent forest was her only reply.

"Holly?" She stood up, a sinking feeling hitting her in the pit of her stomach. She tried not to be alarmed. "Darling? Can you hear me? Holly? Holly?"

*   *   *

Jilly thought she'd heard commotion outside, but only for a short time. She didn't dare look out from the curtains, feeling a knot in the pit of her stomach.

"What if he's out there? What if he sent someone to get me?" She had a vivid remembrance of the goblins that hunted Lluck last December and decided that it didn't bear thinking about.

So, she paced the sitting room floor, wandered out of that room and into another of Granny's makeshift library chambers, where she paused, fretted, wandered some more, and found herself back in the sitting room again. She stopped and listened; all seemed quiet now, but she didn't trust her ears.

"Maybe there's a spell you can use to see whoever's out there? Oh right, because that worked so well when you spied on Blip, you fool!"

She commenced pacing again. After another minute or two, she decided she couldn't stand it anymore. With care, she crept to the front window and, trying ever so hard not to disturb the curtains so as not to give any potential intruder a tip-off, she peered around the side of one of the drapes to get a view of the street.

No one was there. She sighed in mild relief. "But just because I can't see them doesn't mean they aren't around somewhere."

She risked looking out a second time. Again, nothing. She waited a few minutes and tried yet again. All was quiet, peaceful, and normal, whatever that meant these days.

"This is stupid! I can't just stay here all night. I'm tired, and I want to get to sleep and... oh no. Oh, no!"

The realization that she'd forgotten about Moirin hit her like a hammer. Or maybe more like a slap in the face with a wet fish. Only less pleasant.

"I can't believe I forgot Moirin. What have I done? Where's Qwyrk? She was supposed to pick me up. Except she probably came by and couldn't find me, because I'm over here instead of at home! Did she end up going to meet Moirin with Holly? Did they leave me behind? Actually, I hope they did. Oh no, what if they didn't? What if poor Moirin is all by herself out there in the woods?"

She panicked. She had to get home.

"Right, I'll just have to face whatever's out there. If Blip's waiting for me and he tries anything, I know a few spells that might put him off."

She threw on her coat and went to the front door.

"Come on, Jilly, you can do this! Just open the door. You're strong. You've got talents."

She took a deep breath.

"Right. Here I go!"

With a sharp exhale, and more than a few flying creatures of some kind seeming to circle about in her stomach, she threw open the door.

*   *   *

Moirin fled into the darkness. She could barely make out shapes or forms. She stumbled on roots and rocks as she crashed through the tangle of trees, trying to escape the voice, trying to escape her destiny. Her ancestor had fallen silent again, but she knew that wouldn't last for long; the taunts and temptations would return, maybe in an hour, maybe in a minute. No amount of running could stop them, but she ran anyway. She had to go somewhere that wasn't here.

She was aware of dashing across an old wooden bridge and hearing the water rushing underneath. Not long after, she came to a break in the trees, and spied a dirt path under the moonlight that led away toward some hedge in the distance. She heard passing cars beyond it.

She darted down the path and a minute later, found herself looking up at a tall hedge growing parallel to a raised motorway, but there was no way to get up to the road. The sound of the occasional car driving by brought her back to her own reality, back to temporary sanity.

She collapsed to the ground and sat there, breathing in deep gasps of autumnal air and trying to get her bearings. The voice of her ancestor and the coldness of that primal presence had receded, and she was herself again, for whatever that was worth. She took a moment to revel in being alone, in the silence of her own mind. Looking ahead, she saw that the path led forward, and then...

"Wait," she said, lifting herself into a crouch. "It curves and passes under the road. Maybe I can get up there from the other side."

She sprang up and jogged through the tunnel under the

motorway in hope, only to find that the path turned to concrete for just a few feet before becoming dirt again on the other side, leading away into more forest.

"Great. Back into the wild."

"It's where you belong," the voice said to her, calm and cool. "It's where all our kind belong. Come back to us, daughter. Come home. We're waiting for you."

"Feck off!" she yelled, looking for any means of climbing up to the motorway. She was ready to risk her life flagging down a car, if need be.

But she saw nothing, no path, no ladders, no way out, except back the way she came, or forward into the unknown. She could try to scramble up the bank, but it was wet and covered with slippery leaves. Far too dangerous in the dark.

She looked around again. And then she saw it: a faint glow coming from somewhere up the path in the heart of this new wood. Everything inside her told her to stay put, to let it be. She breathed in the damp forest scents, exhaling her misty breath, and took a few steps forward.

"This is wrong, Moirin," she whispered to herself. "Don't do it. Get out of here. Go back, do something. Don't go that way!"

But her body seemed to resist her mind's command, and she took tentative steps toward the flickering light. As she did so, she started to feel calmer, less tense, less panicked, though she had no idea why.

"Maybe it's all right. Maybe it's something good. Maybe it's someone who can help."

She realized how absurd her words sounded. She told herself to get away, to run, but just like when she sang all those months ago, she now felt herself being shoved to one side in her own mind, as if sharing space with another. And that other was soothing, reassuring. She picked up her pace and started to walk with confidence along the dirt path.

She came to a clearing on the right-hand side of the trail. It was lit as if by firelight, but she saw no flames flickering. There, a short, squat figure sat on a log. It held a staff of some kind, its black robe worn and rough around the edges. Moirin couldn't tell what it was, a misshapen creature that seemed to be a blend of many parts, human and animal, Fae and goblin, all melded into one. It gazed at her with piercing amber eyes that seemed to see into her soul but did not threaten. She should have been terrified, but for reasons she didn't understand, she wasn't afraid.

"Welcome, child of the bean chaointe," it croaked in a voice that was both ugly and majestic, rough and harmonious. It held up a gnarled hand, beckoning her to come closer.

Moirin didn't know how to react, didn't know if she even could react. She took a few steps forward, having no idea if she wanted to, or if the presence sharing her mind forced her to do it. And for some reason, she no longer cared. She knew that this creature was an ancient herald of beings long banished, creatures that shouldn't be in this world, but still, it comforted her. Somehow, its presence was like an invitation to a place of belonging, a place of "kin" as Aileen had put it. Whatever remaining resistance she had to the intrusion into her head fell away, and she began to see something she'd not noticed before in her interactions with these strange and ancient folk. She saw kinship and ancestry, and she understood.

The creature stood up and extended the same hand. "I speak on behalf of those who have come before you, and for the noble lineage of which you are a part. If you will permit me, I have an offer to make to you. One that should please you greatly."

Moirin took a few more steps. Something still tugged at her, told her to flee, to run as fast as she could. But she pushed that warning aside. Being here was the right thing to do. The only thing to do. She smiled a little and extended her own hand.

*   *   *

Jilly faced an empty and quiet street. She looked up, she looked down, she took a few hesitant steps into Granny's front garden, ready for anything. Nothing in any direction. She waited for another minute, not daring to believe that she could be this lucky. When nothing untoward came forward to claim the prize of unwelcome antagonist of the evening, she locked the front door, uttered Granny's protection spell, and crossed the street. She didn't linger, didn't bother to check anywhere around the outside of the house, didn't dare to think about what might be lurking in the dark corners of the other houses nearby. She just wanted to get home.

With haste, she jogged up to her front door. Opening it as quietly as she could, she slipped in, locking it behind her. All was well inside; Odin slept soundly in the front room, oblivious to her very late homecoming.

Some guard dog you are. But in this case she was grateful for his inattentive laziness. If he'd started barking, that would have been the end.

She crept up the stairs, slowly and deliberately, well aware of the few steps that made loud creaks if she put too much weight on them. She sighed in relief as she made it to the top, snuck down the hall, and slipped into her bedroom without creating any significant sounds. Luck was on her side.

If they heard me, they'll just think I was in the bathroom, or getting a snack from the kitchen or something. Yes, I did it!

Closing the door behind her, she heaved a much louder sigh and looked around. She saw no sign that Qwyrk had been here or even left her a note.

"Didn't she even bother to stop by?" she whispered in disappointment as she searched for something, anything that showed her friend hadn't gone off without her. She went to her window and looked out over the back garden, which was quiet and undisturbed.

"That's something, at least."

Looking at the clock on her wall, she saw that it was now well past one in the morning, which only made her feel more guilty that she'd forgotten Moirin, who might well be standing all alone in a cold dark forest at this very moment, confused and upset.

"I should see if she's texted me," she whispered in a moment of clarity, looking around for her phone. "I can text her and let her know that there was a big screw-up, and that I'm sorry. That'll be something, at least."

"Ms. Pleeth."

Jolly froze as she heard the familiar voice of her would-be mentor behind her, the last thing she wanted to hear. She turned around. Blip stood there, looking up at her with an inscrutable expression, hands clasped behind his back.

"S-sir?" She turned over in her mind what spells she had at hand; it was a pathetic list.

"Indeed. I do apologize for the late-night intrusion, but seeing as you are still awake, I'm glad to find that I have not disturbed you. Which is for the best. I believe we need to have a talk."

CHAPTER EIGHT

Holly wandered into the denser portion of the woods, and saw a glow in a small grove of trees. She looked back, but now couldn't see the edge of the forest or Qwyrk scrying the ground.

"That's odd. I only left her a minute ago."

The dim light of the clearing in front of her caught her attention. Clutching her stick, she took a resolved breath and walked toward it.

"Maybe I'll find some answers on my own."

As she drew nearer, a thick mist swirled inside the grove, a localized fog that stayed within the confines of this circle of trees and obscured whatever might be there. The glow came from somewhere inside and barely escaped into the surrounding darkness.

Holly shook her head. "I'm probably going to regret this, but it seems like it's here because it's waiting for someone to go in. May as well be me."

She stepped into the mist and found herself disoriented for a moment. She took a few more steps and picked up her pace. The glow grew brighter, the mists parted a little, and she saw herself surrounded by a rocky terrain.

She raised her stick in a defensive posture.

As her glance darted around, she saw a familiar figure moving through the veils of swirling fog. It seemed to float toward her, though it hugged the uneven surface of the ground. It wore a plain, dark red robe, with its arms folded and its hands tucked into the opposite sleeves. She could see a chin under its hood, the skin a pale grey color unlike anything she'd seen on any being before. Once again, Holly had a sense that her visitor was female, based only on that small portion of exposed body. The figure stopped some distance away, and Holly had the uncomfortable feeling of being observed.

Bringing her weapon up in front of her, she took one step forward. "All right, I'm getting tired of these meetings that I don't remember. Who are you?"

The figure was silent for a short time. "You know who I am," it answered in a woman's voice that was both deep and little more than a whisper.

"No, I'm fairly certain I don't."

"I have been with you, all this time, and yet you will not allow yourself to see."

"See what? All this time, since when? What are you talking about?"

"You came to me. You sought knowledge of what was to come. I spoke words of truth unto you, words that were harsh to hear, but that foretold what must be. Wyrd unfolds as it will, for each and for the whole."

Holly held out her weapon in a threatening manner. "I've no idea what you're talking about. All I know is that you keep showing up in my dreams, taunting me with half-arsed warnings that I never remember when I wake up. Sometimes, you're present in my waking hours, too, aren't you? Like in York all those months ago. Who the hell are you? How dare you invade my mind?"

The being was eerily silent for a moment before drifting a bit closer. "I dare nothing. I invade nothing. I simply am. I see what is and what shall be, and I offer such knowledge to those who seek it. I bring no comfort but no threat, no animosity but no friendship."

"Well, I've never sought you out, so leave me alone."

"Have you not? And what was it that sent you on an aimless wander, desperate to flee from your destiny, while in truth running right toward it?"

"What destiny? I've never fled from anything! I've never... oh."

Holly took a step back as a spark ignited in her mind, hints of a memory of wandering in the rain fifteen years ago, in a cold human city that was not welcoming, that knew her not, and wanted nothing to do with her. She found a haven from her misery in a world of mortal make-believe. And there, did something she would never have done otherwise, and from that, a unique new life was created.

"Wait," she said closing her eyes and shaking her head. "I came to you? Because I wanted to know something, something about my future. How did I know to seek you out? What did I want to know?"

"Those answers remain inside you, but you buried them so as not to face the turmoil that they caused."

"You're not making any sense."

"All I have said is all you need."

Holly scowled. "Damn it, stop with the riddles! I don't need your cryptic nonsense. For all I know, you're just lying to me."

"Only the truth may I utter."

"Oh, I see. Well, since you're in the habit of 'uttering' truths, I'd like to know why I'm here. If there's something hidden in my past, why are you taunting me about it now, instead of waiting until I'm asleep again?"

"It was not your time. Not yet. Only in such circumstances may I interfere, so that your fate may be maintained."

"Not my time? What on earth are you talking about, maintaining my fate? Wait, was I going to die? Back in the forest?"

"The attack would have taken you by surprise and mortally wounded you. That cannot be permitted while there is yet more of your fate yet to weave."

"Attack? Oh Goddess." She nearly dropped her weapon and put one hand over her mouth, panic nearly consuming her. "Something's out there, in that forest, isn't it? Did it take Moirin? Oh no, Qwyrk! I have to go. I have to get back to her!"

She turned about, looking in every direction for some means of escape. "I have to leave here, now!"

"Your destiny can only unfold as it must."

"Shut up! I'm sick of your riddles! Whoever you are, you've no right to hold me here." She held up her stick in a clear threat and started toward her mysterious intruder. "Let me go!"

The figure remained impassive, unmoving.

"I'm not joking," Holly growled. "You've been messing with my mind for months, haven't you? Well, it stops now!"

A wave of agony surged through her, just like it did in the training room. But now, memories came back. They flooded her pain-wracked head as her barriers to keeping them away broke down. She cried out and fell to her knees, dropping her stick and closing her eyes against the onslaught of old images and feelings she'd buried long ago. She could do nothing but take it all in, remember what she wanted to forget then, and forget what she wanted to remember now.

* * *

Jilly swallowed hard and her heart raced. "T-talk, sir?"

"Indeed." Blip hopped up on the bed and sat, bidding her to do the same. "It has come to my attention that there may be an issue of conflict between us."

"Conflict? Oh, no, no! I wouldn't say there's any conflict. I mean, none that I've seen. Why would there be conflict? Conflict is for those who are, um, conflicted, and I'm definitely not conflicted. Nope! Not I!"

Blip stared at her with an impassive expression. "Are you quite finished, or shall I be subject to more protestations about your utter lack of conflict? Because you seem rather conflicted about it."

"Sorry."

"Thank you. Now then, as I said, I sense that there has been some conflict recently, and I wish to clear the proverbial air."

"Well, I don't know that the air needs cleaning. I mean, I think it smells pretty good and all, but maybe with a little incense or air freshener—"

"Ms. Pleeth."

"Sorry. Again."

"Now then. The source of this conflict is..."

Jilly swallowed hard again and couldn't look him in the eye.

"...the fact that I've been gone for an inordinate amount of time in recent months with no good explanation as to my absence or whereabouts."

"Um, it's really not necessary for you to explain, sir. I mean, it's none of my business, anyway, and it's not like I'd want to spy on you to find out what you do, or that I even could." *Damn it, Jilly!* She struggled not to grimace.

"Yes, quite. But that is not my concern."

"It isn't?"

"No, of course not. I am worried that my time away has led me to neglect my duties as your imaginary friend and tutor. I fear that I have failed to instill in you a love and a comprehensive grasp of the great philosophical ideas that are so near and dear to me and are at the very foundation of good intellectual discourse and proper critical thinking."

"Oh. Oh!" Jilly almost gasped in relief. "Well, I mean, that's all right, really. I understand that you're very busy, and you can't always dally away your days at my house when I'm sure you've a dozen other important things to do."

"I rather think our epistemological interactions are a tad more than mere dalliance, Ms. Pleeth."

"No, no! Of course they are! Absolutely!" She waved hands, palms forward in an apologetic gesture.

"In any case, the reason for my frequent absences is…"

Her stomach tightened as she had no idea what he was about to say but feared that he was about to confess to something. Was he going to invite her to join his villainy?

"I am currently on the planning commission for a jirry-jirry reunion."

"A… reunion?"

"Rather like your university and school reunions and such, but on a much grander scale. It will be the finest gathering of our folk in centuries!" He clapped his hands with a triumphant smile. "A week or more of reminiscence, stimulating exchanges of ideas, salient debates, the savoring of good wines and spirits in convivial company, and so much more. As such, the amount of planning is extraordinary, and since I was chosen to be one of the chief facilitators of the event, it has meant that my time here must, of necessity, be limited of late. And for that, I do truly apologize, as I have neglected your education. Alas, such is the way of things. I do promise to try to make amends as soon as possible."

"Oh, um, well, that's quite all right, sir. I mean, I completely understand if you have such an important job to do. Take all the time you need."

"Nevertheless, I feel I have been a bit rude in not being more forthcoming, but there was a reason for that, as well, you see. This whole soirée is meant to be something of a surprise for the majority of our company, and while I know that you have no interactions with others like me, and in any case, would keep news of the affair in the strictest confidence, I still felt that I should be cautious, just to maintain the whole unexpected nature of it all."

"That's, um, very clever of you sir. But you're right, of course. I won't say anything about it."

"I thought not, and it's very good of you, my dear. Can I rely on your continued confidence about this matter? I'd hate to spoil the whole shindig, so to speak."

Jilly nodded. "Of course. Absolutely."

"Excellent! Splendid!" He hopped off the bed. "Now then, here is where I would normally suggest that we begin again with our study, but seeing as it is so terribly late, or early, I think a good night's rest would be a better use of your time."

"I, um, I think so too. I'm quite tired."

Blip nodded. "I shall take my leave of you therefore, feeling far better for having cleared the proverbial air, and laid all our playing cards on the table. Good night then, my dear!"

"Good night, sir. I'll see you tomorrow?"

"Absolutely, without a doubt. Oh no, wait, terribly sorry. I shan't be available tomorrow, or for a few days after. Gala business, you see, very important. Planning and coordination, and all of that. But soon, child, soon. And then we shall renew our distinguished pursuits once more. Cheerio!"

And with a wave, Blip disappeared into the opposite wall, leaving Jilly alone and lost in thought. Thoughts that turned to confusion, then skepticism, and then anger. She furrowed her brow and stewed over his alleged confession.

"He's lying to me. And I'm going to prove it!"

*　　*　　*

"Holly? Um, this isn't funny. I know you're out there. I just saw you leave, like, about a minute ago."

Qwyrk looked at the slender ring on her finger and concentrated on the small green stone. "Holly, love, it's me," she said in a much quieter voice. "Can you hear me? Can you answer me? This isn't like you, and I'm a bit worried. Actually, I'm a lot worried. Please talk to me if you can."

She waited, but there was no answer. She fretted, the knot in her stomach getting tighter. She clenched and unclenched her fists and shook her hands out as she started for the trees.

"Right, if anyone has hurt her, even messed up her hair, I swear I will end them. And that means you, Moirin. If you've gone back over to Aeval's camp and you've done anything to her, my prohibition on harming humans is going right out the window." She frowned as she remembered the defenestration jest she and Holly had shared earlier.

Stepping into the forest proper, she saw nothing, heard nothing. It only took a moment for her eyes to adjust, but a scan of the immediate area revealed only trees and darkness. No sign of Holly, no sign of Moirin, nothing but a quiet wood in the early hours of the morning, a place that once may have evoked fear in mortals who braved venturing into it. But for her, it was just another sylvan landscape, small but charming enough.

"There's nothing even remotely off-putting about it," she noticed. "It's almost a bit boring."

She ducked just in time as something swung over her head, hearing its approach only a second before. Something that might well have been a weapon intended for her. She rolled forward and turned, ending up in a crouch. Her glance darted all around, trying to catch sight of her attacker.

"Damn it! Where are you? Where—"

Something sharp as a dagger whizzed by her arm, grazing it.

"Ow!" She grabbed at the cut. "All right, you bastard, I'm done. When I see you, I'm not going to be kind. I'll kick your arse to the World Tree and back!"

"Oh, I doubt that, Shadow scum!" An emaciated shape moved

back and forth in the distance, or rather, hopped. It looked like a withered, diseased tree.

Qwyrk squinted, trying to get a better view of her opponent. As her vision adjusted, she saw it in all of its horror: a tall and slender being that might have been human or Fae-shaped, but for the single, large, bloodshot eye on its otherwise-featureless face, the single, withered arm protruding from its chest and the single leg holding it upright. Its claw gripped a spiked club with lengths of sharp chain dangling down. The creature was covered in black, tattered feathers.

"You're a bit far away from home," she said in defiance, as much to prop up her own courage as to issue a challenge to him. "But then, Fachan aren't known for their loyalty to any home, are they? Or to anything? What the hell are you doing down here? Shouldn't you be scumming up Scotland?"

"Hunting," it spat. "Fae, Shadowsss, humansss, whatever takes my fancy. I care not, only that I make a kill. Though I regret that the magnificent Yakshi escaped my grasp. Her kind are especially deliciousss."

"What do you mean, escaped your grasp?" Qwyrk's anger overcame her fear of an opponent she knew to be very dangerous. "Where is she?"

"I know not. She was whisked away into a pale mist before my poisoned whip could claim her. Some accursed ancient Fae magic, I have no doubt." Its growl betrayed a festering hatred for its enemies. "I shall have to settle for you."

"Look mate, two things: First, I'm glad you just told me she escaped from you, because that makes me a lot more relieved. It also means you're not as fast as you think you are. And second, never tell a girl you're settling for her." She clenched her fists. "It just pisses us off!"

She darted to the left behind a tree, barely avoiding a chain from the Fachan's weapon, which took a chunk out of said tree before whipping back.

This twat wasn't fooling around. But she couldn't just pop away and leave it there. She knew she had to take it down, permanently. She ducked to the next tree, and the next, only to be closely pursued by the Fachan. If she teleported, she'd give away her position. Unless...

"Hide from me, Shadow. Try to prolong your little life, make my hunt at least somewhat entertaining, let me... arrgh!"

Qwyrk timed her jump to materialize in mid-air right behind it. She unleashed the full force of a punch on the back of the thing's head, delivering a blow that would have killed any mortal. She could only hope it would do at least some damage to this monstrosity.

The creature stumbled forward on its one leg and hit the wet ground hard. Qwyrk wasted no time and jumped on its back, delivering punch after punch in a devastating series of blows. This thing played a different game, and she had to, as well.

It grunted and gasped with each blow, but still would not yield, much less die. Qwyrk grabbed the back of its head; the oiliness of its mottled feathers disgusted her. Taking a good hold of some of them, she slammed the creature's face into the dirt, again and again.

"Not so bloody tough after all, are you, you piece of crap? Let's see how well you are when I'm done!"

She relished laying into the beast, working out her frustrations over the whole ward business, the arrogance of the council, her fears over Aeval's return, Holly's disappearance, and whatever else was lurking inside her, waiting to burst out as she raged. Each blow felt empowering and vital in the moment, and maybe that's all that mattered right now.

But it still wasn't enough to take out the creature. It managed to jerk its arm free from underneath its prone body and with a snap of its hand, whip one of the club's chains back behind it. The sharp, jagged edge caught Qwyrk's right lower leg, tearing her jeans and leaving a nasty cut. She knew its poison couldn't kill her, but it sure as hell hurt. She cried out, and with her pugilistic pummeling momentarily interrupted, the Fachan seized the advantage. It twisted around and struck her with the club, sending her flying backward and crashing to the damp earth. Agony surged through the side of her head.

Dazed, she pulled herself up, feeling a trickle of blood down the side of her face. "Cheap shot, wanker. It won't happen again."

The monster hopped up onto its foot and swung its club around, whipping up the chains into a deadly vortex.

"Oh, I know it won't. For in the next act, I will simply kill you."

"Act? What, are we in a play or something? Oh crap, I'm not in some secret audition for Bogtrotter's stupid Prometheus play, am I? Is this some Nighttime Nasty hidden camera reality show, or something? Did he put you up to this? I swear, I'll kill him if he did."

The creature growled and took a few hops forward.

"Yeah," she sighed. "I didn't think so. All right then." She stood and limped as pain surged through her leg again. She clenched her fists and clenched her teeth, trying not to show any weakness. "Let's move on to act two, shall we?"

"It will be my delight, and your doom," the creature hissed, chains rattling as it renewed swinging its horrid club.

Qwyrk feared that it spoke the truth.

*　*　*

Jilly couldn't sleep. She tossed. She turned. She looked at the clock. She rolled over. She rolled under. She tried counting sheep. She tried counting goblins, which was rather unsettling and didn't work at all. She thought of using magic or brewing up some potion. But instead, she fumed and fretted about what she'd seen and heard, not only in her magic mirror, but from Blip himself.

She sat up.

"There has to be more to this than him planning some big party!"

She turned on her light and took out her laptop, calling up Goggle.

"Right, what to search for? Jirry-jirries who have betrayed their friends and started helping the forces of evil? Yeah, I'm sure there are all sorts of websites about that! Gosh, Jilly, you really are pointless sometimes." She sighed. "Where was he? Who were those people with him? What did they say? Come on, think! Hail to something, what was it? The deadly something? Eye! The deadly eye? The deathly eye, that was it!"

She typed in those words and searched.

"'Visit the **Deathly Eye**patch, the newest, scariest pub in Bum-on-Sea, Cornwall. Just in time for Halloween! Our pub/house of horrors experience on a cliff's edge will be even funnier if you're right pissed.' Yeah, what could go wrong there?"

She scrolled down. "'Allergies making you feel **deathly**? **Eyes** gone all itchy and awful? Try new PollenBollocks™, guaranteed to give your allergies the bollocking they deserve!' Um, not sure that's the best ad I've ever read. What else?"

She scrolled more. "'**Death-li: Eye** of the Dangerous Dragon, martial arts classes, now offered several times a week in Much Itching, Derbyshire.' Yeah, no. Oh, none of this is helpful!"

She scrolled a little further and noticed another entry, a plan-text description next to the link. "'A name for a being of legend, whose origins are lost, said to be highly esteemed by the Fomorians.' The Fomorians? Oh, crap!"

She clicked the link, but it led to an expired page. She swore.

She backtracked and tried searching for more, but no other pages showed up. She tried entering combinations of "Fomorian" and "Deathly Eye," but didn't find anything useful.

"It's like it's a name so old that nobody knows anything about it. This is not good."

She scrunched up her face, livid at the thought. "I knew he was lying to me. I knew it! Ooh! If he's gone over to the Fomorians, Qwyrk is so going to kick his arse, and I'm going to watch and love it!"

But her anger gave way a minute later to feelings of hurt, loss, and grief. Tears started to flood her eyes. "Why is he doing this? Why would be betray us? Me? He was my friend, even if he's annoying and all. Why would he want to hurt us, after all we've been through? I don't understand!"

Her tears unraveled into full-blown sobs, and she struggled to keep quiet, lest she wake her parents. She made every effort to choke back her crying, but she couldn't choke back all the awful feelings. For the first time in a good while, she felt helpless, hopeless, and had no idea what to do.

*   *   *

Qwyrk had no idea what to do. Her leg throbbed, and she struggled to hold herself up. The Fachan hopped lightly back and forth, taunting her with its agility, as if showing her that it could do with one leg what she couldn't do with two.

"Now then, Shadow," it hissed. "Are you prepared to meet your end? Alas, I cannot promise that it will be quick or painless. Where would be the fun in that?"

"Yeah, keep talking, you piece of feathered crap! And if you're so sure you're going to end me, why not answer a few questions? Like, why the hell are you actually here? I highly doubt you've chosen to set up shop in some random little forest on the outskirts of a city, just to trap ramblers out late at night. Can't be too many of those about. So, what is it?"

"Ha! Very well, my prey, I guard the way for the young one who is soon to come into her own. Her esteemed ancestor placed me here as watch to prevent those who might interfere with her ascension to her heritage. A rare event, indeed: a human that I do not wish to slay, for she has a greater purpose, unlike most of her kin, or you, or the Fae."

"Ah," Qwyrk said with horrible realization. "So Aeval's back inside Moirin's head. Lovely. She knew Moirin would come out here and sent one of her flunkies to keep us away from her. It all makes sense now. No other reason something as worthless as one of you would be stationed down here."

"Do not utter her name! You are not worthy for it to pass your lips!"

"What, Moirin? Oh, come on! A mortal girl can't mean much to you, even her. Oh wait, you mean... Aeval?"

"Shut up!" It swung its club around, chains rattling with menace.

"Ooh, hit a nerve, have I? Aeval, Aeval, Aaaaaeval! Aevaaaaal!" She waved her arms in the air as if she were cheering at a football match or dancing at a nightclub.

The beast screeched and hopped toward her, which would have been comical, if it weren't so deadly. But Qwyrk hoped its rage would make it sloppy, a gamble she knew she might regret. She lunged to the right, missing its chains, and though her leg burned, she had no intention of revealing that to her foe. She struggled to come up standing, but somehow managed, fists clenched and determined to end this monster, however she needed to do it.

"That all you've got?" she taunted with a heavy breath. "I must've hit your head harder than I thought. Shall I do it again?"

The creature swung its club once more, and a link of chain just caught her injured leg as she dashed out of its way, enough to sting in an area already weakened. She swore but kept herself standing by sheer will alone.

"You know we heal pretty quickly, right?" she shouted. "You can keep taking small nips at me, but that's not going to bring me down, or stop me from killing you!"

"Oh, but I don't need to bring you down, little fool," it snarled. "My weapon has already done that."

"What are you talking about? I'm still here, aren't I?"

"Indeed, but while my chains deliver a deadly poison to humans and Fae, to Shadows, the effects are... different."

"Different? Well, sorry to disappoint you, slim, dark, and ghastly, but I feel fine. So, maybe your big bad weapon isn't so big or bad, after all."

"Perhaps. We shall see."

"Yeah, we shall, because I'm going to finish you off and not be merciful about it!" She circled her hand in the air and willed herself to appear directly above him.

And nothing happened.

She forced herself not to betray her shock, but she knew something was very wrong, and she realized her adversary knew it, too. Without drawing attention to her actions, she made a smaller circle and willed herself to move away to a safe distance.

And still, nothing happened.

Oh, crap!

"You see," it mocked, "I am very sorry to tell you that the poison on my chains has robbed you of your magical abilities. No, actually, I am elated to tell you that. Your teleporting, flight, levitation, strength... all gone. You may as well be a pathetic little human now, which makes your capture, torture, and impending death all the more fun."

"Yeah, I have a feeling you're bluffing." Though she absolutely feared that it spoke the truth.

The creature shrugged. "Come here and try. Please, teleport to me and deliver your deadliest blow. I am weakened from your attack. It should be easy enough for you to finish me off."

Qwyrk scowled at him and weighed her options.

"Just as I thought. The toxin has taken hold. You are no longer a threat. I could let you flee and find your friends, tell them that you've failed. But where would the amusement be in that?"

Qwyrk took several steps back. Her leg hurt like hell, and she knew she couldn't outrun this horrid thing.

"Your death will be only the first of many for those who oppose us." It took one hop toward her. "And, as the forces of the ancients gather, we prepare the way for the one who shall reign over all, the Deathly Eye, who shall return to claim this world at long last."

"Deathly Eye?" Qwyrk summoned some false bravado. "Oh, come on, why can't these slimeballs ever come up with something more original, like 'the Magnificent Daisy Face' or 'the Infernal King of Kittens,' just to throw everyone off for a change? I mean, at least it'd be different!"

But she couldn't back up her sarcasm with force, and she was running out of time. Her leg bled, and she felt weaker by the minute. The poison had quickly sapped her strength.

"You are full of jests, aren't you?" It hopped closer.

"Yeah, well, what's a good scrap without a few laughs, I always say."

"You would have been a worthy warrior for our side, insufferable though you may be."

"You know, I've heard that before. And thanks, but sod off, I'm still not interested."

"I did not think you would be, nor would I have cared if you were."

The Fachan swung its club again, and its chains connected with Qwyrk's left calf before she could dodge them. Pain surged into her whole body, and she fell to the ground. She almost cried out, but she would not give this thing the satisfaction.

It knelt beside her on its singular knee.

"Going to finish me off with a cheap shot, eh?" Qwyrk muttered through her agony.

"Oh, no. First, we're going on a little journey. There is someone who wants to see you."

And with that, it reached down and bound her ankles with its chains, before hopping off into the forest, dragging her along behind. Her strength drained, her magic depleted, she could do nothing but endure this humiliation. If not for the sheer pain that coursed through her body with each yank along the cold, wet ground, she would have been mortified by the indignity of it all. Worse, she had no idea where they were going.

CHAPTER NINE

Each bump along the uneven ground hurt more than the last. Qwyrk squirmed and struggled, but she couldn't get those damned chains around her legs to untangle. The Fachan hadn't even bothered to tie her hands, but she was becoming too woozy and weak to pull herself up. A link of chain bit into her leg, and she cried out, but the creature paid her no heed.

It's enjoying this. "What the hell am I going to do... ow! No powers, no one else out here. Holly, where is she? Damn, damn!"

"Hold your tongue, little worm, or I shall cut it out," the Fachan snapped without looking back.

Right, that is it. That. Is. IT!

Her vision had lost some of its nighttime sharpness, but the moon was full enough that she could still see. They neared a clearing in the trees on the far side of the wood. Her shoulder bumped into a particularly large rock, one that she had the sense to grab a hold of.

Not to try to stop her captor's advance, but to pry out of the ground. She gritted her teeth and worked it loose just before the Fachan took another leap.

It didn't even notice.

She gripped the rock in her right hand, ignoring the pain of being wrenched along the ground. She began to plan her attack.

They left the forest, and she saw that they were on a dirt path that led to a... motorway?

Well, that's unexpected, but good. More moonlight. I can get a better shot.

She forced herself up, almost into a sitting position, hoping it wouldn't notice. The creature stopped abruptly. It sniffed the air and started to turn its head.

Right, you're only going to get one shot at this, so make it count.

She threw the rock with all the strength she could muster, aiming directly for its skull.

She missed.

*   *   *

Jilly hadn't felt so awful in her entire young life. As the reality of what she'd seen hit her—*really* hit her—she fell into despair. Worse, she had no one to tell, no one to comfort her. She sobbed, trying hard not to make any noise. The last thing she wanted was her parents hearing her and coming in to ask what was wrong, without an ounce of genuine interest between them. Knowing she couldn't sleep, she contemplated sneaking back over to Granny's for a while.

"But what if he was lying? What if he's waiting for me to do that and then just grabs me and carts me off somewhere and I can't tell anyone? Oh Jilly, you're being an arse! If he was going to do that, he could just walk right out of your wall and kidnap you."

And that thought unleashed a whole new wave of anxiety, leaving her feeling helpless.

"So, you're basically a sitting duck, no matter what you do. Lovely. I wonder if Lluck's up. No, that's stupid, of course not! But maybe I could phone him?"

She resisted doing it.

"It'd be rude. And his phone's probably off."

She picked her phone up.

"But what if I'm really in danger? Qwyrk's not here."

She put the phone down.

"Come on, Jilly, you're being paranoid!"

She picked the phone up and looked at it.

"Maybe just a quick call? I mean, how annoyed would he be?"

She put the phone down.

"Probably very."

She picked it up.

"Just ring him, just to see."

She dialed his number before she could change her mind. Astonishingly, he answered.

"What are you doing up so late?" he said in a half-whisper.

"Uh, I could ask the same thing of you," she answered. His voice was almost music to her ears.

"Yeah, well, it's half-term, isn't it? Might as well take advantage of that and live it up. Be wild and crazy students, right?"

"So, how are you being wild and crazy, then?" Jilly wasn't convinced.

"Eating cheese crisps with Marmite and watching crap old horror movies."

"That sounds revolting, and kind of awesome."

"Told you. We're pretty over-the-top here at Chateau Woldham. So, why'd you call?"

"Um, I think I might be in trouble."

"What'd you do? Finally turn someone into a toad or something?"

"I wish it were that simple."

"So, like big trouble? Brilliant! Go on, then, what is it?" He crunched a crisp.

"I think I've been betrayed by someone."

"Betrayed? Did someone like, steal your wand, or something?"

She wanted to reach through the phone and smack him. "I don't have a wand."

"I thought all you witch types had wands?"

"This is reality, not fairy tales."

"So, how do you do spells, then?"

She sighed in frustration. "I've told you. Magic is the ability to alter physical reality by applying one's will and directing the flow of the energy that surrounds us."

"Um, yeah, you lost me a bit, there."

"Look, we're getting off topic." Why was he so annoying... and so strangely charming?

"Yeah, all right, fine. Someone betrayed you. Who?"

"Someone close to me, who I think might actually be working for the dark powers."

"Dark powers?"

"You know, like the Erlking and his army? Or Moirin's banshee?"

"Lovely. Charmers, that lot. So, who is it?"

"I'm not sure I should say."

"It's not Qwyrk is it? That'd be a right pisser."

"No. And it's not your mum, either."

"Oh, so it's Blip."

"Wait, I didn't say that."

"You didn't have to. I figured it wasn't the bloke with the plats, and who else do you know? Process of elimination. Also, you're pretty crap at keeping secrets."

"I am not!" She almost hung up on him.

"Yeah, you kind of are."

"Look, we're off topic again, all right? This is serious. If Blip's gone over to the bad guys, we're in real trouble. He knows everything about us."

"How do you know he has?"

Jilly relayed what she'd seen and heard.

"I mean, it doesn't look good, it must be said," Lluck said, "but maybe there's a proper explanation for it?"

"Yeah, well, I'll stay suspicious, thank you, very much. Better safe than sorry." Jilly was in no mood to be giving the benefit of the doubt to anyone right now.

"So, what are going to do?"

"I don't know," she sighed in frustration. "I just needed to tell someone. Someone who'd understand. Qwyrk's not around right now. She's with Holly, and I think they went to see Moirin in Nicewood Park, but I haven't heard back all night. I was supposed to go with them, but I think something's happened."

"I could call on my mum."

"Oh, could you? That'd be brilliant, thank you!" She wished she could hug him.

"Yeah, hang on a second."

Jilly heard him talking to his ring.

"Mum? You there? It's Lluck. Can you get back to me, like ASAP? Jilly's worried about something, and she needs to talk with you and Qwyrk. I'll let her explain, but it sounds right serious. So, just contact me soon, all right? Gotta go, she's on the phone with me, bye for now."

"So, she didn't answer, again? That's odd, isn't it?" Jilly tensed at the thought.

"Yeah, I mean, it's late, but usually she'll call right back if she can."

"All right, we'll just wait a bit then, shall we?"

"No worries. I can narrate the movie for you, if you like."

"What's it called?"

"*Vampires vs. Werewolves III: Full Moon Smackdown in Transylvania.*"

"That sounds absolutely terrible."

"Yeah, it's brilliant!"

Jilly smiled, comforted by his sense of humor. Phoning him was the right decision. Now, as soon as Holly got back to him, things would start looking up.

* * *

The rock sailed past the Fachan's head.

Qwyrk looked up at the night sky. "Well, I've had a good long life. I suppose there are stupider ways to go."

But something curious happened. The Fachan had turned its odd-shaped pate in the opposite direction, so it never saw the missile on its close-call fly-by. But it did hear it crash into the nearby shrubbery. Yes, indeed.

And that noise caught its attention.

"What wass that?" it hissed. "Who iss there?"

Qwyrk resolved to take her final shot at finishing this repulsive creature.

Bloody hell, this is going to hurt.

She lunged and grasped the chain binding her legs. Its sharp edges bit into her hands and fingers, and she forced herself not to swear like an army sergeant. Giving the chain the hardest tug she could, she pulled the weapon out of the unsuspecting monster's grip and right toward her. Before the Fachan could react, she yanked the chain again and took hold of the club, at the same time freeing herself from her entanglement.

It shrieked and hobbled toward her, its single clawed hand grasping for its weapon. But she swung the club and caught its spindly leg in the razor chains. Down it went, crashing face-first into the muddy ground. Qwyrk flung herself at the creature. She brought the full force of the club down on the back of its head with a sickening crack.

The Fachan lay still. She took another shot, just to be sure. The second one was a bit squishier. That was quite enough. And rather revolting.

Breathing hard, she dropped the weapon and looked down at her hands, stained with her blue green blood, and throbbing from a dozen small cuts.

"Great, so now what?"

She stood alone in the middle of the night, near a motorway, with the very dead body of a completely not-human-looking monstrosity splatted on the ground. Her hands and legs bled. Her powers were gone. She couldn't teleport away or even heal herself. Her girlfriend was missing. Moirin was missing, about to about to be initiated into Aeval's happy-fun-times screaming death cult.

"Who knows what else is out here, and I can't get any help at all. I am completely bollocked!"

"Well, I wouldn't say you're *completely* bollocked."

Qwyrk whipped her head around. "Who's there?"

A small figure stepped out of the forest, about a foot tall, mottled green with a bulbous nose, two little horns, and glowing yellow eyes. He wore an ill-fitting burlap sack that might have been an attempt to resemble a toga, but which pretty much failed in every way to do so.

"Horatio? Oh, you've got to be kidding me!" She was simultaneously relieved and annoyed. "Do I even want to know why you're out here and just happened to be nearby?"

"Come on, love, you know me. You know us. It's our sworn duty to keep our ears to the dirt and find out what's goin' on all around the magical realms."

"Yeah, so you can run away and hide when things heat up too much."

Horatio made a mocking gesture of a hand to the forehead. "Bit harsh, eh? We provide a valuable service, of which you have made use many a time in the past, I should like to point out."

"I know, I know. But why are you *actually* here?"

"Tryin' to keep an eye on the young lady who came through here earlier, the human I believe you call Chantz? She went off that way a while ago, incidentally." He pointed toward the motorway. "Underneath the bridge, and into the forest beyond."

"And you didn't stop her?"

"I am just one Nasty, and not a fighter so much as a master of espionage. Which, incidentally, is why I did not rush to your defense, either. I was no match for that thing you squashed there, but I never doubted you, not for a second. Glad to see you proved me right."

"You were betting on me, weren't you?"

"No! I would never! How can you even think that? How can you—"

Qwyrk glared and raised the club.

"Yeah, all right, but just a little."

"Bloody hell!" Qwyrk threw the weapon to the ground. "Can you at least help me out now? I'm a flipping mess—literally—and I can't teleport at the moment."

"Yeah, that's a pisser ain't it? Should wear off in a while, though. The poison, I mean."

"How long is 'a while'?"

Horatio shrugged. "Could be a few hours, could be a few days. Depends on the victim, really."

"I don't have a few days if Moirin's about to go bad."

"Yeah, it might be a whole lot worse than that."

"What do you mean?"

"Come on, love. I'll get ya untangled and whisked back to yer home, so I can get you cleaned up and bandaged and seen to. You need it. And I'll tell you what we Nasties are really worried about. Like paralyzed with fear kind of worry."

"The end is nigh again, eh?"

"That's what I like about you, my dear. Always got a place for humor in the face of immanent doom. Makes it all a bit more bearable."

"Wait, I can't leave without Holly. Where is she? What happened?" Qwyrk's stomach seized up in knots again as she thought of her better half.

"It would seem that she was whisked away by something far beyond you or me. I don't know for sure, but my gut tells me we ain't gonna find her hangin' out in this little wood."

"I don't want to leave if she's still here."

"Love, she's not here! As far as I can tell, she's not even on this plane at the moment, and I honestly don't know if she'll even be comin' back, all right? Now, really, we need to go. You're no good to her if you bleed to death."

Anger and frustration swirled through Qwyrk, but she held them in check, just. "If you're lying to me, I swear I will make what I did to that Fachan seem merciful by comparison!"

"You think I want you to lose her? Come on, I nudged her in your direction. Why do I have to keep reminding you of that? You can look for her after we attend to your wounds and regroup with your mates. Now come on. We're going, now!"

Qwyrk was rather taken aback by his unusual show of assertiveness, but she also knew that he was right, even if it annoyed the crap out of her to admit it.

"What about this mess?" She motioned to the pulped Fachan.

"Oh, not to worry. We'll drop it off on the Moors on our way back to your place. Some of me mates'll sort it out and make it vanish for good."

She nodded and reached down to take his tiny hand.

"Hang on," he said with a grin. "This ride ain't gonna be as smooth as what you're used to, but it'll get the job done. I'll have you home in a tick or two."

With a wave of his free hand, the space around them distorted, and she felt herself being sucked into a vortex, like being beset by an enormous hoover. It was one of the most singularly unpleasant things she'd ever experienced. Other than being bound in razor-sharp chains by a one-armed, one-footed Scottish night terror, of course.

*   *   *

"She's not answering," Jilly said after a good quarter of an hour of Lluck regaling her with descriptions of scenes of werewolves armed with wooden-stake crossbows taking on vampires packing heat with pistols loaded with silver bullets.

"It's odd, isn't it?" he said. "I mean, I suppose she might've taken it off again, or something, but normally, she answers really quick. She doesn't like to leave it too long. Which, to be honest, I really appreciate."

"But that's the second time today. Do you think something's wrong?" Jilly's worry crept back in.

"Don't know. I suppose I could go wake up dad and ask him."

"No, don't do that. I'd like to keep this between us right now, if that's all right."

"Yeah, sure, no worries. So, what do you want to do, then?"

"I don't know," Jilly said, out of ideas. "If she contacts you, phone me right away, yeah? I'll leave my ringer on."

"Yeah, all right. You sure you don't want to hear what happens next? The werewolves are about to bring out the holy water rocket launchers. It's mental!"

"Tempting, but I'm going to try to sleep for a little, I think."

"Not a bad idea. I should do that instead of watching this rubbish."

"Hey, at least it's entertaining!"

"Not quite the word I'd use. Anyway, try to get some kip, and I'll phone you when I know something. If I haven't heard from her by early morning, I'm gonna wake my dad and tell him."

"Sounds like a good plan. Talk to you then."

"Cheers, bye."

Jilly hung up, disappointed and worried.

"What is *happening* tonight? Why's everything going so wrong?"

She stewed on that question for a bit, but her eyes indeed started to get heavy, enough to outweigh her worries, and in another minute or two, she drifted off to sleep.

* * *

"Ow, damn it!" Qwyrk swore as Horatio applied another antiseptic cloth to her head. He'd taken them back to her home, a welcome sight after her ordeal.

"Sorry, love," he said. "You took quite a few nasty hits out there, and with your powers suppressed, you're basically human now, so no quick healing for you. Just a lot of pain."

He hopped down from a table to look at her lower leg, which he'd bandaged earlier, though Qwyrk could see that the bandages were beginning to turn blue green.

"Yeah, I need to tighten them a bit," he said. "It's gonna hurt."

"Oh, that'll be a new sensation, at least!" she said with a roll of her eyes. "Is this what humans go through every time they get their arses kicked in a fight?"

"This or something approximate. It ain't fun or glamorous. Now hold still." He adjusted the bandages and applied a bit more pressure to stop any further bleeding. Then he doused the area with more of his NN antiseptic potion.

Qwyrk grunted and ground her teeth in pain.

"Yeah, that chain's gonna leave a few scars. Consider yourself lucky that's all that happened."

Qwyrk glared at him. "I mean, it's not like there was anyone around who could have, oh, I don't know, gone and gotten some help and come back to bail me out."

"Sorry love, would've messed up the betting pool."

"If my leg didn't hurt so damned much, I'd kick you across the room."

"I'm feelin' the love, I am. And cheer up. You're vulnerable now, hence the special old world tonic here to fight off any mortal infections or supernatural unpleasantries. But as soon as your abilities come back, you'll heal up right fast and good."

"Great, so all I have to do is sit around and do absolutely nothing for an undetermined amount of time, and I'll be fine?"

"Something like that."

"Well, I'm not bloody fine, not even close!" Her fears eclipsed the physical pain that wracked her temporarily weak body. "My girlfriend's missing, and I have no idea where she is, my ring can't locate her, and I'm worried sick. Oh, and the whole purpose of the evening got completely botched, and now a mortal girl I'm partly responsible for is missing, and it may be the prelude to something appalling."

"That's one way of lookin' at it."

"It's the only way I'm going to look at it, you pillock!"

He looked down as if hurt, and guilt about snapping at him hit her.

"Look, I'm sorry. Thanks for your help, mate, really. I might well have died out there. You got me back home, patched me up as good as you could. I'm grateful, really. But I can't just sit around here, hoping I get better eventually. I need to go see Jilly. I was supposed to pick her up earlier, and I cocked it up. I know its late, and she's likely asleep by now, but I don't want to wait until morning. She probably hates me, but I need to explain what happened and check in. Can you take me there?"

"Yeah, I can drop you off. But you really do need to rest. You're not invulnerable, even at your best."

"I know, I know. And maybe one of these days, I'll get that through my thick head. But right now, Jilly is probably my best bet for finding Holly, and maybe Moirin, too. I'd feel better, even safer, if I were with her at her house. Or Granny's"

Horatio shrugged. "Suit yourself, love. I've done about all I can for now, anyway. But you do need to know what I've heard. About the next impending disaster."

"Oh right, that. What is it?"

"This one's more than just rumor, but we don't have all the details yet. To be perfectly honest, we may never get them. Your girl Chantz, and her boss the banshee, they're just heralds. Oh sod that, they're more like foot soldiers compared to what's coming."

"And what exactly is coming? Boggie hinted at it last spring, if I recall."

"Yeah, we don't know for sure, but it's old, really old, like among the first of all magical kind, and it ain't nice, not even a little. Its return has been in the works for a long time, and it'll be ready soon, like immanently. The prevailing theory is that with the arrival of Samhain, this bugger's arrivin' too, and then, we're all basically farked, because nothing we've got will be able to stop it. Shadows, Fae, NN's, all magical creatures: we're gonna be completely helpless against it. I mean, that's the theory, anyway."

Qwyrk recalled Aeval's taunts with dread. "There's got to be someone who knows more about what's happening."

"Maybe a few, but you don't really wanna go down that road."

"Why not?"

"Dangerous, ain't it? Consultin' the primal powers for answers. You usually find out things you'd rather not know or have to do things you'd rather not do. Can drive a person mad."

"A risk I might need to take. In this case, the more I know, the better."

"Suit yourself, love. But I'd have nothin' to do with any of those buggers if I was you."

"Where can I find the nearest one? One of these primal power things?"

"Well, legend has it that one of them dwells out in the wilds of the Western Dales, at least from time to time. Her plane occasionally intersects with some creepy old caves out there, or so the tale goes. But that's all I know. Oh, and it's said she wears a long red robe with a hood that hides most of her face. Got odd, grey-colored skin, too."

"Wait, a red robe?"

"Yeah, that's what I've heard, what about it?"

"Nothing, it just reminded me of something else." She held her tongue about Holly's visions, but something about what he said disturbed her deeply. "Any idea how I find her, like specifically?"

Horatio shrugged. "Don't know, and I'd rather not, to be honest, but your mate Qwyzz might, or maybe those detectives your girl-friend employs from time to time. They're a bit too nosy for their own good. Anyway, that's all I know, so we should get you to your young mate's house, if that's what you really want to do."

She nodded. "Yeah, cheers."

He reached out. "Take my hand and hold on. It's always a bit of an unsettling ride."

* * *

She was dreaming, or at least she thought so, if one can think one is dreaming while dreaming. And in that dream she heard a fluttering, like a rush of wind that disrupted whatever unfolded in her dream. Except, if her dream was being disrupted, what was doing the dis-rupting, if not the dream itself?

The question became irrelevant a moment later when Jilly opened her eyes and found that she hadn't been dreaming at all. No, something far stranger happened. She felt a rush of wind and smelled the faint aroma of stale cigar smoke, followed by a dim flash of light, out of which walked Qwyrk and a little creature she'd not seen before, but knew from Qwyrk's description must be her Nighttime Nasty contact, Horatio.

"Not to sound rude or anything," she whispered as she turned on her nightstand lamp, "because I'm really glad to see you, like really, but what's going on, and why're you here now?"

"That's the question, innit, love," Horatio said in a lowered voice, "and Qwyrk'll have all the answers you need. I have to dash off. We have a body to dispose of, but it was lovely to meet you. I'm Horatio, by the way. Congratulations on that whole witchy thing you do."

CHAPTER NINE

"Um, thank you?"

Horatio bowed and disappeared in another dim flash that sucked a bit of the air out as he left.

Jilly jumped out of bed to hug her friend.

"I'm so glad to see you!" she whispered, "but what's going on? What... oh no, your hands! Your ankles! What happened?"

"Long story." Qwyrk looked sheepish. "I'm so sorry about earlier, about not coming back for you. It's been a really bad evening."

"Huh, you're telling me!"

"Can we go on over to Granny's, so we can talk properly?"

"Of course." Jilly reached for her coat. "If you blink us over to the front door, I'll let us in."

"Yeah, um, there's a slight problem with that, actually." Qwyrk looked pained. "We're going to have to go over there the old-fashioned way, sorry to say."

Qwyrk's admission confused and worried Jilly in equal measure.

*   *   *

A short time later, they sat in Granny's sitting room, the heat turned on, while Jilly remained bundled up, rubbing her arms, and trying to get warm. Qwyrk's mild discomfort (a side effect of the poison, no doubt), was nothing like what she knew Jilly must be experiencing. She really had no frame of reference for the whole "being cold" thing.

"So, what is going on?" Jilly demanded.

"I'll just start at the beginning," Qwyrk said, and she did, recounting this horrid, awful evening in detail (except for the ward, for now), and seeing Jilly look ever more worried and upset. Qwyrk knew she couldn't pull any punches, not this time. If things were as

bad as the Nasties were claiming, she had to let Jilly know. And they both had to be ready.

"Oh Qwyrk, I'm so, so sorry!" Jilly took her hand, gently, so as not to cause her any pain. "And please, don't worry about not picking me up earlier. I totally understand."

"I don't know what to do," Qwyrk said. "I can't contact Holly. My ring doesn't work. I don't have my powers right now, so I can't even go out and search for her, and every moment that I don't know what happened, it's like she's slipping away from me, and I can't stop it from happening." Tears stung in her eyes. "I can't lose her, Jilly. I just can't. We've only just got together, and now I'm worried I'll never see her again."

"Hey, we'll find her." Jilly touched her shoulder. "We'll figure out something. We'll get help. She's out there. I know it."

"The thing is," Qwyrk sniffed, "this isn't the first time something's tried to take her." She recounted what she remembered about that awful night at Beltane, when a black hole invaded her home and tried to abduct Holly.

"That's really bizarre, and really scary!" Jilly said, rubbing Qwyrk's back in comfort.

"You're telling me! The strangest thing was, we both completely forgot about it until just earlier tonight. I don't know what happened, but someone was able to wipe it from our minds. I think it was the bloody Shadow council, but they insist it wasn't."

"Why would it be them?"

Qwyrk let out a disgusted sigh and decided to tell Jilly everything she'd learned about the ward and how she and Holly couldn't even touch anymore without being flung apart from each other.

"What?" Jilly nearly yelled. "They can't do that! How dare they? What kind of stupid, awful, bigoted nonsense is that?"

"The kind that's been in place for thousands of years, apparently, and to which we have no recourse or appeal. Oh, don't worry. We're going to figure out a way around it, even if I have to kick every arse in Symphinity to change the law. And we're going to let everyone know about it."

"Too right, you are," Jilly growled. "And I'm going to help. Just tell me who to punch, and I'm there!"

"Thanks, love, but I can't worry about it right now. I have to find Holly. I feel like I can't do anything else until I know she's all right. My stomach is twisted up something awful, and I can't even concentrate. And being temporarily human and hurting like hell isn't helping, either. I want my powers back! I have things I need to do, and I can't just sit around and wait to get better!"

"Well, I don't think I can do much about that. Maybe I can try to locate Holly with magic. I did it earlier tonight. Not with her, I mean, but with, um, Blip."

"Blip? Why Blip?"

"Well, I've got some terrible news of my own, I think. I really hope I'm wrong, but I don't think I am." Jilly looked very distressed.

"What are you talking about?"

"I'm pretty sure he's betrayed us."

"Betrayed us? How? What do you mean?"

"That thing? That big bad you were talking about? I think he's part of a group that's trying to bring it back."

"That... doesn't make any sense! Blip? Come on! How could you know that?"

"Because I saw it. I heard it from his own mouth. I used a moon location spell to find out where he was, since he's been so secretive lately. Yeah, I know, it was an invasion of privacy, but it turns out I was right."

"Are you sure he wasn't just rehearsing for some daft play, or something?"

"Not unless the play was being put on in an old hallway that looks like a creepy cellar."

"Maybe it was a meeting of like-minded philosophy nerds."

Jilly shook her head and told Qwyrk the details of her scrying. "He said 'Hail to the Deathly Eye.' That can't be good. I think it's some sort of creature that invaded Ireland, a long time ago."

Qwyrk sat in stunned silence for a minute, unable to take it all in. It was absurd, even preposterous, but somehow, on some utterly ridiculous level, it made sense. And coupled with everything else that had happened tonight? A lot of unpleasant things seemed to be falling into place.

"I hate to say it, Jilly, but I think we're in really big trouble."

All Jilly could do was hold Qwyrk's hand softly and nod.

*　　*　　*

Jilly finally looked at her phone. "Oh, no!"

Qwyrk looked up from her fretting. They'd been sitting for the past quarter of an hour or so, Qwyrk worrying about what to do next, if they even could do anything, while Jilly researched online.

"I've got three texts from Moirin, but they were sent ages ago, before and after midnight. This is the first I've seen them."

"What do they say?"

"That she was waiting for us in Nicewood. She sounds worried in the last one. She really was there. She needed our help, and we let her down. We totally failed her, and now she's, she's—" Jilly started to tear up.

"Hey, we're going to do what we can to find her. It'll be fine." Qwyrk put a painful arm around Jilly's shoulder, but she couldn't bring herself to believe her own words.

"And Holly," Jilly sniffed.

"Yeah, and Holly. We'll figure something out, we have to. How's the spell coming?"

"I don't know. I mean, there's a few that may work, but mine kind of backfired."

"But you said you thought that Blip could see you, even if he didn't. If the same thing happens with Holly, maybe we can let her know we're looking for her. Get a message to her. Find out where she is."

"It's worth a try, but I still seem to be pretty rubbish at everything magic I do, so I can't promise anything."

"Hey, you're far from rubbish, all right? You're the only person keeping me sane right now. I'd trust you with my life, and I mean that. Give it a go, do whatever you think's best."

"Thanks, it means a lot to me that you still trust me after I've cocked up so badly."

"You haven't cocked up things. You've been learning. It's like when people are figuring out how to cook, right? They put stuff into cooking pots or ovens or on spits, or whatever, and it comes out different than it went in—which is kind of magical on its own, by the way—and sometimes you mess it up and ruin it, but other times, everything works out fine. Nobody gets to be a master chef after only a few months. And obviously Granny believes in you. I can't even get in her house without your permission! And you've literally helped save the world, what, three times now? All before your thirteenth birthday? I don't know any other human that can say that!"

Jilly's face lit up. "All right, you've convinced me. Let's give it a go."

She got up, went into the kitchen, and returned with a bowl filled with water.

"It's the same idea, just a different way of doing it."

"Water scrying?" Qwyrk eyed the bowl.

"Yeah, pretty much. I'll try a chant to see if we can locate Holly, get some clue about where she is. If it works for her, we could try it on Moirin, too."

"Brilliant, let's have a go."

Jilly set the bowl on the coffee table, and they sat on opposite sides. She held her hands over the bowl and started to chant a simple, repeating verse:

"Water clear, clean of flow | help my sight, oh magic eau | aqua mirror, liquid screen | show me that which must be seen!"

"That's it?" Qwyrk interrupted.

"Shh! There's more."

"Oh. Or, eau, maybe?"

"River, ocean, creek, and stream | show me things as they might seem | give me truth and inspiration | and some mental irrigation."

"That's... kind of crap. Sounds like one of Bogtrotter's poems."

"Shhh!"

"Sorry, sorry."

Five times Jilly recited the poem, and five times nothing happened.

"I... don't think we're getting anywhere." Qwyrk didn't want to discourage her, but still.

"Wait!" Jilly said. "Something's happening. I can see a mist. It's faint, but it's there."

"Mist? That's what the Fachan said Holly disappeared into!" Qwyrk dared to hope. "Where is it? Can I see it?"

Qwyrk leaned in closer but saw nothing. She squinted. She turned her head this way and that.

"Are you sure something's there?" She reached out to move the bowl closer to her. "All I see is... arrrghggh!"

A sharp shock jolted her and sent her reeling backwards into the side of the sofa, spilling the bowl in the process.

"No!" she yelled. "No, no, damn it!"

"What is it?" Jilly said, looking horrified as she ran to Qwyrk.

"It's that bloody, gods-damned ward! It got to me, even here, even across worlds." She started to cry. "We had her, Jilly, you found her, and that means she's alive! But I can't reach out to her because of that horrid thing. Even now, it's keeping us apart."

Jilly knelt and put her arms around Qwyrk.

"I'm never going to see her again, and even if I do, I'll never be able to hold her again, to even touch her. Oh, Goddess!"

She buried her head in Jilly's shoulder and broke down and sobbed. All hope fled from her, and for the first time in a long time, she gave in to despair.

CHAPTER TEN

She staggered out of the forest at dawn, shivering, exhausted, numb, not even sure where she was, or who she was. She saw the faint light of a quiet autumn morning casting its pink glow over a frosty and empty field of green. She could barely remember anything. What had happened the night before? Where had she gone? For how long? Hours? Days? In her head, a jumble of images competed for attention, each claiming to be the truth, but she couldn't decipher what was false and what wasn't.

A heavy chill ran down her back. She fell to her knees, rubbing her hands on her arms to try to grasp at some little warmth, but the effort was futile. She wanted to curl up in a ball on the almost-frozen ground, close her eyes, and never open them. She could just let it all go, never worry again, never be afraid again.

Just drift off. Let it come.

Her heavy eyelids began to shut as numbness overtook her. *Just drift off, just...*

"N-no." She opened her eyes, forcing herself to stay upright. The cold came rushing back into her, and she shivered hard again.

"I can't. I h-have to f-find... Qwyrk, Lluck..."

She held up her trembling right hand and looked at the slender gold band with a small green stone set into it. And she remembered.

"Lluck," she said, teeth chattering uncontrollably. "Lluck, can you hear me? P-please... answer. I n-need you. And Carl. I need your h-h-help."

"Mum?" a teenager's voice sounded soon after her plea. "Is it you? Where are you? Are you all right? I've been so worried! You don't sound good."

"I'm in..." She struggled to remember. "N-Nicewood P-Park? Can you come to me? I'm out b-by the t-t-trees."

"Oh hell, mum! Yeah, we'll be right there. I promise! Please, *please* don't move, don't go anywhere! Dad and I are on our way, like, right now. I'm going to go get him up, and then we'll come for you. Just, just stay there, all right?"

"Y-yes. I'm here. Please hurry. S-so cold."

"We will, I promise. Just stay right there, all right? I love you!"

"I l-love you, t-too."

Lluck's voice faded, and Holly turned her attention to the other most important person in her life. The one who made everything worthwhile, the anchor that had kept her sane during an ordeal that she couldn't even remember much of now.

"Q-Qwyrk? Darling, c-can you hear me? I'm here, in the park, where I w-was with you, maybe last night? Right where I left you, I th-think. Can you hear me at all?"

But there was no answer.

"Qwyrk, p-please, if you can hear me, p-please, can you answer?"

There was only the silence of the park at dawn.

"No!" Holly whispered. "The ward. It's b-blocking us? No, please no!" She wanted to break down, to let out her pain, but no tears came. She remembered crying about something, perhaps all night, and now there was nothing left for her to give. Her whole body reeled in anguish as desolation overcame her, and she collapsed to the ground.

"Please, dear Goddess, please Kubera, h-help me! Don't leave me alone here! Don't leave me like this!"

*   *   *

Dawn broke over Knettles, and Qwyrk paced Granny's sitting room while Jilly slept on the sofa. She looked at her hands for the hundredth time and felt at her ankle. Still painful, still not healed.

"Damn it!" she whispered. "I can't just sit here. The sun's almost up. I've got to *do* something!"

There was a sensation in her right hand, a momentary surge of warmth, as if...

"Holly!" she said, a little louder than she intended. "Holly, are you there, love? It's me, it's Qwyrk, I'm with Jilly, back in Knettles. We're all right. Are you well? Please answer if you can hear me!" She raised her voice in desperation, which made Jilly stir a little.

"Come on, please!" she whispered again. But nothing else happened; there was no answer.

She wanted to hit something, anything, but she didn't want to damage Granny's home (or herself) any further.

"Qwyrk?" Jilly mumbled. "What happened? What time is it? Is everything all right?"

"No," Qwyrk slumped down on the sitting room floor. "Nothing's all right. I think Holly just tried to contact me but couldn't get through. And I'm still not healed, so there's absolutely nothing I can do about anything: not finding her, not figuring out what's going on with Blip, not saving the bloody world again. Arrrrgh!" She punched the floor with her fist, which only made her hand hurt more. She rubbed it and cursed to herself.

Jilly yawned and sat up, looking very much the worse for wear.

"Sorry I woke you up," Qwyrk said. "I'm just sick of sitting around. I've been keeping an eye on you while you slept, just in case Blip or someone else tried anything, but it's all been quiet."

"That's kind, thanks." Jilly blinked and squinted.

"No trouble at all. I just wish I could do more. How do you feel?"

"Exactly as bad as I figured I'd feel after a few hours of sleep."

"Yeah, sorry about that. I don't have any frame of reference, sad to say, but I've seen enough humans lose sleep over the centuries to know it doesn't look very pleasant."

"Eh, I'm young. I'll live. So, what's this about Holly?"

"I think she just tried to contact me, through the ring. I mean, my hand felt a bit warm, but nothing happened. I spoke to it, but—"

"The ward?"

Qwyrk nodded. "Probably. At least I didn't get thrown across the room this time."

"I was going to say, we could try to find her again, but it might not end well."

"No, it's not going to get us anywhere." Qwyrk wanted to cry again at the thought.

"So, what should we do now?"

"I need to find a way to get to Qwyzz's. He'll know what to do.

He might even have some magic workaround I can use while I'm getting this damned poison out of my system."

"Okay, but how will we get to him?"

"I have absolutely no idea. I'm not even sure it's possible."

"Maybe..."

"Maybe what?"

"Maybe instead of Qwyzz..."

Qwyrk raised an eyebrow. "Yes?"

"You could, you know..."

"No, I don't know. Come on, I'm all ears here. Any suggestion you have, I'll take!"

"Maybe you could go see Bogtrotter?"

"Yeah, except that one. Next!"

"Qwyrk."

"No, absolutely not! The last thing I need right now is to have to sing or dance or act for that scruffy pillock when time may be running out for Holly and the world."

"But he might know where she is! Maybe he's heard something. Maybe one of the NNs has. Come on, it's for Holly. She'd do it for you, you know. Put away your pride, and go see him. She's the one, right? For you, I mean. You can't let anything happen to her. You just can't!"

Qwyrk looked away, humbled by her remarkable and wise young friend. She nodded, even managed a faint smile. "You're right. I'd do anything for her, even face that walking rug again. Yeah, come on. If you can help me get in touch with Horatio, he can set up a meeting."

"How do we do that?"

"Oh, it's not difficult. We can probably use my ring, since it's probably only blocking Holly. But I'm not magical right now, so you'll need to cast a simple little contact spell on the stone to reach him. It's like using magic to get his mobile number, or something. Not that I know much about those things."

"Count yourself lucky," Jilly said. "I've only had mine for a few months, and I pretty much love it and hate it at the same time."

"Why are people so obsessed with them, anyway?"

Jilly shrugged. "Maybe they just don't have enough real magic in their lives, so they have to settle for the made-up kind."

"That's both profound and kind of sad."

"That's the state of humanity, isn't it?"

"You're sounding awfully wise for whatever hour of the morning it is."

"Probably an accident."

But Qwyrk smiled wider, because she didn't think it was.

*   *   *

"Drive faster!" Lluck gripped the dashboard, his stomach in knots.

"I'm drivin' as fast as I dare at this hour," Carl said. "The last thing we need is to get pulled over. Then we won't be able to get to her at all. We're almost there, son. Just hang on. We'll find her, I promise."

A few minutes and a few twists and turns later, Carl pulled the car up on a street bordering Nicewood. No sooner had he parked than Lluck shot out the door and sprinted across the green. He didn't care about waiting for his dad. All he wanted was to find Holly.

"Mum!" he yelled, oblivious to the early hour or the concerns of anyone that might be within earshot and not awake yet. He scanned the tree line frantically.

"Come on, come on, where are you?"

He stopped and closed his eyes for a moment. "Can I use my luck powers to find her? Let them guide me to her?"

It was like a switch turned on in his head. And he knew. He started off again at full speed, vaguely aware that his father was approaching from behind.

"I know where she is!" he yelled back. "Come on, follow me!"

He dashed into the woods and soon saw a small little grove of trees off to the right. In the middle, he could see a shape. Someone, dressed in black, curled up in fetal position, not moving.

"Mum?" Tears rushed into his eyes. "No! Please be all right. Please be safe!"

He made his way across the uneven and damp ground, plunging into the grove.

"Mum!"

He knelt beside her and gripped her shoulders, shaking them gently.

"Mum, are you all right? Can you hear me? Mum?"

By now, Carl had caught up and was at his side, catching his breath in deep huffs and puffs. "Come on. Let's get her turned over."

They gently rolled her over so that she was facing up.

Lluck reached out to touch the side of her cold face. "Mum, please..."

Holly shuddered and took a gasping breath.

"Mum!" He wiped at the tears running down his cheeks.

"Holly, can you hear us?" Carl took her hand.

Holly groaned and started to open her eyes. "Carl? Lluck?"

"We're here, mum. We came for you, just like I promised."

"You did, darling. Thank you." She gave him a faint smile.

"You're gonna be all right mum, everything's gonna be all right."

"Come on," Carl said, "help me get her up."

They helped her sit up, taking great care not to force anything too soon.

"Can you move? Can you walk?" Lluck asked.

She nodded. "I think so. We'll find out, I suppose."

"We need to get her to hospital," Lluck said.

"That's not gonna work, son," Carl cautioned. "They couldn't help her anyway. She probably needs magic, and that means Jilly or Qwyrk, or somebody like that. Let's just get her home and warmed up, and then we can figure out what to do. Try to contact them."

"I forgot and left my phone at home, or I'd text her right now," Lluck grimaced.

Holly nodded. "Your home. Please? That sounds lovely. I just need to be s-somewhere safe. And w-warm."

"Come on, then, let's get you out of here," Carl said. He and Lluck gently helped Holly to her feet and lifted her arms over and around their shoulders. They slowly made their way out of the trees and back to his car.

"It's all gonna be fine, mum. You'll see. We'll look after you, and you'll get better. Everything's gonna be fine." Lluck didn't care if anyone saw them. He didn't care about anything else. All he wanted was for her to be safe, and more importantly, to find whoever had done this to her.

*   *   *

"You know I wouldn't do this for just anyone," Horatio said, pacing about Granny's sitting room waving his hands about. "Oh," he looked at Jilly, "and cheers for allowing me in here. Quite the place ol' Granny has. l can cross this one off the bucket list, now. A bit of an achievement, innit? I wouldn't normally be able to get within ten yards of this place without bein' thrown half a mile into the air."

"Remind me to bring you back here after this is all over," Qwyrk said. "I really need to see that."

"You are cold." Horatio pointed directly at Qwyrk.

"Can Boggie see me, like now?" Qwyrk had no time for his drama.

"Yeah, for you, he'll make an exception. Ain't even gonna ask you to do anything to earn it, either. But he'll want you to make it up to him at some point, just so you know."

"Fine, whatever. I'll sing or dance, or ride a unicycle, or whatever the bloody hell he wants. But right now, I just need his help, as much as it pains me to say so."

"If it's about findin' your missus, I don't have any info meself, but the day is early, and others might well have some news to which I am not yet privy."

"How did you know Holly's still missing?"

"'Cause she ain't here with you, yeah? And that strikes me as highly unlikely in this time of heightened tension. Ergo, I have to presume she's still missing, and you need to find her, which I highly endorse. The upside is, I haven't heard anything bad, and in my experience, bad news travels faster than good."

"Thanks. I do appreciate it." Qwyrk relaxed a little.

"Well, I do have money ridin' on you, don't I? You two are quite the power couple, and the talk of the proverbial magical town, so I need to protect me investment."

"Your concern is overwhelming me."

"As it should. Right, I'll just nip off to the boss, set it up, and pop back in a jiff. Cheers!" He disappeared in another puff of stale cigar smoke.

"Talk of the town, eh?" Jilly smiled. "Why am I not surprised?"

"Yeah, I wouldn't go that far."

"But it sounds like you two've made quite the splash in the magical world."

"I suppose that's one way of putting it."

"So," Jilly said. "What's your ship name?"

"What?"

"Your ship name?"

"What are you talking about? I don't have a boat."

"No silly, 'ship' is short for 'relationship.' When you say you 'ship' two people, it's because you want them to be together."

"Oh. Um, all right."

"So, a ship name is a name for a famous couple. It's usually a combination of their two names into one word. Like, if they were named Gary and Susan, they might be Garisan. Or if they were Joanne and Claire, they might be Clairanne. See?"

"But we're not famous. I mean, not like *that*. We're not celebrities, or anything. At least I don't think we are."

"Horatio said that Nasties and Fae are betting on your success as a couple. Which is kind of weird, really, but if you're popular enough to gamble on, that means you're famous. And if the council is making such an effort to keep you two apart, it must mean you're important. So, you need a ship name, if you don't have one already."

"I have no idea if we do, honestly. If so, I've never heard it."

"Well, let's give you one, and then we can spread it around, so that people will know what to call you. It's a good way of flipping off the council, too."

"I'm not sure—"

"Let's see." Jilly was clearly and annoyingly in no mood to take no for an answer. "Maybe, Hwyrk?"

Qwyrk grimaced. "Sounds like an Anglo-Saxon curse word, or the sound of someone about to throw up. Or an Anglo-Saxon who's about to throw up and is cursing about it."

"All right," Jilly said. "Um, Qwolly?"

"Isn't that an Australian marsupial?"

"Qwyrlly?"

"I'm pretty sure he was one of the Three Stooges."

"Hmm, this is harder than I thought." Jilly rested her chin on her hand.

"Maybe we should just forget about it," Qwyrk said, hoping to change the subject, and still too wrapped up in worry to be enthusiastic about this nonsense.

"What if we combined Holly's real name with yours, instead?" Jilly thought aloud. "Something like... Qwyrshala! Ooh, I like that! What do you think?"

"Um, I guess?"

"Brilliant! It's settled, then. I mean, we'll ask Holly when she's back, of course, but I'm sure she'll like it."

"I'm sure she will. Look," Qwyrk insisted, "I don't want to sound rude or anything, but can we get back to the main topic here?"

"Of course, sorry. We still have to find out where she is. I mean, at least Horatio doesn't think anything bad's happened."

"No, but she's obviously been away all night, like not in this world, which means she was taken somewhere by someone. And that worries me. Is she being protected, or held prisoner?"

"I'm sure Bogtrotter will help."

"I'm not, but thanks for the encouragement." She took Jilly's hand. "I need whatever I can get at the moment."

With another whiff of mystical stogie, Horatio appeared in the sitting room. "Crackin' job you did keepin' that portal open for me love, cheers!" He nodded to Jilly. "Uh, I don't suppose you could keep it open on an ongoing basis? Ya know, just in case I want to pop 'round here for tea with Granny now and then?"

"Yeah, she wouldn't be too happy with me if I did that." Jilly shook her head. "And she'd probably toss you like a mile or so into the air."

"Maybe you should do it, just to see what happens," Qwyrk suggested.

"Ya know, I'm doin' you a big favor here." Horatio glared at Qwyrk. "I could just call the whole thing off right now."

"Yeah, all right, sorry." Qwyrk held up her hands in apology. "So, what's the deal?"

"The deal is, the boss will see you now. Let's just say that he has some concerns of his own about how this is all shakin' down, and he'd like to ally himself with you again, if you're amenable."

"Quite, for once."

"Righty-ho, then. Let's get on with it."

Qwyrk stood next her diminutive helper and said to Jilly: "I'll be back as soon as I can, and I'll make sure to keep you in the loop about everything. I promise!"

"Thanks," Jilly said with a reassuring smile. "I'll be here."

With a nod to Jilly, Qwyrk looked down to Horatio, who nodded too.

"Away we go, then," he said, and with a wave of his tiny fingers, they were hoovered through a mystic portal and off to destinations if not unknown, at least unpleasant.

*   *   *

Winston opened his eyes with a start and a sharp inhale. He was fairly certain that he'd slept horribly, but for some reason, he was quite energized. Indeed, it was as if he'd had a luxurious eight or nine hours of uninterrupted slumber, something that never happened.

He sat up and looked at the time: half past seven. "That's preposterous! I can't have slept for more than a few hours. What with all that nonsense last night, being outside and losing an hour of time, and masked cultists or what have you, how am I so refreshed?"

He got out of bed and threw on his favorite wooly robe. He grabbed the key, which he'd left on the nightstand nearby, and kept a tight grip on it. He bounded downstairs to the kitchen with the intent of making his morning coffee.

"I don't really need it, do I?" he realized as he reached for a mug. "I don't even think I want it. This is most peculiar!"

Deciding to forego his usual dose of morning inspiration, he strode into the sitting room and opened the curtains, taking in the morning sun and contemplating his agenda for the day, the plans he had for this potentially priceless little trinket he still clutched in his hand.

"I can get a good start on researching it, try to find out more—"

His voice trailed off, and he froze in place. His vision blurred, and something inside of him spoke. Spoke? Yes, he had vague memories of the same voice calling to him last night, maybe even while he dreamed.

Go to the source, it said. *Find it. You will know where it is. Make preparations and depart as soon as you can. Nothing else matters, and time is of the essence.*

"Go to the source," he repeated in a rather dull, monotone

voice. "Yes. I know where it is. I know how to get there. The source for where it will begin. Where the gate will be opened."

His vision returned to normal, and he felt like himself again, if a trifle off.

"What just happened?"

He glanced down at the key. It exuded warmth, and seemed to pulse with a life of its own. He stroked it with his index finger. It called to him, beckoned him. It knew things: secrets, purposes, locations. His thoughts wandered, and the memory of the voice's instructions came to him, perfectly clear. He sensed his own mind merging with something else, something outside of him. It needed his help, help he would be happy to offer. This other, this being seemed to blend with him, until he could no longer tell who was who. And he knew what he had to do.

He picked up the phone and dialed.

"Penelope? It's Winston."

"Winston? My goodness, you're phoning early! I hope nothing's the matter?"

"Nothing at all. Quite the contrary, in fact. Something extraordinary has come to light, and I need to see it through. Penelope, make yourself ready. We're going on an excursion!"

*   *   *

"Right. No songs, no dances, no bloody sonnets in costumes, no performance art, or anything else. I need your help, and yeah, I'll owe you later. But right now, I need to find my girl, and I need to know what the bloody hell is going on. If you wind me up, or throw any of your damned explosions at me, I swear I will kick your arse, just as soon as I've recovered!" Qwyrk truly was in no mood for any games or Nasty shenanigans.

"Agreed." Bogtrotter nodded, a bipedal highland cow in a fancy blue velvet doublet, sitting on his makeshift rock throne. He'd dismissed all his sycophants so they could speak in private.

"Uh, you do?"

"Yeah, this ain't the appropriate time for gags and whatnot."

"Oh, um, all right. Glad you see it that way. So, what's happening? Where's Holly? I mean if you have any idea. Do you have any idea?"

"The best intelligence we've got is that she's now with her son and the lad's father in Leeds. They was spotted a little while ago helping her out of the trees at Nicewood park, and spiriting her away in an automobile, presumably theirs. That's all I got. As to her condition, I really cannot say, apologies for that."

A flood of relief washed over Qwyrk. "Oh, thank Goddess."

"Well, your lady's presumably in good hands, and I'm sure you'll be wantin' to go to her as soon as you can, but, as you may have noticed, things are startin' to go to hell in a proverbial hand basket."

"Just what is going on? I feel like I've been pummeled over the last day, and not just by that rat bastard Fachan. What's really happening?"

"Something's out there, love. Something big and bad, wut this world ain't seen for hundreds of generations. This is the big one, the one folks've been fearin' for centuries. If this fellow gets his way, we're all done for, and I don't just mean you and me. I mean Fae, Shadows, humanity, Nasties... we'll all be under his proverbial boot forever, if we even survive."

"Okay, fine, but who exactly are we talking about?"

"We still ain't absolutely sure, but were I predisposed to gambling, which I'm not, I'd lay odds on none other than... Balor." He said the name with a change in tone that was apparently meant to unnerve. Only, it didn't.

"Um, sorry, who?"

"Balor?" He threw up his hands. "The biggest of the bads? The ruler of the Fomorians? The one that crushed ancient Ireland so bad that it took an army of literal gods to finally beat him? Ringin' any bells?"

"Oh, *that* Balor."

"Yer messin' with me. You gotta know who he is."

"Kind of? I mean, yeah, all right, if you're talking about ancient battles and such. But aren't those accounts all heavy on the mythology, anyway?"

"What's the meaning of myth? It's 'story.' The kind of story that may or may not have happened, but the essence of which is always happening. Balor might have been turned into a bogey man to scare faery children over the centuries, but he was—is—very real, and he ain't playin' games. Word is that he's got followers among your kind and elsewhere that've been working for a long time to bring him back. His body was destroyed in the battle that banished him, but if what I'm hearin' is right, he'll have a new form real soon. And when he gets it, he'll start drawin' all his servants to him, and he'll have the power to open the gates to the realms of the dead where—"

"Where the Fomorians like Aeval and the rest of the banshees are, and then they'll be able to descend on earth."

"Bingo! They come back, humans are farked, we're farked, everyone's farked."

"But we can stop him, right? There's enough of us. We can mount a defense. The council must be prepared for this."

"From what we've heard, nothin' in our worlds'll be able to stop him. He's too ancient, and he's immune to our magic."

"Brilliant. And all of this starts on Samhain? Tomorrow night?"

"That is the general consensus."

Qwyrk let out a heavy sigh.

"It ain't all doom and gloom, though," Bogtrotter said after a short silence. "There's a prophecy that Balor can be taken down, with the right weapon and the right person wielding it."

"All right, so what weapon? Who wields it?"

"No idea, sorry to say."

Qwyrk blew out another heavy sigh and face-palmed. "So, we've got a day and a half to find some mythical weapon and whoever's supposed to use it. I've got no powers, my girl is in Goddess-knows-what state, one of my mates may have betrayed me to this Balor bloke, and a human I'm technically looking after is probably going to go join this creep's army with her great-great-great-whatever grand-mother, who incidentally taunted me and warned me six months ago that this very thing was coming, and I mostly ignored her."

"Yeah, it's all a bit shite, ain't it?"

"You're not helping, like not even a little!"

Bogtrotter shrugged.

"What will this Balor look like? How will we know?"

"Not sure. Like I said, he'll be gettin' a new body, but if it's anything like the old one, it won't be pretty."

"Meaning?"

"Well, he was famous for having only one eye that glowed, or flamed, or something."

"The Deathly Eye..." Qwyrk shuddered, understanding now what Blip had said.

"Huh?"

"Oh, the one who betrayed us? According to my human friend, he said, 'hail to the Deathly Eye.'"

"Yep, that's Balor confirmed, then. We are well and truly farked."

"Look, maybe we are, maybe we're not. But I sure as hell am not going to sit around making my final peace with things, all right? We have today and tomorrow, and I'm going to try to do something, anything, whether I have powers or not. There's no way I'm going out without a fight!"

"And that's why you're a hero, and I'm not. Get yerself on over to see yer girlfriend, then. You've earned your snog, that's for sure."

"Yeah, about that. Thing is, we can't do that. We can't even touch."

Bogtrotter furrowed his very shaggy brow. "What're you talkin' about?"

Qwyrk very briefly filled him in on the whole situation.

"That's, that is utterly heinous," he said.

"Yeah, you're telling me! You've never heard of anything like this before, then?"

He shook his head. "Sounds like your council wants to keep it on the down low. Don't reckon it'd be too popular with the general population of Shadows or Fae if word got out about it."

"Um, yeah, it's not too bloody popular with me! No ideas on how we can fix it, then? Or do an end-run around it?"

"Not off the top of me head, but I'd be more than happy to set a few of my best researchers on it to find a way to muck it up. It'd bring me some real pleasure to see your council humiliated, I must say." He chuckled.

"You and me both, mate. I've had it with them. I think I've pretty much quit already. If not, I'm sure I've been sacked by now."

"You'd be better off on your own, anyway."

"Maybe, but first things first. If we don't stop Balor and his hordes of Fomorians, we're not going to be doing much thinking about anything else."

"Agreed. I'm tellin' most of my folks to go to ground, really lay low. This ain't somethin' they can handle. Not in the slightest."

Qwyrk nodded with a frown. "For once, Boggie, I don't blame you."

* * *

Jilly waited until her parents got in the car and drove away. Then she waited just a little while longer, in case they came back for some reason.

"This would be the one morning they forget something and come rolling back up just as I go home."

After a few minutes she was satisfied that they were well and truly gone for the day. She selected a few more books that might be of some use. Stepping out of Granny's house, she locked the front door and made a protection sign with her hands while uttering a short chant in an ancient language she didn't even know.

She crossed the street, trying to look as casual as possible, just on the off chance that some other neighbor saw her leaving the home of the neighborhood eccentric. A quick glance of the nearby houses didn't reveal any self-appointed security guards peering out from behind curtains. She walked up the short flight of steps to her front door and pulled out her key.

Just in time to hear her parents' car roll up.

*   *   *

"Everything go all right with the boss, then?" Horatio paced about with his arms behind his back, looking impatient.

"Depends on how you define 'all right,' I suppose," Qwyrk said as she emerged from the ravine where they'd spoken.

"Good news and bad news, then?"

Qwyrk nodded. "The good news is that Holly's with her son, at his dad's house, and that's where I need you to take me next."

"That can be arranged. And the bad news?"

"Just about everything else."

"I was afraid you was gonna say that."

"No, seriously, like pretty much everything else is completely, utterly bollocked." She sat down on a boulder and sighed dejectedly. "I'm not sure we're going to make it out of this one."

Horatio nodded. "That's what I've been hearing." He jumped up to sit beside her. "But ya know, I've learned never to underestimate you or your mates. How many times have you snatched away victory from the proverbial mouth of defeat, eh? A lot, or you wouldn't be sittin' here right now. And that's gotta count for something."

"This is different. If what Boggie's saying is true, nothing can hurt this bastard: not magic, not brute force. Just some mythical weapon, which probably doesn't even exist."

"Which means you'll have found it by nightfall."

Qwyrk laughed softly in spite of her gloom. "I'm glad everyone else thinks so highly of me. I sure as hell don't."

"You've got quite the fan club, I can assure you. Even more now that you and Holly have hooked up. Talk about a power couple!"

"I suppose that's something. Thanks."

"And, the odds are swingin' even further toward a long-term success. I think you're up to about 80-20 in favor of, which means I've made a nice bit of cash on calling it before everyone was convinced."

"Cheers for ruining the moment."

"The point is, a lot of folks from the different worlds believe in you, because you've given them something to believe in. Word's gotten out about you and your merry little band of heroic misfits. You ain't gonna let your fans down. And if your stupid council can't see that, then sod 'em and the snails they rode in on! You've got till tomorrow night to save the world again, Ms. Qwyrk. So, what're gonna do?"

"When I figure that out, I'll let you know," she said with little resolve. "Cheers, mate. Now, can you take me to my girlfriend? We've got a lot to think about if there's actually going to *be* a day after tomorrow."

"Your wish is my command, love. Take my hand."

"Hang on," Qwyrk said, "I think someone's trying to contact me by my ring…"

* * *

"Hi mum," Jilly stammered.

"Jilly," her mother said as she stepped out of the car, "what are you doing out so early? Where have you been?"

"Um, I couldn't sleep and decided to go for a quick walk, you know, get some fresh air and all that? I've been sitting around too much lately. Need to get out more?"

Jilly was quite certain her shoddy lie (and her lies were never good to begin with) wasn't going to be remotely convincing. She held her breath. "But why are you back? Didn't you just leave?"

"Oh, your father forgot some papers in the office."

"I can run and get them for you!" Jilly volunteered, opening the front door.

"Thank you, dear, that'd be nice. They're in a blue folder on the desk."

Jilly dashed into the house. Her mum seemed to have actually bought her fib. She located said folder and ran back out to hand it off.

"Here you are! Um, have a nice day, I guess?"

Mrs. Pleeth gestured at her bundle of tomes. "Why are you carrying books?"

"What?"

"Books. If you were out for a stroll, why are you carrying books?"

Oh no! "Oh, um, well… I never know when I might want to stop for a few minutes and read, you know? Just in case I get the urge. It's silly."

Her mother gave her a blank stare and then got back in the car. "Have a nice day, dear."

"Thanks, um, see you tonight?"

But the vehicle was already pulling away.

Jilly stepped back inside, closed the front door, leaned against it, and sank down to sit on the floor, breathing a heavy sigh of relief.

"That was way too close!"

Odin came over and nuzzled her, and she gave him a good scritch on the head.

Her phone buzzed. Surprised and excited, she pulled it out to see that she had a text message.

Hey Jilly, sorry to text you early. I'll be in the area soon and really want to see you. Can I stop by your house? Lemme know if now-ish is a good time. Got a surprise... ST.

She paused for just a moment. "ST? Who's that? Wait... ST, Star Tao!"

CHAPTER ELEVEN

Wrapped in a warm blanket and embracing a comforting mug of hot tea, Holly sat on Carl's couch, while he and Lluck camped on either side of her, keeping a close watch.

"It's all right, really," she said, looking back and forth between them. "I'm starting to feel a bit more normal again. Whatever that means."

"Are you sure, mum? You looked like you'd really taken a beating out there. What happened?"

"Yeah," Carl echoed. "What's going on?"

Holly sighed. "I'm not quite sure, to be honest." She relayed how she and Qwyrk had gone to see Moirin in the park, and how she'd wandered off into the forest looking for their wayward human charge.

"Then, I strode into some kind of glowing fog in the grove of trees where you found me and ended up somewhere else."

"That makes no sense," Lluck said.

"You're telling me!"

"So, you were teleported away?" Carl asked.

Holly nodded. "I think so. I wasn't where I'd been a moment before. But I've no idea where I ended up."

"So, what happened?" Lluck asked.

"I met someone, someone I've seen before, several times, I think. Only, I never remember her, or what she says. Except this time, my mind was flooded with images of events I'd forgotten, experiences I'd had when I saw her in the past, I think, but it's all a muddle right now. I'm hoping my head will clear up in a bit, so I can remember more."

"This is right strange," Lluck said. "You remember that there's stuff you can't remember, but you might remember it sometime later on, if you don't forget it again?"

"That's basically it." She took another drink of her tea, feeling better with each sip.

"Who is she? What's her name?" Carl asked after a short silence.

Holly shook her head. "I don't know. I think she's some kind of seeress or speaker of prophecies and such. It's all a mess in my head at the moment. I don't know why she keeps showing up in visions and in my dreams, and now for real, apparently. It's like I need to be reminded of something, something important, but she won't tell me what it is. I think she's trying to coax it out of me, without telling me anything meaningful."

"That's bloody rude!" Lluck said.

"Isn't it?"

"So, she took you away, by magic or something? Why?" Carl asked.

"I think she saved my life. There was some terrible danger in those woods, and she said it would have... would have killed me."

"Mum!" Lluck took her hand.

"Hey, it's all right! I'm fine. I'm just worried about what might've been out there, and... oh no. Qwyrk! I have to try to contact her! I tried back in the forest, but I couldn't."

She put down her mug and spoke into her ring. "Qwyrk, are you there, darling? Can you hear me? Please tell me you're there!"

"Holly?" a voice answered back.

"Holly teared up. "Where are you, what's happened? Are you all right?"

"Holly, thank Goddess it's you! I'm with Bogtrotter and the Nasties now. It's a long story. But you're with Lluck and Carl in Leeds, yeah?"

"I am. I'm right here, sitting on the sofa, in a lovely, warm house, completely safe! But, how are you hearing me?"

"I think Nighttime Nasty magic might be mucking up the ward, making it malfunction, which is fine by me!" Qwyrk sounded utterly relieved. "Hang on, love. Horatio and I are on our way."

"Horatio? Why is he coming with you?"

"It's... another long story, but I'll explain when I see you. Believe me, there's far too much to say. We'll be over really soon! Please don't go anywhere, all right?"

"Wasn't planning on it," Holly said. "Then again, I wasn't planning on it last night, either. Bye for now, darling. I miss you so much and can't wait to see you!"

"Bye, love. Goddess, I can't wait to see you, too! I'm going now, just in case the ward kicks us off again."

Holly looked at Lluck and Carl as the conversation ended.

"Sorry, I hope I didn't sound too sentimental or personal. I've had a traumatizing night and really needed to hear her voice."

"Quite all right," Carl said. "We're just happy we found you."

"I am too. I'm ever so grateful."

"So, what'll you do now?" Luck asked. "I mean, once you're better and all that?"

"I need to find out more about this mystery woman, why she keeps invading my thoughts, and why I can never remember anything properly after I see her. I'm starting to understand, I think? But I need some confirmation."

She held up her hand again and focused on her ring.

"Who're you calling?" Lluck asked.

"Some friends who might help shed some light on this," Holly said with more certainty than she'd had for a while.

*   *   *

Penelope arrived at Winston's home precisely when he'd requested; it wouldn't do to be late. She rang the bell and waited. And waited. And waited some more.

"That's not like him," she said to herself, looking around, wondering if he'd wandered off, or gone to the shop around the corner, or some such. Another minute of uncomfortable fidgeting and the door opened. "Oh, thank goodness, I was getting... Winston?"

The man standing in the doorway couldn't be the one she knew. He was dressed all in black: a suit, a long coat, and a scarf. Not quite formal wear, but certainly a good sight more dapper than his usual charming-if-slovenly array of browns and academic tweeds.

Stranger still, his hair was combed and slicked back, not sticking up in random directions as usual.

"W-Winston?"

"Good morning, my dear!" he said in a confident, baritone voice as he took her hand and gave it a light kiss. A little shiver went down her back as a bundle of nerves washed over her.

"This is, I mean, it's all rather, um... I mean, you look, rather, um, rather..."

"Thank you, dear Penelope."

"Grand?" she managed to utter. "What happened?"

"I've been feeling in a bit of a rut lately, you see, and decided it was time for a drastic change. Certain circumstances have led me to believe that I need to step things up a bit, in several areas of my meager existence. Does my new sartorial refurbishment please you?"

"It's, well, it's all rather, I mean, you look, I think..."

"Splendid! Then I've achieved the first of many goals! Now then, the day is crisp and clear, and getting out of Knettles for a bit would do both of us some good, don't you think?"

"Well, I suppose, but what did you have in mind?"

"It's all a part of the research, you see, concerning the key." He pulled it out of his coat pocket, gazing at it with admiring, almost worshipful eyes. "I was going to spend the day in the stuffy old records office, but I had an epiphany overnight. I think the very best thing I can do now is follow up a lead, well, call it more of a hunch. It came to me all at once, rather like someone whispered it in my ear. Come to think of it, maybe someone did. Ha!"

"All right, but where are we going?"

"To the town of Pateley Bridge. There's something there I should very much like to see!"

*   *   *

With a whooshing sound, Qwyrk and Horatio materialized in Carl's living room. Carl and Lluck seemed more than a little astonished by her sudden entrance—though really, they should have been used to it by now—but the one she really wanted to see sat between them, all smiles. Qwyrk's heart raced as Holly threw off her blanket and stood up, smiling ear to ear.

"Qwyrk!"

"Holly!"

Qwyrk forgot about all her troubles. She forgot about the threat looming over the world. She forgot about all the crap that had happened in less than a day. Only one thing mattered now. She ran to Holly, arms open. Holly ran to her. A sweet embrace awaited them.

Only it didn't. Just as they touched, Qwyrk felt as if she had run into a concrete wall. She was propelled several feet backward, landing hard on the living room floor. The anger and humiliation were just as bad as before.

"Damn it! Bloody fecking hell!" she swore, and then swore some more. And then a lot more. She wanted to punch something, to break things, as rage and frustration overwhelmed her, and tears stung her eyes. She sniffed and looked up to see Holly sprawled back on the sofa, holding her head while Lluck and Carl panicked.

"Mum! What the hell? Are you all right?"

"Stupid, damned, sodding ward!" Qwyrk grumbled as she propelled herself into a standing position, her weakened body still aching.

Horatio spoke after a moment of awkward silence. "Uh, is this gonna to affect my betting pool?"

Qwyrk glared at him. "I'm going to drop-kick you into Lancashire if you say one more word about your stupid betting pool."

"Fine! Fine!" He held up his hands in mock submission.

Qwyrk limped to a nearby chair and sat down, trying very hard not to break down and sob in front of everyone.

"Seriously," Lluck offered in a quieter voice. "What was that?"

"I can barely even speak right now." Qwyrk said to Holly in a broken voice. "Can you tell them?"

Holly wiped her eyes and nodded. She relayed a short version of the awful situation, and for Qwyrk, it was like being stabbed by a needle, a little more with each word that Holly spoke. She was so happy that her girlfriend was alive and safe, and yet...

"That's right messed up," Lluck said. "I mean, they can't really do that, can they? It's gotta be illegal or something, right?"

"They can do whatever they like, I think," Holly answered, looking back at Qwyrk with sorrowful eyes. Qwyrk could only nod in confirmation, while inside she was breaking apart.

"That's not right, not at all," Carl said with a shake of his head.

Even in her turmoil, Qwyrk knew that this all must be awkward for him, and she found herself pitying him.

"Our situation isn't even the worst of it, sorry to say," she offered up instead, eager to change the subject. "Turns out there's a new big bad out there, the biggest bad, apparently. Oh, and he's showing up tomorrow. Yeah, on Halloween, because of course he is. And there's literally nothing we can do to stop him, except maybe by one way, which may or may not even exist. So, all's normal, then?"

"Wait, what?" Lluck shook his head in disbelief.

"Qwyrk, what are you talking about?" Holly asked, wiping away her tears and sitting up.

"Balor, love. The king of the Fomorians. He's found a way back from his banishment in the realms of the dead, with a little help from a few well-placed traitors—oh, and that's another whole story—and we have until tomorrow night to figure out how to stop him from crushing us and this whole world under his boot. I mean, if he wears boots, which we have no idea, because apparently, he's getting a brand new body, and we have no clue what it looks like, or where he's going to show up, or who will be with him, or even the exact time it's going to happen. And it's all been in the works for ages, right under our flipping noses, and no one saw it coming, except maybe me, when Aeval practically gave the whole game away to me at Castlerigg six months ago, and I basically ignored her. Bloody magnificent, eh?"

A stunned silence fell over the room, or rather, it crashed through the roof and made quite the silent scene.

"So, what do we do then?" Carl asked after a moment, breaking the tension.

"You tell me, mate. I'm pretty much out of ideas. And on top of it all." Qwyrk held up her bandaged hands.

"Qwyrk, darling! What happened?" Holly started toward her but stopped herself and stayed seated.

"Short version? I have no powers right now. I'm basically human, thanks to the poison from a weapon carried by a particularly nasty piece of work called a Fachan, a Scottish Darkfae who attacked me in Nicewood. It was keeping watch to prevent us or anyone else from interfering with whatever plans Aeval has for Moirin, which is why we couldn't find her after we cocked up and showed up too late for our meeting. Anyway, the thing's club and chains got me a few good times. I killed it, but I was a wreck by then. Horatio here got me out, patched me up a bit." She nodded to him. "The poison's effects'll wear off eventually, but who knows when?"

"Thank goodness you're safe," Holly sighed. "It means she was right. It could have been me. I could've been killed, but she saved me!"

"Who?" Qwyrk shook her head.

"The woman from my visions, in the red robe. That's where I was last night. She took me away to… somewhere, told me it wasn't yet my time to die, that I still had something else to do. She flooded my mind with memories, but of course, I can't make sense of them now. They're just a jumble of images and thoughts, and I've no idea what's real and what isn't. But we've met before, she and I, I'm sure of it. She's spoken to me in the past. She's been in my head for years now, but I keep blocking her out, or maybe something else is blocking it from me."

"You know, I'm getting really bloody tired of having our minds screwed with," Qwyrk said in exasperation. "But this could be really important. Holly, love, can you remember anything, make any sense of it?"

"I'm trying, but it's all very confusing. I put out a call for some help, though."

"A call? To who?"

The doorbell rang.

"Who's that?" Carl asked, standing up to go to the door.

"If it's who I hope it is, we might be able to get some real answers," Holly said. Qwyrk was confused.

Carl returned a moment later followed by two gentlemen wearing long, black trench coats, black bowler hats, and dark sunglasses. One might have been just a hair taller than the other, but they were otherwise identical. Qwyrk found herself smiling a little, despite the doom and gloom that hung over them all.

"Good morning to you all," one of them said in a soothing, if slightly mechanical voice. "I trust you remember who we are, but on the off chance that is not the case, I am Mr. Dill, and this is my associate, Mr. Chives. We investigate unusual situations and lend our expertise in rectifying problematic ones where we can. Ms. Vishala informs us that she has just such a problematic situation on her hands?"

"Mate," Qwyrk said, shaking her head, "wait till you hear the whole story!"

*   *   *

Jilly sat on her sofa, laptop in lap, phone at the ready. She'd texted Star Tao back, and then tried to keep herself occupied with Twitface while she waited for him to drive up.

"I wonder what his surprise is?" she mused, looking out the window for the umpteenth time. No sign of his multi-colored van.

Her mind wandered. She wondered what Qwyrk was up to and how her meeting with Bogtrotter had gone. She worried about Holly. Then Moirin. Her thoughts turned to Blip and what he was really up to. She hated not knowing.

She sighed and gave up on social media as a remedy for her anxieties and concerns (a wise idea, in general). If anything, it just made them worse.

"What if Blip *does* come back? He said he wasn't going to be available for a few days—well, now I know why—but what if that was a lie, too? What if he did see me when he was in that tunnel, and he's been waiting for my parents to leave so he can come and grab me?"

Her worries flooded back. She felt like a sitting duck. She considered returning to Granny's, but if she did, Star Tao wouldn't be able to find her, at least not unless she kept looking out the window. But that would be odd if anyone were watching, and what if the neighbors kept seeing her go over there and told her parents? And what would they think if they saw him drive up in that van of his and come to the front door and she let him in? She wished she'd told him to park a few streets away and walk up.

A flash of pink in the room shocked her from her obsessions over unpleasant possible scenarios. Jilly jumped up onto the sofa and held her hands out in desperation, trying to think of anything magical she could call to mind. Odin cowed in his bed and growled.

"Crap! This is it! Blip's here for me!"

But instead, a circle formed from the light, and out of it walked three very distinct individuals: a Shadow woman with bright pink hair in a bob, blue jean overalls, and black Doc Martens; another Shadow woman with long, dark brown, curly hair wearing a too-tight, too-short white dress with too-tall, sparkly high heels; and a human with a scraggly beard, a tie-dye shirt, green cargo pants, and a brown coat. He'd had long, brown, platted hair, but now it was cut short. She could barely believe it as they stepped into her living room, and she was overjoyed to see them.

"Qwypp! Qwykk! Star Tao!"

"Hello, Jilly!" Star Tao smiled, running up to give her a hug. "My surprise is bringin' these two with me! Long time, no see, eh?"

"Too right! But what did you do to your hair?"

"Well, it was time for a change, wasn't it? Me old look didn't feel right, anymore. I mean, I'm gonna grow me hair out again normal long-like, but I needed to let the strands of old things go, so to speak, to become like a caterpillar emerging from a cocoon into a new life."

Jilly was happy that his mood seemed to have picked up from the last time she'd seen him.

"I think it looks right handsome," Qwypp said, running her hand over the top of his head.

"What are you all doing here?" Jilly asked. "Not that I'm unhappy about it, or anything. I thought you were going to come driving up in your van?"

"Well, I would have," Star Tao answered, "but apparently, there's some bad news about somethin' goin' down?"

"So, you know about it, too?" Jilly asked.

Qwypp nodded. "There's a lot of chatter in the Shadow world right now about what might happen."

"And what might *not* happen could be even worse that what *might* happen!" Qwykk offered with calm self-assurance.

Jilly gave her the briefest of blank glances and raised her eyebrows. "Right, so, what *is* happening there?"

"Bad stuff, love," Qwypp said. "Stuff we wouldn't normally involve a human in, but you're Qwyrk's mate and like, Granny's apprentice, right? And you do magic and all that really well?"

"I don't know about 'really well.' I mean, I guess I've gotten us out of a few bad places a few times."

"Don't listen to her," Star Tao assured. "Jilly's brilliant. And if the old lady's taken her on, she's done it for good reasons."

"That'd be a right fun television show, wouldn't it?" Qwykk

mused, twirling a strand of hair with her finger and gazing off into some undefined distance, smacking her chewing gum.

"What would?" Qwypp looked annoyed.

"You know," Qwykk went on, "have try-outs to be the new sidekick for a powerful wizard or something, and they have to compete against each other every week, until only one's left. They could call it: 'The Sorcerer's Apprentice.' Ooh, I like that name! I bet no one's ever thought of that before!" She looked very proud of herself.

Qwypp joined Jilly in giving Qwykk a blank glance that wasn't so brief this time. "Anyway," Qwypp said, "we wanted to get in touch. We need to see Qwyrk. We called round her house, but she wasn't there. Besides, she's been, you know, a bit pre-occupied this summer with her new girlfriend and all."

"It's so sweet!" Qwykk exclaimed, looking wistfully out the window, before looking frustrated. "But I can't believe we still haven't met her yet!"

"That's really not the point right now." Qwypp rolled her eyes.

"But it is, though!" Qwykk shot back. "We're her best mates, and it feels like she doesn't even have time for us, anymore. I mean, I get it, but come on! We did our part to save the world from that William the Shoeless bloke, didn't we?"

"De Soulis," Qwypp corrected, with a further round of eye rolling.

"Whatever. But we did, right?"

"Yeah, we did," Qwypp confirmed. "But again, not the point right now. Qwyrk's like a sister to us, but we don't own her, and we don't have any right to demand her time. We'll meet Holly when she wants us to. But we have more important things to worry about!"

She turned to Jilly. "Can you call her, text her, send her a Faegram, whatever you do? It's important."

"Yeah, that's a bit of a problem, actually," Jilly winced. "I don't really have a good way to get in touch with her, and it's taken me this long to realize that's not a great setup."

"Oh." Qwypp frowned. "That's not good. Any idea where she might be?"

"She went to see Bogtrotter earlier."

"She did what?" Qwypp almost yelled.

"Oh no, it's all right," Star Tao interjected. "That Bogtrotty bloke helped us out last winter didn't he? Brought reinforcements when we was gettin' overwhelmed by the Erlking. He was all right."

"He's a complete pillock!" Qwypp swore.

"Yeah," Jilly agreed, "but like you said, everything's messed up right now, so we need all the help we can get."

"I suppose," Qwypp sighed. "Is she still with him?"

"No idea." Jilly shook her head.

"This isn't going how I thought it would," Qwypp observed.

"I mean, I can text Lluck and see if he's heard anything," Jilly offered. "He's sometimes more in the know than I am."

"Lluck?"

"Holly's son."

"Wait, Holly has a son?" Qwypp looked very confused. "But she's... am I missing something here?"

"It's a long story. Probably better if Qwyrk tells you," Jilly assured her. "Let me try him."

She picked up her phone and texted him: "Any news?"

"It's kind of amazing isn't it?" Qwykk asked.

"What is?" Qwypp answered, looking for all the world like she didn't want to know.

"Like, we can teleport, but they can send instant messages anywhere in the world. How come we can't do that?"

"Maybe because... we can teleport?" Qwypp said.

"Yeah, but we still can't find Qwyrk, can we? But she can tap a few words out," she made a tapping motion in the air, "and find out where she is faster than we could chasing her all over."

"And your point is?"

"What?"

"What point are you trying to make?"

Qwykk blew a bubble but didn't answer.

An agonizing minute of silence ensued, and Jilly wasn't really sure what to say. As luck (or Lluck) would have it, her mobile buzzed, breaking the uncomfortable hush that had embraced them all like that annoying relative one always has to be nice to at the holidays.

She looked at her phone. "Oh!"

"What is it?" Star Tao asked.

"He got back to me! He says: 'Q&H here. Everybody here. Sorry not to text b4. Can you get here ASAP?' Bloody hell, they found her! They found Holly!"

"Was she missing?" Qwypp looked confused.

"Kind of, yeah. It's another long story. We can fill you in when we get over there. Can you take us all to his house?"

"In theory, yeah," Qwypp said, "but since I've never been there, it makes it more difficult. I don't want us to flash into a bunch of trees or the side of a wall, or anything."

"Yeah, that would be nasty. Wait, have you been here before?"

"No, but he has," Qwypp nudged Star Tao. "So that works."

"Well, I've been to their house," Jilly offered. "Can I show you a map?"

"Is there any kind of open space near where they live?"

"There's a small park not far away, but if we all just blink into it in broad daylight, that could be really awkward if anyone's there. Especially if they see you and Qwykk."

"Hey! I'm dressed up real nice!" Qwykk protested.

"And no one can see what you really look like," Qwypp said, for what Jilly knew must have been the millionth time, at least.

"I know that! I'm just saying," Qwykk pouted. "Even if no one can see you, be sure to stand out! That's my philosophy!"

"Kant and Hegel would be proud," Jilly muttered.

"Can't bagel what?" Qwykk smacked her gum.

"Nothing," Jilly lied. "I think we're just going to have to take our chances with the park. If Star Tao and I stand on either side of you, nobody who sees us will really notice, and we can make up some daft story about how we didn't really just appear out of nowhere."

"I could tell them we got dropped off by aliens," Star Tao offered.

Jilly shot him a skeptical look. "Because that's so much more believable than that we teleported there with two Shadows because we need to talk to another Shadow, her faery girlfriend, that girl-friend's extra lucky son, and his dad, who's a superhero."

"It ain't more believable," Star Tao said with a shrug, "but it won't take as long to say it."

"Fair point," Jilly conceded. She looked at Qwypp. "So, I'll show you a map of the park, and you can pop us over there? We'll just have to hope nobody's around. Or that they're not paying attention."

"Sounds like the best plan we've got," Qwypp said, "Goddess help us."

* * *

"It would appear that we have quite the situation," Dill said. Or was it Chives? Qwyrk still wasn't sure.

"Yeah, that's one way of putting it," she said. "Myself, I'd prefer to say that we're totally screwed, but then, you do you."

"If it is indeed the case that Balor's return is immanent, then your observation in the earthy vernacular is, I'm afraid, quite correct," Dill (or Chives?) said.

"So that's it, then? We're just screwed, and we can't do anything?" Lluck asked, taking Holly's hand. She put her other hand over his, and Qwyrk could almost feel her protectiveness.

"Well, allegedly, there's some kind of special weapon that can stop him," Qwyrk said, "but I have absolutely no idea what it is, or what it does, or where we can find it."

"It would not surprise me if there were something that could exploit a weakness in Balor's defenses," Chives (or was it Dill?) said. "A guarantee should something like this happen and he returns, despite being locked away."

"A sound strategy," his partner agreed.

"But that doesn't do us any good if we can't actually find it," Qwyrk protested. "You don't happen to know what it is, by some chance?"

"Unfortunately, that is not something of which we are aware," Chives (?) answered.

"Is there anyone out there who might know, Mr. Chives?" Holly asked.

So it is Chives! Qwyrk was glad to clear that up.

"Such information would be well guarded, even from the councils and the wise of the many different magical species," Dill said instead. "A few ancient beings might know, such as those who were present when the Fomorians were banished, those beyond the factions."

"What about the woman from my visions and dreams?" Holly looked at Qwyrk.

"Visions and dreams, ma'am?" Dill looked perplexed.

Holly described the mysterious woman in a red hooded robe with grey skin, how she'd been recurring in various ways in recent months and had saved her life only hours before. "She said I wasn't meant to die last night, that I had some purpose to fulfill. Who is she? What does she want?"

"I cannot be absolutely certain, ma'am, but it would appear that you have been in contact with Fayette," Dill replied.

"Fayette?"

"A being of very ancient origins," Chives elaborated, "so ancient that they are lost in the mists of time. Her true name is unknown, but she has been given that moniker as a convenience. It's merely the French word for 'Fae,' of course. Some shorten it further, and call her 'Faytte,' a clever bit of wordplay, as she is wont to speak of the destinies of those who seek her out."

"She is not fully present in this world or any world, nor is she anchored to one temporal location," Dill continued, "she sees past, present, and future simultaneously, and perhaps dwells in all three."

"But what does she want with me?" Holly demanded.

"Unknown, ma'am," Dill said, "but if she is a presence in your life, it is doubtless something of import, and not only to you, but to the world, by the sound of it."

"So would this... Fayette have any idea what the weapon we need is, or where we can find it?" Qwyrk asked, getting antsy.

"She is blessed with the sight of those things that are hidden, though her own eyes can never be glimpsed," Chives answered.

"Yes, why is that?" Holly asked. "Whenever I meet her, her upper face is always hidden in very dark shadows under her hood."

"It is said that because her eyes see all," Dill answered, "they also reflect those infinite sights outward. Were anyone of lesser power to behold them, the sight would drive them mad at best. Or kill them."

"Or drive them mad, then kill them," Chives added.

"Charming," Qwyrk sighed.

"But she would know," Holly pressed, "she'd know how to stop Balor?"

"It is probable, given her vast pool of knowledge."

"Right! Brilliant!" Qwyrk clapped her hands and sat forward. "So, how do we find her?"

"That may prove to be problematic, ma'am," Dill said. "As we have said, she does not inhabit any one world, and where she chooses to be at a given time is entirely up to her."

"But she was here in Leeds just last night," Holly said. "She saved my life."

"A most unusual intervention, it must be admitted," Dill nodded.

"Then she must be receptive to us, to me. If she thought to keep me from harm, she may well be willing to help us again?"

"It is conceivable," Dill nodded again.

Qwyrk was really becoming impatient. "So, if we were—hypothetically—to go looking for her, where would we go? Where would we even start?"

"According to some English folk traditions," Chives said, "a woman in red is said to haunt the Gaping Gap cavern in West Yorkshire, where she gives prophecy to both the willing and the unwary. It is not beyond possibility that said legends refer to Fayette. Such a natural formation may be a point of intersection across the dimensions between this world and hers."

"The Gaping Gap cavern," Holly said, looking as if something had clicked for her. "That's not too far from Manchester, is it?"

"Due north, though still some distance, ma'am," Dill offered, "not immediately adjacent. Why do you ask?"

She shook her head. "No reason."

Qwyrk knew there must be some reason, but she didn't press the issue. "So," she said instead, "a visit to that cave is in order, then? And as soon as bloody possible by the sound of things."

"But you're hurt," Holly said, "and my head is still a bit of a mess, and we can't—" She stopped without stating the obvious.

"I do recommend that in attempting to meet her," Dill added, "you should be at your best, or whatever said best may be under the circumstances. Fayette is a force of nature and can cause great peril to the unwary. Indeed, many mortals who have met such beings have not survived."

"Lovely." Qwyrk's hopes sank yet again. "And I'm effectively mortal at the moment, thanks to that bloody Fachan."

"Yes and no, ma'am," Chives said. "You are still from magic, even if you are not of it at the moment. That should afford you some protection, though, yes, possessing your Shadow abilities and traits would be preferable."

"How do I get them back?"

"Time, ma'am."

"Which I don't have."

"I have an idea," Holly said. "If we're going to try to meet with this Fayette, we need to be prepared first, yes?" She looked at Qwyrk. "You should go to the council, tell them what's happening, and demand they remove the ward. We might well need to touch each other in case we encounter any danger, and this is an emergency that clearly overrides their absurd segregation law. Also, see if they can neutralize the poison or power you up somehow. And don't take no for an answer!"

Qwyrk smiled. She loved to see Holly be forceful and take charge. "And what are you going to do?" she asked Holly.

"I'm going to get some answers. I'm starting to make sense of what Fayette showed me in that other realm, and it's time I ask some serious questions."

"Of who?"

The front doorbell rang again.

"Cor, it's like bloody King's Cross here this morning!" Carl looked exasperated but got up to answer.

"Oh! I wasn't expecting you," he said a moment later, "but good morning, come on in. Everyone else is here. The more the merrier, I suppose."

Qwyrk's jaw dropped as Jilly, Star Tao, Qwypp, and Qwykk strode into the room, and for some inexplicable reason, everything seemed a bit better. Perhaps providence was providing, after all.

CHAPTER TWELVE

"Qwyrk!"

"Jilly! Qwypp? Qwykk? Star Tao?"

"Qwyrk!"

"Qwyrk?"

"All right, Qwyrk?"

"Qwyrk?"

"Holly!"

"Jilly! Star Tao!"

"All right, Holly?"

"Mum?"

"Holly?"

"Lluck!"

"Hey Jilly."

"All right, Carl?"

"Star Tao."

"Dill? Chives?"

"Ma'am."

"Ma'am."

"All right, everyone shut up, this is getting far too confusing!" Qwyrk put a halt to the greeting tennis match mid-game. "Folks on the sofa: Jilly and Star Tao you know, Qwypp and Qwykk you don't. Qwypp and Qwykk: this is Dill, Chives, Carl, Lluck, and yeah, my girlfriend, Holly. Everyone good now?"

"Um, I'm standin' right over here, ya know." Horatio folded his arms and looked to be taking some umbrage at being ignored.

"Right, sorry." Qwyrk felt bad about overlooking him. Almost. "You all remember Horatio?"

"How could we forget?" Qwypp sneered.

"Well, love, the last time I saw you two," he answered, "you was doin' the whole naughty nurse routine quite well, if I recall. It suited you."

Qwypp took a step toward him with a fist, but Qwyrk held up her hand. "Can we not have any bloodshed here, please? There's probably enough of that on the way as it is. However this happened, I'm glad you're all here. We're going to need everyone we can get to have any kind of chance of beating this thing."

"What thing?" Qwypp asked. "And come here and give me a hug, you gorgeous pain in the arse!"

Qwyrk obliged and Qwykk ran to join in with them. "It's been too bloody long."

"Too right it has!" Qwykk said. "So, what's going on? Is this another end-of-the-world thingie?"

"Afraid so, love, the worst one of all." Qwyrk told them everything. Or at least everything that she could condense into something not resembling a nineteenth-century novel in length. No matter, Qwykk still looked confused, as expected.

"So," Qwykk said. "Basically, you just need a mobile?"

"Congratulations on completely missing the point again, love." Qwypp rolled her eyes at Qwykk.

"I so did not miss the point!" Qwykk protested. "None of this would've happened if we could text instead of teleporting!"

"Anyway." Qwypp turned her attention to Holly and went to her, arms extended. "Holly, it's so nice to meet you at last! We've heard lovely things about you, second-hand of course, but I have a feeling they're all true."

"Charmed, I'm sure." Holly smiled taking Qywpp's hands in her own. "And I've good reason to suspect you're the best friends Qwyrk could hope for."

They exchanged pecks on the cheeks, and Qwyrk once again marveled at how bad she was with introductions, and how easy everyone else seemed to do with them. "Look, this is brilliant," she said, "and I'm amazed and astonished that we've all somehow ended up here, but we don't have a lot of time to catch up."

"Where's Blip?" Holly asked. "Shouldn't he be here as well?"

An uncomfortable silence descended.

"What?" Holly pressed. "What's going on?"

Qwyrk winced and looked at Jilly. "Do you want to tell him?"

Jilly looked down and sighed. "Blip... the thing is, he's, well, he's betrayed us."

This was met with a chorus of "whats?" and general disbelief, and Jilly gave them a version of what she and Qwyrk knew.

"I can't believe it! He always seemed so loyal. Annoying, but loyal," Holly said.

"It is not impossible ma'am," Dill said. "The machinations and plotting behind the scenes in this affair seem to be far more complex than even my good colleague and I might have guessed. Unfortunately, the fact is that anyone might be untrustworthy under the circumstances, not only Mr. Blippingstone, but anyone at all."

"Including those present in this room," Chives added, which clearly made everyone uncomfortable at the thought.

A chill rushed down Qwyrk's back. "No," she said. "No, we're not going down that path. The last thing we need to be doing right now is second-guessing each other. We'll all be paranoid, and nothing will get done, and that's exactly what our enemies want."

"I agree," Holly added. "As difficult as it is, we have to trust each other."

"Well, I don't believe it," Star Tao countered, a scowl on his face.

"Look mate," Qwyrk started. She was afraid he would react like this.

"No, sod off, Qwyrk. I'm not listening to this rubbish. You may think something's up, but Lord Blippingstone wouldn't turn on us. I know it."

"I know you don't want to believe it," Jilly said, putting a hand on his arm, "but I know what I saw."

"There has to be an explanation." He jerked his arm away from her, which left Jilly looking hurt.

"Look," Qwyrk said, "I don't know what the truth is, but right now, we can't trust him, and as far as we can tell, he doesn't know that we know, so we have to keep it that way."

"Why, Qwyrk?" Star Tao was more defiant than she'd ever seen him. "Because you say so? The last time I tried to help you lot out, that banshee took over me head, and I could've killed people. I gave up channelin' because of it, cut meself off from a major part of who I am, and it's all your fault!" He pointed an accusatory finger at her.

"Love, come on," Qwypp said, going over to him, "that's not fair."

"Yeah, there's a lot of things that aren't fair, apparently," he said. "Whatever. I'm gonna go sit out in the garden and meditate for a bit... uh, if that's all right with you, Carl?"

"Yeah, knock yourself out. I mean, you know what I mean." Carl said with a shrug.

"Cheers, mate." Star Tao gave him a nod. "At least someone around here isn't talking nonsense." And with that, he stormed out to the kitchen and then on to the garden.

"I'm sorry." Qwypp looked around the room, embarrassed.

"It's fine. We're all on edge," Qwyrk said. "And he's not completely wrong, is he? Every time our world crashes into this one, crap gets stirred up, bad things happen, and it makes me feel like we'd be better off never having contact with each other."

"You don't mean that," Holly said.

"I wish I knew what I meant," Qwyrk said. "But look, I'm going to do exactly what you suggested and head on over to the council to demand they undo this whole segregation thing, because it's interfering with my job, namely, to stop the end of all things. Again."

"And you think they'll actually listen?" Holly asked.

"They have to!" Qwyrk said. "They can't possibly keep this stupid charade going when we've got a full-blown crisis on our hands!"

"We didn't exactly part from them on the best terms," Holly reminded her.

"Oh, come on, what's a little bit of flipping off between work colleagues, eh?"

"I don't know, Qwyrk," Qwypp said. "I think Holly's right. You know they're pretty damned stuffy, and they don't like anyone questioning their authority. They have to be the bloody be-all and end-all of everything, don't they?

"What other choice do I have?" Qwyrk demanded. "I have no powers right now, and this stupid ward makes us all weaker. They've got to suspend it, at least for a few days."

"I just wouldn't get my hopes up, if I were you," Qwypp said, shaking her head. "They're a right bunch of bastards."

"On that we agree." Qwyrk nodded. "Would you mind popping me over there? You know, with me not having powers and all that."

"You want me to come, too?" Qwykk offered.

Qwyrk was touched by the sweetness of her tone. "No, you stay, love. We need to have at least one Shadow around to keep an eye on things over here, yeah?" That seemed to please her.

"Everyone else, wait here until I'm back," Qwyrk instructed. "Then, Holly and I are going to try paying a visit to someone who quite honestly, scares the crap out of me, but it's the only choice we've got."

"We shall not be able to accompany you in that venture, I'm afraid, Ms. Qwyrk," Chives said.

"Indeed, we cannot be in the presence of such an entity," Dill added.

"Do I even want to know why?" Qwyrk asked.

"Not particularly," Chives answered.

"All right, then." Qwyrk was happy to let it drop.

"While you're gone, I have something I need to do as well," Holly announced.

"What's up, love?" Qwyrk asked.

"I just want to be fully prepared for our encounter," Holly answered.

She didn't elaborate, but Qwyrk had a good idea of what she meant. She wished she could be there for her, and her heart ached that it wasn't possible.

*   *   *

"Are you quite sure about this, Winston?" Penelope still had no clue as to why they were driving to Pateley Bridge, lovely though the green scenery and autumnal foliage were at this time of year.

"Never more sure, my dear," he answered with an assurance she'd never seen in him before.

Being called "my dear" flustered her a little. This new Winston seemed unsettling, but undeniably charming.

"And what are we doing when we get there?" she asked.

"We're going on a hunt for something very special. It's directly related to the key, its history, and its purpose. I'm terribly excited, and I know you'll be, as well."

"But how did you find out about it? I thought last night, you were a bit stumped, and wanted to do some more library research."

"It's all a bit complex, but I went for a night walk and gained some clarity. Then I came home, fell into a sleep and my intuition took over and blessed me with some honest-to-goodness revelations. I just need to confirm them once we get there."

"And where is 'there,' exactly? I mean, besides in the town? I assume that's where were going, into the town?"

"Oh yes, quite. No need to worry. I shan't be dragging you across dale and fell on some wild goose chase, invigorating though that might be. No, my dear, what we're looking for should be in a very precise place, if my insights are correct."

"And what place is that?"

"We're almost there."

Penelope realized that they'd entered the charming little town in question and now navigated its narrow streets. Winston pulled the car off to a side lane, little more than an alley, and parked.

"It doesn't look like much," she said, looking around.

"Of course not, but this is not our final destination. Come along!"

He hopped out of the car with a spring and confidence she'd never seen before. It excited and disturbed her all at once. But she followed him as he strode toward the cross street.

"Here we are!" he declared.

A few steps more and they reached the street in question and turned the corner. And abruptly stopped.

"Behold!" he said proudly, making a grandiose gesture with one hand.

Penelope looked at the shop, then back at him, then back at the shop again, more confused than ever. "A bakery?"

*　*　*

Jilly struggled with everything. Too much moved too quickly: Blip's treachery, Qwyrk's powerlessness, Star Tao rejecting them, Qwyrk and Holly forced apart by some bigoted magic, an awful new evil looming over them that they knew almost nothing about. She wanted to cry, to run away, to just be Jilly the artist again, sitting under a tree and dreaming about fantastic worlds instead of being forced to live in one.

She looked around the room at this strange band of misfits. They'd done some remarkable things together, but would it be enough this time? Could it? She looked at Qwyrk and Holly, frustration and grief on their faces. They couldn't even console each other with the simple act of touch, and it broke her heart to see the pain they were trying to hold in for everyone's sake. Forgetting her own worries, she knew what she had to do.

"Um, can everyone else leave the three of us alone in here, just for a bit?" She motioned to herself, Holly, and Qwyrk. One by one, the others nodded and filtered out of the room, going upstairs, exiting out the front door, going anywhere that wasn't here.

Dill and Chives tipped their hats. "We're off to investigate further," one of them (which?) said. "But do call on us if you have need."

"I'm sure we will," Jilly said.

After the room emptied out, she sat down on the sofa and patted it with both of her hands. "Come on, sit down."

Qwyrk and Holly heeded her request and sat on either side of her, Qwyrk on her left, Holly on her right. She looked back and forth between them. They both seemed as if they were about to cry, and Jilly worried she might join them. This magic was so cruel, so wrong, so bloody stupid.

"I don't know what to do right now about the bigger stuff," she said, "I guess that's sort of up to you. But I'm not giving up hope that we'll fix this separation thing. I won't. Ever. In the meantime." She held her right hand up to Qwyrk's face. "Here. Kiss my palm."

Qwyrk gave her a momentary confused look, but she did as Jilly requested, and Jilly placed said palm on Holly's left cheek. Holly put her hand over it and teared up.

"Your turn." Jilly smiled at Holly who did the same to Jilly's left palm, which she then placed on Qwyrk's cheek.

"I know it's not much," Jilly said, feeling so sad for them, "but it's something."

"It's more than something," Qwyrk said, squeezing her hand. "It's everything. Thank you."

Jilly took both of their hands in her own and brought them to her lap, holding them no more than a few inches apart. She looked back and forth between them. "I wish it could be more, but we're going to get this sorted, I promise."

Holly leaned in a little and laid her head on Jilly's shoulder. "I know we have so much to do, but can we just stay here for a while, like this?"

"Yeah," Qwyrk said, through a choked-up voice, as she did the same on Jilly's other shoulder, "I'd really like that, too."

Jilly welcomed both of them and nuzzled each of their heads in turn with her own. "We'll sit here as long as you want, as long as you need."

*   *   *

"Not just any bakery, Penelope. It's the gateway to a site of power, very ancient power. The Brigantes who roamed these parts over two thousand years ago knew about its properties, for good and for ill. And they were charged with a special task, you see."

"What kind of task?"

"Let's go in."

She followed him, not understanding how he knew any of this, let alone how he could have learned it from a dream.

"Good day, sir!" Winston greeted the owner with a smile, though Penelope thought it seemed insincere. Something about this venture began to feel off to her.

"Good mornin' sir. May I help you?"

"Oh, you may, and you can, friend. Far more than you currently realize, I assure you."

"And how may I do that? You have a party or an affair that needs caterin'? We are well equipped to handle all sizes of gatherings."

"A grand gathering *is* in order, funnily enough, but no, we won't have need of your fine baked goods for the occasion."

The owner looked as confused as Penelope felt.

"Uh, then what can I do for you?"

"I need access to your cellar."

"My... cellar?"

"Indeed. There is something there I should greatly like to see."

"I don't understand. Are you an inspector? Some estate agent tryin' to assess property value values, or some such?"

"Oh, nothing so mundane, my friend, I assure you. No, this is in the service of something far more august and splendiferous."

"I still don't understand."

"You needn't. Just direct us to your cellar, and we'll be on our way."

"Excuse me, but, with all due respect, this here is my business, and I am not obligated to do anything I don't want to, unless it's by order of the police or the town council, or some such. So, if you're not from either of them, and you don't want baked goods, I'll bid you good day and ask you to leave."

Winston sighed and looked irritated. "Oh dear, I was afraid you might react this way." He marched up to the hapless shopkeeper and threw a punch across the poor fellow's face. The man went down in an instant, sprawling on the ground, unmoving and out cold.

"Winston!" Penelope yelled in horror.

"Sorry you had to see that, my dear, but he rather left me no choice." Winston rubbed his knuckles.

"No choice?" She stepped back, ready to run in an instant. "What on earth are you talking about? You hit him! How could you do that?"

"Now, now, Penelope. He'll be quite all right, though he might have a sore jaw for a while. But it wasn't exactly easy on my hand, either!"

Penelope shook her head and began to back away in earnest.

"Oh, no. I'm afraid you can't leave, not when we're so close."

He waved his hand, and the door banged shut and locked.

Penelope shrieked.

"Rather impressive, isn't it?" Winston declared. "Something I picked up in a dream. Come now, we have an exciting bit of exploration to get stuck into!"

He strode to a door at the back of the shop and opened it, motioning to her. "Please."

Keeping her eyes on him, she warily approached and saw stairs leading downward.

"Let's be off, then." He turned on the light. "After you."

She descended first with more than a little trepidation and heard him following uncomfortably close behind.

"Can't be having you run off, now, can I?"

The basement itself seemed unremarkable and rather typical of what one would expect in an aged building. It smelled musty and clearly hadn't had a proper clean in quite some time. But on the other side of it was a very old-looking door that not only had been bolted shut, but also had boards nailed across it.

"A wise precaution, I should think," Winston said, walking up to it. Penelope had no idea what he meant, but she did have the thought to dash back upstairs and try to escape. However, something told her she wouldn't even make it halfway up the steps before he caught up with her, so she stayed put.

"Hmm." He looked up and down at the old door. He reached for the first plank and pulled it straight off with no effort, sending it crashing to the ground. Penelope stared in disbelief and started to tremble; what was happening?

One by one, he tore away each board, tossing them to the floor in a clatter. When they were all off, he took hold of the tarnished old doorknob and gave it a firm tug. Sure enough, the door opened; well, more like it almost came off its hinges in his grasp. He flung it wide open and pulled a small torch from his coat pocket. As he shone it inside, Penelope saw a rough, tunnel-like passage leading away into the dark. A shiver ran down her back, but she was too astonished even to move, much less say anything.

"Splendid!" he said, shining the light over the ceiling, walls, and floor. He motioned with his head for her to enter. "Come along, Penelope. A grand adventure awaits us!"

※　　※　　※

With a flash, Qwyrk and Qwypp stood in front of the council hall, where she no longer had the slightest desire to go.

"Really getting tired of seeing this place," Qwyrk sighed, her stomach in at least a few knots over what she knew awaited.

"You sure you don't want me to go in with you?" Qwypp asked.

Qwyrk shook her head. "This is my fight. No sense in you getting in trouble, too."

"All right, but check in when it's over, yeah?"

"Shall do."

Qwypp flashed away. Qwyrk took a deep breath and entered, walking straight to the council chamber. As expected, all six of them were seated around their semi-circular table, wearing their white robes, looking calm, official, and pompous.

Bunch of pillocks.

She looked at each one in turn, their faces expressionless and cold. Whatever they were thinking, they betrayed nothing, not even her hated Qwalm.

She took another breath, gritted her teeth, and spoke. "Undo the ward around Holly and me. Now."

"That is not possible, and you know why," Qworum answered in a voice as cool as his demeanor.

"I know your reasons are ridiculous, but that has nothing to do with rationality, decency, or even common sense. Thing is, this isn't even about her and me being together. You know damned well what's about to happen, and I need her by my side so we can fight. Oh, and thanks, by the way, for keeping me up to date about what's coming. It's not like I had to go off and find out all about it on my own, or anything."

"If I recall, you told us in no uncertain circumstances that you were done with this council, and your service to it. I believe you and your would-be partner showed us a very specific salute upon your exit." Qworum glared, but with restraint. His words "would-be partner" really stung.

"And knowing what was coming, you didn't call me back, anyway?" She didn't want to give him the satisfaction of knowing he'd hurt her. "You're well aware of what I can do, but you couldn't bury the bloody hatchet and put this argument aside for a few days, so we could work together to stop this threat? You didn't think I'd do that?"

"To be honest, we don't know what you think," Qwalm said, with less venom than she expected, "nor do we care."

"So that's it, then? You'll risk the bloody end of everything, Balor coming back and enslaving us all or worse, because you're too damned stubborn and proud to set aside a dispute? Because you don't like how I do things, or who I choose to spend my time with, or Goddess knows what else? Wow, I guess I really did underestimate how utterly pathetic and useless you all are. How long have you known about this whole return thing?"

"It is no longer your concern," Qworum stated.

"How long?" Qwyrk raised her voice. "A week? A month? A year? Has this been in preparation for the last decade, and you just conveniently never mentioned it? Because honestly, nothing would surprise me, anymore."

"It has only come to our awareness recently," Qworum answered. "Those seeking to bring about Balor's return have been very careful not to reveal themselves. As such, we are assessing the situation, and will take appropriate action in due course."

"Appropriate action in due course? What the bloody hell does that even mean? Are you going to invite Balor over for a summit meeting? Serve tea and biscuits and ask him real nicely not to attack? Because honestly, that's about the only strategy you've got at the moment, and you know it, don't you?" She looked at each of them in turn. "Don't you?"

"Our best scholars and wizards are currently devising a defense strategy," Qwote said, "and if necessary, we can make an appropriate evacuation."

"Evacuation? To where, exactly? Are we going to go hide in Valhalla? Or maybe the Isle of Apples? Hell, why don't we all just go crowd into Little Gobbling in Cambridgeshire? I'm sure he'd never find anyone there, and we could hide in barns. Have you all gone completely, utterly, mental?" She threw her hands up in rage.

"It is no longer your concern, Qwyrk," Qworum reiterated.

"It bloody well is, and if you won't let me help, I'll just do it on my own."

"And how will you do that?" Qwalm sneered. Yes, there it was at last. "Sickened by a Fachan's poison, you're in no condition to do anything, except complain and make empty threats."

"I can still beat the crap out of you, Qwarter-brain."

"Qwyrk, cease this and leave us," Qworum said. "I will not ask you again."

"I'm not giving up," she said in defiance. "I'm going to figure out how to beat him, and Holly and I *will* destroy your stupid ward. I'm going back to her now, just so you know. We may not be able to touch at the moment, but I have no intention of leaving her, ever."

"As I expected. But it will soon not be up to you."

"And what's that supposed to mean? Why is it that no one's apparently ever defied this order in the past?"

"Some have tried to do so," Qworum answered. "But if they will not obey the law, there is another recourse."

"And that means what, exactly?" She clenched her injured fists, struggling keep her fury in check.

"The ward expands into their minds. They soon forget about one another, that the other even exists, and eventually that anything ever occurred between them."

Qwyrk reeled. *So that's how they do it, by violating our minds if we resist.*

"A fitting end for you two," Qwalm taunted. "A wretched pairing of two different orders that brings shame on Shadowkind. Be grateful that if we survive, you'll have at least some chance to redeem yourself and be rid of that lesser creature."

With those hateful words, Qwyrk snapped. Whatever she'd been holding back, whatever she'd been trying to suppress in the name of diplomacy, it all went right out the window, a window that no one had bothered to open first. Before she herself even knew what was happening, she'd jumped up onto the table in front of Qwalm, grabbed him by the cowl of his robe, pulled him out of his chair, and begun hitting him with a savage ferocity that she would never have used if she'd had her full strength. Each punch sent shockwaves of pain through her hand, maybe even breaking bones, but she ignored it, blocked it out, blocked everything out, so she could vent all of her rage and frustrations on this one odious Shadow whom she hated with a passion. His blue green blood stained her fingers, and she heard shouting and screaming all around her as she gave full force to her fury and exasperation.

It wasn't until she felt the strong hands of guards pulling her away from her nemesis that some sense started to return to her, snapping her back to the moment. She came around to discover that her own bleeding hands were being bound behind her with tight rope. She tried to kick at her captors, but one of them seized her feet and lifted her up to bind them, as well. She kicked and struggled to break free, but her strength still hadn't returned. She was trapped.

"Damn you!" she screamed. "Damn you all! You'll condemn us to slavery and death, you complete, utter idiots! You can't just sit around debating this! Let me go!"

"Get her out of here, now! Lock her away!" Qworum commanded.

She squirmed and twisted and was aware of someone tending to Qwalm, who lay in a heap on the floor behind his chair. "I should've bloody killed him!" she yelled as several guards dragged her out of the chamber and toward a cell from which she feared she might never escape.

*   *   *

Holly stepped out of a grand oak tree and into the green forest clearing to her home, her refuge, her safe haven.

"But is it, really?" she asked, a sinking feeling inside of her growing ever stronger. "What if nothing means anything, anymore?"

As she pondered uncomfortable possibilities, a familiar feline meandered toward her. "I have a bit of a situation—"

"Not now, Mango." She shook her head and walked past him with a determined stride, in no mood for his whining.

"It's rather dire, I fear." He trotted along to keep up.

"I highly doubt that." She rolled her eyes.

"No, really! Do you have any idea how long it's been since—"

She stopped, reached down, put her hands under his front legs and lifted him up, staring him face to face. "Not. Now."

Mango gulped and nodded. She set him back down, turned away, and left him to whatever imagined tragedy he'd concocted.

Inside, she took in the familiar scents of comfort, but they did nothing for her now. She strode through the reception area, where Qwyrk had been questioned—humiliated, really—by her mother many months ago. Just thinking about it made her work up a head of steam. She stomped into the main sitting room, where sure enough, Vishala sat, looking composed and regal as always. It only made Holly more irritated. Vishala stood with a look of both concern and confusion on her face.

"Beti? Where have you been? You've been gone all night!"

"We need to talk, mother. About Fayette."

CHAPTER THIRTEEN

"So much for your grand adventure," Qwyrk muttered, sitting in a sparse jail cell, the only one in a plain stone room; she'd been abandoned and left alone. Across from the cell stood a single door, presumably also locked shut, just for added effect.

"This is it. This is the end. I cocked it up, and now everything's going to blazes."

She looked around again, but saw no way out, not even a window. The guards had untied her feet, but her hands remained bound behind her back. Her fingers stung from bleeding, while her hands ached from the punches she'd thrown at Qwalm.

"At least that bit was satisfying," she said with a grim smile. Her satisfaction faded when she realized what she stood to lose: Jilly, Holly, everyone else. It was a punch to the gut, though she forced back the urge to cry, just in case anyone spied on her.

I'm not giving them the satisfaction of breaking me.

She tried to snap the ropes binding her hands, but they were as tight as when first tied, and if anything, the effort made her weaker.

"Of course, they're probably enchanted. When is this damned poison going to get the hell out of my system?"

She heard a latch click and the door opened. She tensed as it swung inward. A guard stood with a vague smile on his face. She recognized him as one of those who'd dragged her from the council chamber and forced her into this cell.

Well, this is not good. She made sure not to show him any expression.

"You've caused a lot of trouble, haven't you?" he said.

"If you mean I've done my bloody job, protected people, and not taken crap from anyone who tried to stop me, then yeah. I'm quite the troublemaker."

"You've got a really sarcastic mouth, too. Everyone knows it."

"Everyone, like literally, *everyone*? Oh wow, I had no idea! I'm famous! Look, if you want my autograph, you'll have to get me out of this rope. It'd be really hard to sign your cast with my hands tied behind my back."

"What cast?"

"The one you're going to need over your whole body if you lay one finger on me for any reason other than to untie me and let me go."

"Yeah, you have a real attitude. But no, we're not here to do anything sordid. We're not undignified like that."

"We? Oh." The rest of the guards who'd subdued her now stood behind him.

"No, we're just going to take you on a little trip out to the forest. Call it a short day out. We've been ordered to do some extra-judicial roughing up, you see."

"Ordered? So, there *is* a traitor on the council, then? Not surprised, and I bloody well know who it is!"

The guard said nothing as he stepped into her cell, followed by the others. "See, we're supposed to beat the crap out of you, give you as good as you gave. But, if we get a little too ambitious and make the beating a bit more... permanent, we've already been assured that the authorities will look the other way. You'll just go missing, and when anyone asks about you, no one will have a clue."

"How nice for you. Does it feel good to be traitors? How much did Qwalm pay you to do his dirty work? What's Balor promised him in exchange for selling out his people and all the other beings and worlds?

The guard just smirked. "Come on then." He took hold of her arm, forcing her to her feet. "You've got a date with destiny."

"A date? Well, thanks but I'm already taken. See, that's a big part of this whole mess, and why I'm in here, isn't it? So, it wouldn't do for me to back out of that now. I mean, unlike you lot, I actually have a sense of loyalty."

They forced her into the hallway and took her down a different passage, presumably so no one could see them.

How deep is this conspiracy? How many are in on it? Why are the rest of the council so stupid, when Qwalm's acting like such an ass and practically flaunting his treason in front of them?

She winced in pain as one of them shoved her, which brought her mind back to the moment. At least they let her walk this time.

Marching to my own execution.

Only, something started to happen. Call it a tingle, a little surge of energy, the pins and needles of circulation coming back to a limb gone to sleep. Yes! The pain started to fade from her hands and her leg, as magic reasserted itself over her and began to heal her wounds.

She tugged ever so slightly at the ropes, hoping that she'd soon be able to break them with ease. She forced away a smile and played along, even once pretending to stumble and succumb to the pain, which elicited a small bout of laughter from her captors.

Bastards, every last one of them. Take me out to the forest. Let's just see what happens...

* * *

"Keep up, Penelope! Good gods, you're starting to become a bore! One would think you don't want to see this adventure through."

She stumbled and struggled and sagged and stooped as she followed him through an old, dank tunnel that was a bit too low for comfort, but at least she didn't have to crawl... yet. Still, she didn't dare to turn back now, even though she wanted nothing more.

"How much farther?" she asked instead, trying to humor him and hide her own fear.

"I'm not sure, but it doesn't matter. We'll walk the length of the Dales underground if we have to. The destination surely lies down here somewhere."

"What destination?"

Sometime later (she had no sense of time at all in this wretched place), the tunnel split in two.

"Now what?" she asked.

"Quiet!" he snapped.

She held her tongue but could barely contain her upset. She wanted to cry. What had happened to her Winston, her charming, beloved, disheveled, retired professor? Why was he acting so horrible, and what on earth were they looking for?

"This way!" he said with confidence after a moment of listening for something she didn't hear.

He started off to the right, and she followed on, having the brief thought to dash into the darkness of the left tunnel. Like or not (and she most certainly did not), she was stuck with him until the very end of whatever mad plan he'd hatched. And it seemed to get madder all the time. The colder and damper air down this passage made her shiver.

"Watch your step," he called back, "it's going to get a tad more uneven from here on, I suspect. I don't have time to carry you."

Though not prepared for this change of terrain, she was glad not to have worn heels, at least. The tunnel soon gave way to a nat-ural-looking cave. Winston shone his light around the area.

"There!" he pointed.

A small exit lay on the other side. After crossing to reach it, she saw a larger cavern beyond. A green, unnatural, and sickly light swirled within it, but she couldn't tell where it was coming from. Something about it made her uneasy. She could see two other exits leading off in unknown directions, but something else caught her attention. In the very middle of this grander cave was a stalagmite. No, more like a monolith, rather like a standing stone, only down here, hidden where no one could see it.

Where no one should see it, she thought, but she didn't quite know why.

"Yes, yes!" Winston said. "I knew it! My dream was right. You see, Penelope, sometimes following one's intuition does bring great rewards!"

"What is it?"

He turned to her, the look of excitement evident on his increasingly twisted and non-Winston-like face.

"It's a portal. A door, if you will."

"A door to what?"

"To the return of something marvelous."

"H-how do you know?" She started to tremble again, now shaking from cold and fear.

He smiled and pulled out the strange little implement that had started all of this. "Because this is the key that opens it!"

* * *

Holly stared at her mother, making it quite clear that she wouldn't take no for an answer and was in no mood for being brushed off. "It was bad enough that you hid the Erlking from me, but there's something else, isn't there? What is it? I need to know, now!"

The elder Vishala gazed at her as if terribly pained, as if keeping a dark secret for too long. She looked down, sighed, and spoke, her eyes fixed on the floor: "I have dreaded this day, for so long... centuries. I feared it was about to happen fifteen years ago, but thankfully, it was not yet the time. But now, everything will unfold as it must."

"What are you talking about?" Holly sat down next to her. Her anger began to wane, replaced by pity, though she didn't know why. "Mother, please, I must know what's going on. The fate of all the worlds might well depend on it."

"It might, indeed." Vishala looked up. "And that is what sometimes keeps me awake at night."

"You know what's happening, don't you? About the return of Balor and the Fomorians?"

"I have heard stories about those ancient creatures and their plots, though I don't know the details. I suspect it will be up to you, your friends, and your lady to find out."

Holly held her tongue for the moment about how far the ward had progressed, how it now kept them completely apart. "Tell me everything," she said instead. "I need to know about her. About Fayette. Why does she keep appearing to me? In my mind and in reality? Why the headaches? Why now?"

Vishala paused, her face betraying her trepidation. "After the Erlking murdered your father and we fled to safety, I wanted to be sure that I could protect you in our adopted land. I mean, of course, we would continue to live on this side of the veil, yet we bonded with England and left Indian lands behind to hide our trail. But in that chaotic time, I did not know what dangers lurked, and I needed to learn what we might face. So, I went to see her, the one called Fayette. I knew that doing so was dangerous, that I might learn things that I did not wish to know, that such a being was powerful beyond comprehension and cared little for the affairs of Fae, much less humans. But I was stubborn. I ignored these warnings and sought her out anyway."

"Who is she? What is she?"

"No one knows. One of the elders who preceded us, I suppose. Something like a Norn, a Fate perhaps? A force of nature? I'm not sure it even matters. What does matter is that she dwells outside of time and can see things that we cannot: past, present, and future. Ask her a question, and she may deign to answer it. It will be the truth, but it may not be what one wishes to hear. That is the risk the seeker takes. Only, it is her reading of that truth, and so it may not always mean what one thinks it means."

"What did you ask her? What did she say?"

"I wanted," Vishala's voice faltered a little. "I wanted to know your fate. How I could keep you safe after what had happened with the Erlking. She told me," she paused.

"What? Mother, please!" Holly took her hand.

Vishala fought back tears and looked Holly straight in the eyes. "She told me that one day, you would face the worst of evils, the return of the greatest of adversaries, and that as a result of that battle, you would die."

Lightheadedness overtook Holly. She reeled as visions and memories from her own encounters with Fayette flooded her mind. It was as if her mother had unlocked the final door. Hearing it out loud made it real. She realized that her headaches had been a defense, an attempt to keep these memories at bay. She shook her head to regain some sense of balance. "That's why you've trained me for my whole life, pushed me so hard to learn Silambam, been so stern with me."

Vishala nodded, squeezing her hand. "I wanted to give you the best chance you could have against whatever dangers you might face. I knew you were strong, and I hoped against hope that if I could teach you enough fighting skills, I could perhaps find some way of changing your fate."

"But why didn't you just tell me?"

"And have you live with that terrible knowledge clouding your life? That was fifteen hundred years ago! You were only a child of fifty years. I had to live with it, and one of us was enough. I didn't want you to have to endure it, so I kept what I knew from you."

"But I knew something was wrong, on some level, didn't I? And... fifteen years ago, I finally realized that you'd been to see her, so I sought her out to discover what you'd asked her." Holly's mind continued to clear as the past came back to her.

"Yes," Vishala nodded, avoiding Holly's gaze. "I couldn't stop you from going. In the end, I didn't even try."

"And I found her, somehow, in that cave in Yorkshire, a place where the human world intersects with her own plane of existence."

"There are no such locations in our world, so yes, she must be sought there."

"And I asked her what you'd spoken of, and she told me. She seemed cold, uncaring. She told me my fate, spoke with such truth that I knew it must be real. But it didn't stay in my mind. Maybe I pushed it out, maybe it was something I couldn't retain. Sometime later, I found myself in Manchester. I'm not even sure how I got there. I was upset, but by then, I couldn't remember why. I wandered into that convention, drank a lot of whisky, and met Carl. And well, we know what happened next."

"When I learned you were with child, I was actually relieved," Vishala said.

"I always wondered why you weren't angry," Holly admitted. "To be honest, I thought you'd be furious, or at least disappointed."

"No, I hoped that perhaps the prophecy had been circumvented, short-circuited, to use a human expression. Fayette had never revealed to me that you would bear a son, and I thought that somehow, maybe you had accidentally changed your fate. Since it is so rare for a human and a Fae to produce a child, I saw it as a favorable omen."

"Even though I couldn't keep Lluck with us?"

"The very act of giving birth to him seemed to me to be enough, though I know how much it broke your heart to leave him."

"But now he's in my life again."

"And for that I am glad. But when I heard that the Erlking had returned and I heard whispers of other things stirring in the darkness, I feared that the course had been reset, if it had ever been changed to begin with. Still, with the Erlking, another blessing came to you, beyond reuniting with your son."

"You mean Qwyrk?"

"I do."

"But I've never been sure if you even like her."

"I adore her."

"Well, you have an odd way of showing it, it must be said." Holly sat back and crossed her arms. "To be honest, you've been more than a little rude to her, and it's not made me happy at all."

"I could not give her the sentiment I would like, not yet. I needed her to train with you. To become stronger than she already is. I hope that once again, some mischievous portion of fate is tipping the odds a little in your favor. With Qwyrk by your side, I think you might have a chance to fight this evil, to win, to survive."

"You really think Qwyrk and I can do it?"

Vishala gave her a soft and warm smile. "I think she is the one for you, Beti, the one you have yearned for. I cannot believe that she and Lluck would come into your life at the same time, only for you to be taken from them, for this evil to triumph. I have more faith in the workings of destiny than that. The question is, are you ready?"

"I wish I could say yes, but I've no idea. Qwyrk's own people are forcing us apart." She told Vishala about the ward, of the void that had tried to consume her last spring, of the Shadow council and their intransigence about it all.

"What is this madness?" Vishala hissed in fury. "Those ridiculous fools will not keep my Beti from her true love with their archaic laws! This is vile and wrong. We will fight this, and we will win!"

"I'm afraid we have to stop the end of the world, first. Again, as it turns out. And there's something Qwyrk and I have to do together, even if we can't touch."

"Beti, please tell me you are not going to—"

"We have no choice, mother. We have to seek out Fayette. She's the only one who knows how we might be able to defeat Balor. It's dangerous. I might learn more things about my fate than I want to know—and I might not forget them this time. But she saved me from being killed in Nicewood last night. She told me it wasn't yet my time, so maybe there's hope? Maybe she's actually on our side?"

Vishala sighed and squeezed her daughter's hand again. "I'm so sorry, Beti. So sorry for everything." She began to tear up. "I never wanted any of this for you and now, just when it seems that all good things have finally come to you, this Balor, this horrid evil, returns and may take you away from me, from all of us."

She broke down and cried in a way that Holly had not seen since her father's death. The stern woman whom Holly loved and admired—but often felt in conflict with—gave in to her vulnerability and her caring, maternal side, after all.

Holly drew her in and held her close, her own tears now flowing. "I promise you, mother, we'll find some way. Some way to win. I'm not giving up now, and I don't care what that weird old seeress says. I'll see this through, and with Qwyrk and my friends and family with me, I think I can do it."

"You can, my dearest, you must!"

*   *   *

The light hurt Qwyrk's eyes as she and her jailers stepped outside, but the guards paid no heed to her discomfort, and the lead captor shoved her forward from the prison exit and into the thick autumnal woods that grew to its very edge.

"Convenient having this tree cover right here," he said.

"Yeah, I'll bet it makes it real easy to murder people and dispose of their bodies discreetly," Qwyrk snarked.

"Something like that."

"So," she pressed, feeling stronger by the moment. "How many have died out here over the years? Decades? Centuries? Is this where anyone who you take a disliking to meets their end? Does Qwalm have a nice little hit operation set up to do away with his enemies? Goddess, he must have been planning my demise for ages!"

The guards said nothing but forced her to keep on moving. A few minutes later, they stopped in a clearing. They were in deep woods now, far from earshot or sight. This was going to work out just fine for her.

"So, what's it going to be, gents?" she asked, eyebrows raised and voice sounding in mock curiosity. "Bare hands, or do you have weapons hidden nearby, like in a tree stump, or something? Hey, do you have a secret club house where you all meet up, recite the secret password and make the secret handshake, and talk about all the yucky enemies you want to off? Do your mums come out here and interrupt your meeting with lemonade and biscuits and totally embarrass you? Because I could absolutely see that!"

"You never shut up, do you?" one of the other guards asked.

"Actually, it's a bit of a bad habit," she said. "See, I do it on two occasions: one, when I'm really nervous about something."

"And what's the other one, then?" the same guard taunted.

"When I'm about to beat the living crap out of a bunch of traitors threatening to kill me for their equally treasonous master, whose arse I am going to royally kick the first chance I get."

"Bold words," the leader said with a grin. "Got anything to back them up?" He clenched his fists and loomed over her.

"Actually? Yeah, I do, you tosser."

She jerked her hands away from each other, snapping her binds with ease. Whipping her right fist around, she landed a solid punch on his jaw, sending him sprawling backward a dozen feet to slam to the ground, and knocking him out cold in the process. The other guards stood in stunned silence, looking back and forth between her and him.

"So," she said with a rather wicked smile, "who'd like to go next? To be honest, I don't have a lot of time, so if you want to double up, that'd be a real help, thanks."

One of the guards pulled out something like a billy club from his belt and lumbered toward her.

"Oh good," she said. "I love when they bring out the toys. Then, I really don't have to hold back!"

He took a swing at her, missed, and stumbled. She took the opportunity to unleash the full force of her booted foot on the side of his head. He staggered to the side, dropped his weapon, and fell in a heap to the ground, as unconscious as his companion.

"Next?" she yelled.

The remaining three looked at each other, with more than a touch of nervousness.

"Oh, come on, don't give up now. We're just starting to have fun! Well, all right, *I'm* starting to have fun, anyway, and that's all that really matters."

Her would-be executioners' hesitancy turned to anger. Two of them drew long knives and ran toward her, the third following close behind, fists raised.

"That's the spirit! No pain, no gain! Well, I mean, pain for you, and me gaining my magic back."

She held off until they were almost on her.

I hope this works!

She waved her hand, stepped into a purple circle of light, and disappeared.

Her attackers stopped short, glances darting around, as she rematerialized above, dropping down on top of them. Grabbing two of them by their hair, she slammed their heads together, and released them in a pile on the leaf-covered forest floor. She landed on the ground and turned to face the last one standing. He held up his knife, but instead of threatening her, he put the edge to his neck.

"What? Wait! No!" Qwyrk rushed toward him.

"Hail to the Deathly Eye!" he shouted.

"Bollocks to that! I need answers!"

On instinct, she reached out to slap the blade away. But she also hit him hard enough to send the weapon flying as he also crashed to the ground, unconscious and useless.

"Damn it!" She looked around at the five of them, all taking unexpected naps in various contorted positions. She sighed.

"No answers from this lot then, and I don't have time to wait until one of them comes round."

The momentary thrill of being magical again faded, leaving her with a very unpleasant realization.

She had escaped from their prison. But now she was a fugitive.

* * *

"It's like a prison, you see," Winston said, holding the key in hand and pointing it at the monolith. "A very long time ago, so long ago that no one really remembers if it even happened—though I assure you, it did—there was a brave and wise ruler who fought to bring order to the shores of Ireland, then a lawless and chaotic land plagued by violence and all manner of awfulness. He and his loyal forces fought against that chaos and subdued it, brought stability and the rule of law to an island in desperate need of it. They would have stretched out and taken these islands, as well, but something happened. They were thwarted by new invaders. Long did these horrid newcomers wage war against our brave king, and in the end, in a cursed event known as the Second Battle of Magh Tuireadh, they subdued him. Chronicles say that his own grandson, one who claimed to be of the sun itself, killed him with a sling stone. But they couldn't really kill him, you see. He and his faithful subjects were banished, locked away, forbidden ever to walk this Earth again, while the newcomers infested that island and spread out to this one, as well. Even now, their descendants still come and go as they please while he is locked away."

She had no idea why he was telling her all of this. He loved his history, it was true, but he now seemed so utterly unlike the Winston she thought she knew.

"But that will change." He waved the key again. "You see, this opens the gate that barred him! The Brigantes were tasked with keeping this little key secret, long after that fateful battle, and they hid it so well that it passed out of all reckoning. Only recently has it been found, by those still dedicated to his return. And they left it for someone—a human—to find, and I found it! Don't you see, Penelope? Fate chose me to be the means by which he can come back. This will change the world! It will usher in a new age, one that will see the problems of our times swept away like so much dirt. Oh, Penelope, it will be glorious, and all it will take is me using this little key!"

"I don't... understand any of this, Winston," she said, forcing back a sob.

He put a hand on her shoulder. If he meant to be reassuring, he most certainly failed.

"You don't have to understand. I don't understand it all, either. I just need you to trust me. Can you do that for me, Penelope?"

"I, I mean... no. No, Winston, I cannot. I don't know what you're asking of me, and you're not acting like yourself at all. You've dragged me down to this horrid place after hitting that poor man, you've been terrible to me all morning, and now you're going on about all sorts of nonsense about ancient kings returning to rule Ireland and Britain. I know you're an enthusiast for ancient tales, but I think you've proper lost your mind, if I'm being perfectly honest!"

"If you're being perfectly honest?" he sneered. "Well, that's very good of you. Honesty is, as they say, the best policy. But let me be clear." His tone became angry and menacing. "You are here because I have been fond of you and thought to have you share in the glory of what is about to happen. If you will not take part in it, then I cannot guarantee there will be a place for you in his retinue. That decision will be up to him."

Anger welled up in her and she stood fully to face him. "I'll not be threatened by you, Winston. I don't know what barmy foolishness has gotten into you, but I'll have no part in it. I'm leaving! I'll find my way back in the dark if I have to, but I won't stay in this ghastly place another moment."

"Oh, dear Penelope. I'm afraid you have no choice in the matter now. You can't leave. You might tell others, and that could create problems ere the ritual completes on Samhain tomorrow night. No, you'll be staying here to await his judgement."

Penelope had had enough. She turned to leave. Only, she found that she couldn't take a step. Not a single one.

"Winston!" She turned back to look at him in shock. "What's going on? Stop this!"

Winston held one hand up, and somehow stopped her from moving. "I'm sorry, Penelope, but I meant what I said. You'll just have to stay and bear witness to this glorious beginning, but I promise you, you'll never have seen anything like it!"

With a confident air, he approached the monolith and ran his hands over it a few times, as if searching.

"It should be just about... here! Yes!"

He placed the key into a crevice that she couldn't even see and turned it. A low hum began to fill the cavern, and the eerie lights around them started to flicker, then flash, like random bolts of lightning. She saw a glow emanating from the crack where he'd put the key, growing brighter, more intense. Winston had not taken his hand off the little implement, but stood staring at it, as if transfixed, perhaps even in a trance.

Light and mist flowed out of the keyhole, snaking around both the rock and Winston. Penelope wanted to shout, to scream, to do something, but her voice caught in her throat and felt as immobile as her feet. She had no choice but to watch in horror as the strange mists swirled up his arm and all about him. They seemed to infuse him with their essence, as if invading him.

He let go of the key and raised his hands into the air, a broad smile on his face.

And he started to change.

He began to grow taller and rip out of his clothes, his skin becoming the color of ash. His form started to morph into something else, something awful, something so foul and forbidden that it could scarcely even be imagined by a mortal mind. Penelope watched in wide-eyed horror as the impossible unfolded in front of her, as this ancient thing he'd praised only a minute before possessed his body and made itself manifest in this world again after aeons of banishment. This horror was the king he awaited? The ruler who would bring peace? No, this was nothing but evil and madness. And as she feared that her own sanity might dwindle and blow away like dust in a gust of wind, she at last found her voice and screamed.

CHAPTER FOURTEEN

Qwyrk stepped out of a cascade of purple lights into the welcome mundanity of Carl's living room, where Qwypp, Qwykk, Jilly, Lluck, and Carl sat about, tea and snacks arrayed on a nearby table.

"Nice to see everyone's been snacking while I'm off having a crap day!"

"Qwyrk!" Jilly exclaimed, standing up at once. "You've got your powers back!"

"Thank Goddess!" Qwypp quipped. "We were getting worried. You took your sweet time getting back here. Must have been one hell of a long meeting!"

"Yeah, not so much," Qwyrk sighed. "They actually arrested me, threw me in a jail cell, and then the guards tried to take me out to the woods behind the council building and murder me on the quiet. So, you know, sorry if I'm a bit late."

"What?" the rest shouted all at once; they shouted several other things as well that don't need to be repeated. Qwypp and Jilly ran to her and threw their arms around her, and she had to admit to herself that she was glad for the attention. Qwykk followed close behind them and joined in, and Qwyrk soon worried she was in danger of being crushed by the love.

"Uh, yeah, thanks, really. It's fine. I'm fine." She delicately extracted herself from the tangle of loving limbs around her.

"I'm glad you're back," Lluck said to her, "but if it's all right with you, I'll stay over here."

"No worries, mate, cheers."

"So, what happened?" Jilly asked, wearing a horrified expression.

Qwyrk recounted it all, from her losing her temper at Qwalm, to being dragged off, to the attempted murder, thwarted by the nick-of-time return of her magic.

"This is awful," Qwypp said, flopping back down on the nearest chair. "You mean that twat's been working against you? Against us? For how long?"

"No idea," Qwyrk shrugged, "but yeah, this conspiracy has officially reached the highest levels of the leadership, and we're in a really bad way right now." She looked at each of them in turn. "I can't stay here. Someone—Qwalm, I'm guessing—will send his flunkies after me. And honestly, I don't know if they have any intention of obeying our directive not to harm humans, so I need to not be around you."

"If they try anything, Dad and I can handle them," Lluck said, making fists and puffing himself up.

"No, you can't." Qwyrk shook her head. "I know you mean well, but if a squad of those tossers comes here looking for me, I don't think even your luck powers will do much good."

"But what are you going to do?" Jilly asked, taking her hand. "Where can you go?"

"There're a couple of things I need to take care of, but Holly has to come with me. She's not back yet?"

"No," Lluck shook his head. "Dill and Chives gave her a lift. Said she had something important to take care of but wouldn't tell us."

"I think she went to see her mum," Qwyrk said.

"Why?"

"It's probably better if she explains it, if it's what I think. And it's connected to what we've got to do. Look," she addressed everyone, "things are not good. I've never faced anything like this, and I'm not sure what to do, but I need all of you to be ready at a moment's notice. If Balor is back, if he strikes tomorrow night, you all have to mobilize right away."

"You mean to fight?" Lluck asked. This time, he didn't look too eager. Good.

"Maybe," she answered, "but maybe also to run for your lives, and there's no shame in that. I don't know how this is going to play out, but I'll be honest with you, it isn't looking promising right now. The whole world may be flipped upside down in a few days. There's a chance, a small one, that we can turn this back, but I won't know for sure until later."

"What are you going to do?" Jilly asked.

"I'd rather not say, but I promise I'll fill you in when and if it goes well, or not." She looked around at all of them and then at Qwypp. "Where's Star Tao?"

"He's still out back, I reckon," Qwypp answered. "I think this business about Blip really hit him hard, and I wanted to leave him to think about it, and maybe meditate on it."

"That's good of you," Qwyrk said, "but we need him here now. I want everyone accounted for, because we'll need to split up into groups. So go fetch him."

Qwypp nodded and left the room.

"Lluck, can you contact your mum with your ring? I'd like her back here as soon as she can be."

"Yeah, no worries, I'll just pop into the kitchen so you lot can keep talking."

Qwykk, who had been silent until now, spoke up. "This is bad, isn't it? Like, really bad?"

"I'm afraid so, dear." Qwyrk put a reassuring hand on her shoulder. "But we're not beaten yet, yeah? You, me, and Qwypp, we've been through a lot over the centuries, so let's not give up hope."

"I just want to go back to what I was doing," Qwykk lamented. "I don't know why some folks have to be so horrible, try to hurt others. They never win in the end, anyway."

"Thing is," Qwyrk said, "they might win this time, if we can't stop them. Look, I know you think you don't have it in you, but remember what you and Qwypp did last year? You escaped from the cellar, you kicked the crap out of Redcap. That was brilliant... and hilarious."

"It was pretty fun, it must be said!" Qwykk brightened up.

"Well, if things go our way, maybe you'll get to do it again! But you're going to need to change into something a little more, um, practical?"

"Oh yeah, I know! Should I go for the camouflage aerobic outfit, or the ninja night-warrior cat suit?"

Qwyrk sighed. "Never change, love."

CHAPTER FOURTEEN

"Mum's on her way back with Dill and Chives," Lluck announced as he came back in. "She'll be here in just a few minutes, actually. She sounded, I don't know, worried, upset?"

"Brilliant," Qwyrk said. *Things must not have gone well.*

"Um, we have a bit of a problem," Qwypp said as she returned.

"Now what?" Qwyrk was quite sick of bad news.

"He's not out there!"

"What do you mean, 'not out there'?"

"He's gone! Like vanished, and no sign of him anywhere. Oh Goddess, Qwyrk! Do you think someone's kidnapped him?"

Qwyrk shook her head. "He's angry at us, and he's probably gone off to try to contact Blip somehow to prove his innocence. Which means he's going to tell him that we know he's up to something, which tips our hand to our enemies and gives us away. Bloody hell!"

*　*　*

Holly stepped out of the back of Dill's and Chives' car and paused outside the driver's side window.

"Thank you both, gentlemen, for assisting me whilst I took care of my affairs. And for bringing me back here, of course. I assure you that I'll make it worth your while when this is all sorted out. If this is all sorted out."

"Understood ma'am, and thank you." Dill tipped his hat. "But don't trouble yourself with thoughts of payment. Under the circumstances, it seems a bit premature to be speaking about future plans at all, at least until this whole inconvenience is sorted."

"I think it's rather more than an inconvenience." Holly managed a weak smile. "But thank you for your understanding. I've no doubt I'll be calling on you again soon. If you can stand at the ready, we're likely going to need you."

"Of course, ma'am," Chives answered. "This affair concerns all of us."

"It does, indeed." She waved as they drove away, before stepping up to Carl's front door, and letting herself in with a spare key. Rather surprised that no one came to greet her, she entered the living room to see most everyone there, a veritable pall hanging over the room.

"Hey mum," Lluck said with a wave. "Glad you made it back."

A few others made tepid waves and comments.

"Well, everyone's looking rather morose," she said. "Goddess, I hope nothing too terrible has happened while I was away!"

"I'm glad you're back, love, but it's gotten worse, way worse," Qwyrk said, coming over to her, but holding back from getting too close. Her hesitance pained Holly, and she knew it pained Qwyrk, too. "The good news is," Qwyrk went on, "I've got my powers back, and I'm feeling much better. The bad news is, well, pretty much everything else."

"I've some rather wretched news of my own to share," Holly said. "So, shall you go first, or shall I?"

Qwyrk volunteered and recounted everything that had happened to her, while Holly listened with increasing disbelief. No, actually, she was prepared to believe almost anything at this point, no matter how absurd and awful.

"Darling, that's horrible! And the treachery reaches all the way up to Qwalm? Good Goddess, this is bad. I don't even want to think about what could have happened to you. Are you sure you're all right?"

"I'm fine, but I have to get away from here," Qwyrk said. "I can't put the others in harm's way, and we're all going to be needed before this is over, I suspect. So, we have to stay in touch, no matter what happens or where we end up."

"What do you want to do?"

"We have to split up for a bit, keep a low profile, but I need you to come with me. We have to go to Qwyzz's first, and after that, we've got to seek out Fayette."

"Yes, about that." The knot in Holly's stomach tightened as the truth about her situation came to mind. "Can we talk in private? There are some things I need to tell you."

"Mum?" Lluck asked. "What is it? What's wrong?"

"It's all right, darling. I just want to tell Qwyrk about a strategy that might help us. I imagine that the fewer people who know about it, the better." She hoped it was a convincing lie.

"Yeah, fair enough," he said. "Do you want us all to go out of the room again?"

"No, that's all right," Qwyrk said to him, before turning back to Holly. "Why don't we go out to the back garden, seeing as Star Tao's not there now. Oh sorry!" She glanced over at Qwypp, who winced at her words. "I didn't mean to upset you."

"Of course not, love," Qwypp answered, placing her hands on her chest, "but I can't stay here, Qwyrk, I've got to find him."

"Yeah, you do, and soon, before he figures out a way to contact Blip," Qwyrk said. "Look, Holly and I'll be out back for a bit, and then after that, I need you to pop her over to Symphinity with me. Then you and Qwykk should get on with locating your bloke, all right?"

Qwypp nodded as Holly and Qwyrk exited to the garden.

"So, what happened at your mum's?" Qwyrk asked, after they

sat down on opposite sides of an outdoor table. "I mean that's where you were, right? Asking her about your past? She knows something, doesn't she?"

"You're far too good a detective for your own good!" Holly tried to maintain some kind of cheerful demeanor, but it was getting more difficult with each passing second.

"What's going on? You obviously didn't want to say anything in front of Lluck. Tell me?" Qwyrk's eyes pleaded for information, and Holly wanted to reach across and take her hand, to hold her, to comfort her. It tore her apart that they couldn't touch, and she knew Qwyrk felt the same; it was written all over her face.

She let out a sad sigh. "The night we first met, I told you that I found myself in Manchester, that I was upset. I said it didn't matter why, and I never mentioned it again."

"I remember. Honestly, I've never wanted to push you about it. I figured you'd tell me some day, when you were ready, if you were ready."

"Well, the truth is, I fibbed. I'd forgotten why, and how I'd ended up there. That night, it changed so many things for me, but today, I learned it was because of something that had happened earlier that day, something I'd initiated that left me despairing."

She told Qwyrk everything she'd learned from her mother, and how it had all seemed to almost conspire to bring things together and cause events to unfold. She didn't hold back about Fayette's prediction, or her mother withholding that information.

"Damn it!" Qwyrk said when she'd finished, "just, bloody hell! Holly, love, look: no matter what Fayette said to you, I honestly don't think these things are written in stone. We have some control over our futures, yeah? And even if Fate with a capital 'F' conspires to make certain events happen, we can still change the outcome. And just because the bloody council is trying to keep us apart, it doesn't mean we can't fight back. It doesn't mean you're going to—"

"Die? I don't know, darling. I wish I could believe that. I really do. But she's been in my head now for six months, nudging me to remember, to understand. I don't know why I'm so important, but if Fayette is to be believed, I'll help stop this awful thing, but I won't survive it." Her heart sank at the thought.

"Well, she's bloody wrong!" Qwyrk pounded the glass tabletop with her fist. "Look, we need to go see Qwyzz first, and ask if he can come up with a way to throw those bastards off my scent for a while. And maybe he can do something to help us? I don't know. But I do know that I want you by my side, no matter what. And since we have to face Fayette and her obnoxious words of wisdom about the future, we'll do it together. If she knows how we can defeat Balor, we have to see it through, no matter what else we might learn."

"You're right," Holly said, feeling reassured. "Another rousing Qwyrk pep talk. One of so many things that makes you special."

Qwyrk stood up and came over to her, kneeling down; so close and yet so far. "I want to hold you right now. I need to, so much." Holly teared up.

"I want to tell you everything's going to be all right," Qwyrk continued, "that by this time next week we'll be laughing about how wound up we got over nothing. But I don't know what will happen, none of us do, and that's my point. Fayette's vision of your future could be just one of many outcomes. Maybe it's the most likely one, but it can't be the only one. I won't let it be. I'm not going to lose you, no matter what. I'll fight every last enemy in the cosmos for you. For us."

Holly wept and reached out for Qwyrk, pulling back at the last moment.

Qwyrk held up her palm, facing Holly. "Since Jilly's not here."

Holly responded by reaching out her hand, bringing it to within an inch of Qwyrk's. Wiping tears from her eyes with her other hand, she nodded. "I can feel the magic in your hand," she said, "the heat. That's you. You're like a warm winter hearth to me, my comfort against the unknown, the cold, the dark."

"And you're my springtime sunset," Qwyrk said. "You glow with the beauty of life, and you're my welcome at the end of the day, with the promise of even more light to come in days ahead."

"I do believe you're becoming quite the poet, darling." Holly smiled through teary eyes.

"I have the best inspiration I could hope for." Qwyrk smiled back. "This is nowhere near over, so let's get on with it and show everyone what we can do!"

Holly stood, her mood lifted. "We'll do more than that. Let's make some deeds worthy of a mention in a history book, or two!"

"You mean like in the *Book of DawdleTwaddle?*"

"Exactly so! But we really *do* need to come up with better names for your fake tomes."

"I think they're quite imaginative, thank you!" Qwyrk folded her arms in mock offense.

"That's one word for them."

"Honestly, I should get hired to name the next line of bath bombs!"

"Goddess help us."

*   *   *

A short time later, they all gathered again in Carl's living room.

"Right, listen up," Qwyrk said. "Things are going to get rough over the next day, and maybe beyond. It's not safe right now for us to all be together, much as I'd prefer it, so we're going to split into smaller groups. Under no circumstances is anyone to get separated from their group or go off on their own, understood?"

The rest nodded in general agreement.

"Good. Jilly? You, Lluck, and Carl are one group. Stick together. You've got a lot of talents between you, and I think you'll be fine here. But, Lluck, if anything happens, you call on your mum."

"Wouldn't it be better for us to wait it out at Granny's?" Jilly asked. "All her books are there, and it's got magical protections around it. And she comes as goes as she pleases, so she might well head on back there herself. She must know what's going on."

"If it feels like the right thing to do," Qwyrk said, "then trust your gut. But remember: Blip knows you spend time there, and he might be trying to set up a trap. As far as I know, he's never been here, and he may not even know where 'here' is. I'll leave it up to you, but be careful."

Jilly nodded.

"And speaking of Blip." Qwyrk turned to Qwypp and Qwykk. "You've *got* to find Star Tao as fast as you can. We can't risk him meeting up with Blip and saying anything, even if he's not meaning any harm. Do you have a way of contacting him at all?"

"Well, I'm kind of tied into his mobile," Qwypp said, "I can teleport to where I sense it is, but it's off right now—probably on purpose—so that's a no-go at the moment."

"All right, but try to think of something. Holly and I are off to see Qwyzz, and I'll need you to drop her there first, but after that, get on with it, yeah?"

Qwypp nodded.

"Right, that's it. Um, where's Horatio?" Qwyrk looked around, a bit concerned.

"Oh," Jilly said, "he said he had some folks to talk to and things to do, and ta or now, and all that."

"Of course he did. Probably just as well. The Nasties will have to look after themselves, I'm afraid." She looked at Holly. "Dill and Chives are on speed dial?"

Holly nodded. "They're ready if we need them."

"Good. They're odd, but I'm glad they're on our side."

She looked around at this group, this weird and wonderful band of misfits and heroes who all meant so much to her. Each of them had their own strengths, and together they were something of a force to be reckoned with, but would it be enough?

"All of us are important now, and we need each other. As soon as Holly and I have done what we have to do, we'll be in touch and go from there, figure out where to meet up. I have absolutely no idea what's going to happen, or what to do next. I wish I could say it's all going to be fine, but honestly, I don't know. What I will say is you're brilliant, each of you. Good luck, be careful, and we'll see each other soon, all right?"

There was more general agreement and nodding of heads. Jilly got up and ran over to Qwyrk, throwing her arms around her and holding her tight. Qwyrk responded in kind.

"Be careful? Please?" Jilly said.

"I'm not going to be reckless, dear," Qwyrk answered. "I have a lot to live for these days."

＊　＊　＊

Qwyrk and Holly hid in the trees and peered out at Qwyzz's ever-charming, ever-odd home.

"Everything looks normal enough," Holly whispered. "I mean, as 'normal' as it's going to look. Do you suppose someone's already come and questioned him? Or even taken him away?"

"No, I doubt it," Qwyrk said. "The guards that wanted to take me out? They weren't doing it on the official orders of the council. Whatever those pillocks think of me, they wouldn't try to pull off some extrajudicial murder here. But Qwalm, he's obviously got some of them on his side, so whatever he's doing, he's keeping quiet about. Sending some ruffians around to try to intimidate Qwyzz would be a really foolish thing to do. Qwalm's an arse, but he's not stupid. He won't tip his hand when they're so close to getting their master back. Asking about me would make them look suspicious, so I'm guessing they haven't said anything to anyone just yet. But that doesn't mean they won't try to find me."

"And why you didn't want to stay with Lluck and Carl. Thank you for that." Holly gazed lovingly at her, and Qwyrk had never wanted to take Holly in her arms more than at that moment.

"Come on," Qwyrk said. "I think we're safe to pay him a visit."

"What about our dancing friend?" Holly smiled.

Qwyrk sighed. "Yeah, we'll just have to get past the rocky horror gargoyle show as fast as we can."

They made their way to the house, and Qwyrk rang the bell. No one answered. Qwyrk shot Holly a worried look and rang the bell again. Again, they were met with silence.

"This is not good," Qwyrk whispered.

"What now?" Holly whispered back.

"Let's give it another twenty seconds and then break the door open."

"Is that wise? It seems a touch overly dramatic. And it's a lovely door."

"We don't have a choice. If he's in trouble again, or if Qwota's been freed and she's come after him, we have to help."

Holly nodded. "Right then, shall we?"

Qwyrk nodded back. "Here we go!"

The door opened just as she rushed it, and she barreled into Qwyzz, knocking him to the ground and landing on top of him.

"Oh, Goddess!" Qwyrk scrambled to get off of her master. "I'm so, so sorry! You didn't answer the bell and Gargula didn't show up and yell at us and we were worried that something might have happened and I kind of panicked and charged the door just as you opened it—"

"It's quite all right, my dear," Qwyzz chuckled, sitting up and dusting himself off. "My gargoyles are in for repair, so I didn't hear you at first."

"Repair?" Holly asked.

"It's nothing major," he said with a wave of his hand. "Gargula's been having a bit of trouble with his ballet slippers not fitting properly, so I'm making some small adjustments to the shape of his feet. He's deactivated at the moment, but I'll revive him shortly."

"Wait, you *know* about the ballet dancing?" Qwyrk scrunched up her nose as she offered him a helping hand up. He took it and stood up with an agility that reminded her that his somewhat wizened appearance was largely for show and his own amusement.

"Of course I know of his dancing!" he said. "I think it's delightful that he's taken up a hobby! How do you know about it? He's rather shy about sharing it."

"Oh, um, well, we happened by here one day when you weren't home, and he was practicing, I suppose? We kind of walked in on him, or he walked in on us."

"I think it's a lovely endeavor," Holly offered. "I've studied ballet myself, though I haven't kept up with it as much as should like. Qwyrk dances too," she added teasingly.

"Does she?" Qwyzz looked at Qwyrk, who was horrified, mortified, and several other kinds of "-ied" all at once.

"Indeed," Holly continued with no mercy. "In fact, she has a very special piece that she's preparing, and she's going to dance it for me at some point."

"That... may or may not be true," Qwyrk interrupted in a desperate attempt to derail the conversation, lest this nightmare progress any further.

"Well, I should be delighted to see it, when it's ready," Qwyzz said.

"As would I." Holly gave a triumphant nod. "I'm positively a-tingle at the thought of it."

Qwyrk glared at a grinning Holly. "Setting that all to one side for the moment, if you're all right, we need to get inside, right now! It's not safe."

Motioning to Holly, she fairly barged passed him. He closed the door as soon as they were in.

"I assume you know what's going on?" she asked him, point blank. "I'm being hunted right now, by some tossers who've betrayed us all."

"I've heard the news," he said with a nod. "Please, come through. You'll both be quite safe here. I promise you no traitorous hooligans will ever find their way into this house again."

Qwyrk was struck by his words. He meant Qwota, his hopeful-ly-still-imprisoned former wife, who'd locked him up and betrayed him to help William de Soulis.

"So, what the hell is going on?" she asked instead, as she and Holly took seats on his sofa (but kept their distance from each other) and accepted the port he offered them without any hesitation.

"Bad things, I should think. Very bad things," he said as he sat himself down opposite them. She noticed that he looked visibly disturbed. "Hidden forces are working hard to bring about the return of Balor, and it looks like they're about to succeed, if they haven't already."

Qwyrk nodded. "And there's a traitor on the council helping them out," she said after taking a gulp.

"So it would seem," he agreed. "And that is very upsetting news indeed. We cannot know how much damage has already been done, what intelligence might have been leaked. It all has the potential to be catastrophic."

"It's Qwalm," she said after another big sip. "He's hated me for a long time, and it makes sense that he'd try to have me killed after I went off on him in the council chamber."

She recounted her brief but forceful incarceration and attempt on her life, while Qwyzz grew ever more distressed.

"Oh dear, oh dear," he fretted.

"Worrying about it isn't going to get us anywhere," Holly inter-jected. "We have to act. Put a stop to this, any way we can."

Qwyrk nodded. "Even with this stupid ward on us, we need to do something. Is there anything you can do?"

"I'm afraid this kind of magic can't be directly negated," he said, with a sad shake of his head. Qwyrk's heart sank.

"However," he said, flashing a mischievous look, "I might be able to tweak your teleportation magic temporarily to let you both at least get to the same place together. That should prove useful if you need to go on a fact-finding excursion or flee from danger." He motioned toward Holly's hand. May I see your ring, Ms. Vishala?"

"Of course." She took it off and handed it to him. He held it up close, squinted and examined it, turning it about to view it from several different angles.

"Yes, good. Ingenious, even," he remarked, turning to Qwyrk. "May I see yours as well?"

She handed him hers, which he subjected to the same level of scrutiny. "Good, yes, this should be quite easy, in fact. I think I can link them, magically speaking. How would those young folks say it, I'll get them 'rigged up.'"

"Oh yeah, that's definitely what the young folks, say," Qwyrk said, holding back a smirk. "I heard at least three of them say it today, in fact."

"Really? How remarkable!"

Qwyrk didn't have the heart to tell him she was being sarcastic, so she let it go.

"Rig them up to do what, exactly?" Holly asked.

"Ah, well, there's the trick. If I'm correct, I can configure them so that when Qwyrk teleports, you can use your own ring's magic to follow her to her next destination."

"That would be brilliant," Qwyrk exclaimed. "Thanks Qwyzz! At least we could move around again and get on with something, anything."

"Well, unfortunately," he added, looking apologetic, "it's an unstable enchantment. You won't be able to get many uses out of it, only a handful, I'm afraid. But it will work for a time."

"It's better than nothing." Holly tried to sound encouraging. "Being connected in any way is a blessing."

Qwyrk looked at her with a longing she could barely contain. She turned back to Qwyzz. "We'll take it! Right now, we're relying on others to shuffle us around."

Qwyzz nodded. "I'll make the necessary adjustments. It shouldn't take too long." He stood up. "I'll just take them through to my workshop. Please make yourselves at home and have all the port you like!"

With that, he scampered off.

"His enthusiasm for things is so charming," Holly said. "He still has a child-like wonder, even in dire circumstances."

"I know," Qwyrk agreed. "I think it helps him cope with everything that's happened since last year. First his wife, and now the bombshell that others in high places are working against us. It's a lot for someone so sweet and trusting to take on."

"I wish we could do something for him."

"Well, despite appearances, he's a pretty tough old lad. I think he'll rise to the occasion if we need him, and I imagine we will before this is all over."

"Are we gathering an army, then?"

"Something like that. I don't know how we're going to stop Balor, *if* we can stop Balor, but we have to call on every resource we have. Do you trust Dill and Chives? I mean, *really* trust them? I know they've helped you out—all of us—but we need to be really careful here."

"Honestly, I'd trust them with my life."

Qwyrk smiled, relieved. "That's good enough for me."

"So, we wait for Qwyzz to do his tweaking, and then off to you know where?" Holly shifted, showing some discomfort at the thought.

"It's got to be done. The only way out of this is through."

Holly sighed. "I really need to hold hands right now."

"So do I, love. So do I."

*   *   *

He sat in the gloom of the cavern on a makeshift rocky throne, newly awoken and clad in a tattered and hooded robe that his servants had prepared for him. Not the kingly garb that he deserved, but for the moment, it would have to do. When this world was his, he would present himself in something more suitably resplendent. For now, he kept his face shrouded, knowing that the time had not yet come to reveal it. He looked down at his clawed hands, held up his arms, impressed by the size of this body; he stood well above the heads of the average man-creature. The little human who had freed him served his purpose well as a physical host. He would find a more suitable host eventually, but for now, this sufficed.

The other mortal, the female, cowed in the corner, bound by the ropes he'd instructed his faithful to detain her in. He hadn't yet decided what to do with her.

"Perhaps you will be of some use," he said, breaking the silence of the cavern, the silence of being alone in his thoughts.

"W-what?" she whispered.

"Why do you always do this?" he sneered.

"Do what?"

"Not you, you fool, the lot of you, the human plague that infests this world that is mine by right! Why are you always cowering, sniveling, running away? Why can you not grow strong, face the dark majesty of the true nature of reality, embrace it? Thousands of your years have passed since last I stood in this world, and yet I see nothing has changed. You are weak, worthless. I should kill you."

He heard her sob. Pathetic. Still, an idea amused him. "I will give you a great honor, instead. You will join me in my revelry tomorrow night. Under the Samhain moon, my kin will be called back to this world, and we will reclaim it. You will be my herald, and set the task of informing your people that where once they ruled, they will now serve, or they will perish. Indeed, once you have beheld the glory of our kind, you will surely have no desire other than to serve us. Nothing you could do would ever achieve the same purpose as our mere existence."

He watched as she tried to retreat farther into the shadows, to make herself small against side of the cavern.

"Small, so small. But soon, your role will be grand, indeed."

CHAPTER FIFTEEN

Qwyrk stood at the bottom of the Gaping Gap cavern. Water trickled down around her, and a number of small falls filled the air with watery mist.

"Going to get soaked if we stay here too long," she said to herself. "Come on, Holly, make it through, please!"

As if on cue, there was a bit of a warp in the air in front of her, and Holly stepped out of a split in the fabric of reality, looking astonished to be there.

"Yes! It works!" Qwyrk clapped in triumph.

"Well, that was a bit of an experience!" Holly said, taking a few uncertain steps forward and finding her footing on the cavern floor. "Rather like a blend of being drawn though a hoover and some horrific amusement park ride, to be honest. Nowhere near as smooth as your teleporting."

"Sorry about that! I'm just glad Qwyzz's little upgrade works. I mean, I'd much rather hold your hand, but at least we're here."

"It's a remarkable place!" Holly exclaimed, looking up and around through the spray of water and mist.

"These cave formations are pretty amazing," Qwyrk nodded. "I imagine you'd need to be a geologist to really appreciate everything down here."

"My sediments, exactly," Holly quipped.

"I can't believe you just said that. Like, really. I just can't."

"What? I saw a chance for a joke. It's not my... fault."

"Oh, bloody hell."

"I think Moirin would like it down here," Holly continued, oblivious to Qwyrk's exasperation. "I mean, it's dark, spooky, there's no people, and she's quite the... rocker." She failed to suppress a grin.

"Are you sure you didn't bump your head on the way down?"

"So, you want me to just cave in and stop, then?"

"Why are you doing this?"

"Oh, come on! You can rattle off the wretched names of your bath bombs with impunity, but I can't have some fun?"

"Yeah, fair enough, but is now really the best time for it?"

"There's no time left at all, darling, so why not live in the moment? Make each other moan a bit?"

"I'm... not commenting on that."

"Oh. Pity."

"Look, joking aside, we have to figure out what to do next. And honestly, I have no clue. What did you do when you were here before?" Qwyrk looked around again.

"I don't know if I was ever here, to be honest," Holly admitted. "That's something I still don't remember. I may well have met her up above."

"Oh, now you tell me."

"Well, I didn't do it deliberately! She obviously knew I was coming. Maybe she wanted to be sure that I ended up in Manchester that night. I don't know."

"Sounds like she's a bit more keen on interfering with the flow of events than she's willing to admit."

"Yes, I've thought so, too."

"Right then," Qwyrk said, turning her attention to the network of caves leading out of the cavern in random directions, "may as well try the direct approach."

She took a few steps forward and held a hand up to the side of her mouth.

"Fayette! You know we're here, and you know who we are, and I'm guessing you know why we're here, too. We've come to you freely, and we're asking for your help. Things are about to get pretty terrible here on Earth if Holly and I don't do something about it. We don't have time to beg or solve riddles. If you have something you can tell us, please do it. Um, thank you."

Qwyrk's voice echoed around the cavern and faded, but no response came.

"Fayette!" Holly called out. "You saved my life last night, because you told me it wasn't yet my time. If I'm being kept alive for something important, this must be it. We really can't wait and mull about and fret over this. We need to know how we can stop Balor, and I think you can tell us. Please, if I'm to fulfill whatever it is I'm supposed to do, can you come to us now, in this place? Can you help us?"

They were greeted with only silence.

Qwyrk cursed. "Maybe this was a waste of time. It sounds

like she's just a capricious old force of nature that does whatever she wants."

"Gæð á wyrd swá hío scel…" A voice, both sonorous and wisp-like, sounded from somewhere in the darkness and echoed off the walls.

A sharp chill ran down Qwyrk's back. "Um, yeah, never mind."

"I recognize that phrase," Holly said. "It's from *Beowulf.* 'Gæð á wyrd swá hío scel.' It means something like 'Fate goes wherever she will… or must.'" She raised her voice. "Are you referring to yourself, then? Or are you saying that you are fate itself? That's a bit presumptuous, I should think."

In answer, a grey mist illuminated by a dim light began to form in one of the cave openings, and edged toward them.

"That's what I saw last night," Holly said. "That's what took me to her!"

"So now, she's telling us she wants us to walk into it, right?"

"Apparently so."

"Right then! Let's get on with it. The sooner we get answers, the better." Qwyrk started toward the swirling fog but turned back to see Holly hesitating. "Hey, I know this isn't going to be easy for you, but I'm here. I'm with you, one hundred percent. I know we can't hold hands right now, but nothing changes that."

Holly nodded. "I know, thank you. There's just a finality about it all that's giving me pause. I feel like once we start this, there's no going back, and things are going to change forever, no matter what happens."

"Then we'll face it together. And kick its arse if and when it needs kicking!"

Holly smiled. "Well, I couldn't possibly turn down an offer like that."

"Didn't think so. Come on, then. Let's go hear what she has to say. Find out what the hell we have to do, if there's anything we can do. And if there *is* something we can do, I have no doubt it's going to be a complete, utter pain that'll be nearly impossible."

"That's the spirit, darling!" Holly's smile widened as they walked into the mysterious mist that seemed to beckon them.

* * *

Star Tao hid in a little copse of trees in a park, a good long walk from Carl's home, gazing up at the already-darkening sky. Qwypp wouldn't be able to find him, at least not right away. But was he ready to take the chance he knew he had to take? He had to try. He closed his eyes and opened his mind in a way he hadn't done for nearly six months, not since the whole nightclub disaster.

"Right, I ain't stayin' open very long," he declared to whoever might be listening. "I need to find Lord Blippingstone, wherever he may be. I don't want nothin' from anyone else: no Council of 27, no elf ladies, no banshees, nothin'. Just put me in contact with the one called Blip, or at least let me leave a message, like a cosmic voice mail or something."

Nothing happened.

"It's really, really important."

Still nothing.

"Like, maybe the most important thing I've ever done."

A grand pile of nothing.

"Just a quick message? That's all."

Ginormous amounts of nothing.

"Please?"

More nothing then had ever nothinged in the history of nothing.

He opened his eyes, frustrated and defeated. "I guess that's it, then. I'm a failure. I'm useless. I'm—"

"Great northern beans, lad!" Blip stepped out of a nearby tree. "Was that you calling out to me? How on this Earth did you find me?"

Star Tao fell to his knees in supplication. "Praise be to you, Lord Blippingstone! My wish has been granted. Please forgive your imperfect servant and grant an audience that he may find some comfort."

"Well," Blip said with a satisfied smile, "I suppose I could spare a small bit of time. Now tell me, my boy, what troubles you?"

"Quite a lot my lord. You won't believe what the others are sayin' about you."

"Really? Do tell..."

*   *   *

Qwyrk and Holly emerged from swirls of fog into a dull and rather uninteresting cavern, reddish-brown in color and lit by a yellow light from an undefined source.

"Not very impressive," Qwyrk observed. "But that," she gestured to the glow, "that's almost always a sure sign of magic. I don't think we're in sodding Kansas anymore."

"No, we're not," Holly agreed with a sense of foreboding, "but it has the same feel as where I was last night. Something about it gets to me. It's unsettling. Wherever we are, we're not on Earth any longer."

"I suppose we've come to the right place. So, yay us?"

"Huzzah?"

Qwyrk cocked her head. "Do you hear water? Something like the shore of a lake?"

"I do."

"So, what next? Do we ask for her to show up? Chant something? Do an interpretive dance? I'm not sure how to summon a Fate, or whatever she is."

"I don't think we'll have to wait very long. Look." Holly pointed to a tunnel at the far side of the cavern.

From it emerged a figure in a deep red robe. It seemed to float over the rocky floor, its arms folded within its voluminous sleeves, while a hood was drawn over the upper portion of its face. Qwyrk could make out the features of the lower half: female, young-looking, with grey skin and lips of a darker grey. But these features seemed more like a mask than anything real. Qwyrk shivered again.

"That's definitely her," Holly confirmed.

Fayette glided toward them, stopping some distance away.

"So," Holly said, "we meet again. It seems like only yesterday. Except, it was, of course. Last night, when you abducted me and flooded my mind with all sorts of memories and then left me for dead in the chill of the forest at dawn. So nice to see you again! How have you been?"

Fayette did not respond.

"Uh, hello?" Qwyrk said, "anyone in there? The lady spoke to you. A bit of courtesy would be appreciated. Just staring at us isn't going to accomplish anything."

"You would have died. I intervened," Fayette whispered.

"Yes, so you say," Holly answered, a distinct anger in her tone, "but was it necessary to dump me back in the woods in that state? You know my kind are sensitive to the cold."

"The danger had passed by dawn. You were safe."

Holly scowled. "I was damned well *not* safe! You filled my mind with more than I could take. Memories, feelings, all sorts that overwhelmed me. I thought I might not come back from it."

"I did nothing. You perceived the visions. You already held them. Your mind simply unlocked them when it was ready at last to face them."

"I was *not* ready!" Holly fought back her fury.

"Yet, you stand here, now. Strong, unbroken, determined, avidious for the knowledge to save a world. Just as I have foreseen."

"Oh, so just because you knew it would happen, that makes it all right?"

"The way of Wyrd unfolds as it must."

Holly let out disgusted sigh and turned away.

Qwyrk whispered to her. "Hey, careful. I'm worried that things are already going tits up, and we might ruin our one chance to get the information we need. She unnerves me, and her haughtiness grates, but let me try to smooth things over, all right?"

Holly begrudgingly nodded.

"Look," Qwyrk said to Fayette, "things are obviously rather tense right now. We didn't mean to get off on the wrong foot. We're just overwhelmed by everything that's happening, right? We came to you because we need your help, but this is all pretty strange to us." She held up one hand. "If you don't mind my saying, you seem like a bit of all right under that hood. Why not pull it back so Holly and I can see you? It might make us both feel a bit more at ease."

"I can assure you, it would not," Fayette answered. "Mine eyes reflect all that has been and all that shall be across a multiverse of possibilities. No one, mortal or otherwise, may look into them and retain their sanity."

"All righty, then. Sod that idea. Let's move on, shall we?"

"You cannot do otherwise."

Qwyrk took a couple of steps forward. "Right, I'll be blunt. I mean, that's normal for me, but in this case, I just thought I'd mention it, so you don't think I'm being rude. You know why we're here, I'm sure you do. We're in a pretty big rush and all, so... how do we do it? How do we defeat Balor? I mean, I'm assuming there's a way, or we wouldn't even be here chatting with you right now, would we?"

Fayette was silent for a moment—there was a surprise—before inclining her hooded head forward just a bit. "You must seek out and obtain the Spear of Scáthach, called the Gáe Bulg, the deadly wrath of Cú Chulainn. A weapon of immeasurable power, even the greatest of the Fomorians shall fall from its piercing."

Qwyrk looked at Holly in some confusion.

"Cú Chulainn was a great hero in Irish legend," Holly answered. "Scáthach was the legendary Scottish warrior woman who trained him and gave him the spear, so it must have had a lot of power."

"The greatest power. Even the new form to be taken by Balor cannot survive its wounding," Fayette continued, "and he will be banished from the mortal realms again, if the death blow strikes true."

"All right, brilliant, so there *is* a way," Qwyrk said, looking back to Fayette. "That's a good start. But I'm assuming that we can't just go and pick up the Spear of... Scat Hag at 'Spears R Us,' or 'Marks & Spearers,' or what have you. So, what do we have to do to get it?"

Fayette took a moment to respond. "The Spear was lost long ago."

"Of course it was." Qwyrk rolled her eyes. "But?"

"But it may yet be summoned by those who are worthy. One perhaps, two are better, three for the best chance of all."

"Brilliant, always got to love those 'worthy' summoners. So, who are they? Where are they? What do they do? I mean, I'm assuming they're not solicitors, or politicians, or anything? And if you tell me they're on the bloody Shadow council, I'm storming out of here right now."

Again, Fayette paused. "Gáe Bulg may be called to the mortal realm in time of greatest need by those who are from magic, but not of it. Thus was it preserved from abuse and theft by those whose magic was infused with evil."

"There's that phrase again," Qwyrk whispered to Holly, before turning back to Fayette. "What does that mean? 'From magic, but not of it?'"

Fayette didn't answer.

"Oh, come on!" Qwyrk snapped, exasperated. "Give us something? A clue? A crumb? A crossword puzzle hint? Charades? You know, first word: two syllables, and all that?"

"You will know the answer to that question when the time is right."

"Well, that's lovely, but we're running out of time, and there isn't much of it left for things to feel 'right' to us, got it?"

"Seek among those that you already know for what you must find and do. I can say no more, for the balance of the procession of time and the ways of Wyrd must ever be maintained."

"Don't try getting any more out of her," Holly said with disdain, and loud enough that Fayette could hear her. "All she does is speak in riddles and sow confusion. What little value you get from her rarely outweighs the ordeal that she puts you through." She looked at Fayette. "You've been in my head for the last six months, apparently just so you could tell me I'm going to die because of all of this. I don't know what offense you took at my coming to you for answers fifteen years ago, but I can't imagine it was so bad that you have to torment me as you do. I don't know what you are, and honestly, I don't want to know, but if you're not going to be of any more help, then let us leave, and we'll get on with trying to decipher your riddle. Apparently, playing childish games suits you when the fate of every world hangs in the balance."

Qwyrk clenched her teeth and whispered, "Yeah, pissing her off is probably not a good idea."

Fayette floated a bit closer to them, though not in a way that seemed menacing, but as if she wanted to be better heard. "I saved your life in those woods, when I did not have to."

"Yes, you did," Holly acknowledged, "but if it was only so I could live one more night before dying while fighting Balor, I'm not sure you did me any favors."

"There is time aplenty to prepare for this battle, if you use it wisely. Think with your hearts and minds together, and understand what must be done, if you would stop the return of the Fomhóraigh."

The sound of lapping water distracted Qwyrk again. "Sorry, is there a lake back there, or something?" She pointed to the tunnel from which Fayette had emerged. "Not exactly the kind of place I'd want to book a seaside holiday, to be honest, but maybe it appeals to selkies, or something. You could rent out spaces on the beach, get some proper cheer in here, maybe an ice cream vendor, or something. This place could use it, to be honest."

"The Pool of Segais offers boons to the deserving," Fayette answered, "and the potential for extinction to those who would abuse it or enter in with a dishonest heart."

"Goddess, you really don't do anything by halves, do you?" Qwyrk said.

"Does the water feed the Well of Segais at the River Boyne in Ireland?" Holly asked, now intrigued.

Fayette inclined her head. "Indeed, daughter of Vishala. Long have those folk venerated the waters there which arise from here, seeking its gifts of prophecy and renewal."

"That was going to be my next question, just so you both know," Qwyrk spoke up.

"So, you can ask it for something by wading into it?" Holly looked in the direction of the tunnel.

"Once only," Fayette answered, "and only if it finds you worthy. Before you are tempted, Vishala the younger, know that it will not tell you how you may find the spear, so think not to use it for such a purpose. It will only grant a wish born of a higher calling, one with the goal of a fundamental transformation."

"Pity," Holly said. "I suppose it's no surprise it wouldn't be that easy."

"Well, we don't have time for a swim, anyway," Qwyrk added, "but we'll keep it in mind should we need to make any drastic, life-altering changes in the next twenty-four hours, which to be honest, is highly doubtful. So," she looked at Holly, "I guess we need to get on and find this spear, eh? There's got to be some worthy folk out there who can conjure it up for us? Magical, non-magical beings. Those should be easy to find."

"Look within and without," Fayette said.

"You know, you really stopped being helpful a few minutes ago," Qwyrk said. "So, if there's nothing else you can tell us, like *really* tell us, that's going to actually be useful, can we leave?"

Fayette didn't answer.

"Yeah, that's what I thought," Qwyrk said. "Righty-ho, this has been charming and all, but we should be off. Maybe we'll pop by again some other time for tea or something. I'm sure that'd be lovely."

Fayette said nothing.

"You've really got no sense of humor at all, do you?"

"She's got nothing but her apparent mystique as the keeper of deep knowledge she'd rather not share, and quite a bit of spite, apparently," Holly sneered. "Easier just to invade someone's mind with vague torments about their future, which they don't even remember."

Fayette remained silent.

"Come on," Holly added. "We're not going to learn anything else from her right now, which I suppose is what she wants. She enjoys having us jump through hoops. It's just making me angry, and I want to get out of here."

"Your wish is my command, love," Qwyrk assured her, holding back from putting her hand on Holly's shoulder, and looking back to Fayette. "We're going now, so... thanks, I guess? We'll let you know how it all turns out, if the world doesn't end, or something. The spear, that's the ticket apparently, so cheers for that. We'll go find those worthy ones and get it summoned straight away. We'll see ourselves out. Bye then, byeeee!"

They turned and walked back into the mists, still swirling in their swirly manner. A short time later, they found themselves in Gaping Gap again, the spray from various waterfalls wafting through the air.

"Well, that was useful. Sort of," Qwyrk said. "Shall we get out of here before we get soaked?"

"Please!" Holly nodded. "So much water. Here and wherever she was."

"Come on. I'll pop on back to Carl's home and you can follow behind. We'll figure out what to do from there."

"I don't think you ladies will be going anywhere, to be honest," a voice sounded in the gloom.

"It's one of the guards I clocked earlier," Qwyrk said to Holly. "Still wearing his uniform. They're not even trying to hide it now."

She spoke up, giving away no sign of her unease: "Well done on finding us, I suppose."

"Your trail isn't hard to track." He grinned, clenching his fists. "Magical traces are like spilled paint, if you know what to look for."

"Mate," she sighed, "do you really want a rematch? I clobbered the lot of you before, and I wasn't even at a hundred percent. I'm feeling even better now, and there's two of us. And I promise you, she's just as bad-arse as me, and pretty pissed off at the moment." She flipped a thumb in Holly's direction.

"That might well be the case," he sneered, "but I brought some friends with me. A whole lot of them, to be honest."

Qwyrk and Holly looked behind him to see several others dressed in the same manner emerging from the darkness. More than several. Like two dozen or more. A veritable small army had come to recapture her, or maybe just finish them both off here. Holly shuddered.

Qwyrk sighed again. "You know, under other circumstances, I might even enjoy having a go, just to see how I could do, but we really don't have time for this crap, like not at all." She turned to Holly and moved in as close as she dared.

"Change of plans," she whispered. "We can't lead them back to

Leeds. I suspect they'd be more than willing to hurt our friends. I'm going ahead. Follow me."

"Where are you going?"

"To the Moors, though I'd rather not say just where. But follow me, all right? You'll use up another charge on your ring, but we have to. Don't stay here and fight them. I mean it."

"I should hold them off for a bit, so you can hide when you get to where you're going." Holly found herself spoiling for a fight.

"Holly, please don't try to fight them!"

"I have to buy you some time, Qwyrk! Go now, and I'll distract them, just a little. Don't worry, I've no intention of letting them get me. Not with you out there waiting for me."

Qwyrk took a step back. "I want to kiss you so much. You're the best."

"And don't you forget it!"

"Right," Qwyrk's would-be abductor said. "If you two are finished whispering sweet nothings into each other's ears, how about you come here and get what's coming to you? It may not be painless, but we can make it quick enough. If we feel like it." A chorus of laughs sounded behind him.

"Why do it?" Qwyrk demanded. "Why serve that bloody traitor? You know nothing good's going to come of this."

"It's all about choices, isn't it? A new order is dawning. Nothing can stop it, and we want to be on the winning team. You could've been a part of it, too, but you made some bad choices, like her." He pointed. "Bloody Yakki."

Holly bristled at his slur. She snarled and clenched her fists.

"Yeah, no thanks," Qwyrk said. "And if you ever insult my girlfriend again, I'll rip your arms off and stuff them down your bloody throat, and then she'll make things even worse for you. I'm so done being nice with you lot, and I wish I had more time, because honestly? I'd love to tear into all of you, just to see how much hurt I could spread around."

"Bold words, oh mighty Qwyrk," the guard said. "Care to put them to the test?"

"I'd love to, just not right now. But this is to be continued, you arse-womble. You can bloody well guarantee it!" With that, she flashed away in a blaze of violet light.

"Right," Holly said, flexing her fingers, "shall we?"

*   *   *

Jilly sat on the sofa with Qwypp, Qwykk, and Lluck, going over the details about what she'd seen Blip doing. Or allegedly doing, or whatever.

"That's not good at all, is it?" Qwykk asked.

"No, love. It isn't," Qwypp took her hand. "I still can't believe he'd do that."

"I know!" Qwykk said. "He's gonna get sick or something wandering about down in that cold dungeon."

"That's... so not the point. Again." Qwypp tried her best to humor her sweet if not-bright friend. "So what are we gonna do? ST's gone out there looking for this bastard, and who knows? He might just find him. He's got weirdly good skills like that sometimes. And if he does and spills the beans—"

"We're all right screwed," Lluck said. Jilly noticed that he was spending a bit more time checking out Qwykk than he should be, and it irritated her.

"I can probably locate him with a simple spell," she said instead. "I mean, he can't have gone too far in an hour or so, and since he's still in our world, it'll be way easier to find him. You can teleport us to him, right? It's not like with Qwyrk and Holly."

"So," Qwykk said, "they can't touch each other, like not at all?"

"Not right now, I'm afraid." Jilly said.

"That's horrible." Qwykk said with a frown.

"It is, isn't it?" Lluck nodded and inched a bit closer to her. Jilly wanted to smack him.

"The best way we can help them is to stop this all from happening," she said instead. "And that means, finding Star Tao before he accidentally messes up our plans."

"But we don't really have any plans, do we?" Qwypp said. "I mean, we're waiting to hear from Qwyrk and Holly so we'll know what to do next."

"Yeah, all right!" Jilly admitted, now getting annoyed. "But we have to do *something*. I'll look up the locating spell. Let's just go find him and keep him from making things worse."

"I don't really see how things could get much worse," Qwypp said.

"Please don't say that," Jilly implored.

* * *

"Well, well," the guard taunted. "Looks like your lover girl don't care about you as much as she says, Yakki. We'll get on after her in a bit, but what say we make quick work of you, and then drag your nice body along with us to show her just how badly she messed things up?"

Holly instinctively reached for her belt to grab her stick, only to remember that she'd lost it while in Fayette's presence last night. She cursed to herself.

"Well, I hesitate to call you 'gentlemen,' because you're anything but," she called out, "so I'll just think of you as reprehensible troglodytes and bid you all good day!" *Oh dear, that sounded far too much like Blip.*

They closed in on her, menacing and angry. But she held her ground, not giving them the slightest hint of satisfaction that they might be intimidating. She placed her left hand over her right and felt the small stone on her ring, focusing on Qwyrk and where she'd gone. Though she didn't know the exact destination, she trusted in Qwyzz's skill.

It worked fine before. I just need to give Qwyrk a little more time.

They edged closer to her, clearly enjoying drawing this out.

Just a few more steps. She kept her eyes squarely on her opponents, hoping that none of them had any kind of a projectile weapon.

"That's far enough, lads," she said. "How about you stop, before I make things unpleasant?"

They answered with a round of sneering laughs. That was all she needed to hear. Flipping up her left hand, she spoke some ancient words that she half-remembered the meaning of.

A streak of green flame shot out of her palm. It engulfed the first of the would-be murderers to shouts, gasps, and screams. She held them back, pain surging up her arm, knowing her magical weapon wouldn't be enough to stop them all. She couldn't keep it up for much longer, lest it begin to burn her too. The flames stopped them just long enough for her to touch her ring. She let go of the energy and staggered back.

Magic surged from within the stone, engulfing her and shooting her along the path of her dearest Qwyrk, to safety, to somewhere far away, to…

She stumbled out of the whirling vortex and onto rough ground. The smell of the air and the shape of the landscape told her it was indeed the Yorkshire Moors.

"Oh, thank Goddess, darling. I stayed there as long as I could, but they were getting too close, so I actually used my Faery Fire for the first time in absolute ages. I'd forgotten just how exhausting it can be, but it gave them some hurt and… Qwyrk? Darling?"

She darted a hasty glance around the landscape, her excellent eyesight scouring the hills and heather for Qwyrk, but there was no sign of her.

"Qwyrk?" she called out much louder. "Oh no, no! Something must have gone wrong. It must have dropped me near to her but not near enough. Damn it!"

She glanced around again, and panicking, she wandered about in random directions, calling out, but there was only silence.

Qwyrk was nowhere to be found.

CHAPTER SIXTEEN

"Get down!"

Someone shoved Holly to the ground. Someone small, with a familiar voice.

"Horatio, what's going on?"

"Shhhhh!" he whispered, "Stay quiet!"

She did as he asked and lied on her stomach, propped up on her elbows to look around. He crouched next to her.

"What's happening?" she asked.

"Those goons'll be on their way here in a minute, I expect."

"Yes, but lying here isn't going to help us."

"That's where you're wrong, love." He waved his hands about in the air. "Just a little bit of conjuring, some NN trickery that gets us out of tight spots when we've learned too much, or get found out."

A pale blue light appeared and draped itself over them.

"Now don't move and stay quiet!" he hissed.

He'd no sooner given his order when the first of the Shadow guards emerged in the distance, stepping out of various colors of flashing light. They were followed by another group, and another, until at least twenty of them began scouring the area.

"They're not here," one called out after a minute or two.

"They have to be!" said the chief jerk who'd insulted her. "Qwyrk's trail led right to this spot! Maybe she really did give her girlie the slip and somehow ended up somewhere else, but it's Qwyrk we want, anyway. The Yakki would just be a bonus. Keep looking!"

Holly bit her tongue. Horatio crouched next to her, holding his hand up in warning to say nothing. But she so wanted to ask him where Qwyrk went and why none of these goons ventured anywhere near them. He must have put an enchanted cloak over them that hid them from view.

Not a bad trick, really.

They waited for some time for those treacherous fools to stop looking, and she grew ever more angry and impatient. After several minutes and a good deal of swearing and kicking the dirt and even shoving each other in frustration, they conceded defeat and flashed away, one by one. The last few, including the leader, lingered and seemed to be arguing about something. He punched one of his subordinates in the stomach and stormed off in a flicker of red lights. They followed suit, and soon, all of them were gone.

"Wait here just a bit longer," Horatio whispered. After quick look around, he motioned for her to get up and come to him.

"What was that magic?" she said, brushing dirt off her front. "It's remarkable!"

"Not bad, eh? Just a little disruption spell that keeps away unwanted attention. They never even knew we was here."

"Thank you, really, but where is Qwyrk? She had to have come here. I couldn't have followed her otherwise."

"She's right over that ridge, love." He pointed to base of a low hill. "Hidden the same way. Those damned Shadow flunkies? Yeah, they mean business, and even with your fighting skills, I wouldn't necessarily bet on you two takin' all of 'em on. No offense, just sayin'.'"

"Oh, right, because you're always betting on us, aren't you?" She shook her head and followed him as he bounded over to where he'd pointed.

"Would it make a difference if I said it's in favor of you two?"

"Not really, no."

They reached the spot in question, but she saw nothing.

"Well?" She eyed him.

"Well, what? She's still under the enchanted umbrella, ain't she?" He motioned with his hand, and at once, Qwyrk appeared, sitting cross-legged on the ground, an amused grin on her face.

"I've actually been waving at you for like the last thirty seconds," Qwyrk said. "But I wanted to see how well this magic worked, so I stayed here."

"It works quite well, I should think." Holly smiled and knelt next to Qwyrk, relieved and even amused herself. But not being able to kiss, to hug, even to touch was destroying her, and she saw the same sad longing in Qwyrk's eyes. She held up one palm, and Qwyrk did the same, no more than an inch away.

"We're going to fix this," Holly said, even if she didn't believe her own words.

"Damn right we are! When this is all over, we're going to kick so many arses, they're going to need an accountant to tally up the number."

"You have such a way with words, darling!"

"Well, I may not be as posh as you, but I like to think I can get my point across with some vibrancy."

"That you do."

"Right, this is charming and romantic and all that shite," Horatio said, head darting around with a nervous glance, "but we really do need to get the hell out of here. Those twats are gonna come back sooner rather than later, and they may bring reinforcements."

"How many Shadows have turned traitor, do you think?" Holly scanned the horizon, just to be sure they were still alone. The thought of more of them returning horrified her.

Qwyrk shrugged. "I don't know, but see my previous eloquence about arse-kicking. To say that I'm furious right now doesn't even begin to describe it." She turned to Horatio. "So what's the plan?"

"To get you two to safety. I'm takin' you to Bogtrotter."

Qwyrk rubbed her head. "Maybe my mind's a bit fuzzy from meeting Fayette, but it almost sounded like you said we'd be safe if you took us to Bogtrotter?"

"You're a right laugh, you are." Horatio rolled his eyes.

"No, seriously," Qwyrk insisted, "how exactly is he going to 'protect' us? And even if he can do anything—which I doubt—I'm not dancing or whatever just to get his protection, let's be clear about that right now."

"My hopes are always dashed," Holly sulked.

Qwyrk shot her a look but didn't say anything.

"Correct me if I'm wrong, but I just saved both of your arses from that goon squad with my little conjuring trick, yeah?" Horatio waved his hands about as if casting another spell. "So maybe, just maybe, we have some talents that could be of use, yeah? And maybe if I'm offerin' to help you out, you could try bein' a bit more gracious just once, especially since it's the bloody end of the world... again! Yeah?"

Qwyrk looked down. "All right, fair enough. Sorry. We do appreciate your help."

"Thank you." Horatio mock-bowed. "The point was to throw 'em off your trail just long enough for you to get on with whatever you need to do. I assume there's some sort of master plan at work here, wherein you two will go off and do somethin' bloody heroic and then save all our arses?"

"It's a bit more complicated than that," Holly said. "We actually have to find a weapon that doesn't exist, at least not on this plane."

"Oh, that's just brilliant, isn't it?" Horatio threw his arms up. "Honestly, I don't wanna know right now. Let's just get the hell out of here, and you can explain it all to the boss."

Qwyrk glanced to her right and left.

"What is it?" Holly asked. She knew that look on Qwyrk's face, and it wasn't a good one.

"They're coming back. Soon."

"Then take my hands, ladies, and let's be on our way, eh? They won't be able to follow me, 'cause I don't teleport with the same magic as Shadows do."

"Thank Goddess for small favors," Qwyrk said.

Doing as he said, they vanished in a puff of smoke and what sounded like a belch. Not the most elegant way to travel, but when running for their lives, it would do.

*   *   *

"There he is!" Jilly exclaimed, pointing at a cluster of trees in a park that Qwykk and Qwypp had taken them to.

Star Tao sat cross-legged on the ground and seemed to be explaining something, while Blip paced about, hands behind back.

"Oh, no!" Jilly said. "We're too late! Who knows what he's already told him?"

"Yeah, so much for the stealth approach," Qwypp sighed.

"What's that?" Qwykk asked.

"What's what?" Qwypp eyed her with irritation.

"The 'self approach.' Is that like one of them psychological things, or is it more like asking yourself out on a date? Would you even have the nerve to do it? And if you did, what if you said 'no'?"

"The *stealth* approach." Qwypp glared. "As in being quiet, sneaking up on someone, as in those two over there? Got it?"

"Fine," Qwykk pouted. "Sorry I didn't hear you. It's all pretty stressful right now, isn't it?"

"Not to interrupt this very important conversation." Jilly totally wanted to interrupt. "But Qwypp's right. We have to barge over there now, get Star Tao, and get out of here before anything else happens, like Blip taking him away."

"You don't think he'd do that, do you?" Qwypp fretted as she glanced over at the unlikely duo again.

"Right now, I don't know what he'd do, but we can't take the chance," Jilly said. "Let's just pop on over there, you and Qwykk grab him, and then we'll flash on out of here."

"Sounds like a plan," Lluck said. "Anything you want me to do?"

"Maybe be ready to make something bad happen if we need it?"

He cracked his knuckles. "Sound. I don't get to do that enough."

"Right, let's all join hands and get it done," Jilly said, and the others willingly followed. Being Granny's descendent seemed to be a big deal.

With another flash, they found themselves almost right on top of their quarry. In fact, close enough to knock him over.

"Hey!" Star Tao shouted, "what's the hell's goin' on?"

"Grab him, now!" Jilly shouted. She watched with satisfaction as Qwypp and Qwykk lifted the poor fellow off the ground with ease. Before he or Blip could even react, Qwypp circled her hand through the air and the magical charge of Shadow energy surrounded her. In mere seconds, she whisked them away. Only, the "them" in question wasn't all of them. She'd managed to get herself, her boyfriend, and Qwykk away as planned. But she'd somehow managed to forget to take Jilly and Lluck along with them.

"Uh, why are we still here?" Lluck asked.

Jilly glanced over to see an annoyed-looking Blip glaring at her. She shot a glance at Lluck. "Oh crap!"

*   *   *

"Thanks, mate." Qwyrk nodded to Bogtrotter as she and Holly sat down in a patch of gnarled old trees for a chat.

"Under the circumstances, it's the least I can do."

"You *could* ask her to do the dance," Holly suggested.

Qwyrk made to swat her on the shoulder, but swiped the air instead, just in case the ward prevented even that quick contact, which it probably did.

"What?" Holly feigned innocence. "It's merely a suggestion!"

"Ain't got time for dancin' at the moment, love," Bogtrotter said.

"Thank you." Qwyrk was relieved.

"However, I do agree that it is a worthy artistic endeavor which needs to be presented in the near future," he added.

"Thank you," Holly said with a satisfied smile. "I simply want to view the piece and judge it on its artistic merits."

"And I think you'll be quite pleased with said merits," he replied. "The piece blends several elements and styles into a mélange of contemporary expression. There are bits of Graham, Cunningham, and even a little Nijinsky, but it tries not to slavishly copy any one style. I choreographed it meself, you see, so I also threw in a bit of Scottish folk and polka and twerking."

"Well in that case, I simply must see it!" Holly enthused.

Qwyrk cringed. "Bloody hell, can we please get back to the topic at hand? You know, the flipping end of the world, yet again?"

"No worries, love," Bogtrotter said. "We can revisit you dipping your toe into the Terpsichorean delights at another time."

"Thank you!" Qwyrk folded her arms.

"Anyway, you both have sanctuary here, as long as you need," he said. "Ain't no way those Shadow pillocks are gonna find you out here in the Moors. We have a more elaborate version of Horatio's spell goin' on all around us. Rest up, make yer plans, use this as a base, whatever you need to do. Only, speed it up, yeah? Time's runnin' out, and we're all lookin' at you to save our bacon yet again."

"Mmm, bacon," Bogtrotter's trumpet-nosed herald remarked as he happened to walk by. "I could really go for some nice, smoked and salted rat flesh right about now."

"Do you mind?" Qwyrk fairly snarled. "Look, I'm not at all sure we're going to be able to pull this one off, and if not, we still have to mount some kind of resistance. Can you get your folks mobilized and get them out there, to spread the message about what's happening? We're going to need every last bit of help we can get."

"The problem is, we don't know where he'll appear," Holly

objected. "I mean, we're just assuming it's going to be somewhere nearby, but what if it's not? What if it's in the Lake District, or Scotland, or even Ireland?"

"Nah," Bogtrotter said with a shake of his shaggy, cowy head, "I strongly suspect it'll be in the Dales, somewhere north of Pateley Bridge."

"Wait," Qwyrk said, "the town with the bakery? The one I chased your sycophants away from?"

"The very same. There's a definite energy source under that bakery—strong magical stuff that we're pretty sure is to do with Balor—and I was using my scouts to go and have a look, so cheers for chasin' them off and ruinin' me plans."

"Well, how did I know? I mean, they didn't say anything about it! As far as I knew, they were just making some disgusting rat pasties or some such."

"Ooh, a rat pasty'd be right lovely, too!" the herald said, wandering back by.

"Shut it!" Qwyrk snapped.

"They didn't say anything because they was under strict orders from me not to," Bogtrotter explained. "We've been hearin' about this potential comeback for quite a while, and I didn't know who to trust. Sorry, love."

"It might explain why I got so dizzy, too," Qwyrk said. "The council sent me to check it out."

"Sounds like someone from that establishment might not have wanted anyone snooping about, so they sent you to rough up my boys," Bogtrotter posited.

"And we already know who," Qwyrk grumbled.

Holly spoke up. "Is it worth sending some of your fellows back there to investigate now that it's getting dark?"

"Already on it," he said. "Now that we know pretty much for sure it's happenin', I need to know what's goin' on down there. And before you ask, I ain't sendin' you two. You've got your own quest to get on with, and besides, you're too big and noisy. My NNs can get in and get out without any fuss."

"Too big?"

"Too noisy?"

Qwyrk and Holly looked at each other and then back at him in mutual irritation.

"Truth hurts, ladies, but spy craft ain't your strong point, so leave it to the experts. I need my suspicions confirmed."

"What do you think is going on down there?" Holly asked.

"Near as we can tell, it's a seal. Balor and all the Fomorians are basically kept from returning to Earth by a potent magical protection, see? We think that seal is down there, kind of like a locked door, which means there must be a key. And apparently, someone has found it, and has put it in the lock and turned it, or is about to. If that gate's been opened and stays open, nothin'll stop Balor and all his best beasties from surging back into this world, spreadin' out over these here isles, and doin' whatever they bloody well like. I don't want that, you don't want that, nobody wants that. It's likely that he and maybe a few of his mates are already down there, and they'll be doin' some kind of ritual under the light of the moon on Samhain to bring back the rest of them."

"It's always some ginormous magical shindig, isn't it?" Qwyrk puffed in exasperation. "De Soulis, the Erlking, even Aeval. They all have to throw some big, bloody spectacle as a show of power. They love flaunting it!"

"Theatricality is a hallmark of the bad ones, love," Bogtrotter said, "and there ain't none badder than Balor. His will be the epic tragedy to end all epic tragedies."

"So," Qwyrk said, "we're going to need someone down below the bakery to, what, pull whatever the key is out of its lock? And at the same time, we'll need to face Balor and all his minions above ground and nearby."

"Looks that way, love," Bogtrotter nodded.

Qwyrk stared at the ground for a moment, thinking it over. "Something about all of this bothers me. The council asked me to go to that bakery and keep an eye on it. I thought it was a rubbish assignment at the time and was pretty much just chasing those two off from making their revolting dinner."

"Don't judge our delicacies," Bogtrotter interrupted.

"But what if I was sent to stop them because someone knew what's down there and didn't want your spies finding out about it?"

Bogtrotter nodded. "That seems a likely scenario. If it is indeed the gate, then someone on your council already knew that and was tryin' to keep it secret as long as possible. They used you."

"Oh, I already know it's Qwalm," Qwyrk said, disgusted. "And we know what we have to do, so we have to stay focused on that. Given that they're sending Prince Not-at-all-Charming and his score of flunkies to kill us, they aren't even trying to be secret about it now. But the fact that they want to off us tells me that they're still afraid we might just stop them."

"Then let's give them something to be afraid of!" Holly exclaimed.

"That's the spirit, ladies!" Bogtrotter slapped his bovine knees.

"Ooh, spirits!" The herald wandered by again. "I could go for a strong whisky and a lovely rat tripe and kidney pie."

"Oh, for crap's sake!" Qwyrk rolled her eyes.

"My agents will find out what's down there," Bogtrotter assured them.

"Brilliant," Qwyrk said. "In the meantime, we should talk some more about our next move, which, to be honest, is a little unclear at the moment."

"Agreed," Holly answered. "Before that, I'd really like to check in with Lluck, and maybe he can let the others know we're all right? Can I do that?"

"Uh, better not," Bogtrotter answered. "This whole magical canopy of silence is pretty delicate, and using other magic inside might punch holes in it and make us noticeable. We're just hopin' it holds out for now."

"Just hoping?" Holly cast him a skeptical glance. "That's not very reassuring."

"Nothin's guaranteed at the moment, love," Bogtrotter said as he stood up. "Now, if you'll excuse me, there's a lot to do before everything potentially comes crashing down and Balor turns our innards to jelly."

"Jelly?" the herald said as he strode by, yet again. "Ooh, I do love a good vulture brain jelly, especially marinated with spicy beetles!"

*　　*　　*

Qwyrk wandered up a hill to where Holly sat watching the sunset, grateful for a brief respite under the NN's protection.

"Do you ever get tired of it?" Holly asked as Qwyrk sat down next to her.

"Tired of what?"

"The setting sun. I was thinking about how many I must have seen over the centuries, and somehow, they always amaze me. Incredible that something as simple as viewing the star this world orbits around as it disappears each day could be so beautiful and moving."

"I haven't really thought about it that much," Qwyrk admitted. "But yeah, they do get some spectacular ones up here in the north."

"Each one is unique. The clouds will never be the same again, so the light will be slightly different in each one. It's like seeing a marvelous new painting every time."

"It is, isn't it? I'll keep that in mind in the future. I mean, assuming we have a future after tomorrow." That thought darkened her mood at once.

Holly looked at her. "What do you think our chances are? I mean, really?"

"Honestly? I have no clue, but I'd guess not good."

"We should probably get back out there, see if we can find the 'worthy' ones, so we can try to summon the spear."

"The problem is, as soon as we step outside of the magic barrier, they'll just be on to us again. Maybe not right away, but it'll probably mess up any chance we have of being left alone long enough to figure this out. And I don't want to risk going back to Qwyzz's. There may be a dozen of those pillocks watching his home from the forest."

"I know, and I can't even contact Lluck because they're out there, looking for us. It's killing me."

"I'm so sorry." Qwyrk wanted to hold her. Everything in her

mind and body told her to reach out to Holly, to wrap her arms around her. But each time they touched, the reaction had grown more violent. Who knew what might happen now, with even the slightest bit of contact?

"I'm just worried that they've found Lluck and Carl," Holly said after a brief silence. "What if they're being held hostage? What if they're trying to contact us to let us know, but they can't because of this dome around us? What if—" She didn't finish her question, but Qwyrk knew what she feared.

"I wish I could tell you everything's going to be fine, that they're all right," Qwyrk said, "that we'll see them soon. But honestly, I don't know. All we can do is trust that they can look after themselves. I hate it, but for now, that's all we've got."

"You're still fairly rubbish at pep talks, you know that?" Holly managed a slight teary smile.

"Yeah, they never were my strong point."

"But we can't just sit here all night, fretting and fidgeting."

"I keep coming back to what Fayette said. That whole business about being 'from magic but not of it.' I'm still trying to wrap my head around what it means."

"I've no clue. I gave up thinking about it a while ago to give my mind a rest."

"It seems completely contradictory, doesn't it? I mean, how can anyone come from magic but not be 'of' it? If you're from magic, you're *from* magic. That's not really something you can negotiate."

"She also said it was best for three to summon the spear. What if they're all over Britain? All over the world?" Holly looked back to the reddening sky.

"I think she meant three would be the best number, but not

absolutely necessary if we can only find one or two. She's not all that clear, I'm finding out. But I think she's sincere."

"I've a feeling that's just what she wants you to think. Fifteen years ago, she had no qualms at all about telling me I was going to die soon, which put me in such a state that I fled to Manchester. I could have been killed there, Qwyrk. What if I'd wandered in front of a car, or I hadn't met Carl, but someone awful instead? Her words really would have been prophetic."

"But that didn't happen, and maybe she knew it wouldn't."

Holly turned back to her. "So, you're saying she set me on the path to something so it would be a self-fulfilling prophecy? That she's just manipulating things behind the scenes?"

"I don't know. It could be that, or maybe she's just somehow outside of time, normal time, I mean, and sees everything at once, where we can only see it as it unfolds. Maybe our minds just can't hold on to that kind of information for too long."

"Now you're getting all metaphysical on me."

"Well, given our circumstances, a bit of the unknown might be our best chance. I think we're going to have to stay put for now, at least until the trail on our arses goes a bit cold. I don't think they'll waste a lot of time on us, to be honest. If their big, bad boss is about to make his grand entrance tomorrow night, they'll be much more interested in that."

Holly sighed and nodded. "You're right. As much as it pains me, we should probably keep out of sight tonight, try again first thing tomorrow. I just wish I could get a message to Lluck."

"This is the part where I'd suggest that we go to Horatio or one of the others and bribe them with some candied crickets to take a small written note to your lad," Qwyrk said. "But I'm guessing most of the NNs are out and about right now, delivering other messages or spying to find out what they can. Still, if the chance comes up later, you should definitely do it."

"The sun's almost down," Holly said, changing the subject. "I think I'm going to go train for a bit. I mean, I don't have my stick with me, but even a branch would do. I just want to twirl something and swing it."

"I'd suggest Horatio, but I don't think he's around right now."

Holly laughed, and it was a lovely thing to see.

"Or maybe you could bat some Nasties into the dark?" Qwyrk grinned.

"That would be rather rude to our hosts, I should think."

"True, but it'd be funny."

"You're horrid." Holly chuckled as she moved in to kiss the air in front of Qwyrk's lips. The temptation to pull her in for a proper kiss was overwhelming, but Qwyrk resisted. She kissed the air back.

"Yeah, but I'm witty and charming, so I've got that going for me."

Holly winked and stood up. "Apparently, they have a tent for us to share tonight that will keep out the cold. I don't like our chances for food, though."

"Good thing I don't have to eat."

"One of these days, you'll appreciate what a fine thing it is to be hungry and to enjoy a lavish meal."

"Yeah, don't see that happening, but I'll ask Boggie to set aside some decent food for you. Or at least something that's not revolting."

"You're a love. Ta for now, darling."

Qwyrk watched Holly wander off in search of a makeshift staff and turned her attention back to the ever-darkening sky. She kept turning over Fayette's words in her mind.

"From magic, but not of it."

As night descended, she pondered that idea over and over, in light of everything that had happened. Slowly, a realization came to her, and she started to formulate a plan. But she didn't like where it was going.

CHAPTER SEVENTEEN

"What is the meaning of this?" Blip demanded.

"What's the meaning of what?" Jilly sassed, looking around at the trees to find the quickest means of escape.

"Why are you acting in whatever inexplicable and disgraceful way you are? All of you?"

"Um, hello? I might ask you the same thing, 'Mr. Childhood Companion' who bores me to death with philosophy while sneaking off in secret to do all sorts of things I'd rather not think about. Or was that part of the plan all along? Wearing me down and killing me slowly?"

"I've no idea what you're talking about, but you're clearly in a mood."

"In a mood? Oh, you have no bloody idea how much of a mood I'm in, you wanker!" Jilly frantically tried to think of any magic she could lob at him.

Lluck flexed his fingers but did nothing yet.

"Profanity avails you nothing, Ms. Pleeth. Now, come here and we shall discuss this situation like civilized individuals."

"Oh, I don't think so, Mr. Traitor. I wouldn't exactly call you civilized, anyway. Not anymore."

Blip took a step toward her.

"Don't," she growled, holding up her hands, but having no real idea what spells she would even work, if any. Bluffing was hard.

"Do not test me, girl," Blip warned. "I'm in a bit of a 'mood' myself today and have no time for this."

"Oh? Got to get back to helping destroy the world, eh? Yeah, that must be keeping you really busy." Tears came to her eyes, his betrayal slapping her in the face again. "I trusted you! You were my friend, you were—"

"Jilly..." He took another step forward.

"Look mate," Lluck said, pointing an angry finger at Blip, "I don't know you all that well, but I think Jilly's had about enough of your crap, and honestly, I have, too. So why don't you just bugger off now, before things get ugly?"

Blip bristled. "Don't take that tone with me, boy! Having a faery mother and a human father doesn't make you all that, as you younglings like to say."

Lluck took a step forward. "You know, someone else liked to call me 'youngling', and it turned out he was worth way more than you. Oh, and I may not be 'all that,' but I can still do this!"

He flicked his hands out and Blip slipped and fell flat on his froggy bottom.

"Come on!" He grabbed Jilly's hand. They sprinted deeper into the forest at the edge of the park, the darkness of sunset gathering around them.

"Thanks for that!" Jilly huffed and puffed as they stopped to catch their breath. "I was trying to get a spell together, but I needed more time."

"Yeah, well, whatever you've got, you'd better get it ready soon, 'cause he isn't going to be down for long, and if he was pissed off before, he'll be savage now!"

They sprinted for a bit over rock and root.

"Do you think we outran him?" Lluck gasped, pausing again for breath.

"No," Jilly shook her head as she stopped and took great gulps of air into her aching lungs. "Once he's recovered, he'll probably be able to just teleport to where we are."

"Great. So basically, we've got no chance."

"Pretty much."

"Adventures kind of suck, you know?"

"Sometimes they do."

They set off again and soon clamored to the top of a small hill. They eased themselves down the other side, trying not to slip on fallen leaves and damp forest earth in the darkening forest. They almost succeeded.

"Ow!" Lluck yelled out, as they slid to the bottom. He fell down and grabbed at his foot.

"What is it? What happened?"

"My bloody ankle. I think I twisted it. Bollocks!" He rubbed it and grimaced.

"Oh no! I'm so sorry! But we have to keep moving, come on!"

"No, I'm gonna do the whole heroic 'you go on without me' bit. I'll stay here and hold him off. I can make his life a bit of a pain in the arse for a while. Might be a right laugh."

"Listen to me." Jilly grabbed his shoulders. "If you're doing that, I'm doing the whole 'I'm not leaving you' thing, all right? We're a team. We have to be. No one's expendable. So, if you're staying here, I am, too. We'll fight him together."

"I don't think that would be a wise idea," Blip announced in an icy tone as he stepped out of a nearby oak tree. He glared at both of them. "It seems you've injured yourself, young man. How unfortunate. But thank you for yelling so loudly. It revealed your exact location to me and saved me a fair bit of searching time. Now, where were we?"

"We weren't anywhere you posh plonker!"

A shower of pink lights fell all about them and there stood Qwykk, now arrayed in a brown army coat, camouflage leggings, and high-heeled boots. A bit more practical, at least.

"I mean, we're here, right?" she went on, "but not really. Like, we're here in this moment right now, but never again, because you can't cross the river twice and going back would be too much trouble and you'd get wet, and time's a wave and not a participle or something and..." She paused and looked around. "Where are we?"

"If this is the best the Shadows can offer, you lot should have gone extinct a long time ago," Blip said, rolling his eyes.

"Hey! I had a nice bath this morning, and I do not stink, thank you very much!"

"Please go away," Blip sighed.

"Yeah sure," Qwykk said. "That's what I was plannin' on doin', anyway. Off we go, then!"

She grabbed Lluck by the hand, and they vanished in a puff of rosé luminance.

Jilly stared at the empty space they'd just occupied. "Um..."

She looked back at Blip with a mixture of annoyance and confusion. He scowled and started toward her.

There was another flicker.

"Oops!" Qwykk said as she stepped back into the wood once again. "Sorry 'bout that! And before. We got distracted. Come on, then!" She grabbed Jilly's hand, and they poofed on their way to safety, at least away from having to see and listen to the one who'd betrayed her, who'd betrayed them all.

* * *

"Why did you do that?" Star Tao snapped and sulked as he paced about the clearing in the Symphinity forest where Qwypp had taken him.

"I'm sorry love, but I had to," she answered, putting a hand on his shoulder, only for him to shake it off. That stung her, and she pulled back a little.

"Why?" he demanded. "We was just about to get down to talking and having a meeting of the minds, a communion and all that, and you lot came along and whisked me away."

"Wait, so you didn't tell him anything, about our suspicions and all that?" Maybe he hadn't cocked up everything, after all!

"I didn't have the chance. I mean, I didn't want to lead off with that, did I? 'Excuse me, but are you a traitor?' That would have been right rude. So, I was waitin' for me opening. Do you know how rare it is to have the chance for that kind of one-on-one with a divine being? I may never get that again, especially not now."

"Love, he ain't divine," Qwypp said, relieved that he'd said nothing, "and he's definitely not interested in 'communing' with you. He was trying to get answers out of you, to see what you know. About what we said."

"Yeah? So?"

"So, what kind of god needs to ask his worshippers for answers, eh? Shouldn't he know everything already?"

Star Tao looked away, lost in thought. "Not necessarily, I mean, maybe, I mean... oh, crap! Now me head hurts!"

"Well, that's just it, isn't it?" Qwypp pressed, trying to get through to him. "If he's really a god and you're a faithful servant, why would he be puttin' you through the ringer trying to figure things out?"

"Test of faith?"

"Or, he's just been lying to you this whole time, 'cause it feeds his bloody ego. Jilly saw him, love. Saw him doing something bad, praising someone they called the 'Deathly Eye,' which I'm guessing is that Balor bloke. She's good at what she does, and she wouldn't lie to you. I think you know I'm right, on some level."

Star Tao sighed and slumped down on the ground, sitting cross-legged. "First, me channelin' goes all haywire, now this." He looked up at her, like a sad little boy. "I'm kind of losin' everything here. I don't even know what to believe."

She sat next to him and put her arms around him. "You haven't lost me, love, and you're not going to, yeah? We've got a big load of trouble coming up, and we've got to stick together. You, me, Jilly, Qwyrk, everyone. I've a feeling your channeling is going to help us all out again before it's over."

"I doubt it," he said, though he smiled just a little. "I guess this is the crisis of faith, eh? The dark night of the soul?"

"I think it's the dark night of the soul for the whole world. But whether we come out on the other side of it is going to be up to us and what we do. Blip doesn't need you for whatever he's up to, but we need you." She hugged him. "I need you."

He hesitated for just a moment, but hugged her back.

"That's all right, then," he said. "Oh, and likewise."

"Come on, love," she said. "Let's get out of here."

"Yeah," a voice in the woods sounded. "I don't think that's gonna happen."

Qwypp found herself staring at the pointy end of a crossbow, held by an angry-looking Shadow dressed like one the guards Qwyrk had described.

"Um, this ain't good, is it?" Star Tao asked.

She shook her head, but never took her eyes off the newcomer. "Nope. Not at all."

*   *   *

"This was the right thing to do, right?" Qwykk said, "bringing you two back here?"

"Yeah, this is perfect, thanks," Jilly said, flopping down on Carl's sofa, a huge improvement from where's they'd just been. "I don't think Blip'll be able to trace us back to the house. At least, he's not going to try anything with us all inside. I mean, I hope he won't." She turned to Lluck. "How's your ankle?"

"It's all right," he said, rubbing it. "Feels better now. I think I just stepped on it wrong."

"Not very lucky, I guess," she teased.

He sneered at her.

"Sorry about forgetting you," Qwykk said. "I was so into being a rescuer that I forgot to grab your hand, too. Your boyfriend sent me back to get you, though."

"Oh, he's not..." Jilly stated with a vigorous shake of her head, embarrassed.

"Yeah, not at all," Lluck interrupted, addressing Qwykk. "I'm totally single, just so you know."

Jilly glared at him.

"You two sure you're all right, then?" Carl asked as he entered the sitting room with mugs of tea for each of them.

"We're fine, thanks," Jilly tried to sound reassuring, but she was still pretty shaken from having to confront Blip about his betrayal.

"So, did your mate spill the beans?" Carl asked, sitting down next to his son and offering them the mugs. "Are we in even more trouble?"

"I don't know," Jilly sighed. "Qwypp's not back yet?" She took a sip of the most welcome hot drink.

Carl shook his head.

"I think she was gonna take Star Tao over to Symphinity and give him a bit of a scolding," Qwykk said. "I mean, if he gave away secrets and all."

"Yeah, the plan was to get him as far away from Blip as possible," Jilly said. "Maybe she'll just hide him over there for a while."

"But humans get all wonky if they spend too much time over there," Lluck said.

"They do," Jilly said. "But let's be honest, he's already pretty wonky, anyway, so who'd notice?"

"Fair enough." Lluck shrugged and drank his tea.

"So, still no word from Qwyrk or Holly?" Jilly looked at Carl. He shook his head.

"I tried my ring right after we got back, and got nothing, a total blank," Lluck offered.

"Do you think she's not wearing it, again?" Jilly asked.

"I don't know," Lluck answered, "but if I don't hear from her in the next hour or so, I'm gonna go looking for her."

"Oh?" Jilly asked, annoyed. "And where are you going to start with that?"

"I don't know, but it beats just sitting around here, waiting for the bloody world to end!"

"Qwyrk said they'd be back when they got back," Jilly protested. "We have to take her at her word, even if it means feeling a bit useless for a while."

"I mean, I could suit up and head out," Carl offered after a short silence. "Maybe I can find something?"

"But what if Blip's out there, somewhere nearby?" Jilly asked. "Maybe he can't find us in here, or he doesn't want to try, but we shouldn't be going outside and making it easier for him. Especially after dark."

"Yeah, fair enough," Carl conceded, "but I have to say, I'm with Lluck on this one. The mother of my son is out there somewhere, and we've no idea where. She's probably with Qwyrk, which is a good thing, but she's already gone missing once in the last day. The two of us found her in Nicewood this morning, half-frozen to death. Where were you and Qwyrk, eh?"

"That's not fair!" Jilly protested. "I was stuck inside at Granny's up in Knettles, because I was worried that Blip was looking for me— like he's probably doing right now—and Qwyrk did look for her out in those woods, but she got hurt because some horrid thing attacked her, poisoned her, took away her powers. She wanted to find Holly. It was all she could think about!"

"So maybe we should give it a go this time," Lluck said. "You should have a rest, try to work on some new magic and stuff. We'll pop out for a bit, see what we can find. Dad's doing great now. He's got better skills, a better suit, and I'm there to make sure we stay lucky" He turned to Qwykk. "You could come with us, I mean, if you want."

Jilly found her jealousy to be unexpected and irritating. "And just where are you going to go, eh? You have no idea where they are, none of us do, and even if by some miracle you find them, how exactly are you going to help them with whatever they're doing? A bloody superhero and his lucky son and another Shadow probably aren't going to be much use to them."

"Well, it's better than just sitting here, arguing and whining about things!" Lluck snapped, putting his tea mug down with a rather emphatic slam.

"Oh, so I'm whining now?" Jilly grew angrier with each word.

"I didn't say you!"

"You meant it, though."

"Oh, bloody hell!" Lluck stood up. "I'm not doing this, all right? My mum's missing, again, and I don't want to waste time scrapping!"

He stormed out of the room.

A moment later, he stormed back in, picked up his mug, and stormed back out.

"Don't let him bother you," Carl's tone softened. "He's very attached to her, and he's just upset."

"I know, I know. And I'm upset, too. I'll be away from my house again tonight. My parents are going to notice eventually."

"Can you call them? Text them? I could let 'em know where you are. I could just fib and say you're working on a big project with Lluck, and I'll have you back home tomorrow."

"That'd be brilliant," Jilly said, "though I'm not sure how well it would go over. They might be fine with it, or they might get really mad and insist I come home at once. I think the best thing for me to do is text them, and not give them the chance to say no."

"It's your call," Carl conceded. "But you're welcome here for as long as you need to be."

"That's kind, thank you." She turned to Qwykk. "Could you get me back to Knettles and into Granny's house? I mean with the teleporting?"

"Yeah, I think so. I mean, Qwyrk's the best at jumpin' about, but I'm not too bad at it. I could at least get you outside, if you show me where it is."

"Brilliant, thanks! Come on, then."

Qwykk looked in the direction of the kitchen. "Do you think I should check on Lluck before we go? He seemed pretty mad."

"Oh, no, no, you definitely don't want to do that." Jilly shook her head with extra vigor. "Trust me, he's better off on his own right now."

"All right, if you're sure."

"Totally sure. It's best if you don't go anywhere near him, maybe even for days. Or weeks."

"Fair enough." Qwykk shrugged. "So where exactly is this little home of Granny's then?"

"Funnily enough, it's right across the street from my house."

*   *   *

"Run!" Qwypp yelled as she dragged Star Tao by the hand through the thickening forest, having punched the guard just hard enough to slow him down.

"Who the bloody hell is that?" Star Tao gasped as they legged it through the foliage and underbrush.

"One of the guards that tried to kill Qwyrk, I reckon. Keep up!"

"Can't you just blink us out of here?"

"Yeah, but I don't want him to be able to track where I go, or he'll just follow us wherever we end up. I've got to put some distance between us, first. Come on!"

A crossbow quarrel whizzed by her head and she ducked as it lodged in a nearby tree.

"Crap! That was *way* too close. Right, it's gonna have to be here, then. Hang on love."

"Wait," he said, "where are we gooooiiiiiing…"

Qwypp whisked them away from immediate danger (or so she hoped). In a flash of pink and blue light, she found that they were standing outside a peculiar-looking home. A mansion, to be precise, that was a mix of Tudor and medieval styles, situated in a forest clearing.

"Yes!" she cheered, "I bloody well did it!"

"Uh, did what?" Star Tao looked confused. And a bit pale.

"I got us to Qwyzz's, Qwyrk's mate and mentor? If anyone can help us, he can. Come on, then, let's go see him."

Leading him by the hand, she walked up to the impressive front door, with its equally impressive bell.

"Do we ring it?" Star Tao asked, eyeing the bell with some skepticism.

"Yeah, I should think."

"Go on, then. You do it. Just in case there's some sort of spell on it that makes me go mad, or somethin'. I've heard stories about what this place'll do to us mere mortals if we stay here too long."

"Yeah, well, right now, bein' here is our best shot at safety, love. I don't want to have that plonker follow us back to the human home in Leeds."

As she rang the bell, another crossbow bolt shot past her head and struck the door with a decided thud. Their pursuer was already reloading as he strode toward them out of the trees.

"You didn't seriously think you were gonna lose me just by launching yourself somewhere else, did ya?" He pointed his weapon at them. "So, are you gonna come quietly now, or do I have to start shooting at various body parts to get you to see sense? I won't kill ya—not yet anyway—but if you keep gettin' up my nose, I might just change my mind. The next shot's goin' in someone's leg, so which one of you is it gonna be, yeah?"

Qwypp clutched at Star Tao. "Oh love, I'm so sorry!"

"Why not me, instead?" a thin and gravelly voice sounded from above them.

Before Qwypp even knew what happened, a small, stony statue had launched itself off the roof with a creep-inducing screech and sailed right toward the hapless bounty hunter. He shot his bolt in panic at the little creature, but missed, and the thing crashed into him, knocking him to the ground, and out cold.

"Uh..." Star Tao stammered. "That's bonkers, but kinda cool?"

The creature stood up, dusted itself off, and turned to greet Qwypp and Star Tao with a bow.

"I am Babewin," it said in a high-pitched, gravelly voice with a pronounced French accent. "As allies of Qwyrk, you are most welcome here! My wizard-master is a tad busy at the moment, tending to my mate—mon époux, if you will—to give him better dancing feet, but if you will follow me inside, I am sure we can get you sorted with some port. You must mind the infant wyvern, however. Come, this ruffian won't be able to get in, no matter how hard he tries!" She gave the unconscious guard a swift kick.

Qwypp and Star Tao stared at the little gargoyle as it hobbled past them through the main door, and then they looked at each other.

"I literally understood about one-third of that," he said with a head shake.

"Yeah, our world's pretty mental. And I've lived in it for centuries."

"What about him?" Star Tao pointed to their nemesis.

"I don't think he's goin' anywhere for a while. If he gets up, we'll just send that gargoyle back out. Wouldn't mind seeing that again, to be honest! Come on, let's get on."

*　　*　　*

"Down in here, lads," Horatio whispered and motioned as two of his fellow NNs followed him into the basement below the bakery. They crept down the stairs and made their way into the main room. "Well, look at that!"

The door at the far end had been opened wide. Boards were scattered on the floor around it.

"Looks like someone has wandered through here recently and didn't do a good job of hidin' their tracks, probably 'cause they didn't care about who might come after them."

"That ain't the most comforting thought in the world," one of his companions, who resembled a bipedal iguana, grumbled.

"No, Arbunkle, my friend, it's not," Horatio agreed. "And while our normal course of action would be to high tail it out of here as fast as possible, the boss has charged us with plungin' into the dark to get a good look at just what we're all about to be goin' up against."

"I don't really want to know, to be honest," the other, the honey badger whom Qwyrk had chased off in Pateley Bridge, added.

"Nor do I, Felix, but orders is orders," Horatio said with resignation. "And I mean, we do have our diminutive size goin' for us, so if things get really harried, we can probably hide until the danger has passed. I'm a gambling fellow, so I choose my words wisely and never make promises I can't keep."

"He means we're all gonna die," Arbunkle said to Felix.

"You're not helping with morale," Horatio grumped.

"Didn't know we had any to begin with," Felix said.

"That's the problem these days," Horatio lamented. "No team spirit. Remember, there is no 'I' in 'team.'"

"Yeah, but what about eyeballs in spirits?" Felix said.

"Ooh, that would be lovely right about now, wouldn't it?" Arbunkle answered. "A Bloody Mary with real blood and an eyeball on a toothpick."

"I'm more of a gin fellow, meself," Felix said.

"Gentlefellows," Horatio interrupted, starting to realize why Qwyrk got so exasperated with his people, "if I may interrupt, we have a job to do. Let's get it done, and then we can think about culinary and alcoholic indulgences, fair enough?"

The other two grumbled but nodded.

"Excellent. Now, shall we?"

They squeezed into the entrance, since the door was still a bit ajar, and set off down the tunnel, keeping quiet for a good long time.

"Bloody dark in here, ain't it?" Arbunkle finally whispered after a long, silent walk.

"That's the way these overlord types like it," Horatio whispered back. "Always got to be skulking about, plannin' in secret, using the lack of light to make themselves seem even more sinister. 'Look at me, everybody! I'm *so* bloody evil! I'm dressed in all black. Everything around me is dark, mwahahahaha!'"

"You're not half bad at that, you know," Arbunkle whispered. "Maybe you missed your calling?"

"Eh, I ain't got the time or interest to be some bloody dark lord," Horatio protested. "I enjoy what I do too much. Also, me lack of height would probably just have people laughin' at me."

"Yeah, you're pretty short," Felix observed.

"Pot, kettle, black, mate," Horatio said. Well, what do we have here?"

"It's a fork. Two tunnels," Arbunkle piped up.

"Thanks. I was bein' all rhetorical."

"You what?"

"Never mind. My instincts say we should go... right!" Horatio pointed.

"Why?"

"Why not?"

"Good enough for me," Felix said.

"And me."

"I'm glad you both agree. Don't know what I'd've done if you didn't."

Sure enough, a wander over rougher terrain brought them into a small cavern, and in the cavern beyond, they heard thumpy noises and saw flickering light.

"I don't like this, not one bit," Arbunkle said.

"We're not supposed to like it, that's kind of the whole point," Horatio whispered, motioning to both of them to keep their voices down. "Remember, all we gotta do is get a good look, take note of what we see and bugger off on out of here and get back to the boss. It ain't like we need to fight anyone, or anything."

"But what if we get caught?" Felix asked.

"We know the way now, so I can teleport us out."

"But what if they kill you? Step on you and squish you, or impale you on a kebab skewer, or lop off your head with a meat cleaver, or—"

"Yeah, I get the idea. Cheers, mate." Horatio rolled his eyes. "You're just gonna have to hope that doesn't happen, all right?"

"And if it does?"

Horatio shrugged. "Run like bloody mad back the way we came?"

"This is a really stupid mission, I'd just like to point out," Felix said.

"You're the one who volunteered," Horatio said.

"I didn't, not even a little! I was volunteered. By the boss."

"Yeah, he's good at that," Arbunkle added.

"Look, I don't care how you ended up bein' here." Horatio had had about enough. "Let's just get on over there and see what we can bloody see, all right? The sooner we can get the hell out of here, the better."

"I think," a raspy voice sounded in the darkness, "you shall not go anywhere. Ever again!"

An appalling-looking creature with one leg, one arm, and one eye, carrying a wicked-looking barbed whip hopped out of the darkness to stand above them. It trailed its whip on the rock cave floor and glared at them one at a time with that single eye.

"We are so doomed," Horatio said.

*　　*　　*

"I'm just sorry you weren't here earlier," Qwyzz said as Qwypp and Star Tao rested in his sitting room. "Qwyrk and young Vishala did indeed stop by."

"Of course they did," Qwypp said. "Do you know where they've gone off to, then?"

"Oh yes. Yes, I do." He relayed what he knew and what they intended.

"So, they're really doing it, then," Qwypp said. "They've gone off to find that ancient being who knows the future, or whatnot."

"She sounds right creepy," Star Tao added.

"That she is, young man, that she is." Qwyzz nodded with a somber expression. "Fayette is ancient, primal, a force not to be trifled with. I hope they are not making a terrible mistake, but as I'm sure you know, Qwyrk won't be deterred once she gets a plan in her mind."

"No, she bloody well won't," Qwypp agreed.

"In any case, you're most welcome to stay as long as you like. That hoodlum and his ilk won't be getting in here any time soon."

"Thank you, that's very kind," Qwypp said, "but what about him?" She motioned to Star Tao. "He's human. He can't stay here very long, right?"

Qwyzz looked at Star Tao. He squinted. He cocked his head to one side.

Star Tao squirmed. "Everything all right?"

"Human, yes, but you've had more than a fair share of the mystical about you, haven't you, lad? I mean literally inside you."

Star Tao nodded. "Well, I channel. I mean I used to, but something awful possessed me, like six months ago, and I haven't wanted to give it much of a go since."

"Nonsense, my boy! There will always be setbacks, but you've quite the gift, and one that may be very important as these atrocious events unfold. You've used them for everyone's benefit before, yes?"

"Yeah, but then I messed up, real bad. A banshee took hold of me, and I nearly hurt people." He looked down, dejected, and Qwypp put an arm around him.

"But you didn't?" Qwyzz asked.

"But I could've."

"It's more important that you understand the risks and take them, anyway. Things are not always what they seem. People are not always who they say they are."

"Yeah, I've been reminded of that recently." His expression fell.

"But you can trust in yourself," Qwyzz assured him. "And right now, you don't have the luxury of doubt. The end really *is* coming, I'm afraid, and you must be prepared."

"I think we'll stay here for a bit," Qwypp said, "get our bearings and such. But we do have to go back to our friends. We need to be ready to do what we can to fight this."

Qwyzz nodded. "Understood."

"We could use you." She knew it was a long shot, but she had to try.

"Oh! Well, thank you, but I'm not sure how helpful I would be."

"Hey, right now, we need all the help we can get. We sort of need to draft you in, whether you want to or not."

"Yeah, she makes a fair point," Star Tao added. "We can't trust too many folks right now, but you and Qwyrk, you're tight, right? She's gonna need you. We all will."

Qwyzz sighed. "Well, I suppose when you put it that way, how can I say no? I'll need to gather some things: spells, potions, manuscripts, that sort."

"Take all the time you need." Qwypp smiled. "Um, Qwyrk says you serve really good port?"

*   *   *

"Keep runnin'!" Horatio whispered in a harsh voice as he and his diminutive companions dodged the Fachan's deadly whip. So far, somehow, they hadn't attracted the attention of anything else in the far cavern—assuming there was anything else in the far cavern, of course—but maybe that was the point.

"This thing's probably here to keep everyone else away," Horatio reasoned as he hopped, skipped, and jumped to find a place where the creature couldn't get him.

"You could just poof us on out of here," Arbunkle panted amid heavy breaths. "Save all our skins right easy."

"Yeah, but we gotta find out what's in there, don't we?" Horatio panted. "If we go back with nothin', the boss'll skin us alive!"

"If we stay here, we're gonna end up worse than that... look out!"

The whip came cracking down, and they dived in opposite directions. Horatio realized that the entrance to the main cavern was just a short dash away.

"Keep this grotty plonker busy, will ya?" he said to Felix, "and go find our third. I'm goin' in!"

Before his companion could object, he made a mad rush for that entrance; well, one that involved a few detours into the darkness, just to be on the safe side. But sure enough, his crazy plan worked, and he found himself slipping into the much larger cave.

He hid behind a small rock and surveyed the scene. A black obelisk stood in the middle of the cavern with what looked like a small glowing object stuck into it. And in the distance... was that a human woman bound up? A few shadowy robed figures milled about, their mechanized movements perhaps performing some kind of ritualistic folly, but the worst thing of all sat on an enormous pile of rocks, like a makeshift throne. Said figure was large, and Horatio could see its features well enough. It wore a tattered robe, and its hood was drawn back. Horatio's eyes widened and then he squinted to try to get a better look; he immediately wished he hadn't.

"Oh no," he whispered, shaking his head. "Oh, bollocks. Oh, crap. Oh, dammit. Oh, sod this!"

CHAPTER EIGHTEEN

"So, what are you lookin' for?" Qwykk asked as she wandered about Granny's abode.

"I'm trying to find some useful spells in these books, but they're all too complicated, or have too many ingredients." Jilly hastily thumbed through a stack of books in frustration.

"It's a bit like cooking, ain't it?" Qwykk asked. "Like a recipe, where you have to have all the parts just so, or it won't turn out right."

"Kind of, yeah. Sometimes, you can wing it a little, but usually, if you're not prepared, it either won't work, or it can really backfire."

"I tried baking a cake once," Qwykk said. "I just thought it'd be a bit of a laugh, you know? But I confused baking powder with gun powder. I thought it was 'gum powder' and would make it all nice and chewy."

Jilly didn't want to know how she came up with that idea. "So, what happened?" she asked instead.

"Well, it blew up the bloody oven, didn't it? Tossed bits of batter everywhere."

"I wouldn't think an oven would get hot enough to set it off," Jilly objected.

"Yeah, well, turns out this was goblin gun powder, right? It don't take much to set it off. And set it off, I did. Caused a whole lot of damage to the place we were holidayin' at."

"Well, lucky for me, none of my spells need an oven," Jilly said and shook her head.

"That's good! Wouldn't fancy havin' to drag one out to wherever we're goin' tomorrow night."

Jilly was busy scribbling instructions in her spell book, but understood Qwyrk's exasperation with her sweet, if dim-witted friend.

"How much longer you gonna be, then?" Qwykk asked, wandering back into the room where Jilly sat. "I feel like we shouldn't stay here for too long. Intuition, or whatever. I'm not as clever as Qwyrk, but I get sensations sometimes."

Jill stopped writing and looked up. "What are you sensing right now?"

"It feels like something might be outside, or like, it's about to be outside once it knows we're here."

"Good enough for me," Jilly said, closing Granny's book and her own. "Let's get on back."

"Do you want to stop across the way and get some clean clothes?"

"Oh, can we? I'd love that! Can you get me in?"

"I think so," she wandered over to the window. "Just point out where in the house you want to go."

"Well, my bedroom faces the back," Jilly said. "But if you could put us on the roof, we'd be right on top of it. Then we could just pop right down."

"I can do that," Qwykk smiled.

A minute later, and Jilly found herself out in the cold and the dark, and sure enough, standing on her roof. She crouched down at once, lest some neighbor see her up there and have a veritable fit.

"It's right down there." Jilly pointed.

Qwykk made a small circle with her hand, and they popped into her bedroom.

"Oh, thank goodness! Just being back in my room makes me feel so much better." She sighed. "I wish I could stay here tonight."

"Don't think that'd be a good idea," Qwykk said. "That feeling? It's gettin' stronger, so maybe hurry it up?"

Jilly grabbed some extra clothes, but her attention was drawn to an old book on her desk. She stopped and placed her hand on it.

"What is it?" Qwykk asked, looking over her head.

"Oh, it's just something Blip wanted me to read and study, back when—" The hurt flooded into her and she forced back tears.

"Sorry, love," Qwykk put a hand on her shoulder. "But we really should go."

"I don't think you should be going anywhere," a stern and formal voice sounded behind them.

Jilly whipped around to see Blip standing in the corner, fists on hips, glowering at her. "I knew you'd come back here at some point," he said. "Now then, shall we conclude what we began earlier?"

*　　*　　*

"I should very much like to conclude this suicide mission as soon as possible!" Felix shouted, diving out of the Fachan's way for the umpteenth time, "preferably without the bloody suicide!"

Horatio nodded as he dodged the deadly whip again. "You and me both, mate. And no worries, I've seen everything I need to see in there. And it's a flippin' nightmare, believe you me! Get on over here, and I'll have us out in a flash. Where's our third?"

"Don't know. He made a dive for the darker parts over there, but I haven't seen him since before you went into the big cave. I reckon he's hiding out."

"Crap! We gotta find him," Horatio said. "'No Nasty left behind' and all that."

The deadly whip swung around again and barely missed them both, its crack echoing off the walls. If the bigwig in the other cavern knew what was going on over here, he didn't seem to care.

"Well, none of us is gettin' out of here if that thing hits us!" Felix hissed.

"Now that I know the layout," Horatio said, "I can shoot us over to that side, pick up our colleague, and have us all out of here in a jiff."

"Brilliant! How 'bout doin' that right now? Now is good. Nower than now would be better. And better is usually better than good, actually."

Horatio glanced to where they needed to go, too far to run without getting stung to death by their enemy's awful weapon. "Hold on!" Horatio grabbed his companion's arm and catapulted them to the other side of the entrance cave in a trail of musty clouds. They materialized in a dark corner behind a cluster of stalagmites. Felix dashed off right away in search of their companion.

"Right!" Horatio whispered. "Arbunkle? Where are you? We got what we came for, and we've gotta get out of here, now. Come on, mate, we're not playin' around."

"Horatio." Felix's voice was solemn.

Horatio clamored over the rocky obstacles and joined his comrade in the midst of the stone floor spikes. His heart sank at what he saw.

"He didn't make it," Felix said.

Horatio gazed down at Arbunkle's lifeless form. "Crap! I'm so sorry, mate. This war ain't even started yet, and we're already losing good folks. We need to get the hell out of here, now!"

"Yeah, but we're takin' him with us, right? I ain't leavin' him down here!"

"Yeah, mate. We're takin' him, come on."

As the fiendish creature hopped toward them, intent on finishing the job, Horatio whisked them away to safety, but it was a safety he knew was only temporary.

*　　*　　*

"I have nothing to say to you!" Jilly growled at Blip. "Get out of my room. Get out of my house, now!"

"And do you think just giving me orders is going to work?"

"Oh, I have more than orders. Want me to start lobbing spells at you? I may not have Granny's control, but that's actually a good thing. Even if something goes totally wrong, it's probably going to go badly for you, not me."

"I'd listen to her, if I was you," Qwykk chimed in. "She's a regular prestidi-, presidigi-, presidentialdigital... she's a real wizard!"

"I've no doubt. I've seen her progress over these many months and learned what she can and can't do. It's been quite useful, really."

"Spying, then," Jilly glared.

"Gathering intelligence," he corrected with a smugness that angered her even more.

"That's... literally the same thing. And what's to stop us from just zipping away from here, eh?" Jilly asked with a little more haughtiness, knowing that Qwykk could get them out of there in a literal flash.

"Well," Blip paused, and seemed to be thinking. "There is the matter of your parents, who are not home yet, I presume?"

"You... you wouldn't."

"Kill them? Of course not. But they might make useful hostages, and once taken, their fate would be out of my hands. Do you really want to risk that?"

"You bastard!" Jilly sneered.

"All is fair in love and war, child."

"Yeah, and it goes against everything you've tried to teach me in all that bloody philosophy of yours."

"Well, if I recall, you either ignored me or were bored senseless for a good portion of it all, so you might not be the best one to lecture me on consistency of words and actions, which is a whole discipline in and of itself."

"So, what do you want?"

"For you to come with me, of course."

"Why? So you can deliver me right up to Balor? So he can shoot a death ray from his bloody eye, or whatever he does? 'Hail the Deathly Eye' and all that?"

Blip glowered. "How do you know of that phrase?"

"Oh, you mean when I saw you with all those other robed creeps last night, praising your god-king like something out of a bad Mazes and Monstrosities game?"

"So, it *was* you! Thank you for confirming my suspicions."

Crap! "Yeah, well, the secret's out, traitor, so maybe you should just come clean and admit what you've been up to, eh?"

"Don't waste your time on him, Jilly," Qwykk spoke up. "A tosser like him ain't worth gettin' upset over."

"Oh, the Shadow has spoken," Blip's tone turned mocking. "Qwyrk's not about, then? This one's all you have now? I must say, your standards have slipped quite a lot. At least Qwyrk has some good ideas and a modicum of intelligence."

"Ooh, you just watch it, frog face!" Qwykk clenched her fists.

"Oh! I am beside myself with trepidation!" Blip placed the back of one froggy hand over his forehead. "What, pray tell, are you intending to do, to make me 'watch it,' as it were?"

"This!" Qwykk rushed at him, grabbed him by the arm, and vanished a puff of pink light.

"Um," Jilly said, looking around. "Hello? What just happened?"

Her question was answered when Qwykk reappeared with a broad smile on her face, her hair messed up just a little.

"What did you just do? Where did you go?"

"I just took him on a little trip over to the river and dropped him into it from a considerable height. You shoulda seen the look on his face. His yell was a right laugh, too!"

"Thanks, really, but won't he just come right back here in a couple of minutes, madder than ever?"

"Yeah, but we won't be here. Come on!"

"But what about my mum and dad? You heard what he said!"

"He was bluffin'."

"How do you know?"

"The tone of his voice. Look, I may not be as sharp as Qwyrk, but I've been on enough bad dates to know when someone's lyin', and he wasn't even close to tellin' the truth. He ain't gonna hurt them or take them away, 'cause he knows Qwyrk would hunt him down to the ends of this Earth and a few other worlds if anything happened to them."

"But we haven't heard from her in hours. What if she's gone? What if—"

"She ain't love. I know it in my bones. But if it'll make you feel better..." She strode over to one of the bedroom walls and put both hands on it.

"What're you doing?"

"Just a bit of insurance that Mr. Blip don't get no bad ideas." A streak of white light shot from her hands and passed into the wall.

"What was that?"

"Somethin' I learned a good while back. I just stored a little energy in the house. If Blip or any other magic creature tries to get in here, they'll get thrown like a quarter of a mile away and knocked on their arses. It can't affect humans, so don't worry about that, and it'll go away by itself tomorrow."

"That's brilliant? Can all Shadows do that?"

"Nah, it's a thing I learned ages ago. But I like to keep it secret, so don't tell no one, yeah?"

"I won't. But what if Qwyrk comes back here later, looking for me?"

"Um, she'll get an unhappy surprise?"

Jilly sighed. "I guess it's a risk we'll have to take. Let's get out of here before Blip comes back. I mean, I'd kind of love to see him get blasted through the air, but we really should go."

She gathered up her clothes, supplies, and books. Qwykk did her magic, and in a twinkling of pink light and the scent of rosé wine, they were gone.

* * *

"I'm sorry mate." Qwyrk sat with Horatio watching the starry night sky under the Moors.

Horatio sat slumped over, gazing at the ground. "Cheers, love. That was a hard loss, it must be said."

"And to another Fachan, too, damn it! But if it's any consolation, now we know for sure it's Balor, and—"

"And we're well and truly farked, I know. Coulda told you that beforehand."

"But we know he has an actual form, that he's already here, and where he is. And he doesn't know that we know."

"But we weren't exactly super spies, were we? Ol' one-armed bandit there has probably already told his boss everything."

"Doesn't mean they know who you are, or where you are."

"I suppose." He threw a small rock into the darkness, his face a mess of frustration and hurt. Qwyrk patted his tiny back.

"Where's your girl, eh?" he added to change the subject.

"Oh, she turned in already. She's exhausted after her misadventure last night. Boggie saw to it that we have a nice magic tent, one that's way warmer on the inside. She figured she'd be more use to everyone well-rested."

"You should take heed of that yourself. Do a bit of that Reverie thing, or whatever."

"Yeah, I'm going to go and sit with her, maybe try it for a bit."

"And then? What's the plan?"

"I'm working on it."

"Do I want to know?"

"Not really. Honestly, *I* don't even want to know."

"What the hell's that supposed to mean?"

"Nothing," she sighed and shook her head. "Still putting it all together in my head."

She sat in silence with her little companion, turning over everything she'd learned so far, and beginning to accept what she was going to have to do if there was to be any chance of stopping this bloody horror.

* * *

Jilly opened her eyes to the quiet of dawn. She was curled up on the sofa, a blanket wrapped around her. She saw Qwykk sitting cross-legged on the floor nearby, her eyes closed, as if meditating. Reverie always seemed strange: not sleep, but not just resting.

She looked out the living room windows, covered in moisture from a frosty morning. She thought about everything: how they'd gotten to this point, how even her own home wasn't safe. Her mind turned back to her parents, and she hoped against the odds that Qwykk was right about Blip. She also thought of Moirin and wondered what had happened to her. Was she safe? Was she even alive?

She sensed a change in the air, the one that always accompanied a Shadow's arrival.

"Qwyrk?" She sat up as she saw lights begin to form mid-air.

In a flash of blue and pink, Qwypp, Qwyzz, and Star Tao emerged.

"Oh," Jilly said. "It's just you."

"Lovely to see you, too, dear," Qwypp quipped. "Good morning, and all that."

"Sorry, I was just hoping Qwyrk might be back."

"No sign of her, then?" Qwypp asked.

Jilly shook her head.

"That *is* odd," Qwyzz said, with a stroke of his bearded chin.

"She and Holly have been gone since yesterday afternoon," Jilly said.

"They came to see me, before embarking to seek out Fayette," he answered.

"So, they really did it?" Jilly asked, more to herself.

"Indeed."

"What if something went wrong, what if they're hurt, or captured, or—"

"Fayette is not that kind of being." Qwyzz tried to reassure her. "She is an ancient creature who does not take sides, not even in a simmering conflict like the one we face. She is a voice for fate, for Wyrd, nothing more, nothing less. Qwyrk and Young Vishala are quite safe in that sense. I worry more about what she may have told them to do."

"Like, sent them off on some wild goose chase, you mean?" Jilly feared for how little time remained.

"Well, her words are said to be very cryptic, so who knows what they're getting up to?"

"None of which helps us in the here-and-now," Qwypp interjected. "Sorry, I don't mean to sound cold, but we can't wait around for them.

We have to make a plan for tonight, whether they come back or not."

"This is true, I'm afraid." Qwyzz nodded his head. "I brought some extra spell books, Miss Pleeth. They might be useful." He pulled two tomes from his satchel. And then two more. And three extras. Plus, two scrolls. And a map. Oh, and another book and a pamphlet. And one more scroll.

Jilly looked at him, rather astonished. "How did all that fit in there?"

"It's a multidimensional carrier, of course! Very useful when you have an armful of things to bring with you."

"Brilliant. Hey, Star Tao!" Jilly turned to him, feeling bad for ignoring him. "How are you doing?"

He stared at the floor before turning his attention to her. "Been better, I must say, but I have to face facts. I think I've been betrayed."

Jilly frowned. "We all have, but we have to stick together. Blip tried to confront me last night, but Qwykk was brilliant. Stood up to him and got us out of my bedroom after dropping him in the Nidd."

"Aw, it wasn't much really." Qwykk blushed, emerging from Reverie with a yawn and a stretch.

"You dropped him in the river?" Qwypp grinned. "Bloody hell, I wish I'd seen that!"

"You and me both!" Jilly smiled.

"Apparently," Carl said as he lumbered downstairs, "my home has become the secret headquarters for the resistance. Which is bloody brilliant, but seeing as it's possibly the last day of the world, I'd've loved to sleep in for a bit."

"No time, I'm afraid, dear fellow," Qwyzz said with a nod. "We must set to planning for tonight, if we're to have any chance of countering Balor and his forces. We still don't know quite what we'll be up against. And finding the location of the barrier breach to this world is of primary importance."

"Are there any other Shadows you can call?" Jilly asked.

"I'm reluctant to reach out to anyone else at the moment," Qwyzz said. "We simply don't know who has been compromised, I'm afraid. Of course, I'd much rather we had a sizable army on our side, but we daren't take the risk. We'll have to trust that Qwyrk's efforts bear fruit and do what we can."

"Still nothing from mum," Lluck said as he dragged himself downstairs, wearing a t-shirt and sweatpants, his hair a bit of a mess. "I tried twice, and it's empty, not even static. It's so weird. Oh hey!" He looked at Qwykk and started smoothing down his hair. "Good morning! All right?"

"Hey, sport!" Qwykk smiled and winked.

Jilly scrunched up her face.

"I can't find Qwyrk, either," Qwypp added. "Maybe they've both gone undercover. Maybe they can't let anyone know what they're doing right now? Kind of for the same reason we're all laying low?"

"I hope so," Jilly said, forcing her attention back to more pressing matters, though she was finding it ever more difficult to hold on to that hope.

*　　*　　*

The day passed alternately too slow and too fast, depending on one's perspective and hopes and fears. Jilly and Qwyzz pored over arcane manuscripts, looking for offensive and defensive spells that could be rattled off with few ingredients. After all, they had no time to mix dragon's blood incense with henbane and black sea salt in the heat of battle. Lluck and Carl went out to the garden to train. Qwykk offered to go help them, but Jilly manufactured an excuse for keeping her in the sitting room, to turn pages as they read, and act as a living bookmark. Astonishingly, it worked. Qwypp and Star Tao went off somewhere, and Jilly didn't ask. If it was to have and end-of-the-world shag, she didn't begrudge them that at all.

In early afternoon, everyone reconvened in the sitting room for snacks and further discussion.

"So, what have you found out?" Carl asked, munching on a biscuit as he poured tea for everyone who wanted it.

"My best guess is that the ritual for summoning the Fomorians will take place in a remote forested area in Nidderdale," Qwyzz said.

"That doesn't narrow it down much, does it?" Lluck asked.

"Quite right, my boy, but such a calamitous congregation of elder magics will most definitely ripple through the whole enchanted fabric, rather like shockwaves from an earthquake—oh, I would love to experience one of those, sometime! What exhilaration! What—"

"Um, Qwyzz?" Jilly interrupted.

"Oh yes, terribly sorry! The point is that, as these creatures begin to manifest, they'll leave an obvious trace. I very much doubt that they'll be making any real efforts to conceal themselves at that point, in any case. Finding their exact location then will be child's play."

"So, we just have to wait for the first of those bastards to come through, and then we can pinpoint where the whole thing is happening?" Qwypp asked.

"Precisely!"

"Doesn't sound like the best plan," Carl offered, "doesn't give us any chance to get the lay of the land. We'll just have to hide and watch."

"Not many other options, it seems," Jilly said. "We're doing our best."

"When will the first of those buggers start showing up?" Star Tao asked, and Jilly could hear the nervousness in his voice.

"Sometime after sunset, I should think," Qwyzz answered. "They'll draw more strength from the moon than the sun. Fomorians prefer the dark."

"Does that mean if we can stall them till daylight, we have a better chance?" Carl asked. Jilly appreciated that he was trying hard to find advantages.

"I'm afraid not," Qwyzz shook his head. "They're not vampires, after all."

"Wait," Carl said, "are vampires a real thing, too?"

"Well, there may be a handful in the world," Qwyzz said, "but they're nothing to be concerned about. Oh, and the whole business about garlic is nonsense. Why, once I—"

"Qwyzz?" Jilly interrupted again.

"Sorry! At this point, I would advise you all to get some rest, even relax a little, if possible. Yes, I know, that's not easy. But we'll all be better off if we've taken a bit of quiet time for ourselves."

"Good suggestion." Jilly tried to sound positive, even if she didn't feel it.

"I'm heading upstairs for a nap," Carl said.

"Not a bad idea, really," Lluck said. He glanced over at Qwykk as he said it, and Jilly gritted her teeth.

"I'm gonna do some more Reverie," Qwykk said. "All that page-turning was sort of exhausting."

"Reverie is an excellent idea, my dear," Qwyzz said. "In fact, I intend to indulge in a bit, myself. Shall we sit together?"

"That'd be lovely, yeah!" Qwykk was all smiles.

Lluck looked a bit deflated, and Jilly felt a bit better.

* * *

"Can we talk? Like really talk?" Qwypp sat down next to Star Tao on the patio of the garden.

"Yeah, of course." He shrugged, without looking at her.

"Look, love, I know you've had a rough time of it," she started, "but you heard what Qwyzz said. When Aeval possessed you, that was bad, yeah, but it wasn't the end of the world. All right, bad choice of words, but you know what I mean. It's like riding a horse or a bicycle. You fall off, you have to get back on, and right now, you've fallen off and don't want to get back in the saddle, bike seat, whatever. But you know what? You're gonna have to try tonight. I have a strong feeling that we're gonna need you and whoever you can connect with."

"But there are gonna be piles of them Fomorian freaks," he protested. "What if Aeval's there? Or what of some other banshee gets a hold of me?"

"What if they don't? What if Jilly needs your help at some point? What if a bloody meteor hits? That's the whole thing, isn't it? We don't know. Not yet. And the only way we're gonna know is when we're there. It's all right and good to talk about facing our fears, but when the moment comes, we still have to do it. What kind of teachers are we if we don't live by our own words?"

"Don't know if I'm much of a teacher at all, to be honest."

"That's not true! I've seen you wow a room full of seekers. You've got the gift. Qwyzz believes in you, and so do I. You just have to believe in yourself, clichéd as it sounds."

Star Tao sighed and looked away.

"Try? For me?" She laid her head on his shoulder.

"Yeah, all right. I mean, it *is* the end, isn't it? May as well give it a final go. See what's out there. Maybe we'll even live to tell the tale?"

"That's my lad!"

*   *   *

Jilly read through her books and tried to concentrate, but as the afternoon wore on and the shadows grew long, it became impossible. It would be dark soon, the jack-o'-lanterns would be lit, and the streets would be filled with little ghosts and goblins seeking treats. Parties of adults—some in appalling costumes—would be getting underway, and none of them would realize the true danger brewing just north of here, one that might alter the world forever.

She looked over at Qwykk and Qwyzz, so peaceful in their Reverie, as if none of this was happening. She envied them. This was all way more than an almost-thirteen-year-old should have to bear. It wasn't the first time she'd thought that.

As the dark crept in, so did the companions, one by one. Qwyzz awoke from his Reverie and stood up with amazing agility. Qwykk opened her eyes at almost the same time, and he offered her a hand up.

Carl came downstairs next, in full costume. Only, it wasn't the disaster of an outfit she remembered from last December. This one looked cooler, fitted well, had protective padding, and dazzled with dark greens and deep purples.

"You look kind of amazing!" Jilly exclaimed.

"Thanks," he said, beaming. "Lluck helped me with the redesign. Much stronger and more durable. Quite the upgrade."

A minute or two later, everyone had returned. Jilly looked

around at them, this odd group of misfits and strange folk who each, in their own way, just wanted to do some good, wanted to help, to make things a little better. Even if two of its most prized members were still missing, she was proud to call them friends.

"I'm glad we're all here," she said with a smile.

"I am, too," Star Tao said with a little more of his old confidence back, which warmed her.

"You lot are pretty special," Qwypp said as she held his arm. "I don't know where Qwyrk is right now, or what all's going to happen, but I'm glad to be here with you, come what may."

"Yeah, so am I!" Qwykk said as she sidled up to Qwypp, and put her arm around her. "You're all brilliant."

Lluck stayed silent, but he nodded at Jilly, and that was enough. She knew he must be worried, with still no word from his mum.

"So this is it," Carl said. "We've assembled. This is our time."

"Indeed," Qwyzz nodded. "The sun will be setting soon, my friends." He spoke with a solemnity in his voice that Jilly had never heard from him before. He was far from the jovial wine-making wizard she'd grown fond of. "I'm afraid it's time to go."

CHAPTER NINETEEN

In a subdued flash, Jilly found herself in a tangle of forest. Qwypp brought her and Star Tao here so they could scout the area, based on some unusual magic ripples Qwyzz had detected.

"Looks quiet enough," Qwypp whispered.

"Yeah, but there could be anyone, anything out there in the dark," Jilly whispered back. "We need to make sure."

She crouched down and held her open palms a few inches apart from each.

"What are you doing?" Qwypp knelt next to her on one side, Star Tao on the other.

"Is it sort of a magic radar?" Star Tao asked.

"Kind of," Jilly answered. "It's something I realized I needed to learn after our last couple of adventures. If there are any Darkfae or other bad things nearby, the space between my hands will glow yellow. And if not, it'll glow green."

"It's like some enchanted pregnancy test, ain't it?" Star Tao mused. Jilly didn't know how to respond to that and thought it best to say nothing.

"How long's it take?" Qwypp asked.

"Should be right about... now!"

They breathed a collective sigh of relief as a warm, green glow lit up her hands for a moment.

"And you're sure this is accurate, yeah?" Qwypp asked, standing up again.

"Oh, yeah. I mean, I think it is."

"That's not very reassuring, love."

"Look, we'll be fine. Whatever shows up will probably be in that clearing, way over there," Jilly pointed to where the trees parted. "We'll be all right hiding out here, I reckon."

"Unless they decide to send some flunkies out to have a look and make sure that no one, like say, their enemies, are about and planning something," Qwypp said, with more than a little skepticism.

"Go back and tell everyone else to come on over," Jilly said with a confidence she didn't really feel. "It'll be better when we're all here."

"You two'll be all right, then?" Qwypp gestured at them.

"Yes, I'm sure we can manage for thirty whole seconds while you round up the rest of the gang."

"You've gotten way more snark about you since we hung out, just so you know." Qwypp rolled her eyes and transported herself away.

"Hey, I've earned it," Jilly called after her. "How are you holding up?" she asked Star Tao, putting a hand on his shoulder.

"Been better, been worse." He shrugged.

"Well, I think you can do it, honestly. You just have to trust yourself, get out of your own way."

"Yeah, there's nothing to lose tonight, really, which oddly enough, makes it a little easier."

"That's the spirit!" Jilly smiled and patted him on the back.

Soon, Qwypp, Qwykk, Lluck, Carl, and Qwyzz blinked into the woodland. It wasn't going to be enough, but it was something.

I just wish I knew where Qwyrk and Holly were, if they're even still...

She shoved away that awful thought as far as it could go, steeled herself for the task to come, and went to meet the others.

"All's good here," she said, "but let's try to keep our voices down, just in case." She looked at Qwyzz. "The clearing's over that way. You can just make it out over there, where that glow is."

Qwyzz nodded. "We'll need to get a closer look, much as I'd rather not."

"Is anyone else coming?" Jilly asked, almost pleading. "Anyone at all?"

"I have discretely put out the word, and I think there will be a few," Qwyzz said. "But it's hard to know who to trust. I have sent notice to Simon and the Templars, and I've no doubt some of them will be here, but I hate the thought of asking such fine knights to sacrifice themselves."

"It's what they've trained for, though, isn't it?" Jilly said. "And if not now, when?"

"Quite right, my dear," Qwyzz said solemnly.

"So, are we gonna get a better look at what's going on?" Lluck said. "If I'm gonna snuff it tonight, I'd at least like to see it coming."

"You're quite eloquent, you know?" Jilly shook her head, while doing her best to position herself between him and Qwykk. "And yes, we should. I'm going, want to come with me?"

"Do I have a choice?"

"Of course, but not really."

"All right, then. She should come with us, too." He pointed at Qwykk.

"Why?" Jilly tensed and frowned.

"Um, because? If something happens, she can get us out of there in a hurry? I thought you were good at tactics and all that."

"Yeah, you two go on just a bit ahead, and I'll be right behind," Qwykk said.

"Fine," Jilly sighed. "Let's go see how bad it really is."

*　　*　　*

A far-too-short walk later, and they found themselves crouched down behind a fallen tree, long since returned to the forest floor. Near the clearing was a mess of twists and turns, rocks and outcrops to one side, a hill sloping up to a ridge on the other, and opposite, more forest stretching into the dark. A white and eerie fire burned from atop one outcropping; it made no sound and gave off no smoke. Several dark-robed figures stood nearby, but they were as silent as the magical flames that illuminated them.

"What're we looking for, exactly?' Qwykk asked.

"Shhh!" Jilly held up her hand. "Hang on... there."

She motioned to where an old woman was hobbling toward the fire, hunched and small, but somehow imposing. She clutched a walking stick, and streaks of white lined her caliginous, tangled hair.

She had dark circles under her eyes and a countenance of guile, of scheming, of self-satisfied evil. Jilly knew immediately who she was.

"That's Aeval!" she whispered. "She's the one who's controlling Moirin, the singer we saw at Leeds Uni."

"That definitely doesn't seem good," Lluck said.

"She's a banshee, right?" Qwykk whispered.

"You know about her?" Jilly was rather struck by surprise.

"Hey! Just 'cause I ain't as smart as Qwyrk doesn't mean I don't know some stuff!"

"Yeah, right. Sorry."

"But I always wondered, if there are ban*shees*, are there ban*hees*, too?"

Jilly gave her a blank stare and turned back to the clearing. She squinted and strained to see more.

"What are you doing?" Lluck whispered.

"I'm just, I don't... wait."

A taller figure in a grey robe, a woman, emerged from the forest. As she approached Aeval, she knelt and pulled back her hood, revealing a thick and long mane of curly red hair.

"Damn it!" Jilly swore. "It's Aileen, the girl at the club who knocked Qwyrk on her arse and beat up Holly."

"Crap, she's tough, then," Lluck said.

"Yeah, but at least it doesn't look like... oh. Oh, no. No!"

Another robed woman, this time wearing a darker robe, entered the clearing from a different direction. She also knelt before Aeval and then drew back her hood as she stood up. Her long black hair fell around her, a singular streak of green on the right-hand side. She joined hands with Aeval and Aileen and they opened their mouths to let out a low hum that somehow seemed to be vibrating the very fabric of reality.

As Jilly watched in horror, the eyes of all three women faded to white, and white streaks began to line the hair of Aeval's descendants.

"This is it!" Jilly managed to say in a trembling voice. "They're calling him and the others. It's starting. Oh, Moirin, no, no!"

*   *   *

All manner of strange beings began to manifest into this world, fading in at various places in the clearing. Large and small Fomorians, oddly-shaped creatures and perfectly-formed ones, some beautiful, some horrific: all of them gathered in the presence of the magical fire atop the rock, awaiting the arrival of their master. They regarded one another with admiration and spoke words in a tongue so ancient it had not been heard in this world for thousands of years. Some laughed, slapped one another on the back, and made grandiose gestures. At the same time, the banshees' chant increased in its intensity, though they uttered not a single word, merely a continuous tone that started to irritate Jilly's ears, like a persistent insect.

"Some of them look like the Erlking's goons," Lluck said, "but those others, they're like faeries or gods. Those are Fomorians, right? What are they?"

"They ruled Ireland in ancient times," Jilly whispered. "They were tyrants, cruel and awful, but they were overthrown, banished."

"Yeah, I know all that, but I mean, what *are* they?"

"Ancient magical creatures. Some of the first, I'd guess. They're kind of a mix of all sorts, every kind of being, but they serve the strongest one, Balor, and he'll be showing up soon. Especially if the three of them keep up with that bloody humming."

"It's a sodding nuisance, isn't it?"

"And that's really bad, right? The whole thing with Balor showin' up?" Qwykk asked.

"It's the worst thing that could happen."

Jilly saw genuine fear in Qwykk's expression. "I wish Qwyrk was here," Qwykk said. "No offense."

"No, I'm right there with you."

"Nothing from her at all, eh?" Lluck asked.

Jilly shook her head. "Not a word. Still nothing from your mum, then?"

Lluck shook his head. "What if they're—"

"Don't say it. Just don't!" Jilly was in no mood to hear what she feared most.

Without a word, Qwykk put a hand on Jilly's shoulder and motioned to Lluck with her head. Then she smiled and backed away into the trees, where presumably she could still see them.

Jilly smiled back at her in a way that said, "Thank you."

"So," Jilly said to him, keeping one eye on the gathering of the ultimate Unseelies.

"Yeah, this is bollocks," he answered. "All of it. I think I was better off not knowing about any of this."

"That's not true." She shot him a look. "You found your dad, your mum, you have a home and a family now. Would you really give all that up just to sleep one more night peacefully, which might be the last night anyone does, by the way?"

"Fair enough. I suppose not."

"Too right. Look, I don't like this any more than you do, but we have gifts, abilities, and we have to use them. I don't know where Qwyrk and Holly are, or if they'll be here tonight, but even if they show up and kick everyone's arses and figure out a way to send all of these creeps away, we still have to do something. It's like that strange woman who's in your mum's head, who they went to see. She's all about fate. 'Wyrd' I think it's called."

"Weird?"

"No, W-Y-R-D. It's an old word meaning something like fate or destiny. I don't know if we have that—a destiny, I mean—but I want to believe that something's brought us together, something put us in this place tonight, you, me, here."

"It might've. I'd honestly believe anything about now."

"If fate's a thing, and here we are, you and me, maybe that's a good thing, yeah? I mean, I think you're kind of brilliant and all, so maybe, I mean, if we make it through the night, we could, you know, hang out again?" Her heart pounded and her mouth went dry. "But like, sort of... you know, kind of like a... date, sort of thing? Kind of? But not really. Sort of? Maybe?"

To her immense relief, he gave her smile and a nod. "Yeah, that'd be all right."

"Oh! Um, fine! Fantastic! Well, we'll talk about it later, assuming we're not ripped to shreds in the next hour or two."

"That'd be a pisser, wouldn't it?"

"Not how I want to spend the evening, honestly."

"Oh, and by the way," Lluck leaned in just a little. "Qwykk? She's fit and all that, but she's a bit thick, isn't she?"

Jilly gave him a slight slug on the shoulder. "Be nice! She's actually brilliant." But inside, she was doing a little happy dance.

"Uh, that doesn't look good," Lluck gestured, before turning around to motion Qwykk to come back to them. She jogged up with surprising silence (considering she was wearing combat boots with heels) and crouched down with them.

"What is it?" she whispered.

"We have to get back to the others," Jilly answered. "I think Balor's almost here!"

*   *   *

"We must take a closer look," Qwyzz declared, hearing the news of their enemy's immanent arrival, "and gain a sense of just what we're facing. We have three Shadows, so we need to spread out to different parts of this side of the woods and try to obtain a view of this spectacle from different vantage points. The more we can see, the better. I suggest that I take Jilly. Qwypp, you take Star Tao, and Qwykk, you take Lluck and Carl. Find places close enough to the edge of the woods, but still safely within them. We three can teleport easily enough, now that we've seen our surroundings. But do take all care that you are not seen."

"What if they've posted guards out there?" Carl asked. "Or what if they've sent some of them to patrol in these woods? It's what I'd do, to be honest. Last thing I'd want is a super team of heroes marching in and mucking things up. I doubt they've just left the whole place undefended."

"A good point." Qwyzz said with a nod, embarrassed to admit he hadn't thought of that.

"Also, what if the Fomorians can sense magic?" Jilly asked. "Like, when you teleport?"

"Another sound point," Qwyzz conceded, "but I'm afraid we

don't have the luxury of waiting and strategizing, or avoiding and hiding. Help may or may not be on the way, but until it comes, we have to acquire as much knowledge as possible. That will entail some risk. Keep an eye on your surroundings, but try to gather as much information as you can. Let's reconvene here in a quarter of an hour."

Everyone begrudgingly agreed that there was no other choice. Qwyzz didn't know what he would have done if there'd been too many objections, or any objections at all. He berated himself for not being a better planner, and he wished Qwyrk were here, as he knew they all did.

* * *

"This is right bad," Lluck whispered.

"What have we gotten ourselves into?" Carl muttered as they watched all manner of strange creatures gather around the smokeless fire.

"Being a hero means not shying away from threats, no matter what the odds," Lluck answered. "That's what you keep telling me."

"Yeah, for the record, that sounds a lot better on paper that it does in real life."

"Lots of things do."

"What're we supposed to do, then?" Qwykk whispered. "We ain't got the power to stop them, to do much of anything. Without Qwyrk, and maybe a whole lotta other Shadows, we're pretty much done for."

"We're just spying right now, so we can strategize with the others," Carl explained, though he didn't sound too confident.

"Like, trying to look for weaknesses and places to strike," Lluck said.

"I dunno," Qwykk said. "I'd still feel a lot better if Qwyrk was here, and her girl, too." She looked at Lluck. "Oh, sorry, love. I know you're worried about her, and all. But I've got a feelin' she's just fine."

"You can't know that," Lluck answered, a little annoyed.

"Well, not like, for sure, but I got a good intuition, yeah? And I'm usually right about these kinds of things. I'm not all that thick, thank you." She glared at him.

"How, how did?"

"Shadows have really good hearing, so I heard everything you said before, even though I wasn't tryin' to."

"Crap. I'm sorry." Lluck felt genuinely bad.

"No worries. And yeah, you and Jilly should go on a date. That'd be right sweet."

"Wait, what?" Carl said. "You and Jilly, what?"

"What's happening over there?" Lluck said, eager to change the subject.

"It's starting," Carl said.

*   *   *

Jilly and Qwyzz crouched down to hide themselves. A low rumble shook the ground. The clearing darkened for a moment and then something new appeared, something awful. A black dust storm whipped up in the midst of the gathering creatures, out of which stepped a gigantic figure, fully manifesting in this plane, and Jilly knew the moment had arrived; Balor had returned, at long last. He towered over his minions, a wraith in a hooded and tattered robe, and he held their undivided attention, their unquestioned loyalty. Cowering beneath him, she saw a human woman, bound in rope. She stumbled and fell to the ground at his feet, to the sound of laughter and mocking growls.

"I've no idea who she is," Jilly whispered, "but she wouldn't be here unless it was for some reason. Maybe she knows something? Maybe she has some power or knowledge to stop this?"

"Nothing would surprise me anymore," Qwyzz answered.

"Do you think they mean to sacrifice her?"

"Nothing would surprise me anymore."

As the throng of Fomorians murmured their approvals, Balor raised an arm to encourage their cheers, making a fist with one gnarled hand and waving it in the air in rhythm to their chanting.

"Conceited wanker, isn't he?" Jilly snarked.

He opened his fist and indicated that he wanted the sound to cease. "At last, my friends," he spoke in a voice both deep and scratchy, unearthly and grounded, "the time we have hoped for, have longed for, is at hand. Those who have remained loyal to us have striven to bring about our return, and tonight, they have succeeded. Such loyalty will be rewarded in the new world to come. Those who fight against us, those who resist, will have a far less enviable fate, for none can stop us. The magic of all the worlds cannot harm me, and as long as this form remains on this Earth, so shall all of you!"

His audience cheered and howled, arms and claws thrust into the air, taloned feet and knotty hooves stomping the earth, making general mayhem at the promise of unfettered access to this world and all of its treasures. "Oh dear," Qwyzz whispered. "This doesn't look good at all."

"Is there anything we can do? On our own, I mean?" Jilly asked.

"We have to try, I'm afraid. Shhh, he's speaking again."

"And so, dear companions, the time has come to reveal myself. This mortal form has been an acceptable host to allow me to grow and take shape, and now, I shall show you all my dark grandeur." He turned to the woman in ropes, who cowered nearby. "Observe, little one, see what your mate hath wrought in his ignorance and innocence, for his mortal frame hath brought me again to life! Well has he played his part, so be glad for that. It is because of him that you still live."

His clawed hands reached up and drew back his hood. The Fomorians let out a collective gasp as they beheld his hideous majesty.

Jilly stared in shock. She couldn't process what she was seeing. The skin of his face was a dark grey, almost charcoal, rough, yet featureless, save for two things, two terrible things: a large, fanged mouth, and an eye, one horrid eye, that encompassed almost the entire upper half of his head. The eyelid opened and closed rapidly, as if adjusting to the light of the moon. His bloodshot eye glowed a faint orange, enhancing the redness and making it that much worse.

"This can't be real. This isn't happening!" Jilly mouthed in a quiet voice as she started to tremble. She felt Qwyzz take her hand.

"It's all too real, I'm afraid," he whispered.

The Fomorians roared with delight at the sight of their hideous king reborn, breaking into cacophonous cheers and ancient songs in dead languages that soon began to coalesce into a single sound, a single name: "Balor! Balor!" Aeval, Moirin, and Aileen led the chant, like directors for some unspeakable choir.

"This is it," Jilly said, a horrible sinking feeling spreading through the pit of her stomach. "This is the end. We can't beat this." She turned to look at him. "We can't even fight it."

To her dismay, Qwyzz didn't answer; he just stared at the ancient horror that loomed before them.

"And now, my fair and foul siblings," Balor spoke again. "We will, from this place, this most sacred of places that hath witnessed our rebirth, go forth, across this island, and retake *Inis na bhfiodh-bhadh*, and from there, we will spread out over this whole world and make it our own. And then the other worlds beyond will bow to us, and should they resist, they will know true fear and suffering."

Another cheer greeted his words.

"Before that glorious quest begins," he continued, his single eye darting about the crowd, "I would have those come forward who have seen our return and endeavored to aid us. Come forth, my faithful servants, that all may see you and rejoice and honor you!"

Three robed figures stepped forward from the gathered assortment; the crowd parted to let them approach their master. One, Jilly noted, was considerably shorter than the others.

"No," she whispered, tears forming in her eyes. Even now, she didn't want to believe it was true. She still hoped it was all some appalling bad dream, but as this diminutive figure drew back its hood, she had no choice but to face the reality of who lurked underneath.

"It's him," she whimpered, as Blip's smug face looked around at the creatures and then up in reverence to the one who ruled them all.

*   *   *

From their vantage point, Star Tao and Qwypp watched the scene unfold in all its horror, and as Blip revealed his face from underneath his hood, Star Tao was shook to the core.

"It's the worst betrayal," he said, as he clutched Qwypp's hand.

"I'm so sorry, love." She took hold of his hand. "I didn't want it to be true, believe me. I know this must be devastating for you."

He looked at her, and something stirred inside, a fire that he hadn't felt in a long time, if ever.

"Nah, it's more than that. It's a sign, a signal that I've been denyin' meself for too long. I've been afraid 'cause I let one of those Fomorian spooks get in me head, right? And that's what she wanted all along, wasn't it? Make me doubt what I do, make me scared to do it again. Well, I ain't scared anymore!" He squeezed her hand and turned to stride away from the hideous events in the clearing. "Come on. Let's get well hidden back in the trees. I need your help."

"What are you gonna do?"

"I need you to keep an eye on me and beat the crap out of anyone that gets near. I'm goin' deeper, deeper than I ever have before. I'm gonna do everything I can to reach out across the planes, to connect. I'm gonna find a being out there that can help put a stop to this rubbish, and if I have to clobber Lord Blippingstone in the process, so be it!"

Qwypp smiled as they hurried away into the woods. "That's my lad!"

* * *

Jilly knew that all was lost. A sick, sinking feeling washed over her, not so much in a wave, but more like a tsunami. She reached out to grip Qwyzz's hand as the scene unfolding in front of them only became more horrid with each passing moment. She watched as Blip bowed before this monstrosity, prostrating himself in a way that she never would have thought to see.

"Why?" she whispered, wiping tears away with her free hand.

"You have my sympathies, my dear," Qwyzz said in a gentle voice. "I know full well the sting of betrayal. In fact, I fear that I may yet see the one who betrayed me this very night."

"Qwota? Your wife? But she's still a prisoner, right?"

"Probably not, if traitors are in control, as Qwyrk seems to think they are."

"Where is she? Why isn't she here? What happened to her? And Holly?" Frustration, doubt, and fear clawed at her again.

"Only fate knows, my child, and I mean that in quite the literal sense if they have indeed been in the presence of that strange being."

Fate indeed may well have had a strange sense of timing, for as Jilly asked that very question, she caught sight of two figures emerging from the forest at the other side of the clearing.

"No! Is it? Qwyzz, Look!" she almost screamed.

"Can it... can it be?"

Jilly's heart began to soar, the despair lifted a little, and the hopelessness seemed a bit less hopeless. There, against all odds, strode Qwyrk and Holly, confident and proud, right toward this unspeakable rabble. Jilly noticed something odd. They wore long, dark, form-fitting coats that almost matched, and yet...

"Why is Qwyrk wearing a black bandana on her head? She looks like a pirate! It's kind of cool, to be honest."

"I couldn't tell you, my dear, but it seems that perhaps our hopes are not in vain."

Jilly almost smiled. Maybe everything would be fine, after all.

* * *

Sixteen hours ago:

Qwyrk opened her eyes as she descended from her Reverie before dawn. Holly slept in peace next to her on the makeshift bedroll that Bogtrotter had provided. Qwyrk gazed at her for some time, deciding that she would rather just stay in this moment forever than do what she had to do. But she knew that by waiting much longer, she risked Holly waking up, and she had to be gone before that. She just had to.

Taking care to make no sound, she stood up and threw on her clothes. She smiled sadly as she donned her usual garb, reflecting on how she would likely never have the chance to impress Holly again with the possibility of dressing outside of her usual sartorial choices.

She readied herself to leave but couldn't bear not to gaze upon Holly one more time, maybe for the last time. She crept back in and knelt to where her dearest still slumbered in bliss. She smiled, the twinge of a tear in her eye. Leaning forward, she kissed the air just above Holly's cheek as carefully as she could.

Goodbye, love. It has to be this way, much as I wish it didn't. We had a good run, you and me, even though it was way too short. I know you're the one. It's just a damned shame we didn't have more time. But my life's pretty unfair like that. Take care of yourself, no matter what happens.

Knowing she would start to cry if she stayed any longer, she forced herself to step back, to face the dark and the unknown, leaving behind the only one in all the worlds that she wanted. She turned and crept away, her heart breaking, and left the tent without looking back again.

CHAPTER TWENTY

Now:

"You know," Qwyrk announced as loud as she could yell. "You lot are a damn sight more impressive than some of the flunkies we've had to deal with, I'll give you that. But honestly, that's not saying much. I mean, come on, *look* at you! A bloody stupid mixture of the sublime and the ridiculous, but really, mostly ridiculous. You lot actually ruled Ireland? I'm surprised you didn't get laughed back to your boats, or however you got there. How did you get there, by the way? Actually, never mind, more importantly: why the bloody hell are you here now, in flipping Nidderdale, of all places? Not exactly where I expected the end of the world to begin, I must say. Are you like, all going to go get in boats and sail over to Ireland again? Kind of recreate the whole thing? Hey, this could be kind of like a living history event, couldn't it? Except, you all were there for the first one, too, right? So, it's more like history repeating itself."

She took a few steps toward the ghoulish gathering. "But it's not going to repeat, because we're here to kick your arses and send you back to whatever awful little world you've been forced to scrape away in for the last several thousands of years."

A stunned silence fell over the assorted beasties, who looked at Qwyrk and Holly, shot glances at each other in confusion, and looked back at her and Holly again.

"You've always had a knack for talking far too much, haven't you?" asked one of the tall, robed figures standing next to Blip (and yes, it bloody well was Blip) in a mocking and gravelly tone. He too took a few steps forward.

"Oh, cut the crap with the evil, scary voice, Qwalm!" Qwyrk called out. "You're not impressing anyone but yourself, and—all right—maybe a few of these tossers. I know what an absolute wand you are, and you don't scare either of us. I've already beaten the crap out of you once."

"Qwalm may not frighten you, nor should he," the figure answered. "But our intention is not to frighten." He drew back his hood.

"Qworum," Qwyrk said, a sinking feeling collapsing into her stomach all at once, but she didn't want to show how rattled she was. "And you?" She directed her question to the other figure, while still sounding, she hoped, forceful and fearless.

That figure drew back its own hood.

"Qwyll? Oh, brilliant. So the heart and core of the council has been working against it the whole time. Are you all in on this, then?"

"Just the two of us," Qwyll replied in a cold, uncaring tone. Her face was as icy as her voice.

"So, Qwalm isn't a traitor after all," Qwyrk said, more to herself.

"Wow. Remind me again? You two have been sitting your arses in those chairs for how long?"

"A millennium," Qworum said in his own voice, the need for pretense now over.

"And you've been working toward this night the whole time, I suppose?" Holly asked. Qwyrk was grateful for her interjection as she'd lost the ability to form any kind of coherent sentence, much less a smart-arse clap back.

"Not the entire time, no, but it has long been a goal to restore the ancients to their rightful places as rulers of this world and bring the other worlds under their dominion."

"All of this just to get at the innovators?" Holly pressed.

"Ha!" Qworum mocked. "The innovators are fools, easily manipulated. Their war with the ancients was always going to fail, but getting them stirred up from time to time has served its purposes. They supported De Soulis, you see. It wasn't difficult to convince some to throw their lot in with him."

"Like Qwota," Qwyrk managed to say.

"Like Qwota," he confirmed. "And if he had succeeded at Hermitage, it would have made our task easier, but your victory was acceptable to us, as well. It took them down a peg. In fact, you did our work for us."

"Where's Qwota now?" Qwyrk demanded.

"We've freed her." Qworum said.

"Of course you have."

"She may yet have her uses in the future. It's a shame she's not here at the moment to, as they say, rub your nose in it?"

"And the Erlking?" Holly said.

"The Master of the Wild Hunt has long been a favorite of

the ancients and his dominion would have paved the way for the Fomorians' return that much more easily. But again, you lot foiled that, so we decided that we had to weaken you."

"The ward." Qwyrk felt sick.

"An ancient protection that was already in place," Qworum affirmed. "It does take a good while to settle in, giving the offenders time, decades, to rethink their unwise decisions. But I turned it up a few degrees over the past few days. It's been... amusing."

Qwyrk bristled at his words. "You sent that thing, didn't you? That void, into my home? And then lied about it."

"I did. It seemed the fastest way to separate the two of you, and thus weaken you, both physically and morally. It would have trapped the Yakshi in a dark dimension for a year or so, more than long enough for us to complete our task."

"This 'Yakshi' has a name," Holly said, as she took a step forward, "and you will damned well use it!"

Even now, Qwyrk beamed with pride. She reached out and did something incredible, something she wasn't even sure she'd be able to do again. She took Holly's hand, squeezing it to let her know she was right there, right beside her, till the end.

*   *   *

From the edge of the trees, Jilly and Qwyzz watched and listened to the whole thing. At the mention of his estranged and apparently now-free wife, Qwyzz recoiled in disgust. Jilly made sure not to mention it.

"I knew Qwyrk would come, I knew it! And Holly, too!" Jilly kept her voice down to keep them hidden. "We have to get to them,

Qwyzz! They've done it, somehow. They must have found a way to defeat Balor. And look! They're touching again! They're holding hands! I knew they'd figure out how to break that stupid ward!"

"It's remarkable, indeed," Qwyzz answered, "but something is different. I cannot put my finger on it, but it's there, all the same."

"Different how? It's them, right?"

"As far as I can tell."

"Well, let's just be glad, gather up everyone, and march on out there. I'm sure they've got a plan."

"Yeah, I'd hold off for just a bit, if I were you, love," a voice sounded from behind.

Jilly whipped around, ready to launch something, anything at a Formorian attacker, but instead saw Horatio stroll into view from the dark.

"Horatio? What are you doing here?"

"Well, you know, likely end of the world, and all that. Gotta check out things to see if my betting pool will still be viable at sunrise, or whether we'll all be fleein' for our lives. I'm a bit concerned it will be the latter of those two choices, to be honest. Anyway, I sensed magic all about, but since Ms. Qwyrk and Ms. Holly are out there riskin' their necks, poppin' by to see you seemed like a safer bet."

"Sorry, but what is a Nasty doing here?" Qwyzz looked confused.

"Long story, mate," Horatio said. "Actually, it's a fairly short story. Me and some of me mates discovered the source of the Fomorians' power, in a cavern underground, not far away from here. There's a big slab of stone in the middle of the place, with a small but very shiny, very glowy key stickin' out of it, and I reckon it's what's bringin' these creeps to the party, especially the biggest creep of all." He motioned to where Balor stood.

"Of course." Qwyzz mused, stroking his beard. "The key must have opened the dimensional gate, allowing them to cross over. And as long as it remains in the slab, the way will stay open, ergo, we must shut it down."

"Yeah, easier said than done, mate. It's guarded by something really awful—we lost one of our own to it—and anyway, I doubt you can just reach up and pull it out."

"But if we can," Qwyzz said, "we can send them all away. The question is how do we do it?"

"How, indeed?" Horatio responded.

"I suspect that it was used to bring Balor here, and as long as he lives in this form, it can't be removed."

"And ain't that the whole trick?" Horatio said in defeat. "As far as I know, there ain't no magic that can be used against him."

"It is a problem," Qwyzz agreed.

"Shhh!" Jilly said, motioning to them. "Something's happening!"

*　　*　　*

"Both of you are nothing to me," Qworum said with a dismissive wave of his hand.

"Oh, I think we're quite a bit more than nothing," Qwyrk said. "I think you're terrified of us, of what we've done, and what we can do. Otherwise, you wouldn't have gone to such trouble to try to keep us apart. It takes quite a bit of magic to create something like that, doesn't it? A bloody hoover to another dimension, popping into my sitting room. And it didn't work, did it? No, because we have something you don't, you'll never have, you'll never even understand." She traded smiles with Holly. "Our bond, it ruined your little plan, didn't it? So much so that you couldn't even make it work again, could you?

Your void never came back, so all you could do was wipe it from our memories. I hope the backfire gave you a bloody miserable headache that lasted for weeks."

"It was not pleasant," Qworum admitted.

"Good. So, what, then? You just said you turned up the volume on the ward this week. Made it as awful as possible. Were you the one making the bloody trees and rocks go for walkies around my home, too?"

"That was to test the resistance in your world." Aeval hobbled up, bracing herself on her walking stick, to stand next to Qworum. "To see what we could affect. When I procured my descendant, I had to examine the protective magic beforehand."

"Ah, so these things came from different sources," Holly said. "You, making trees wander about—very impressive, by the way: Qworum trying to fling me into semi-eternal darkness, and some bigoted ancient spell to keep us apart if everything else failed. Well, that hasn't worked either." She lifted her and Qwyrk's clasped hands again in a sign of defiance. And again, Qwyrk beamed.

"You have no idea what we've gone through for each other," Qwyrk added. "We're not going to be defeated. Not by tall, dark, and gruesome back there, and certainly not by your pathetic arses. Sorry mate. You've thrown your worst at us and failed. And now, we're going to make you pay."

*   *   *

Sixteen hours ago:

Sometime before dawn, Qwyrk stood at the floor of the Gaping Gap. Spray from the waterfalls obscured the passage to her destination. But she knew that the way would open when she called for it.

She should have been nervous, should have felt something, but numbness had overtaken her. Desperation, grief, and anger all invaded her mind, but she didn't feel any of them now, and hardly acknowledged them. There was only the task at hand, and thoughts of what that meant almost overwhelmed her, consumed her.

I can't believe I'm doing this!

Sure enough, the mists of the otherworld appeared, beckoning her again into the strange world of a strange being, a place she had no desire to return to. But it was the one place that might give her the chance to end this mess once and for all. She walked into the mists, followed the same path, emerged in the same place.

"Fayette!" she called out. "You know I'm here, and I'm ready to do what I have to do to end this, so let me in!"

For a long moment there was only silence, but a fiery glow soon filled the passage beyond. Fayette emerged from the darkness, as always, in her red robe, hood drawn over her head, ever obscuring the upper half of her face. Her presence exuded its eternal calm, emotionless demeanor. She said nothing, but beckoned Qwyrk to enter, to leave her own world behind for something far stranger and far more dangerous.

* * *

Now:

"All of this has been terribly amusing," Balor spoke at last, taking a few steps forward. "The threats, the anger, the nobility of sacrifice, the dissension amongst former allies, and the defiance in the face of certain defeat. Know this, strangers: no one of magic can harm me by spell, by word, or by deed. And so, I shall live forever in this world. And I will rule it as I see fit. None, not Fae, not Shadow, not Firbolg, not even the gods, can stop me. You would be wise to kneel now, accept me as your master, and I may yet be merciful and generous, if it suits me."

"The time has come, Qwyrk," Aeval cackled. "I warned you at the stones this half-year past that you must choose a side. You rebuffed me then, but you could yet be a potent ally."

Her two young descendants now stood on either side of her, silent but ominous in their twisted visages. Qwyrk winced at the sight of them. *I'm so sorry. We failed you.*

"Yes, one called 'Quirk.'" Balor took a few more steps. "Listen to my closest advisor, and take in the wisdom of her words. Kneel before me. Our victory is assured, and you can share in it. But, if you would join us, you must see that whom you would serve. Behold the form of your true god!"

Balor clutched his tattered robe and ripped the front of it down the middle in one grand gesture, tearing it to shreds with his claws, casting it aside to reveal a dark grey and muscled man-like form. Endless spirals, images, and ancient writing seemed to be engraved into his very skin, covering him from neck to foot and glowing with a faint blue light. He looked like a dark tapestry or an ancient book, relaying some horrid story best left untold. And worst of all, his body was nearly unclothed, save for a small, tattered loin cloth.

"Whoa, bloody hell, mate!" Qwyrk swore, turning her head away and averting her eyes, even as she glimpsed Holly doing the same. "Was that really necessary? I mean, seriously? If you're trying to scare us off, you might well have succeeded, except, we really can't run away, tempting as it is right now, believe you me. Couldn't you at least have found a pair of trousers at a big and tall shop? And if you think for one minute I'm coming up and putting a ten-pound note in your knickers, you are sadly mistaken!"

"More jokes, more sarcasm, always the same," Qwyll said. "She doesn't deserve your generosity, my lord."

"I believe you are right, little Shadow." Balor turned to address his fellowship of fearsome fiends. "Kill them in any way you see fit. Rip them apart, if you wish!"

A roar of approval erupted, and Qwyrk and Holly stepped back in haste.

"This had bloody well better work," Qwyrk whispered in Holly's ear.

"You're telling me that?" Holly asked. "You're the one with all the confidence!"

The first of the Fomorians charged at them, a misshapen olive-green creature with a goblin's appearance and three arms, each of which held a club. As it swung at them, Qwyrk and Holly dived to opposite sides. Qwyrk rolled and came back up standing, fists ready for a fight.

Holly launched a kick at the thing's midsection. It gasped, grunted and fell forward. Qwyrk delivered her own angry kick, followed by several punches to the back of the thing's head. She'd had to beat the Fachan by fighting dirty, and she didn't like it, not even for these creatures. But she had no time to contemplate the ethics of her attack.

Another monster grabbed her from behind and tossed her to the side. Her face hit the ground and pain surged through her head. She pulled herself up and sniffed at a trickle of blood from her nose. She wiped it away with the back of her hand and looked at it. It was red.

* * *

Slightly less than sixteen hours ago:

Qwyrk stood before Fayette in the cave.

"You know why I'm here," Qwyrk said. "I have to go into that bloody lake of yours and see what happens."

"As I have warned," Fayette spoke. "The pool does not grant what you wish. It grants only what you need. You must be sure of that need before you enter, and that your need is just, or it will reject you. If it rejects you, it may deny you anything at all, or it may kill you if it deems you unworthy or unjust. It alone decides."

"Lovely," Qwyrk said, rolling her eyes. "I know what I need. I need the means to defeat Balor, and as far as I know, there's only one way I'm going to be able to do that in the time we have, as unpleasant as it is. Can the pool do that? Can it grant me that ability?"

"The pool will decide."

"You know, you're not really all that helpful."

Fayette said nothing.

"Not much of a talker, either. You must be a real laugh on a first date."

"Will you enter the pool, seek its wisdom, know its decision, receive its solution, accept its judgement?"

"Do I have any other choice?"

"Do you still wish to defeat Balor?"

"Obviously!"

"Then enter the pool you must."

"Oh, thank you, master Yoda."

Fayette didn't reply. Qwyrk sighed.

"You're just no fun at all. Right then, let's get this bloody thing over with. What do I have to do?"

"Remove your garments, and when you are ready, follow me to descend into the waters."

"You know, normally someone has to take me out a few times before they get to ask me to do that, and also, I'm already spoken for. Except... that's not an option anymore, is it?" She sighed, her yearning for Holly as aching as ever. "What if I'm making a terrible mistake?"

Fayette did not reply.

"Fine, have it your way. I'll get naked and step into your pool. Then maybe we can get this business started, and I can go save the bloody day again."

"Well, you're not doing anything without me."

Qwyrk whipped around in shock to see Holly standing at the entrance to the cavern, dressed in her usual black, and looking far more stylish than anyone had a right to at this awful hour of the morning.

"How... how did you know where to find me? And how did you get here?"

"I woke just as you left. Since you were gone, but there was no note dumping me, I reasoned you were coming back here. Also, Qwyzz's work on my ring? I can follow you to your most recent location. It had one charge left in it. And this place is pretty much the last chance we have, isn't it, even if we're not sure what it will do?"

"Oh, I know exactly what it does," Qwyrk answered, taking a few steps toward her. "At least, I'm pretty sure I know."

"So do I," Holly answered. "Balor can't be defeated by any magic we have. It's that damned prophecy: the only ones that can destroy him must come from magic, but not be of it. I know what you want to do: you want the pool to grant what you need, the ability to banish Balor forever, and the only way to do that is... is by becoming mortal yourself: to be *from* magic, but no longer *of* it. You want the pool to make you human."

Qwyrk grimaced as she halted her approach, barely able look Holly in the face, but she nodded. "I'm sorry," she whispered, tears forming in her eyes. "I'm so sorry. I wanted some other solution, anything that wouldn't be this, but there's no other way, there just isn't. I was sure you wouldn't understand, so I snuck out. Yeah, all right, I ran away. I figured if we all survived, I'd apologize later, or something, but at least you'd be safe, and the world wouldn't be overrun with those plonkers. I could live with myself in whatever life I got if I at least knew those things had happened."

Holly stepped forward. Qwyrk worried that she'd berate her, even yell at her, but Holly did what she always did. She understood. She smiled and moved to place her hand on Qwyrk's cheek, but held back, again.

"Always thinking of others, always putting yourself last when the stakes really matter. It's what makes you so special."

Qwyrk wept and put her own hand near Holly's. "Then you know why I have to do it."

Holly smiled again. "Yes, I do. And it's also why I'm going with you. Whatever your fate is, it's mine, as well."

"What? Holly, no!" Qwyrk took a step back. "I can't ask you to do this, to give up who you are. You'd be abandoning your whole heritage. No, this is my burden, not yours."

"Your burden *is* my burden, Qwyrk. Where you go, I go. We're a team, remember?"

"But this, this is too much to ask of you."

"You're not asking me to join you. I'm telling you I will."

"But what about your family, your life?"

"You're a part of my family now, Qwyrk, and you *are* my life, you…" Holly's eyes also became teary. "Oh, for Goddess' sake, you silly woman, I *love* you! Crazy, mad love. More than anyone I've ever known. You're my dawn, my evening star, my springtime sunset, my warm winter hearth, all rolled into one. I can't be without you. I won't!"

"I… I love you, too," Qwyrk whimpered, stepping in closer. "I've tried to say it for so long, but I kept tripping over my tongue, kept telling myself it was too soon, not the right time, worrying you'd just push me away and run. I'm such a prat!"

"No, you're not," Holly shook her head. "You're perfect, just perfect, and I wouldn't change a thing about you." She looked at Fayette and Qwyrk's eyes followed. "Answer me this, 'Faytte': do the laws of the Shadows matter here? Or are you immune to them?"

"This place is beyond all concerns of Fae, humans, Shadows, Fomorians, and others. Nothing they decree holds stock here."

"Good, I was hoping you'd say that!" She looked back at Qwyrk, reached out and put her arms around her, drawing her in. "Just come here!"

Qwyrk kissed her beloved with all the passion and force she could muster, which was quite a lot. There was no shock, no repelling across the cavern, just Holly in a perfect embrace. Nothing could spoil this moment, not even the seer that stood nearby in eerie silence. They parted and gazed at each other, wiping away tears of joy and savoring the moment for just a little bit longer.

"Are you absolutely sure you want to go through with this?" Qwyrk asked, baffled that anyone would be willing to sacrifice so much to be with her.

"We've no other choice if we're going to stop Balor," Holly answered. "And wouldn't it be better odds if there were two of us standing against him, instead of one?" She sniffed and grinned. "Also, added bonus, if we're both human, then that horrid ward won't work. We can be together without their interference, and they can't do a damned thing about it. I, for one, would love to give them two fingers up again, after telling them how we did an end-run around it, just to see the looks on their faces!"

Qwyrk's heart soared, and she burst out laughing. "That's it. Oh, Holly!" She held her close and kissed her again. "I can't believe I didn't think of that before. We have a way out of this whole mess!"

"Well, lucky for you I'm a bit of a genius, and I not only figured out what you were going to do, I saw an even better advantage in your strategy." Holly looked again at Fayette. "Years ago, she told me that my life would irrevocably change and that after a battle, I'd die. I was distraught. I ran away. And in my despair, I ultimately did something impulsive which led to the birth of my son, whom I adore and who has brought me so much joy. But it also set me on the path of one day meeting you—beautiful, precious you. I might never have otherwise."

She turned and addressed Fayette. "Seer, you enjoy talking in riddles, so what you said to me is more obvious than it was years ago. Still, I've no intention of dying right away."

"The pool will determine if you are worthy of your request," Fayette answered, "and if not, then yes, you may well perish this very morning. But even if you survive the waters and the coming conflict, the length of a mortal's life is quite short compared to the endless timespan of your people, is it not?"

"I'll take what I can," Holly said.

"Right, there's nothing else for it," Qwyrk said. "We may as well get on with it."

"Something about disrobing, if I overheard correctly?" Holly teased.

"Yeah, normally I'd be delighted to get my kit off with you and go have a bath, but I suspect this is going to be a lot less fun than that. It's that big underground pool. Arcane magic and all that."

"Well, we'll have a dip together, but at least it's not that ridiculously cold lake by your home."

"It's not *that* cold!" Qwyrk protested.

"I'm convinced it's positively arctic in there. I'm surprised it's even in a liquid state."

Qwyrk sighed with a smile. "Never change, my love."

"Not planning to. Well, except for the whole becoming human thing, I suppose."

Qwyrk nodded. "Yeah, that's the catch, isn't it? Right, we need to do this. Now. Are you absolutely sure?"

"Qwyrk..."

"All right." She turned to Fayette. "So, what do we do? Clothes off, then?"

"Disrobe and follow me."

*   *   *

Now:

"What's happening?" Jilly demanded. "It looks like they're getting hurt out there. Why? Come on, we have to go help them!"

"We will, my dear, we will," Qwyzz assured her, "but first, there's something I must do. Excuse me for a moment."

He vanished in a flash of ruby-red lights, leaving Jilly and Horatio alone.

"Well, that was lovely," Horatio said, folding his arms. "Just send up a bloody flare to announce to everyone that we're right here. Yeah, brilliant strategy."

"They're all paying attention to Qwyrk and Holly right now," Jilly said, seeing her friends holding their own, just barely. "But where did he go?"

In answer, Qwyzz returned, with Qwykk at his side.

"Wait, what are you doing?" Jilly demanded, panicking. "She's supposed to be with Carl and Lluck, keeping them safe!"

Qwykk looked just as confused as Jilly felt. "Yeah, what's goin' on?"

"This is far more important, I'm afraid," Qwyzz answered with a wave of a hand. "And besides, the boy is remarkably lucky, and his father is a, um, what do you call them? A mega-hero?"

"Superhero, and he's not really, let's be honest!" Jilly answered.

"No matter, excuse me again!"

He vanished again amid more lights.

"Hello there, everyone," Horatio rolled his eyes, "step right up and see the sparkling light show! All the entertainment of a mixed bag of beings, standin' round for you to slaughter. Fun for the whole feckin' Fomorian family!"

Qwyzz flashed back again with Qwypp, who looked decidedly annoyed.

"There'd better be a bloody good reason you made me leave my boyfriend alone in the woods!" she growled. "He's in the middle of making contact with someone very important, and I promised him I'd stand guard. If he gets hurt 'cause I'm not there, heads are gonna roll!"

"I'll see to him, I promise," Qwyzz said. "But for now, I need you, and you Qwykk and you, um, what did you say your name was?"

"Horatio," he said with an annoyed eye roll.

"Ah yes, good. I need the three of you to go into that cavern and be ready at a moment's notice to pull the key out from the rock."

"Are you freakin' kiddin' me?" Horatio threw up his hands. "Do you know what the bloody hell's down there? 'Cause I do, and it ain't fun, and it killed one of me mates, and no thank you!"

"And there will probably be more of them down there by now. But you don't understand," Qwyzz said. "Between the three of you, you should have enough power to remove the key from the slab when the time comes."

"The key?" Qwypp looked confused.

"Yes, the key that's holding open the dimensional gate and letting those creatures invade this world. But I've a strong feeling that it cannot be removed unless Balor's form is destroyed. If that happens, and you pry out the key, the gate will shut, and all of the Fomorians should be forced back to their own plane."

"All right," Jilly said, understanding him better now, "but who's going to kill Balor? I thought none of us had the power to do it."

"That is where I believe our dear Qwyrk and Younger Vishala will come into the plan."

"You think they've figured out a way?"

"I have a hunch they have, yes."

Jilly glanced back over to the clearing. "Wait!" she cried out in far too loud a voice. "What's that?"

CHAPTER TWENTY-ONE

"Duck!"

Qwyrk heeded Holly's warning and just dodged a blade, swung by a troll-like monstrosity with five eyes, arranged in a random fashion.

"Behind you!" she shouted out to Holly, who swerved and avoided a spiked club coming down on her at the hands of a bipedal wolf creature with glowing yellow eyes that made it look undead.

Qwyrk scrambled to Holly's side. "These buggers aren't messing about. They really want to kill us!"

"Well, I'm happy to disappoint them!" Holly stepped to one side and kicked a small, matted fur-ball of a creature with beady eyes and a large, fanged mouth, sending it sailing through the air and crashing into a four-armed goblin in the distance. The goblin grabbed it with its two hands, and threw it even farther away, and soon the thing was being tossed about like a rugby ball.

"As entertaining as this is, we can't keep them at bay forever," Holly added. "I do hope some reinforcements are on the way?"

"You and me both, love. And there's still the main event. We just have to stall for time."

Qwyrk shot a glance over to Balor and his entourage. He had seated himself on the rocky outcropping and seemed to be watching the unfolding melee with much amusement. Nearby stood Qworum and Qwyll, Aeval and her descendants, and that bloody traitor, Blip.

"I'm going to kick his little amphibian arse to the moon and back and then wring his lousy neck!" Qwyrk growled, as she side-stepped a sword thrust by a three-legged ogre and delivered a stomp to one of its ankles, sending it tumbling to the ground in a howl of pain. But still, more Fomorians appeared. At least a dozen new monstrosities advanced on them, forcing Qwyrk and Holly to inch back toward the tree line.

"This is not good, darling, not good at all," Holly said, edging in closer to Qwyrk. "If there's a cavalry out there, now would be an excellent time for it to make an entrance."

"Sorry, I hope we're not too late," a voice sounded from behind them.

Qwyrk and Holly whipped around to see a youngish man with shoulder-length dark brown hair and a fair amount of stubble, dressed in a white tunic worn over chainmail armor and carrying a rather splendid-looking sword. Behind him were a few dozen others, dressed in the same manner.

Qwyrk fairly blurted out an enthusiastic response: "Sir John bloody Ashley! Great to see you, mate! And yeah, if you lot would like to get stuck in with bringing some hurt, I wouldn't object."

"Say no more. Oh, and Simon sends his regards. He's sitting this one out, rather reluctantly. Sprained his ankle tending a rose bush or some such." John bowed and with a motion of his hand, he and his fellow Templar knights charged into the clearing, rushing headlong at the assorted beasties and bringing said hurt.

"This is going to make things so much more fun!" Qwyrk rubbed her hands together.

"Hang on," Holly said, raising an eyebrow. "Is that the Templar knight who fought de Soulis in Leeds? The one you were fawning over last year? And should I be jealous?"

"I was *not* fawning! Good Goddess, I was admiring!"

"Well, that's fine, I suppose," Holly teased with her ever-charming grin. "You can look, but don't touch."

"Wouldn't dream of it, love," Qwyrk said. "But over there," she gestured, "Balor seems a bit upset now, which makes me happy. We need to keep on annoying him until everything's ready. So, are we going to let those knights have all the fun?"

"Most certainly not!"

* * *

"Those are Templar knights!" Jilly pointed, excited and a little hopeful for the first time.

"Yes, quite!" Qwyzz said, obviously pleased. "Some of the bravest and best humanity has to offer, and Qwyrk has almost certainly brought them here, which means she definitely has some kind of plan in mind." He addressed Qwypp, Qwykk, and Horatio. "And that makes it even more imperative that you three go to the cavern. If we are to have a chance of banishing these revolting creatures, that key must be removed."

"You know," Horatio sighed, "I really hate havin' to be a bloody hero. I so ain't cut out for it. But, yeah, all right, I'll take the ladies down there, and we'll yank out the bloody key… if we don't get eviscerated by those things, first."

"I'm not liking the sound of that, it must be said," Qwypp remarked.

"Yeah, me either," Qwykk added. "Why would they feel sorry for us?"

"What?" Qwypp's face fell.

"Horatio said they was gonna eviscerate with us. If they're the enemy, why would they feel sorry for us?"

"That's com-mis-er-ate." Qwypp stared at her with a flat expression.

"Oh," Qwykk said, confused. "So what's that other word mean, then?"

Qwypp explained it, and a look of horror swept over Qwykk's face.

"Blimey!" she said. "That's right horrible, isn't it?"

"Don't worry, love," Horatio said, "it's gonna be nothing but fun and games down there."

"You're lyin'."

"That I am. Right then, shall we be off?"

"Fine, but if I die, I'm coming back to haunt the hell out of you," Qwypp warned Qwyzz.

"I suppose I could live with that," he conceded. "If any of us live, that is. Here…" He handed her a small ring. "Wear this, and I'll contact you through it when the time is right."

"Thanks," she said. "I think?"

Horatio grabbed their hands, and with a puff of smoke and a small whooshing sound, the three of them vanished.

"Do you really think it's a good idea to send them down there?" Jilly asked. "That sounds like a big responsibility."

"No doubt it is, but I need you here, and our other human friends are far too outmatched to go it alone out there." He looked to the increasing chaos and Jilly's gaze followed his. "Now then, I shall collect our other friends and go check in on the channeling lad. Then, I think it's quite time for us to do some magic and enter the fray, as it were. Are you ready to kick some bum, Miss Pleeth?"

"Oh, I'm more than ready!"

*   *   *

Fifteen-and-a-half hours ago:

Qwyrk and Holly followed Fayette through a short tunnel, which opened into a larger cavern. Eerie, glowing, incandescent white orbs hovered above a grand, natural subterranean pool that reflected the light back across the whole of the chamber.

Fayette stood to one side. "Here, you will be judged, and if your plea be deemed worthy, it shall be granted. I will wait until the reckoning has passed."

"And if we're unworthy?" Holly asked, her voice more than a little nervous.

Fayette did not respond and withdrew into the shadows.

Exhaling sharply, they held hands and walked side-by-side to the water's edge. Qwyrk looked over at her beloved.

"Last chance to change your mind, darling."

"No chance at all," Holly answered, squeezing her hand.

"Right, then," Qwyrk sighed. "Let's do this."

"The water had better not be cold, or I'll be very put out."

"You're really not going to let it go, are you?"

Holly shrugged.

They took a tentative step into the shimmering liquid. It was warm and tingly, even pleasant, rather like stepping into a bath of fizzy water.

"Well, at least it's tolerable," Holly said in exaggerated relief.

Still holding hands, they proceeded forward into the water, wading in until they were about waist-deep. Qwyrk turned and looked back at Fayette. "Do we keep going?"

Fayette did not respond.

"I assume that's a 'yes'?" Holly asked. "She's not very helpful."

"It's like she's not even in her body half the time," Qwyrk said, "or she's really good at falling asleep quickly while standing up."

"I just think she's rather rude. Come on."

They waded in until they were almost up to their necks.

"This seems like far enough, yeah?" Qwyrk said, turning to face Holly.

"I've no clue, but I suppose?"

"Right," Qwyrk raised her voice. "Um, pool? Hi, Holly and Qwyrk here. All right? Things are going good, I hope? Um, we're standing here in you because we have a very big problem that we can't solve, and none of our equally powerful mates can fix it, either. As you probably know, Balor has escaped his banishment, has a new form, and wants to bring back the Fomorians to rule not only Ireland, but Britain and basically the whole human world. That would be a right pain, and pretty much awful for everyone who's not a Fomorian. We—Holly and I—would really like to stop him, stop that from happening, but I guess we need your help if we're going to do that."

She lowered her voice. "I'm talking to a bloody pool of water."

She glanced at Holly and raised her voice again. "So, if you think our quest is worthy, we're willing to sacrifice our immortality to have a shot at stopping this pillock before he succeeds in hurting a whole lot of beings in many worlds. Does that sound good to you? Is that a fair trade? Will you grant our request?"

Her voice echoed in the chamber, and for a moment there was only silence.

"Um, hello? Anyone there?"

"Are you sure we're in the right place?" Holly asked, looking around. "I don't think anything's hap—"

"Holly!" Qwyrk shouted, staring in horror as her beloved was pulled under the surface by a sudden, unseen force.

*   *   *

Now:

"Well, if you're going to kick some bum, you two will likely need my help!"

Jilly whipped around. "Granny!" She ran to her mentor, and practically jumped into her arms. "Oh, I can't tell you how glad I am to see you! Your timing is perfect!"

"I didn't intend on staying away as long as I did," Granny said, adjusting her cardigan and scarf, "but when Qwyzz put out the word this morning, I simply had to rush back as soon as possible."

"Wait, you sent for her?" Jilly demanded. "Why didn't you say so?"

"Because I couldn't be sure she would answer." Qwyzz looked apologetic.

"Oh, Master Qwyzz, you know I could never refuse an offer like this!" Granny beamed. "Now then, what say we go and teach these monstrosities a lesson or two, eh? Our magic may not be able to hurt Balor, but we can make his flunkies rather miserable! Despite our Templar friends' efforts, the Fomorians still have the advantage."

Qwyzz gave her a nod. "Well, now that you're here, I'm hopeful that more of ours will be on their way."

Jilly wanted to believe but didn't share his hope.

*   *   *

Some time ago:

Qwyrk floated in a dream-like state. How long had she been here? Was she in a trance? Was she still in Reverie in the tent next to Holly? Everything seemed unreal. Moving images, like films, of her past, played in the haze around her, several events all happening at once. In the distance, two figures started to emerge.

"Holly? Is that you? Who's with you? Where are you? Where am I?"

The figures advanced, their features becoming clearer, until they stood before her.

"Mum? Dad? How can this be happening? Why are you here? How are you here?"

But they remained silent, gazing at her. Were they angry? Judging? Indifferent? She couldn't tell, and it made her confused, frustrated, sad, even angry. She reached for them, but they drifted back away from her.

"No!" she cried as they faded. "Don't go, please! I need to know, I need to know what happened to you, why you vanished. Tell me, please!" But they said nothing. Maybe they were just illusions, phantoms in her drowning, dying mind.

"Don't you miss me?" she cried. "Don't you love me?"

A look of sadness descended over them, yet they remained in the mists, beyond her reach.

"If you can just tell me where you are, where I can find you. Can you say something, anything?"

Her mother raised one hand in some kind of gesture and mouthed words, but Qwyrk couldn't make out what they were. Her father did the same. They pointed at Qwyrk and then upward, before fading into a fog, as if drawn back in against their will.

"No!" Qwyrk shouted. "Damn it! No!" She thrust her arms out, desperate to reach them, to touch them. But they were already too far away, and in another moment, they were gone. Overwhelming feelings of loss and bereavement struck her, as acute and painful as when they'd disappeared all those centuries ago.

"Mum, dad, I'm sorry," she cried, sinking to her knees on some unseen ground. "I'm so sorry. I've tried to find you, but I didn't try hard enough. I gave up after a while. I failed you. Please forgive me, please tell me it's all right—"

In the next moment, she was choking, gasping for air as she emerged from under the surface of the pool. In desperation, she crawled to the shore. Holly was nearby on her knees, completely drenched, retching and spitting out water. How long had they been under?

"What happened?" Holly coughed.

"I don't know, I... for a minute everything was dark, and then something happened, and I saw my life flash or something."

"I did too," Holly said, in between breaths. "I felt like something was watching me, seeing everything I've ever done and somehow, I relived my whole life in a few moments."

Qwyrk took in another deep breath. "We're still alive, for the moment, anyway. But—"

"Qwyrk!" Holly gasped.

"What? What is it?"

Holly stared at her, her hands clasped over her mouth.

"What happened?" Qwyrk demanded. "Why are you staring at me? Oh crap, I haven't turned into a man, have I?" A glance down at herself, followed by a quick pat-down of all the appropriate places banished that fear. "Oh, thank Goddess! After all this, that would have been really shite."

"No," Holly whispered. She reached out and ran her finger along the edge of one of Qwyrk's ears. Qwyrk reached up and touched it. Her hand fell away in shock before she brought it up again. "It's, it's not pointed!"

She reached out at once and brushed aside some of Holly's wet hair, revealing a human-looking, rounded ear.

"It happened," Holly whispered.

"The pool has found you and your plea to be worthy and just," Fayette interrupted, gliding forth from the shadows. "You have been granted what you have sought. How you live from this day forward shall be entirely up to you. But understand that what you have gained cannot be given back, and should your efforts fail, you cannot retreat back to your former lives."

"If we fail, we won't have lives to retreat back to, anyway," Qwyrk said. "So we may as well fight Balor or die trying."

Fayette tipped her head in a slight nod. "It is as you have wished it to be. May your Great Goddess be with you. Go now, and strive not to enter here again, for only one boon per seeker can be granted, and many have there been before you who have died trying to return."

"I for one will be very happy never to see this place again," Holly said, standing and helping Qwyrk up. "But before we leave, can we at least dry off first?"

"Yeah, that's a fair point, Fayette," Qwyrk said. "We're starkers, dripping wet, and our clothes are back in that other cavern. I don't want to sound ungrateful, but if we could get some towels or something, so we can gather up our kit and get on out of..."

Qwyrk heard a snapping sound, followed by a rustle, like wind through leaves.

"...here. What?"

She and Holly now stood outside, near the cavern's entrance, wearing their clothing, and dry as if they'd never set foot in the pool.

"Well, that was a dramatic exit," Holly said, looking just as shocked as Qwyrk felt.

"Wait," Qwyrk said. "Did that all really happen? Or did we just imagine it?" She reached up and touched her ears. They were rounded, human. Holly did the same, and sure enough, hers no longer had points, either.

"We did it," Qwyrk said, shaking her head. "We really did it. Oh Holly, what have we done?"

Holly embraced her. "We did what we had to. We've given ourselves a chance against this horror, one that none of our friends have. Let's make sure we honor that and get the job done!"

Qwyrk kissed her and held her close. No shocks, no flying thought the air, everything just as it should be. She glanced up at the sky—clear of morning mist now—and noticed something else.

"Hang on, the sun's already past its midpoint. But we got here at dawn! How were we in there for that many hours?"

"Human time and Otherworld time run at different speeds, I

suppose," Holly answered, following Qwyrk's gaze to the sky. "For all we know, it might not even be the same day."

"Well, we have to get back to the others as soon as we can. But that's a bit of a problem, isn't it? If I'm human now, I can't just teleport us anymore, and you've used up the last of your free travel tickets. Damn, I didn't think about that!"

"I may have a solution," Holly said, holding up her hand. The slender gold ring with the green gemstone twinkled in the autumnal afternoon light.

"Right, of course!" Qwyrk said. "You can call Lluck and have Carl come get us."

"No," Holly shook her head. "I'm not ready to tell Lluck what we've done. Not yet. But my investigator friends? I'm sure they could be persuaded to come and collect us. There's a road not far from here."

She gazed into the stone on the ring and closed her eyes. "Mr. Dill? Mr. Chives?" she asked. There was a pause, followed by a metallic chiming that was a bit like a ring tone.

"This is Mr. Dill," a voice sounded from inside the gem.

"Mr. Dill! So lovely to hear your voice! This is Vishala—the younger, that is. Qwyrk and I have found ourselves in a bit of a tight spot, and we could use some assistance, if you or Mr. Chives might be able to avail yourselves."

"I should be most happy to avail myself, Ms. Vishala. Mr. Chives is indisposed at the moment, further looking into our impending doom, but I am happy to report that I am free to offer my help. And of course, we are both at your service for this evening's... unpleasantries."

"I'm delighted to hear it. I shall make it worth your while."

"Of that I have no doubt, ma'am, and I thank you for your attention to such considerations, but again, it may prove unnecessary should the evening, as they say, go south. Now, what can I do for you?"

"Well, it's rather odd, but we need a ride."

"A ride, ma'am?"

"Yes. We're rather stuck out at Gaping Gap cavern and we could use a lift back to civilization."

"And is Ms. Qwyrk not able to transport you both wherever you so wish?"

"Not at the moment. It's a long story."

"Then I look forward to being regaled with a rousing explanation, ma'am. I shall be there within the half-hour to retrieve you both and relay you to wherever you wish to be deposited."

"Thank you ever so much!"

"Always happy to oblige, ma'am."

And with that, the glow in the gemstone faded. Holly gave Qwyrk a proud smile.

"See? Problem solved!"

"This is brilliant! I'm so glad you had the foresight to think this through."

"Well, one of us had to," Holly teased. "But let's just get ourselves rescued. I don't want to think about what we've done. We can process it all later, and I'm quite sure I'm going to need to do a fair amount of processing."

"You and me both, love. I still can't believe it. I mean, I don't feel any different. Do you?"

Holly shook her head. "Not that I can tell, so far. But I'm sure differences will become quite apparent sooner than we'd like."

"Actually, I do feel something," Qwyrk said as they walked together.

"Really? What?"

"It's kind of unpleasant. Like, something creeping up my back, a sensation, and I think I want to put on more clothing?"

"Well, that would be a first," Holly quipped. "Sounds like you're a bit cold, darling."

"Is *that* what it feels like?"

Holly nodded.

"I don't like it."

"You'll get used to it. Come on!" She wrapped an arm around Qwyrk's waist, and they started down to the nearby road.

*   *   *

Now:

Qwyrk wrapped an arm around Holly's waist and pulled her back as a new swarm of Fomorians surged forward. The Templars were holding them off, but she knew that would only work for a while.

"How much longer?" Holly asked, as they kicked and punched and kept their foes at bay.

"Any time now would be lovely." Qwyrk looked around, increasingly anxious.

"Do you think there's been a problem?" Holly backhanded a horned goblin and sent it flying into a group of its fellows, to much consternation and grumbling.

"I hope not." Qwyrk kicked a small, bipedal dragon in the gut.

It expelled a puff of flame into the face of the ogre next to it, causing them to turn on each other.

"Is that Jilly with Qwyzz and an elderly woman on the other side of the clearing?" Holly asked.

Qwyrk tensed. "Yeah it is, and the woman's Granny Boatford. Glad to see her here, but I really wish Jilly wasn't."

"It's not up to us, I'm afraid... watch out!"

Qwyrk jumped to one side as a spear whizzed past her head. "I know, if things go bad, we're all bollocked, anyway. That must mean Lluck and the others aren't far behind. To your left!"

Holly swerved and caught a club that swung down on her from a two-headed troll. She twisted it out of the creature's hand and whacked it across both faces. It slumped to ground and didn't move again.

"Nice shot!"

"Nice club," Holly said. "I think I'll hold on to it for a bit." She glanced over to Granny. "I certainly don't want Lluck here, but there's no way he'd stay behind if he thought he could help."

"Takes after his mum. What happened to your fancy stick, by the way?"

"I lost it when Fayette took me out of Nicewood."

"That's a pity. Be nice if you had it right now."

"I know, behind you!"

A large axe-wielding troll loomed over them, poised to strike. But before it could swing, its eyes went wide, it staggered forward, and fell flat on its face. Behind it, two improbable little winged beings hovered in the air. They were made of stone, and one of them was wearing ballet pointe shoes.

"Alloooooo!"

"Gargula, what the bloody hell?"

"We are here to help with zee battle. Our master has sent us to thin zee herd, so to speak."

"Bon soir, Qwyrk!" Babewin bellowed, before blitzing a bulbous bugbear.

Qwyrk watched in amazement and amusement as the gargoyles flitted to and fro, clonking Fomorians and leaving them annoyed and bruised. Gargula spun about in the air, as if he were dancing, kicking foes and leaping about in a brutal ballet. He and Babewin soared out over the crowd to inflict more medieval misery.

"Aha!" Gargula bellowed as he flew away from them. "Zis will be glorious, like zee Hundred Years' War, all in one night! Vive la France!"

"And you thought it wasn't a good idea for him to learn to dance," Holly quipped.

"If he keeps it up, he can do the Turkey Trot for all I care. I'm just glad that—Holly, watch out!"

Qwyrk shoved Holly to the ground as another club-wielding beastie—a sort of hybrid hippopotamus-gorilla-something-or-other—took a swing at her. It missed Holly, but the weapon caught Qwyrk on her left side. She gasped as pain shot through her. She crumpled to the dirt, her breath knocked out.

"Qwyrk!" Holly screamed. She scrambled across the ground to where Qwyrk lay, heaving and panting, unable to get up, unable to defend herself from the Fomorian, who loomed over both of them with its club raised again, ready to strike. Holly swung out at the creature's knees with her new weapon, but it jumped aside, grunted and snorted, and lifted its weapon up to bring it down on both of them.

"Get out of here!" Qwyrk hissed.

"No!" Holly snapped back. "It's both of us or not at all. To the end!"

Holly brandished the Fomorian club again, but Qwyrk knew it couldn't withstand the next blow. She braced herself for the end.

A screech rang out behind them, and then another. She glanced back, amazed to see two tabbies wearing small suits of armor, complete with helmets. They sprang into action, leaping through the air towards the Fomorian's hippo face, tearing, clawing, scratching. The creature shrieked as it stumbled backwards, desperately trying to pry its attackers off, but failing.

"Mango! Minty!" Holly shouted. "But that means—"

The elder Vishala emerged from the woods, dressed in splendid purple leather armor. She masterfully swung her own Silambam staff about herself, leaving a trail of violet sparks in its wake.

"Get away from my daughter and her lady, you miserable abominations!" She stepped forward and with a swing of the staff, took out two of the creatures in one blow, sending them flying into the Templars' fray, where they were quickly overwhelmed.

"Mother, your timing is impeccable!" Holly cheered, standing and helping Qwyrk up.

Qwyrk struggled to get up, but knew she had to make a brave show of it. Grunting, she forced away the pain and took her place beside them.

"Right," she gasped, her wind and her voice returning. "Let's deal out some real damage, shall we?"

*   *   *

Granny shot a bolt of white light from her wand, striking two of the creatures in front of her and hurtling them backwards into their companions. Qwyzz followed suit and scattered several more. Jilly whipped up a wind spell that blew a few others over.

"That's it!" Granny said as she unleashed another blast that cleared the area in front of them. "Ha! Not so pleasant is it now, eh? You stupid brutes!"

She let loose another bolt, and another. Jilly marveled at the power this little old woman could still wield. Who could have guessed that the eccentric lady from late medieval Knettles was perhaps the most powerful witch in the whole world?

"What do we do now?" Jilly asked.

"We draw their attention," Qwyzz said. "I've a feeling that Qwyrk and Holly are stalling for time."

"Who's that with them?" Jilly asked. "Is that Holly's mum? She's amazing! But why aren't Qwyrk and Holly fighting more? They should be beating the crap out of these things. Why are they holding back?"

"I wish I knew," Qwyzz said. "We've no choice but to trust them."

"I'm rather bothered that Balor is doing nothing at all," Granny observed. "He seems to be enjoying this."

"He can't be killed, not by us," Qwyzz answered. "We can only hope that his confidence will be his undoing."

Jilly glanced back over at Qwyrk and Holly. "Something's wrong with Qwyrk!"

*   *   *

"Has this charade gone on for long enough, my most sovereign lord?" Qworum inquired of Balor, as the battles raged below them.

The great fiend grinned as he turned his horrid eye to him. "Where is your sense of fun, little one? We, who have been trapped, locked away for so long, are not entitled to some respite from that suffering?" He gestured with a great, clawed hand. "Are you not amused by this spectacle? These humans and their pitifully few allies who think they can defeat us?"

"My concern is that we waste time here, my master, when already, you and yours could be spreading across this island and placing it under your dominance, claiming it as your own."

"Your concern should rather be that I might choose to remove your head from your shoulders and parade it about on a pike if you displease me. But, perhaps you are right, and the time has come to proceed, entertaining though this is."

Qworum nodded and looked down to Blip with disdain. "I believe you said you have something prepared? A surprise for those 'friends' of yours?"

"Oh yes," Blip said with a satisfied smile. "Yes, I do."

Qworum nodded. "See to it, then."

"The time has come to bring an end to this nonsense." Blip produced a whistle from his robe and held it up to his mouth.

*   *   *

Jilly, Qwyzz, and Granny advanced toward the Fomorians, who had regrouped and were lining up to face them again.

"I don't feel good about this," Jilly said.

"Tosh, my dear!" Granny exclaimed. "They're not as powerful as they'd have you believe. This is the most fun I've had in ages!"

"You have a strange concept of fun," Jilly answered.

"Actually, it looks like it could be a bit of laugh." Lluck ran up beside them, joined by Carl.

"What are you doing here?" she asked.

"Um, same thing as you?" Lluck shrugged. "Helping save the world? Be honest, my luck is about to get dead useful."

"Yeah, all right. Go on, then!"

"So, where did Qwykk and that lot go off to?" Lluck asked.

"Long story, but they went to get a key, or something."

"A key?"

"It lets the Fomorians into our world, I think?"

"Just slam the door in their faces, then!"

"Something like that. You sure you're both up for this?"

"We don't have a choice, Jilly," Carl answered, pumping himself up. "We can't run now, no matter what the outcome."

"Well, I'm glad you're here, both of you."

"I'm bloody not!" Lluck quipped. "I could be back home watching crap telly and eating my weight in crisps right now."

Jilly shot him a look, but she couldn't hide her amusement.

"Right then, shall we?" Qwyzz said, though Jilly detected more than a little nervousness in his voice.

"You best be careful with that lot," a woman's voice in a thick Scottish accent sounded behind them.

Jilly and the others turned to see Star Tao walking toward them, calm and assured, his eyes glowing gold.

"Who are you?" Jilly didn't dare to hope. The voice sounded disturbingly like Aileen's.

"I am Scáthach, Lady of Dún Scáith," Star Tao's body answered. "Balor is a very old enemy of mine."

"And you're here to fight with us, then?" Jilly was exhilarated and relieved. At last, the plan was starting to make sense!

"No."

"Hang on, what? Then why are you here? Speaking through my friend, I mean?"

"I am here to observe and to advise. There is a way Balor can be brought down, forever, and the means of doin' so is at hand." Having said that, Star Tao's body began to walk past them, into the fray.

"Wait!" Jill tugged at his arm. "You can't just walk out there alone. You've got no protection!"

Star Tao smiled. "Then ya'd best come with me."

*   *   *

Blip blew on his whistle, three times to be precise, once long, once short, and then long again. For a moment, nothing happened as the high-pitched tones disappeared over the din of the skirmishes below them.

"Well?" Qworum demanded. "Is that it? A tune? Are you a pied piper? Will you draw out rats? Will our enemies follow you, merrily skipping on their way to certain doom?" Qwyll laughed. Even Balor chuckled.

"Oh, it's something far better than rats," Blip answered with an assured smile. "And far more dangerous."

A low rumble sounded from beyond the ridge. Quiet at first, its volume intensified, then a vibration shook through the ground beneath them.

"What are you doing?" Qworum demanded. Blip smiled in

amusement as he saw even Balor's expression turn to one of curiosity, perhaps even concern.

"What I've been wanting to do for some time, you insufferable miscreant!"

The rumbling grew ever louder, and as an astonished Qworum looked out, silhouettes appeared on the ridge line: a few at first, then a few more, then a dozen, now two dozen, and more after them. Dragons, crocodiles, Komodos, and more fantastical quadrupedal beasties galloped in no sort of formation, stampeded down toward the nearest hoard of Fomorians, some of whom had just joined the dark festivities. These thundering steeds were ridden by a curious assortment of frog-like creatures: bull frogs, tree frogs, horned frogs, wood frogs, rain frogs, true toads, less-than-true toads, cane toads, common toads, uncommon toads, and even one European fire-bellied toad. They wore a multitude of helmets—Roman, medieval, and pith—and wielded an array of weapons, from sword canes to muskets to lances. Most sported some form of Victorian facial hair, and all looked rather put out.

As they charged down to the base of the hill, they set upon the first of their befuddled opponents with glee, hacking, slashing, pounding, shooting, and mowing down the Fomorians with ease. The Templars cheered as they joined forces to hammer their enemies harder.

Blip rejoiced in work well done. And did he spy Qwyrk and Ms. Vishala in the distance?

"What madness is this?" Qworum demanded.

"Treachery in reverse, boyo," Blip grinned. "You've been played for a fool, you see. I used you to gain information about where this garish little soirée would take place, and now my colleagues and I are going to make your lives bloody miserable!"

He whipped out his sword cane from beneath his robe and stabbed Qworum in the foot. Qworum shrieked and fell to one knee, which Blip found most satisfying. But Balor stood up with a growl, and Blip judged that it was time to make a swift exit.

"To me, Snickerwocky!" he shouted above the chaos, giving his whistle another blow. His trusty Komodo dragon lurched through the throng of panicked Fomorians, and Blip made a mad dash for the beast, before Balor or any minions could pursue him. As he hopped onto his mount, he cheered, grateful that Aeval and her kin seemed to be preoccupied with... someone? Someone they were now making haste to confront on the other side of the clearing.

"Great northern beans, what is that lad doing here?"

*   *   *

Mother Vishala mowed down foes with her staff, sending them flying, yelping, howling, and whimpering. Qwyrk marveled at her skill and grace as she beat back several enemies at once.

Qwyrk's left side throbbed with waves of pain, sometimes so strong that she feared she would pass out, which was a new and very unpleasant feeling. It even hurt to breathe. But she held her ground and managed to push back several creatures intruding into their space.

Just a few paces away, Holly stood firm, keeping a protective eye on Qwyrk, which was both a bit embarrassing and completely endearing. Her own efforts kept at bay the remaining monsters who weren't distracted by the Templars.

"Mother, how did you know we'd be here?" she asked, as she launched an elbow into the stomach of a bipedal warthog. The creature dropped its axe and slumped to the ground, where she kicked it in the face, sending it sprawling backward.

"I had a little help," Vishala answered, eyeing the enemies in front of her.

"Help?" Qwyrk asked.

Vishala motioned with her head for them to look back to the trees as she whacked another creature. They did so just as two decidedly eccentric fellows emerged from the darkness. They were indistinguishable from one another, wore black trench coats, black bowler hats, and despite it being well on into the night, dark sunglasses. They carried large rifles that looked more like ray guns from a 1950s science fiction film.

"We took the liberty of bringing your mother with us, ma'am," said Dill (or was it Chives?). "I trust that is acceptable?"

"More than acceptable!" Holy grinned. "Thank you!"

"And she is not the only one," Dill continued.

"They're here?" Qwyrk's heart raced in anticipation.

"Indeed, they are, ma'am. Indeed they are."

CHAPTER TWENTY-TWO

Eight hours ago:

"An extraordinary tale, ma'am," Dill said, as he drove Qwyrk and Holly along a narrow country road through the Yorkshire Dales. "And a significant sacrifice to make, even in such dire circumstances. Are you quite sure it was the right decision?"

"Well, it's not like we have much of a choice now," Qwyrk answered, looking out the car window as the landscape whizzed by.

"It's funny," she said, "I've only ever been in one of these contraptions a few times."

"What? An automobile?" Holly gave her a rather incredulous expression.

Qwyrk shrugged. "Never needed to. Guess I'll have to get used to it."

"If I may ask, where are we going now, ma'am?" Dill inquired.

"Take us to Richmond, if you wouldn't mind," Qwyrk said. She looked at Holly. "I have an idea."

*   *   *

Now:

"Scáthach!" Aeval spat as she approached Jilly and the others, her two descendants close behind her. "I should have known you'd find a way to come crawling back to this world. And in the body I took hold of last spring. How ironic and amusing. The little fool is good for something, I suppose."

"I'll not treat with you, Aeval," Scáthach replied from Star Tao's body. "I am here for one reason alone, which this fine young lad alerted me to. I'm going to see Balor banished once and for all."

Aeval cackled. "It is too late for that, spear woman. It's been far too late for quite some time. Your magic, the magic you all possess can avail you of nothing." She motioned to Jilly and Qwyzz. "Our tenebrous lord cannot be harmed by anything you do. You would be well advised to surrender now, kneel, and beg for mercy."

Jilly watched as Moirin and Aileen, eyes white and hair streaked with grey, fell in next to their ancestor. Their faces were expressionless, as if they were merely dolls. It unnerved and upset Jilly to see her friend like this, and she almost had to look away.

I have to try to reach her. "Moirin," she said as she took a hesitating step forward. "I know you're still in there. It's me, it's Jilly. You came to us for help, just a couple of days ago, remember?"

"I remember that you abandoned me, just like everyone else," Moirin answered, turning her blank gaze to Jilly.

"That's not what happened, I promise!" Jilly pleaded. "Things got mixed up. We all wanted to be there for you."

"What would you know about bein' there for her, you little brat?" Aileen hissed. "She's with her family now. She's where she belongs."

"And yet," Scáthach interrupted, "are you sure you are where *you* belong?"

"What're you talkin' about, freak?" Aileen demanded.

"So alike, it's almost uncanny," Scáthach answered.

"What?" Aileen demanded. "What's so alike?"

"You look just like me, ya daft bairn! When I was young. And that's how I know!"

"Know what?"

"You may have that old hag's blood runnin' through ya." Scáthach pointed to Aeval. "But know that you're my descendant, too. There's Fomorian magic about you, aye, but there's much that's good, as well. Do right by it, young one, reclaim that part of your heritage, and let this evil go."

"Do not listen to her!" Aeval commanded, as she raised her hands, threatening to work her dark magic.

"Moirin! Aileen!" Jilly took several steps forward, hoping against all odds that Qwyzz had a powerful spell in the works, or that Lluck's luck would be extra lucky. "Listen to Scáthach! Listen to me! You don't have to do this; you don't have to follow her. She doesn't love you. She doesn't want you to be free. She needs you to be her slaves, forever. Is that what you really want for yourselves?"

"Lies!" Aeval snarled as she began to circle her hands around each other.

"I... still don't want to hurt you, Jilly," Moirin said, her voice softening.

"Then prove it!" Jilly said. "Come back to us, both of you! Let go of this madness."

"It's not madness," Moirin protested. "I've embraced who I really am." But she hugged herself and looked unsure of her own words.

"I don't believe that," Jilly answered in defiance.

"Is it true?" Aileen said, looking to Aeval, confused. "Am I descended from her, as well?"

"What difference does it make?" Aeval snarled. "You have found what you sought, and you are mine, now! I will hear no more of this!" A dark light formed in the space between her hands.

"Back, baintsíde!" Qwyzz warned, in as forceful a voice as Jilly had ever heard from him. "You will not harm these mortals, not while I live!"

"Well then, perhaps we should remedy that." Aeval cackled as she lobbed a blob of dark purple lightning at him. It stuck him square in the chest. He staggered back, but managed to stay on his feet.

"You'll have to do better than that!" He hurled his own blast of energy at her, which sent her staggering backwards to collapse in a heap on the ground. In response, Moirin and Aileen both opened their mouths and began to hum in a constant, painful pitch.

"Moirin!" Jilly shouted, hoping to be heard above their voices. "Fight this! You can be better. You don't have to do this!"

But their droning became more intense, and Jilly had to cover her ears. Lluck and Carl did the same. Her knees wavered, and she feared she might fall to the ground. If that happened to all of her friends, it was over.

*   *   *

"Bloody hell!" Qwypp whispered.

"It's not lookin' too cheery, is it?" Horatio said.

"Why do they only have one leg and one arm?" Qwykk asked.

"They're Fachan, love," Qwypp said. "They're real nasty Darkfae from up in Scotland. Wouldn't expect to see them here, but with all this extra nonsense going on, I'm not surprised."

"There was only one of 'em before," Horatio noted. "Now there's three. Bloody hell! There's no way we're gonna get to the obelisk without bein' seen."

"Can't we just teleport over to it and pull out the key?" Qwykk asked.

"Accordin' to your bloke Qwyzz, it ain't comin' out of the rock until Balor is stone cold dead," Horatio said. "And by the sounds of it, that won't be easy to accomplish, if it's even possible at all."

"So, we just sit here and wait for him to contact us, then?" Qwypp asked, looking at the ring he'd given her. "I'm not happy with hiding behind this rock and just hoping they don't see us."

"Yeah, it ain't the most brilliant plan in the world, it must be said," Horatio added, "but as long as we keep quiet, we shouldn't attract attention."

The sound of a whip cracking directly over their heads shocked them all back into the moment.

"Well," Qwypp noted. "So much for that idea!"

*   *   *

As Jilly struggled against the increasing intensity of the young banshees' voices, she rummaged through her mind for something, anything, that could neutralize their awful sound, even if only for a few moments. Her head vibrated, and she didn't dare take her hands from her ears. She could barely move, presumably what they were counting on. She glanced at the others, and only Star Tao seemed unaffected. He took a few steps forward but seemed unable to advance any farther; it was like they were all stuck in treacle.

Over it all, she heard a rumbling sound in the distance, something that wasn't coming from Moirin and Aileen. She looked to the ridge line and saw something that made no sense. A horde of various animals carrying all manner of frogs and toads and other creatures thundered down the slope and crashed into the lines of Fomorians battling the Templars.

She could hardly believe what she saw next. A Komodo dragon charged toward them, running roughshod over every creature in its way, breathing short bursts of fire at those that got too close. Several Fomorians shrieked and fled, swatting at flaming body parts. And sitting atop the beastie swinging his sword cane about and shouting, was...

"Blip?"

Snickerwocky bounded in front of Jilly, crashing into Aeval before she could react, and sending her through the air to slam into one of the nearby trees. Moirin and Aileen broke from their trance, shattering the sonic spell they'd cast.

Before Jilly could say anything else, Blip gave her a quick bow, and the dragon turned tail and launched itself toward the fray in the clearing. And in the distance, she saw a multitude of mounted animals advancing, mowing down the Fomorian ranks. She'd regained her senses but had no magic prepared. In desperation, she ran to Moirin and took hold of her shoulders. Aileen was doubled over on her knees, holding her head.

"Moirin, please, listen to me," Jilly pleaded. "Don't do anything else for her. It's wrong. It's all wrong, and you both know it. Come back to us. Let us help you. Both of you."

"Jilly?" Moirin asked, confused and dazed.

"Yes, it's me! I'm here!"

"Get away from her!" Aeval yelled as she hobbled back toward them with surprising swiftness, the hideous dark light again glowing around her hands. Qwyzz let fly another burst of energy, but she swatted it away and pressed onward. Lluck and Carl tried to get in her way, but she punched Carl and shoved Lluck aside with ease. They went down, unconscious... or worse.

"Aeval!" Scáthach shouted. "Your time of reckoning has come. Release these two from your thrall. Release my descendant, whom you've no right to constrain!"

Aeval howled and jumped at Star Tao, reaching for his neck. They fell to the ground, rolling about like angry alley cats, each struggling to gain the upper hand.

Jilly felt completely helpless. She looked down, frantically searching her mind for something that she could use, some spell to force them apart, something to stop Aeval without hurting Star Tao. But she drew a blank.

When she glanced back up at them, her mouth fell open in shock. "No!"

Aeval stood over Star Tao's motionless body, her wicked smile triumphant.

*　　*　　*

Six hours ago:

Adjua the Ghanaian dream-seer answered her front door.

"We're so sorry to intrude," Qwyrk said, "but this is kind of an emergency, and I'm pretty sure you can help us. You may be the only one, actually."

"You seem... different," Adjua observed as she stood to one side and let Qwyrk and Holly enter.

"Yeah, it's a bit of a long story," Qwyrk said. "We'll try to summarize it as we go, but for now: how do you feel about trying to help save the world?"

"Do I have a choice?" Adjua asked, amused.

"Of course!" Qwyrk said. "But... not really?"

"That is what I thought. Come, tell me everything."

After they'd explained everything as best they could, Adjua sat in silence, trying to take it all in. "So, the three of us can summon a spear, a weapon that will destroy this Balor?"

"We think so, yes," Holly said.

"And we only need to meditate to summon it?"

"Well, that's the whole thing," Qwyrk said. "We don't really know how it works, and Fayette was annoyingly short on details. But I figure it's the best shot we have, if you'll give us a hand? I mean, literally, we join hands and maybe it just... works? Maybe?"

Though skeptical, Adjua sat down cross legged on the floor with them, forming the third side of a triangle, and taking their hands.

"I heard words, when I was in the pool," Qwyrk said. "My parents mouthed something. It's coming back to me now. It was like they *wanted* to be heard. I think it's how we summon the spear."

"Well let's have a go, shall we?" Holly said. "No time like the present."

Qwyrk spoke the phrase she'd heard in her head, and they clasped each other's hands tightly. The air began to pulse around them, and Adjua felt a force being conjured. She opened her eyes and saw a faint light appearing in front of them all.

"I think it's happening!" she said.

And for a moment, an energy glowed between them, but just as it began to take shape, it faded and disappeared, and they were left with nothing.

They looked at each other in confusion.

"What happened?" Holly asked. "Why didn't it work?"

"I do not know," Adjua answered. "There are three of us here, yes? The three who, as you say, would fulfill the need to bring it to us?"

"This should have brought us the spear," Qwyrk said, disheartened. "This was our best shot."

"Perhaps you've said the words wrong?" Holly offered. "Maybe you forgot something?"

"No," Qwyrk said. "But I've just had a thought, an awful one. We did it right. That's not the problem."

"What do you mean?" Adjua asked.

Qwyrk looked at her with regret. "I'm sorry, but it's not you. You're not the third. I see it now. It's your daughter. It's Ashanti."

*   *   *

Now:

"Run! Duck! Whatever!" Horatio dived out of the way as a Fachan's whip just missed him. Qwypp and Qwykk teleported about in the smaller cavern, staying one step ahead of the deadly weapons that could rob them of their powers.

"How are we supposed to get to that bigger cave with those awful things out here?" Qwykk asked, holding tight to Qwypp's hand.

"I think that's the bloody point!" Qwypp answered. "As long as they're chasing us, we can't get to the key, can't pull it out."

"That's not fair!" Qwykk pouted.

"Fair's got nothing to do with it, love. Jump!"

Qwypp teleported across the cavern again as another Fachan's chain-whip swiped far too close for comfort.

"I just need to get a view of it, so we can get in there," Qwypp said. "Horatio! Where are you?"

A few seconds later, Horatio puffed into view next to them. "This ain't exactly going' accordin' to plan, is it? Not that we had a bloody plan, of course."

"Look," Qwypp said, "Qwykk or I just need to get a look inside that bigger cave, and then we can blast all of us in there, yeah?"

"Ain't gonna stop them from comin' after us," Horatio protested, "and for all we know, there's a dozen more of these buggers in there. And trust me, ladies, you do *not* want to get hit with one of those weapons... watch out!"

They avoided another attack, and Qwypp blinked them to the opposite side of the cave.

"Maybe if we can get close enough to that entrance, I can go in and have a look," Qwykk offered.

"Are you sure, love?" Qwypp squeezed her hand. "We have no idea what else is in there."

"Well, we've gotta do somethin', right? We can't keep on teleportin' out here!"

"We could just toss him through the entrance and see what he finds out?" Qwypp looked at Horatio and then back at Qwykk with a grin.

"Oh, thank you so much for your support!" Horatio glared. "And besides, I've already been in there. You're the ones wot need to see it, so you can get us close the slab."

"Why don't you just take us in there, then?" Qwykk asked.

"Because my teleportin' isn't as fast as yours, and right now, speed is the only thing keepin' us from gettin' pulped!"

Qwypp shook her head and glanced back to Qwykk. "Fine. Just get in there, get a good look, and head right back, yeah?"

Qwykk nodded with surprising confidence. "They don't call me Qwykk for nothing! Go over there with me, and I'll be in and out in a jiff."

Qwypp concentrated, and in an instant, they were at the entrance to the large cavern, with no Fachans nearby.

"Look! There it is!" Qwykk said.

"Now get in there, have a look," Qwypp ordered, "and then get out!"

Qwykk flashed away and materialized right next to the stone. Qwykk looked about, nodded, and gave her the thumbs up.

Before Qwypp knew what was happening, a barbed chain lashed out at Qwykk from the darkness and wrapped around her ankles, bringing her down.

*　　*　　*

Five-and-a-half hours ago:

Adjua let go of Qwyrk's hand with an angry jerk. "What are you talking about?"

"No, Qwyrk," Holly begged.

"The three must be *from* magic, but not *of* magic," Qwyrk explained. "That's Holly and me, obviously, but it isn't you, Adjua. It's your daughter. She comes from your lineage, so she has magic in her blood, but she's not yet magical. You've said it yourself, she'll come into her power when she's older. It's why you didn't want Jilly to meet her yet, right? You wanted her to have more time to be a child. And that's why the buggane tried to kidnap her, because Balor knew she could help unleash the one weapon that could take him down. Only, he didn't anticipate what I came up with, so I suspect he was looking for other children from similar backgrounds. Jilly might have been one. Lluck too, but they're already manifesting their magic, so it's too late for either of them to be part of this. But Ashanti, she fits the bill perfectly. She comes from magic, but she's not part of it, not yet. She's our third. She has to be."

"We can't do this," Holly said, shaking her head. "There must be some other way. This is awful. It's too much."

"No, Qwyrk is right," Adjua said, an awful, sinking feeling working its way into her heart. "I have feared more than anything that Ashanti would be called before she was ready, before I was ready. I don't want to believe it, but it is the truth. My daughter must help you summon this weapon. She is the third, and she must go with you when you face Balor. But I will not let her go alone. I must go with you."

"Are you sure?" Holly asked. "We've no right to ask this of either of you. And yes, I know I'm projecting my own guilt about Lluck onto her, but I'm no more willing to put her in danger than I would my own son. I'm not sure how I'll live with myself if something terrible happens."

"If something terrible happens, we'll all be dead, anyway," Qwyrk said. "Sorry to be blunt, but we're really down to that at this point."

Holly squeezed her hand. "You're right. I'm getting really tired of the world nearly ending, I must say."

"You and me both, love. But I feel like this will be the last time. All right, that didn't quite come out right. A bit of unintentional gallows humor, but you know what I mean."

"Qwyrk is right, there is no other choice," Adjua said. "Ashanti must grow up tonight. It is not fair, she's only seven. She deserves to be a little girl, to run about, to play with her dolls, to feel safe and surrounded by love. She will see things that she can never unsee. But, perhaps we can shield her from the worst of it, keep her away from Balor and his minions long enough for us to do what we need to." She fought back tears as everything she'd resisted overwhelmed her.

"We'll do what we can, I promise you," Qwyrk sighed. "Go and get her."

Adjua nodded and left the room.

*   *   *

Now:

Jilly wanted to scream, to run, to do something, but her eyes were fixed on Aeval. The banshee's maddened expression betrayed that she moved in on Star Tao for the kill.

Star Tao was down. Carl and Lluck were on the ground, alive at least, but in no state to help. Even Qwyzz seemed incapacitated. Moirin and Aileen began to recover, struggling to their feet.

Jilly was alone. She picked up a stone and threw it at the banshee.

"You!" Aeval growled, turning to look at her. "You heinous, vexatious brat! You are the one who took my Moirin from me, the night she should have been reborn. You are nothing more than a child playing with magic, with no sense of what it really is! I've had enough of you and your meddling! Die now, wretchling!"

Aeval summoned her dark fire again. She opened her mouth, releasing a low-pitched hum, mixing with the energy held in her fingers and making it grow.

Jilly's eyes went wide. She felt frozen to the ground, a deer in headlights.

The pulsing around Aeval's hands grew larger, stronger.

"Great ancestor!" Moirin call out. "What are you doing? She's just a kid!"

But Aeval ignored her, if she heard her at all. Jilly searched her mind in panic for something, anything that could counter Aeval's deadly attack. Running away would do no good; Aeval would just cut her down.

Determined to stand her ground, Jilly took a deep breath and started to formulate something, a simple spell that might confuse Aeval for a short time. Might. She mouthed the words as her enemy approached.

The fire around Aeval's hands glowed a sickly, luminous, blackish purple. Jilly knew that if it hit her, she wouldn't survive. *Just a few more steps,* Jilly thought, as she finished the words to her incantation. She felt a momentary warmth grow up around her, surround her. *Maybe? Please?*

Aeval stopped, snarling in anger and confusion.

"Jilly!" Moirin called out. "Where'd she go?"

"She vanished," Aileen said.

It worked! Jilly sighed with relief. But it only bought her a minute, if that. *And if I move too much, the illusion will break. Now what?*

"I will find you, you miserable hellion!" Aeval threatened. "And when I do, I will tear your head from your little body!"

"I don't think so, you Fomorian trash."

Granny strode toward the banshee, clutching her ornate wand in one hand.

Granny? No!

Aeval's eyes narrowed. "Out of respect for your centuries of magical life and the rich strain of our blood that runs within you, I will allow you to leave this place, if you go now."

"Oh, you're quite the amusing one, aren't you?" Granny asked in mockery. "Do you think we're going to cede this world to you and your horrid fellows? As we humans like to say, kiss my arse!"

Granny waved her wand at Aeval, shooting a pulse of lavender lightning toward her foe in an explosive flurry of sparks.

Aeval blocked the attack with her hands, but not without staggering back several steps. She responded by lobbing a bolt of her own black fire. Granny deflected the majority of the blow, though she too stumbled back a little.

Jilly's head started to tingle and she knew her spell would wear off any second. She had to think of something, anything.

"There she is! Great ancestor!" Aileen shouted.

"Aileen! Be quiet!" Moirin shouted.

But it was too late. Aeval grinned and let loose a wave of the same deadly energy at Jilly.

She covered her face with her hands. *This is it, it's over!*

Except that it wasn't. Before she knew what happened, someone manifested right in front of her. Someone who took the direct force of the blow. Someone...

"Granny, no!" Jilly screamed as the old woman fell into her arms, shuddering and shaking. Jilly collapsed from the force of her fall as they both tumbled to the ground. The wind knocked from her, she was trapped under her mentor.

"An unexpected bonus," Aeval taunted, as she stepped forward. "To kill you both at once. What a joy this night has become!"

She raised her hands and began her otherworldly hum, the deathly energy around her fingers taking shape and growing again.

*   *   *

Five-and-a-half-hours ago:

Adjua returned to the sitting room holding a sleepy Ashanti, who hugged her mother close and rested her head on Adjua's shoulder. The two of them sat down on the floor between Holly and Qwyrk. "Now, my precious one," Adjua said, fearing what would come next. "Do you remember these two?"

Ashanti smiled. "Yes, Auntie Holly and her friend, Auntie Qwyrk."

Holly seemed pained by the girl's words, but she smiled and answered. "That's right, sweetheart, I told you a story the first night we met, remember?"

"Yes, it was lovely, thank you. But I can see Auntie Qwyrk now! She doesn't look scary. She's very pretty, just like you said, Auntie Holly."

Qwyrk blushed. "You're very kind, Ashanti. Do you know why you can see me now?"

Ashanti shook her head.

"It's because I'm like you and your mummy now."

"Does that mean you're not a faery anymore?"

"Something like that," Qwyrk answered.

"Remember when I showed you my pointed ear?" Holly said.

Ashanti nodded.

"Well, look now." She pulled her hair back. "See? It's just like yours! And so's Auntie Qwyrk's." Qwyrk motioned to her ears and turned her head back and forth to show them off.

"But why wouldn't you want to be a faery?"

"It's not that we don't want to," Holly said, "it's because we have a very important job to do, and we need to be human to do it, because humans are very special, too. They can do some things that even faeries can't. And you know what? That's why you're here. We need your help!"

Ashanti looked up at her mother, who gazed at her with a gentle smile, even as her heart broke. "It's true. There is something very special about you, my sweetest one, and Holly and Qwyrk need you to help them do something wonderful."

"What?"

"Remember how I told you that magic is all around us?" Holly said. "Now we're going to show you. With your help, we're going to do some magic and make something appear right here in front of us. At least for a while."

"What is it?" Ashanti's eyes widened.

"It's a special tool that will help us stop something very bad from happening."

"What do I do, Auntie Holly?"

"It's simple." Holly answered. "All you have to do is hold our hands. We'll take care of the rest."

"It's all right, my darling," Adjua said, setting Ashanti on the floor and sitting herself down a short distance back. "Nothing will hurt you. I will be right here the whole time. I promise you will be safe." She only hoped that she spoke the truth. "Can you be brave for me and help them?"

Ashanti looked as if she was mulling it over for a moment, but she smiled and nodded.

"Good, my beauty," Adjua smiled, caressing her head. "Now, do as they tell you, and I will be beside you. I will not leave you. Not ever."

"I wish I'd brought Effie with me," Ashanti said. "She's very brave, and she makes me feel brave, too."

"Well, now you've a chance to protect Effie, and all the children of the world, and their bears," Holly said, reaching out. "Take my hand. It will be all right."

Ashanti nodded and reached out to hold both of their hands.

"Right, let's try this again," Qwyrk said.

Adjua took a deep breath, knowing that nothing would ever be the same again.

✳   ✳   ✳

Now:

Qwyrk breathed a heavy and painful sigh of relief as she saw a young woman emerge from the trees carrying her young daughter in one arm, while holding an ornate staff in her free hand.

"Adjua!" she called out as she and Holly hurried to her, taking advantage of the confusion the mounted jirry-jirries had sown (why they were here, Qwyrk had no idea, but they were most welcome; honestly, not something she expected to feel). "Thank Goddess, and thank you!"

Adjua seemed terrified and she held Ashanti close, putting her daughter down to stand on her own. Holly went to the girl and knelt to give her a big hug. Dill and Chives closed rank in front of them, their strange but no doubt deadly weapons aimed at anything that dared get too close.

"What you must do, do quickly," Adjua commanded.

"The quicker the better, I promise," Qwyrk nodded. She wanted this finished, and soon; the pain in her side was becoming unbearable.

"Right, darling," Holly said, one hand on Ashanti's shoulder. "Do you remember what we did earlier, back at your home?"

Ashanti nodded and smiled.

"Good! Let's do it again, shall we? Only this time, it's for real. This time, we'll make the monsters go away, forever."

Holly took Ashanti's hand, and reached out to Qwyrk, who took hers and Ashanti's as she knelt.

"This had better bloody work," Qwyrk muttered to Holly.

"We saw it before, didn't we?" Holly whispered back.

"But it didn't last!"

"That was then. Say your words."

Qwyrk closed her eyes and recited the words she'd heard in the pool in a simple and short chant, over and over, growing in intensity each time. She held on to Holly and Ashanti, their hands swaying in rhythm to her words.

"It is happening!" she heard Adjua say. "It is returning!"

Through her closed eyes, Qwyrk sensed a warm glow rising up in front of her, accompanied by the faint aroma of peat smoke.

"Do not stop!" Adjua urged.

"I would suggest hurrying, if at all possible, ma'am," Qwyrk heard Dill (Chives?) say. "I have the distinct impression that this endeavor is beginning to attract the sort of attention that we don't want."

"I have no doubt, Mr. Dill," Holly answered. "But if you can hold them off with those splendid weapons of yours for just a bit, we'd be ever so grateful."

"We shall do our best, ma'am."

Through it all, Qwyrk never faltered, never stopped her chanting, even as her side ached, and her breathing became difficult.

"Is it working, mama?" she heard Ashanti say.

"It is, my dearest," her mother answered. "You are helping magic happen. Stay with them. Do not let go of their hands. I am right here, right beside you."

Qwyrk risked opening her eyes, and to her great relief, she saw a glorious sight. A spear, surrounded by white light, floated in mid-air between them, the tip pointing to the night sky. Words and markings decorated both the shaft and the blade, each wrought in exquisite perfection, like the handiwork of the gods. Her heart raced in excitement.

Just a few more times, she thought. Twice more, once more. She held her breath as she ceased her chant.

"Please stay," she whispered to the spear. "Please don't vanish or fall apart."

For a moment, no one dared move or say a word. But the weapon remained, and they all exhaled a sigh of great relief. The spear had returned to this world.

"At least now we have a chance," Qwyrk said.

"Did we do it, mama? Did we do what Auntie Holly and Auntie Qwyrk wanted?"

"Yes, my love." Adjua wrapped her arms around her little girl. "You did so well, and I am so very proud of you."

"What will they do with it?" Ashanti asked.

"We're going to stop the horrible monster that's bringing all these other monsters into the world," Holly said, as she grasped the spear and lifted it into the air. "And we're going to make them run away and never come back."

"If you are referring to the Most Tenebrous King Balor, ma'am," Chives said, pointing his rifle in the direction of a crowd of creatures eyeing them from a safe distance, "he seems to have spied this activity, and if I may say, he looks rather put out."

*   *   *

Qworum's foot throbbed from Blip's stabbing, but he knew to kneel when Balor rose. Something had caught his master's attention in the distance and for the first time, the dark king looked troubled, even worried.

"W-what is it, my lord?" Qworum asked.

Balor paid no attention to him, but took a few steps, his single-eyed gaze fixed on something. Qworum looked in that direction, over the struggles of Fomorians against Templars and Blip's fellows on their mounts. He saw a spear surrounded by white light, floating in front of... Qwyrk and Holly?

"All of this has been very amusing," Balor interrupted Qworum's train of thought. "But now the time has come to put an end to it, to crush those who oppose us, and to reclaim these lands."

"Wisely said, my master." Qworum was eager to please and show his loyalty.

"Another word from you," Balor said with an eerie calm, "and I *will* separate your head from your body and place it on a spike for all to see."

Qworum swallowed hard and began to tremble.

"The end begins now," Balor announced in a raised voice, attracting the attention of those nearest him, both servant and foe. He stood atop a rocky outcropping and held out both arms. The glyphs on his skin began to glow in a sickly pale blue light. He opened his maw wide to let out a terrifying cry that echoed across the clearing and brought everyone and everything to a standstill.

Qworum quivered, and for the first time, he began to realize just what horror he had helped to unleash into this world.

CHAPTER TWENTY-THREE

Qwypp panicked. In a moment of not thinking things through, she teleported herself to her best friend's side. Qwykk was lying on the ground writhing in pain, her left leg showing a nasty gash, blue-green blood staining her camouflage trousers.

"Lie still, sweetie. Don't try to move." Qwypp ripped off the bottom of one trouser leg and tied it around Qwykk's wound.

"We can't lie still!" Qwykk protested. "That thing'll come back and finish us off."

"I know, which is why I'm getting us out of here." She heard the thumping of one foot, slapping against the hard cavern floor, getting closer. Then another.

"No! We have to stay here. Qwyzz said so. The three of us are the only chance of gettin' that key out."

"We can worry about that later. Right now, we have to get out of here!"

"No, we don't," Qwykk grunted in pain as she struggled to sit up. "We've gotta stay here. Tell Horatio to get his tiny arse over here."

Qwypp hesitated.

"Do it!"

The flapping single foot grew closer and louder.

"Horatio!" Qwypp called out into the dark. "Get in here, now! We need you!" She looked back at Qwykk, who had started to limp in a circle around the obelisk, one hand touching the ground.

"What are you doing?"

"Just trust me, all right?"

Qwypp shook her head, certain they were all about to die in a decidedly horrible manner. "Horatio! Now!"

A dull shockwave and a puff of stale cigar smoke later, and he stood at her feet. "Um, what are we doin', exactly? I mean, besides makin' ourselves proverbial sittin' ducks?"

"Just stay by the obel-, obli-, the big rock thingie, all right?" Qwykk ordered as she continued her uneasy orbit around said thingie.

"What exactly are you doin'?" Horatio looked her askance. "This ain't no time for the Hokey Pokey, love, and personally, I'd rather not be reduced to a pulp waitin' on you to finish."

The flapping foot became a stomping foot, and the sound of a cracking whip echoed around the cavern.

"He's got a point, love," Qwypp said, her nerves very much on edge. "Whatever you got planned had better work. I don't know if I can get us out of here before that whip falls."

Qwykk stumbled and grumbled before picking herself up. "Damn it! I can feel my magic drainin' away, just like Qwyrk said. I've gotta finish this."

"Finish what?" Horatio demanded. "What the bloody hell are you doin'?"

"This!" Qwykk announced in triumph, just as her leg gave way, and she slumped to the ground. "Get in here next to me. Come on, snuggle up!"

Qwypp glanced at Horatio and saw that he looked as confused as she was. "Fine, but if we die horribly, it's all your fault, and I'm never forgiving you." She sat down next to Qwykk, and seeing that she was shivering, took her in her arms.

"I don't feel so good," Qwykk said.

"I know, love. It's the poison in that damned thing's weapon. It drains our powers, but only for a little while. You're gonna be fine." *If we're not all dead in the next few minutes.*

Horatio sidled up to Qwypp. "Ya know, normally I'd be thrilled to be sitting in close proximity to two ladies such as yourselves, but in these circumstances, all I can think of to say is, if whatever this is don't work, it's been an honor to serve with you. You're brave and not nearly as stupid as you seem."

Qwypp glared at him.

"Yeah, fair enough, that didn't come out right."

"Look out!" Qwypp looked up in horror to see the Fachan towering over them. In one swift motion, its single arm swung forward, bringing the deadly whip down.

* * *

"Good shot, Mr. Dill."

"Thank you, Mr. Chives, I've been practicing."

"So I see. Any maneuvers in particular?"

"Indeed, though now is perhaps not the best time to discuss them. Broadsword to your left, Mr. Chives."

"Much obliged. And mind the battle axe, Mr. Dill."

"I see it, thank you, Mr. Chives."

"Shall we discuss new tactics later over a pint of something local?"

"An excellent notion, assuming we survive the evening."

"That would be a precondition for said quaffing."

"Indeed, it would, sir. Indeed, it would. We can only hope that we last through the night."

"A worthwhile hope, indeed, Mr. Dill. For the moment, we might wish to step to one side to avoid the incoming flaming arrows."

"Another excellent notion, Mr. Chives."

"I have my moments, Mr. Dill."

"Indeed, you do, sir. Indeed, you do."

*   *   *

Aeval leered as she towered over Jilly, now trapped under Granny's motionless body. "It is a pity," the banshee said. "The two of you could have been valued allies, but alas, it was not to be. And so, I must put an end to your meddling, so that my own girls can flourish."

"They're not your girls, you wretched creature!"

Jilly turned her head to see Star Tao rousing himself, or rather, Scáthach; her voice spoke through him still. Jilly's heart raced.

"Why will you not stay down?" Aeval demanded, shooting a hateful glance his way.

"Because this world is not yours," Granny said in a weak voice, "and it never will be."

"Granny!" Jilly whispered, joy and hope returning to her all at once.

Aeval flew into a rage. "Shut your mouths, all of you!" The dark magic began to surround her hands again. "I will destroy each of you in turn, and I will enjoy it as I make you watch each other die." Waves of purple and black light spun around her hands.

Jilly searched for anything that might counter it, even the silliest of spells, but she couldn't prepare anything in time, had no spell components, and could barely breathe under the weight of Granny, much less recite any kind of proper enchantment. She wrapped her arms around her mentor and waited for the end.

"I'm sorry," she whispered, as tears formed in her eyes. "I've failed you. I've failed us all."

"No," she heard Moirin's voice sound with force and authority.

"No, what?" Aeval spat.

"You won't harm them."

"Will I not?" Aeval mocked.

"Your hold over me is over."

"Is it, now? Aileen? Your companion is bothersome. Teach her a lesson, and if she persists, you have my permission to kill her."

"Remember who you are, Aileen," Scáthach said. "You may be of her blood, but you're also of mine, and that means somethin', somethin' more important than the lies she's told you."

"Aileen," Moirin said as her eyes returned to normal, the streaks in her hair fading. "This is wrong, you know it is. Look around." She pointed at the chaos all around them. "Is this what we are? What we want to be? Do we want these monsters and freaks loose in the world? What right do they have to be here?"

"I..." Aileen hesitated. "I don't, I mean—"

"Do not listen to her!" Aeval howled. "She has been corrupted by this child and her master. I will only tell you this once, Aileen: you defy me at your peril."

"At your peril?" Moirin snapped. "Is that love? Is that family? Do you hear what she's saying, Aileen? I spent years trapped by those damned kobolds, only to escape into this?" She looked back to Aeval. "You dare threaten her? Yeah, missy, I've got somethin' to say to you: feck off!"

Aeval lobbed a pulse of her dark energy at Moirin, who let out a piercing shriek in defense. Jilly watched in awe as these two primal forces collided, neither giving way to the other. Moirin's voice grew louder as Aeval screeched to amplify her own magic.

"Aileen!" Jilly managed to shout. "Help Moirin! Be there for her, please!"

"Remember who you are, Aileen!" Scáthach cried out again.

Aileen seemed confused, lost and shook her head a few times.

Aeval's magic began to overpower Moirin's voice, as the dark energy inched ever closer to her. Jilly knew that if it reached her friend, Moirin would die.

"Aileen! Please!"

Aileen held her hands over her ears, as if trying to block out the opposing forces tugging at her. She glanced up again, looked at Moirin, and to everyone else in turn.

"Please!" Jilly screamed, her voice going hoarse.

Aeval's magic had almost reached Moirin's face.

Aileen drew herself up, as if at last understanding what was about to happen. She unleashed a powerful wail of her own. It joined with Moirin's failing effort, bolstering it, becoming one with it. Their voices merged into something new, something powerful, something that would not be denied.

And for once, Jilly realized, Aeval looked genuinely afraid.

*   *   *

As Balor threw his head back, the markings covering his body glowed ever brighter. He fixed his one enormous eye on the night sky above, on the moon that illuminated his hideous visage. He uttered words in a tongue that Penelope didn't understand, but she knew this was the beginning of the end. She still clung to the hope that all of this was some horrific dream.

The monster's minions were fixated on his actions.

She thought of sneaking off. They'd never know, except that she was still tied up. And what about Winston? Her poor, dear Winston? She was about to give in to despair when something nudged her mind, a tug, a poke.

Penelope!

"What?" she whispered. "Who's there? Who said that?"

It's me! It's Winston!

"Winston!" she cried, hushing herself at once and glancing around to see that no one had heard her. "I don't understand!" she whispered.

I'm inside him, or rather, he's using my physical form to create the monstrosity that you see, but I am still very much a part of his mind, and right now, he's distracted, reciting some ancient text in a language that sounds to me rather like a proto-Celtic variant, but it can't possibly be that late, if these creatures were already in Ireland thousands of years earlier. It makes me wonder if they had an influence on those later tongues, so that—

"Winston, darling? Not now."

Oh, yes, right, sorry! Now listen: while I'm in here, I share his thoughts and some of his knowledge. He greatly fears that spear conjured up over there, which is why he's now resorted to some enchantment to try to stop its use. But here's the thing: the weapon will only work on him by a stab to that blasted eye of his. It's his proverbial Achilles' Heel. If the weapon hits anywhere else, it will simply bounce off. You have to get to those ladies and relay that information, or their efforts will be in vain.

"But, but how can I tell them? They'll never hear me over the clamor."

Ah, that's where I think I can come in. His followers are all distracted at the moment?

"Yes."

Good, then you simply need to slip away.

"But I'm bound."

Not to worry. I can access some of his magical power, I believe, and use it to undo those wretched ropes. Give me just a moment.

Penelope waited, pulling at the bonds around her hands and feet, trying to force them apart.

There!

At once, the ropes slipped off and fell to the ground, as if they'd never held her.

"It worked!" she said, a tad louder than was advisable.

Excellent! Now get to them quickly, before you're seen!

"Will I... will I ever see you again?"

I don't know, my dear. But I'm terribly sorry about how I treated you before. It wasn't me.

"I know. And in that case, I have something that I simply must say." Tears welled up. "Winston, I—"

There's no time, Penelope. He's coming out of his trance. Go! Now! Run!

*　　*　　*

"I don't like the look or sound of that," Qwyrk said as Balor raised his voice in a piercing cry. She threw up her hands. "Why do they always have to glow like they're about to explode? And raise their arms like that? And make a bloody spectacle out of it?"

"I've a feeling it's now or never for us, darling," Holly said, clutching the spear, and turning it about.

Qwyrk heard a rustling sound and turned to see someone emerging from the forest, a short yellow-colored creature with a nose shaped like a trumpet. She recognized Bogtrotter's herald as he hopped into the clearing.

Qwyrk shot him an exasperated glance. "About bloody time you lot showed up!"

"Yeah, um, about that." The herald shuffled his little feet on the ground. "The boss sends his apologies. Says they're gonna be a bit late."

"A bit late?" Qwyrk couldn't believe it. Actually, she could. "What, are they waiting for a replacement bus service, or something? How are they late to the flipping end of the world?!"

"He's busy, you know."

"Busy doing what? Rewriting his crap play for the tenth time?"

"Excuse me, but that is a work of genius!"

"Oh, I'm sure it is! 'The Desiccation of Proboscis,' or whatever the hell it is. So, when are they getting here?"

"Soon."

"That's not helpful!"

"It's all I've got."

"Well, we don't have time to wait. *If* he gets his arse here, tell him and his bloody minions to do whatever they can to keep those bastards away from us, especially Holly, all right? I'm in a bit of a bad way right now, and she's going to need some assistance."

Adjua stepped forward. "I will help."

Qwyrk shook her head. "You've done enough already. You need to keep Ashanti safe. I'm guessing that all three of us have to be here to keep the spear on this plane. So, you two stay with Dill and Chives, and I'll be right over there, keeping away whatever comes.

"I can't do this alone, darling." Holly said. "I need you by my side. We're a team, right?"

"I'm hurt, love." Qwyrk took her hand. "First time out in a new body, and I go and get myself beat up bad. Typical, eh?" Another round of pain shot through her, and she winced.

Holly gripped her hand, now looking very distressed. "Oh no! Oh, love, what happened?"

"Took a hit to my left side. I'm still standing, so I don't think it was enough to do me in, but I doubt I'll be much use to you if we try to push through that mob to get to the final boss over there. As much as I hate to admit it, I'm better off here protecting Adjua and Ashanti." She put her hand on Holly's cheek. "I'm so sorry, love, but if I mess up, if I get hit again, it'll only slow you down. And if I go down... permanently, I'm not sure you could get it done, not in the time we have."

Holly began to cry as she let go of the spear—Adjua rushed to retrieve it—and cupped her hands around Qwyrk's cheeks. "I love you," she said as tears streaked down her cheeks, "more than anything, more than life."

"And I love you," Qwyrk answered, taking Holly's face in her hands as they touched foreheads, not holding back her own tears. "Listen to me: this isn't goodbye, all right? And it bloody well isn't the end. We've come way too far for that. Now, you get out there, and you do what needs to be done. I'll be here, and I'll damned well be waiting for you when this is all over!"

Holly broke down and sobbed. Qwyrk broke down and sobbed. They hugged and held one another. They parted and kissed, then hugged, and kissed again.

"I *will* come back to you, I promise!" Holly insisted.

"I know. Now go kick some arse!"

"Come, Beti," Vishala said, approaching them after having waited in the distance. "We will finish this together."

"And wherever my lady goes, so go I!" Mango announced as he sauntered up next to her.

"And me! And me!" Minty meowed, as he took his place next to his brother. He had a small dent in his little helmet that somehow made him look a bit more fierce.

Holly laughed, in spite of the dire situation. "Well then, how can we fail?"

"Thing is, for all your good intentions, you ain't gonna get far without our help," a deep, gravelly voice said from behind them, coming from in the woods. Bogtrotter strode out, in full kilted Highland finery and carrying a rather impressive-looking axe. At his side were his many, many minions, carrying crude weapons and wearing comical excuses for armor, though Qwyrk admired their tenacity; the perpetual cowards were here, at the end of all things, ready to sacrifice everything.

"All right, Boggie? About time you showed up, yeah?" Qwyrk smiled.

"I do apologize, but I was a bit busy, rounding up some more help." He turned his head and nodded. Behind him, trolls, ogres, goblins, dark elves (yes elves!), and all sorts of unpleasant creatures Qwyrk would normally enjoy pounding into the ground emerged from the woods. Line after line of them, all armed and looking quite dangerous. In their midst, she even recognized those odious goblins, Silktassel and Sneezewort, armed with clubs.

"What's this?" she demanded, amazed.

"Darkfae," Bogtrotter answered.

"Yeah, I bloody know that. Why are they here?"

"Partisans of the faction of the innovators," Bogtrotter explained. "They ain't happy about the ancients tryin' to make this play. So, it weren't hard for me to convince 'em to join us. 'The enemy of my enemy is my friend' and all that. They've agreed to a two-day truce to get this mess sorted out."

Qwyrk shook her head and laughed. "Boggie, you are a marvel!"

"This is true. Now then, shall we?"

"Who's that?" Holly interrupted, tugging at Qwyrk's arm.

A human woman, perhaps fifty years old, slipped through the last line of Fomorians who were still captivated by Balor's light show. She looked frazzled, and her dress was dirty and torn. She stumbled toward them, arms held up.

"Please!" she said. "I can help. I know something!"

"Who are you?" Holly asked. Qwyrk clenched her fists, worried this might be a trick.

"My name is Penelope. Um, that's not important. It's him, that horrid Balor creature. I know how to defeat him!"

*　　*　　*

The Fachan's whip bounced off of an invisible barrier and back to strike it in its featureless face. The force of its own blow sent the creature flying across the cavern to crash into a wall. It slumped to the ground, obviously (and amusingly) stunned.

"What the bloody hell just happened?" Qwypp looked on in disbelief.

"A little trick I learned a long time ago." Qwykk smiled, even as she winced in pain. "Wasn't quite sure it'd work, but I'm chuffed it did!"

"Hang on." Horatio shot her a look. "So, you had us crouch down with you in the hopes that your little spell was going send tall, dark, and gruesome flyin' away? As much as I found it funny to watch, that was one hell of a huge risk!"

"Yeah, well it worked, didn't it?"

"So how long does this nifty little enchantment last?" Qwypp asked, impressed by her friend's ingenuity.

"In my state? An hour, I reckon, maybe less. Long enough for our mates to do what they have to up there, anyway."

They heard another foot stomping on the rocky ground.

"And you're sure they can't get to us?" Horatio asked.

Qwykk nodded.

He clapped his hands together. "Oh, this is gonna be right fun to watch..."

*   *   *

Aeval shrieked as the force of two voices struck her full-on, knocking her down and breaking her spell. Jilly stared in shock. The power of the banshee's human descendants—awesome, raw, unchecked—thrilled and terrified her.

She'd rolled Granny to one side with all due gentleness, but still clung to her, afraid of letting go, afraid of what might happen if they were separated.

"You insolent brats!" Aeval howled as she pulled herself to her feet. She looked to be in tremendous pain, but like an injured beast, Jilly knew that only made her more dangerous. "I will do more than kill you!" She advanced on Moirin and Aileen, ignoring Jilly. "I will obliterate every trace of you. I will erase you from all memory, you who taint this bloodline with your betrayal!"

Her warning snapped both young ladies out of their call. Their eyes returned to normal, and Jilly saw fear in them. Moirin took a step back, then another. She took Aileen's hand and pulled her along.

"Normally, I would enjoy the chase," Aeval hissed, "the thrill of hunting you down. But not this time. No." She advanced on them with astonishing speed and caught each by the throat, lifting them up in the air with ease. "This time, I will forego that pleasure and rip you apart with my bare hands, here and now!"

"No!" Jilly screamed. "Stop!"

"Take the wand, dear." Jilly looked to Granny, who offered up her magical implement.

"What? I can't do it. I need you!"

"No, you don't. You're ready. You've been ready for some time. Do it. Save them. They saved you."

Jilly grasped the wand and felt its warmth, an elder enchantment that surged into her hand, running up her arm. Drawing a deep breath, she nodded to Granny, and stood up.

She took one step, and another, and another. Which each, her resolve strengthened, even as fear gripped her. She ignored her shaking hands, ignored the instinct to run.

"Not this time," she said.

Just in front of her, an eldritch force was about to murder two humans, one of whom was her friend. They struggled in her grip and Jilly knew they wouldn't last long. Hands still shaking, she pointed the wand at Aeval.

"All right, you banshee bitch!" she yelled. "I've had quite enough of you!"

Jilly willed something from deep inside, a force unlike anything she'd ever sensed before. A surge of primal magical power welled up in her hands and directed itself through the tool in her grasp. Just as Aeval turned with a snarl, the force of that power hit her with all of its supernatural fury.

*　*　*

"It's the eye!" Penelope gasped. "That awful, horrible thing. It's the only part on him that's vulnerable to the spear."

"And you know this how?" Qwyrk asked, more than a bit skeptical.

"Winston told me!"

"Winston...?"

"A charming fellow, a retired professor. He's trapped inside Balor's body. He accidentally unleashed that monster when he found the key and put it in the obelisk. I'm sure he was already possessed then. He'd never have done something like that willingly! He told me everything by some sort of telepathic message, which means he's still alive, trapped inside that horrid creature!"

"I didn't... get most of that." Qwyrk struggled to understand as pain began to make her feel light-headed.

"It makes sense, though," Holly said.

"How do we know she's not just a Fomorian trick?"

"We don't, but I don't think we have a choice right now."

"Look, I swear to you, I'm telling you what he told me," Penelope insisted. "Please! You have to help him, help all of us!"

"That's good enough for me," Holly said. She looked at her mother and the felines. "Shall we?"

"We shall," Vishala gave her a determined smile. "Kubera protect us."

Holly glanced at Qwyrk for what Qwyrk hoped wouldn't be the last time. She mouthed the words, "I love you," and then, with spear in hand and her family beside her, she charged into the fray.

* * *

Aeval absorbed the full force of Jilly's attack. She lurched forward, dropping Moirin and Aileen. They collapsed to the ground, coughing and wheezing. But Jilly didn't relent. If anything, her confidence grew and she tried to increase the force of the power flowing through her. Aeval cried out and stumbled, falling to one knee. She whipped her head around and glared at Jilly with pure hate. Her eyes glowed white with an unearthly luminosity. For all the power that Jilly directed into her enemy, she knew that this ancient creature, this force of nature, was stronger. But she didn't care. She wouldn't give up. She couldn't.

And in the next moment, everything changed.

*   *   *

Holly tore through the first line of Fomorians, striking them down with ease.

Right beside her, her mother whipped her staff about with effortless grace, felling one enemy after another. Even the little felines showed their prowess, leaping back and forth between the hapless creatures, sowing confusion, pain, and fear, softening up the Fomorians for the deadly blows that their mistresses delivered in their wake.

Holly reveled in the power this ancient weapon bestowed on her, but she kept her focus. Balor loomed directly ahead, his glowing body a beacon that seemed to dare any to come and challenge him.

"Challenge accepted," she said as she felled another of his minions. She saw that the Templars were starting to falter; more than one had fallen already, and even the jirry-jirries and their steeds struggled to keep these ancient creatures at bay.

"This is it, Beti!" her mother shouted. "We must make for him now!"

Holly nodded as Balor's luminosity intensified. "We'll do this, mother!"

And then it hit them all.

*　*　*

A wave of grey washed over the clearing, like a thick fog. Everything in its grip simply stopped moving. No, they were moving, but almost imperceptibly so.

"What's happening?" Qwyrk shouted in panic. "Is this another one of those... time things? Because I really hate time things. What do we do?" She looked back. Adjua, Penelope, Dill, and Chives seemed frozen in place. "Lovely."

"Mama!" Ashanti shouted.

Qwyrk swore as she dashed over to the little girl.

"Auntie Qwyrk, what happened to mama?" Ashanti cried, tugging at Adjua's motionless hand.

"I'm not sure, honey, but I need you stay with her, all right? Don't leave her. She needs you. I'm going to get help, but you'll be safe if you stay here. Can you be brave? Can you do that for me?"

Ashanti nodded through her tears. "Yes, Effie taught me to be brave."

"Good." Qwyrk kissed her on the head. "Remember, stay here."

She turned and plunged into the haze.

"Qwyrk!" she heard Holly's voice calling to her.

"Holly! What's happening?"

Holly came into view, spear in hand. "Balor's hit everyone with some kind of time magic, I think, slowed everything down."

"I bloody knew it! I hate time things! But why aren't we caught up in it?"

"I think because we summoned the spear. Ashanti's unaffected, as well?"

Qwyrk nodded. "She's fine. She's scared, but I told her to stay with Adjua, not to leave her side. What about your mum? Your cats?"

"Frozen, just like everyone else. Looks like it's you and me, after all."

Qwyrk held her side and winced in pain again.

"I hate seeing you hurting," Holly said, placing a gentle hand on Qwyrk's shoulder.

"Nothing for it now, I'm afraid," Qwyrk said. "We have to do this."

"At least take my mother's staff," Holly said, handing Qwyrk the elegant weapon.

A deep and insidious voice called to them through the gloom. "Come to me, chosen handmaidens of Scáthach. I have waited long enough to claim this world. Let us finish this once and for all, if you have the courage. Bring Gáe Bulg to me."

Holly looked at Qwyrk and reached out to take her hand. "Together."

"Until the end, love." Qwyrk squeezed her hand.

Side by side, they pushed on through the murkiness and the multitudes of the frozen, and marched right toward the lucent horror that beckoned them from his place on high.

*   *   *

Blow after blow struck at them as they huddled by the obelisk, but none cracked the enchanted shell of Qwykk's making. After each round of being hurtled into the darkness, the three Fachan in the cavern—yes, there were bloody well three of them—would come hopping back to try again.

"Aw, whatsa matter, you repulsive goons?" Horatio taunted. "Havin' some performance problems? Not surprised, really."

"You might want to ease off on the taunting there, just saying," Qwypp suggested.

"Duly noted, but come on, you have to admit, it *is* pretty funny!"

Another round of attacks sent them flying again. Horatio dissolved into a fit of guffaws.

"How's your leg doing, love?" Qwypp squeezed Qwykk's shoulder.

"Not good. It really hurts!" She clutched her ankle.

"I'm so sorry. We can still get you out of here if you need."

"No! We ain't goin' nowhere, not till Qwyzz tells us to pull out that key."

"You always were the most stubborn one of us."

"Yeah, but you love it!"

The creatures hopped up again and brought down new blows on their protective shield.

But the Fachan were not thrown back. They lingered for a moment in a fit of crackling, hissing, and sparking. They glanced at each other as if in surprise, and then struck again, with the same result.

"I do not like the looks of that, I'm sayin' right now!" Horatio exclaimed.

"What the hell's happening?" Qwypp demanded.

"Don't know," Qwykk said. "The protection is supposed to last for an hour at least. Maybe down here, it just doesn't?"

"Or maybe because you're hurt, it's already wearing off? Right, we have to get out of here," Qwypp said. "We'll come back."

"No!" Qwykk grabbed her. "We're not leaving! Not without that key."

The whips lashed out above them again, to the sound of cracking glass against the shield.

"Love, we may not get the chance," Horatio said.

"Just a bit longer? Please?"

Qwypp nodded. "But the first sign of one of them breaking through, we're out of here!"

"That's the thing, love," Horatio said, "they're already breaking through!"

*　*　*

Qwyrk and Holly strode toward Balor, pushing aside the near-frozen forms of his servants.

"I'm telling you, mate," Qwyrk snipped, "that whole supernatural speedo look is just really not working for you. I know you wanted to show off all those nifty markings and whatnot, but speaking for myself, something a little more modest would really have helped me not want to heave. You know, maybe a 1950s two-piece bikini? Something with a little more class? I mean, if you're going to rule the world, you should probably try to dress the part. A robe, maybe? Preferably a long one."

"Banter from a weakling about to meet her death," Balor taunted with a cruel laugh. "I do admire your hubris in the face of obliteration. It amuses me, in truth. There is much to salute in warriors such as you, but since you will not acknowledge your true god, I have no choice but to destroy you."

"We've heard it all before," Holly said, now whipping the spear around with the same remarkable skills as with her stick. "But there's fear in your repulsive eye. You know what this is, and we know what it can do to you. Am I right, would-be god?"

"You know what it is," Balor scoffed, "but not how to use it."

"They know enough, you abomination!" A woman's voice sounded from the gloom.

Qwyrk saw someone emerging from the dark... "Star Tao?"

"Scáthach." Balor directed his attention to the newcomer. "How amusing. Will you now wield the weapon and destroy me?"

"I would fight," she said through Star Tao, "but this tiny body is far too weak and puny."

"Then the game has ended," Balor mocked. "Though I will allow you to watch as I kill these two."

"Oh, how generous of you," Qwyrk sneered. "You're welcome to try."

Star Tao smiled and held out his hands, which began to pulse with some kind of sparkling energy.

"Mate, I really hope you know what you're doing," Qwyrk said.

The spear began sparkling, too. "What's happening?" Holly asked.

"I've imbued the sacred weapon with a portion of my essence," Scáthach said. "It will guide you and finish the task. Now go and, as you folks say, kick his bloody arse!"

"Best words of encouragement I've heard all day." Qwyrk grinned through her pain.

As if sensing the balance of power may have shifted, Balor clenched his fists. The markings on his body began to glow brighter.

Holly pointed the spear at their enemy. "Shall we?"

"We shall!" Qwyrk smiled.

Holly broke into a run, Qwyrk right behind her. They pushed their way through the last of the frozen Fomorians and up the side of the hill to where their ghastly foe waited. Holly thrust the spear at Balor, but he sidestepped and lashed out with a clawed hand, just missing her. Qwyrk delivered a blow to his back with Vishala's Silambam staff. It hissed and sparked, but did no damage.

"Heh. Do you think that little Yakshi trinket will harm me?" he taunted.

"Oh, I'm sure it won't," Qwyrk said. "I just have to piss you off enough to make you careless. And good Goddess, you are bloody appalling up close! Is this really the best face your sycophants could come up with? Did they just, what? Run out of time and say, 'sod it, let's just make one ginormous eyeball and stuff it on his head'? I mean, come on!"

Balor swiped at her, but he missed. Qwyrk landed a blow on his head. It bounced off again, but it did indeed piss him off. He shrunk back as Holly thrust the spear at him, grazing the side of his face. It left no mark, but he grunted, as if in pain. She followed with another attack, but he was too fast and ducked away. He spun around and stepped back. A blue fire manifested between his clawed fingers, and he blew it in Holly's direction. The flames tore through the air, almost hitting her as she rolled to one side. She held up the spear, and its blade cut through the flames, slicing them in half and snuffing them out.

"Good to know it's a shield, too!" she said.

Balor growled in clear frustration.

Good, Qwyrk thought, approaching him with caution. *Keep him off balance, make him careless. He's no different than any other pillock we've ever faced.*

Balor reached out and seized one of his enspelled, immobile Fomorian flunkies. He opened his maw and bit into the creature's neck. It didn't cry out as he drank several gulps of blood from the wound and cast the body aside. In the next instant, he seemed to grow a bit taller.

"All right, maybe he is a bit different." Qwyrk stopped short.

At the same time, Holly maneuvered behind him.

"What the hell was that?" Qwyrk blurted out, drawing his attention. "Some kind of Fomorian energy drink? Yeah, you're probably going to have a few problems marketing that one, mate."

Holly moved to strike again, and Qwyrk charged forward, swinging her own weapon at his midsection. Her blow bounced off, but a shower of sparks flew into the air, striking him in the face. He growled and swiped to disperse them.

Holly stabbed with the spear, and lurched forward, unharmed by the attack.

Qwyrk swore. *We're not getting to him. And we don't have our strength and stamina anymore.*

Balor sidestepped another swing, but instead of retaliating, he moved to where Qworum stood, frozen in place. One touch brought him back. Qworum looked around in shock.

"Finish that one." Balor pointed to Qwyrk.

"Gladly," Qworum smiled. With a flash of yellow lights, he vanished. The next moment, he stood beside Qwyrk. Before she could react, he backhanded her across the face, sending her crashing to the ground as a wave of pain spread across her jaw and neck. She tasted iron in her mouth and spit blood. Red blood.

"Oh, but you had to make such a terrible sacrifice, didn't you?" Qworum stepped forward, fists raised. "To try to save this world? To be with her? What a shame it's all been in vain."

"I did the right thing, the only thing, which is something you'll never understand."

She dragged herself to her feet, clutching the stick she could barely use. She saw Holly in the distance, keeping Balor at bay, just. "Truth be told," she said as she drew herself up, "you've always annoyed the crap out of me, even when I thought I could count on you."

"Well, the feeling is mutual, I assure you. The only reason I didn't have you killed a long time ago is that you are popular in many circles, and there would have been repercussions, difficulties."

"Wait, I'm popular? Do I have like, a fan club and likes on social media? Aw, brilliant! Thanks for letting me know, you knob. It'll make kicking your arse *so* much more satisfying!"

She swung at him, but he teleported away, only to appear behind her and strike her again. The blow to her back made her lurch forward, fall to her knees, and drop her weapon. Before she could regain her stance, she felt a kick to her side. Her injured left side. Another wave of agony shot through her as she collapsed to the ground. Her eyes watered. She felt sick and light-headed. Somewhere in the distance, she heard Holly call her name.

"You were saying about kicking my arse?" Qworum taunted as he paced nearby.

"Yeah," she whispered, "I may have to rethink that." *Come closer.*

"I would imagine that would be prudent." He stepped forward.

She reached out to grab his ankle and, pulling his leg toward her with a violent jerk, sent him crashing to the ground. She was not on top of him as fast as she wanted to be, but she stunned him as she delivered the first punch to his jaw.

"Yeah, I've decided to straight up kill you, instead!"

She struck him again and again, grabbing his robe and slamming his head into the ground. She slapped him, elbowed him, and punched him again. She unleashed years of frustration and rage on this traitorous vermin, and she reveled in it. Blows that would have left a mortal long dead only made a little impact, but it was enough to stop him, enough for her to exhaust herself. He lay beneath her, unmoving as she paused for breath, human adrenaline being the only thing keeping her upright.

"Qwyrk!" Holly yelled from somewhere. "I need you, help!"

*　*　*

Holly's blows couldn't pierce Balor's hide, and she couldn't get to his eye. He grinned with his hideous, fanged maw as he closed in on her. He reached for her, but she stumbled back. He did so again, and she now realized his tactic, too late. He wasn't trying to hurt her; he'd backed her into a crevice. Her heart pounded as she realized she was trapped.

"Qwyrk! I need you! Help!"

"There is nowhere for you to go," Balor taunted. "You have the weapon, and you have the spirit of Scáthach within it, and yet, still you cannot defeat me. Do you not see? I am the absolute. I am eternal. Kneel to me as your god, and perhaps I will yet be merciful. Perhaps."

The words of Fayette came back to her, and the words of her mother, who for so long had lived with the dreadful knowledge of this moment. In the darkness of this small ravine, she would meet her end.

"I'm sorry, mother," she whispered. "I'm sorry Qwyrk." Tears formed in her eyes. "I wasn't good enough to do this. Fayette was right after all."

She tightened the grip on the spear and made ready to make one final charge.

"Hey, Admiral Underpants!"

"Qwyrk!" Holly shouted.

Qwyrk emerged from the haze, swinging the staff about and leaving trails of sparks in its wake. "If you're going to send idiots to do your work for you, at least make sure they're not bloody useless."

"Why will you not die?" Balor demanded.

"Oh, I don't know. It's more fun staying around and pissing you off, you twat!"

Holly knew this was her moment. Taking advantage of Qwyrk's momentary distraction, she charged at Balor, thrusting the spear at his muscled chest. She knew it wouldn't pierce his magical skin, but it just might be painful enough to give them an advantage.

Indeed, he roared as the spear scraped against his glowing flesh. Meanwhile, Qwyrk swung her staff at the back of his head. It was enough of a blow to knock his noggin to one side, and she swung at him again and again, batting his head about like a grotesque piñata.

Holly spun the spear around and slammed its end into his midsection. He gasped and lurched forward.

"Didn't expect that, did you?" she taunted, whipping the spear about again and managing to scrape the side of his jaw with its blade. He roared, and in that moment, she realized.

"Qwyrk! The closer the spear gets to his eye, the more it hurts him!" The spear began to glow, as if in response.

"You will not vanquish me!" Balor thundered. He punched toward Holly with a magical shockwave that knocked her back, sending her sprawling to the ground. She hit her head on the ground and felt a wash of pain, followed by the light-headed sensation that her consciousness was leaving her.

CHAPTER TWENTY-FOUR

Two chain whips bore down on the magical shield to the sound of crackling and hissing.

"Qwykk, love, we can't stay here." Qwypp held her tight. "Those things are gonna burst through any minute."

"And then, we're all fecked." Horatio filled in the blank that none of them wanted to admit out loud.

"If we leave now, we won't get another chance," Qwykk protested. "You can go if you want, but I'm stayin' here."

"Oh, don't be daft!" Qwypp snapped at her. "Do you honestly think I'd leave you here with those things?"

"Thanks," Qwykk said. "I've just got a feelin' we need to stay."

"I have no idea why I'm agreein' to this," Horatio grumbled, "but she's right. This is our best shot, and if we bugger off now, they might bring in reinforcements. So, just a bit longer?"

Qwypp shook her head. "If we get killed, I'm gonna drag you both around as companion spirits for all eternity!"

"Aw love," Horatio said with a toothy grin, "didn't know you cared."

"I don't," Qwypp snarked as another whip laid into their defense and the sound of cracking glass got louder.

* * *

Holly was stunned, prone. If Balor reached her before Qwyrk did...

Qwyrk's side was in agony, her head was spinning, and she knew her weapon was useless. But she had to act. She took off in a quick stagger, knowing that her failing human body wouldn't let her do what she wanted it to do.

Balor didn't seem to care about her anymore. All he wanted was the spear. And if he got it, then the game would indeed be over. She tried to think of something, but without her Shadow powers, she was weak and muddled.

Come on! Her mind reeled as she approached him from behind. *Think!*

Balor loomed over a dazed Holly. She tried to sit up, but seemed on the verge of passing out. In that last, desperate moment, a memory came to Qwyrk from when they'd sparred on the mats a few days earlier, when they'd had no cares in the world. But now at the end, Holly's words returned: "What would you do if you couldn't teleport?"

"Strike him where he's vulnerable and catch him off-balance," she said to herself in a sudden realization. "Hit him where it hurts. Not very sporting, but hey, he's the one wearing that appalling loincloth!"

Balor reached out to wrench the spear from Holly's grasp. Qwyrk winced at what she was about to do, but her beloved's life and the fate of all the worlds were on the line. Grasping the staff, she drove the end straight forward, straight toward the loincloth, straight toward what she hoped was there.

* * *

She felt like she'd been coated in sticky toffee pudding. Qwyll looked about, sensing that things had gone wrong; all of their best-laid plans and so on. Straining her head to move as sensations returned to her, she saw Qworum sprawled on the ground, only a little conscious and obviously in pain. As she began to move, the memory of the Fomorians battling enemies and failing came back to her.

"This was not supposed to happen!" she hissed.

But without Qworum hale and hearty as her ally, she risked capture if Qwyrk and her companions succeeded, or torture and death if the Fomorians surged back to claim victory. Their master seemed preoccupied with...

"Qwyrk? Of course, it would be her!" she spat. "Nothing for it, then. I'd best remove myself from this disaster while I'm still breathing. Farewell, Qworum! I always hated you, and if this is to be your end, it's a richly deserved one!"

She wanted to give him the proverbial kick while he was down but decided that slipping away under cover of dark and the general bedlam of the moment was her best option. And so, she eased her way down from the rocky outcropping and crept into the woods, disappearing into the night.

*   *   *

Qwyrk's attack struck true. Balor let out a sharp, high-pitched yelp that would have had her bursting out in laughter if not for the gravity of the situation. She jerked back the staff and landed a blow behind his right knee. In his tender state, it was enough to bring him down. He collapsed to his side, hitting the ground with a terrible thud. Qwyrk seized the moment and rushed at him. She brought her weapon under his jaw to choke him and pulled him toward herself with what strength her mortal body had left.

Balor grasped at it, trying to shake her off. She scooted out of the way, so that the back of his head hit the ground, but she held on to her grip, kept on choking him with the staff.

"Holly! I need you. Do it now, love. Do it now!"

Holly staggered forward. She seemed weak and woozy, but she held the spear in both hands, a look of determination on her weary face. Unable to free himself, Balor fell into full-on panic: squirming, grasping, and thrashing about, his hideous eye widening as his maw attempted to cry out.

Holly stood over him and raised the spear.

"Love, I can't hold him much longer!" Qwyrk warned.

Balor let out a choked cry as Holly thrust the tip of the spear down with full force into his hideous orb. He screamed a scream that even Qwyrk's choking couldn't muffle and thrashed his arms about.

But Holly was not done. Planting her boot in his chest, she drove the spear in deeper, until it made a sickening sound as it tore through the back of his head. Greyish-black blood gushed forth, running in all directions.

Balor's screams withered into whimpers, and his arms became ever more still, but Holly would not relent.

She drew the spear up and brought it down again. She cried out and struck him over and over. With each attack, the ancient creature moved less and less, until he was finally still.

"Holly," Qwyrk whispered. "We did it. You did it!"

The sound of their heavy breathing filled the cold night air. Holly let the spear fall from her hands.

Before Qwyrk could climb to her feet and go to her love, an acrid, burning smell stung her nose, and she saw dark smoke begin to pour out of Balor's lifeless maw.

"That... doesn't seem good." Qwyrk inched herself away from the gigantic corpse, feeling too weak to even stand up.

In the distance, Holly swayed from side to side, as if about to fall over.

"Holly, get away from it!" Qwyrk pleaded. Holly looked over at Qwyrk, dazed, but she took a step back, then another.

The smell intensified, and a crackling sound came from inside the body, which began vibrating and convulsing. Qwyrk knew that something was about to happen.

"Holly! Get back, get—"

There was a flash and a boom, and Qwyrk had the momentary sensation of an explosion, but she felt herself thrown some distance and then she knew no more.

* * *

Qwyzz raised his head up and found himself slumped against a tree. He saw Jilly, Aeval, and the others nearby, frozen in a grey haze, caught in mid-battle. But they were just beginning to move. In the distance he saw the entire clearing shrouded in the same substance, all of the combatants frozen the same way. Above the whole surreal scene, there was a cloud of smoke rising into the cold night sky.

"We were frozen in time, and now we're not," he said. "And that plume... can it be? Did they succeed?"

He had no more time for musing, as he heard the sounds of conflict resuming in the clearing. Aeval and Jilly began to unstick from the enchantment in mid-fight.

"I have to tell Qwypp! If Balor is defeated, they have a chance!"

He lifted his hand up to call them, but something was missing. "Good Goddess, no! Where is my ring? It must have fallen off! Oh, dear, where is my ring?"

*　　*　　*

Fomorians, Templars, jirry-jirries, Nighttime Nasties, and Darkfae all looked up to the rocky ledge in confusion.

"I daresay, chaps," Blip announced with satisfaction. "It looks rather like your overlord is no more. How disappointing for you. In that case, I would advise you all to surrender now, lest it turn into quite the beating!"

"Master! Where's the master?" A Fomorian called out, fear and panic in its voice. Black smoke billowed high into the air, mingling with the magical murk that was now releasing its time-trapped victims.

"Our lord cannot be gone!" another Fomorian insisted. "It is a trick by these creatures, these mortals and Fae and all of their foul ilk."

"Whatever you choose to believe," a Templar somewhere spoke up, "we will not stop until you are all vanquished and sent back to your own stygian realm!"

Other voices sounded, and soon a din of cacophony and confusion spread over the clearing as fast as the smoke from Balor's corpse, with no one seeming to know whether they should resume fighting or not. But animosity and bloodlust won the moment and in due course, isolated fights began to break out, spreading until a general donnybrook once again engulfed the entire area.

*   *   *

"It has to be around here somewhere. It has to be!" Qwyzz searched frantically for the ring. "It must have fallen off during the commotion. Oh dear, oh dear! How will I tell them?"

"You looking for this?" Lluck said, limping over with his palm facing up, a small item resting in it. He looked a bit worse for wear, with a dirty face, ruffled hair, and a tear in his coat.

"Yes, yes, my boy! That's it! Oh, splendid! How did you find it?"

"Must've fallen off when you took a hit from Lady Creepy out there. It landed on me, and when I came to, there it was."

"How utterly extraordinary! What are the odds?"

"Almost impossible, but I'm the lucky one, remember?"

"Quite so, quite so. May I?" He took the ring from Lluck and examined it. "Oh dear."

"What? What is it?"

"There's quite a split in the stone. I hope that won't be a problem."

"Here, let me try." Lluck took back the ring and placed both hands over it, closing his eyes. A green glow flashed from between his palms. "Try it now."

As soon as Qwypp took it back, a voice sounded through the stone, cracked and fuzzy, like radio static. "Qwyzz?"

"Oh my goodness!" Qwyzz exclaimed. "There you are! It's been quite the spectacle up here, simply extraordinary! You should see what's been happening—"

"Qwyzz! Not now! What do we do? We're trapped next to the obelisk, and some very nasty things are about to finish us off. Please tell me you have some good news?"

"Oh yes, yes I do! In fact, that's why I'm checking in: to tell you, it's time! Balor is gone, and the key should come out easily!"

"Are you sure?"

"Well, as sure as one can be about such things, I suppose, I mean it's possible that—"

"Fine, thanks, that's good enough! We'll be in touch, bye!"

Her voice faded, leaving Qwyzz and Lluck to witness the growing chaos.

"Um, we'd better do something," Lluck said. "They're coming around."

"Indeed, my boy! Shall we?"

*   *   *

"This is it!" Qwypp yelled. "Qwyzz says we have to do it, now. You were right to make us wait, love."

Qwykk gave her a weak smile. "Help me up?"

"Let's get it done, ladies," Horatio urged. "I reckon we've got less than thirty seconds before this whole barrier comes tumbling down, takin' us with it."

A loud crack above them shocked everyone back into the moment. The creatures hit the barrier harder and faster, confident that they were nearly through.

"Come on!" Qwypp yelled, as she lifted Qwykk up to stand beside her. "Horatio, get up here!"

He hopped up onto her shoulder and ran down her arm. The three of them took a hold of the key. "Right," he said, "What do we do?"

"We pull it out?" Qwypp suggested.

"Yeah, I figured that, but is there any special way to do it, or do we just give it a right old tug?"

"A keyhole is a keyhole, I think."

"Loves," Qwykk interrupted as she slumped forward, "I'm not feelin' so well."

"No, no, stay with me, darling," Qwypp said in desperation. "We have to see this through. Come on, everyone! Let's give it a pull, yeah?"

"On three?" Horatio suggested.

"One..."

"Two..."

"Three!"

They heaved. They pulled. They tugged.

And nothing happened.

*   *   *

Moirin's fingers began to tingle. She wiggled her toes, which burned as her awareness returned. She struggled to turn her head, still unable to fully feel her body. Beside her, Aileen stood, mouth open. She let out a gasp as she emerged from the haze, moving her arms slowly, as if swimming through treacle.

And on the other side, Aeval and Jilly started to return to their skirmish, the spells that they'd been throwing at each other also stilled, but now springing back to life.

Beyond them, deeper in the forest, Moirin could hear others approaching, but she didn't know if they were friend or Fomorian.

"What do I do?"

And just as quickly as everyone had been petrified, they returned to battle. Aeval howled as she hurled dark energy at Jilly, who held off the attack with Granny's wand, but only just.

"We must help our ancestor!" Aileen started toward Aeval, but Moirin caught her by the arm.

"No, wait, please! Look at what she tried to do to us. Please, stay here. Jilly saved us!"

Aileen said nothing, but Moirin saw the confusion, the conflict, the feeling of betrayal on her face, because she felt the same. Aeval had just tried to kill them, and yet Moirin still heard the call, the lure toward her ancient heritage, and it started to pull at her again.

*   *   *

"What the hell?" Qwypp shouted. "It's supposed to come right out!"

"Love, in my experience, almost nothin' ever goes the way it's supposed to," Horatio said.

"No, it's gotta work!" Qwykk said, as she struggled to stay on her feet. "We've gotta try again. Come on!"

They tried again, and again, and... nothing.

"Damn it!" Qwypp swore.

Three whips lashed over their heads and a crunch like glass about to shatter only made everything worse.

"Crap!" Horatio looked up. "A few more hits and we're done for. I'm open to suggestions?"

"We may still have to run for it," Qwypp said.

"No!" Qwykk gasped. "We've gotta do it! We have to! We're so close. Please?"

"Think, ladies, think," Horatio said. "Why would a key be stuck in a lock? It ain't like we've got any magical liquid to loosen it up. If it got turned the wrong way or... oh hell. Oh, bloody hell, it can't be that easy!"

"What? What?" Qwypp demanded.

Another attack of the whips brought hot sparks down on their heads.

"Which way does it turn?" Qwypp cried out.

"It doesn't matter, just turn it!" Horatio shouted, flinching as their attackers moved in for the kill.

Qwypp grasped the key again and turned it with some effort. Sure enough, it moved clockwise, and made a crunching, clicking sound.

"That's it!" Qwykk shouted "Try again!"

The whips struck again. The protective bubble crashed down around them in a shower of lights.

"Now!' Horatio yelled.

The three of them took hold of the key and tugged. It slipped, it loosened, it gave way, and popped out in their hands. They fell back from the obelisk and crashed right at the foot of the nearest Fachan.

Its eye glaring at them, the creature raised its whip for the killing blow and brought it down. Qwypp covered her face with her hands. But its weapon dissolved like a parting mist, and this dissolution traveled up its single arm to engulf its whole body. As they watched in astonishment, the Fachan faded away above them, followed by its two companions, leaving the cavern silent.

"What... what just happened?" Qwykk asked in a weak voice.

"I think we won?" Horatio said, sitting up.

Qwypp stared at the empty cave around them. Relief came to her. Then excitement. Then giddiness. "We did it! We bloody well did it!" She let out a yelp of joy that echoed off the cavern walls.

"Uh, love?" Horatio poked her. "It's brilliant and all, but that ain't lookin' good." He pointed to the obelisk, which had begun to glow brighter as the cavern started to shake. "I'm gonna hazard a guess that we don't wanna be down here much longer?"

"Point taken," Qwypp nodded. "Qwykk, love, hang on to that key."

"Got it!" Qwykk held it up.

Qwypp took hold of both their hands and in flash of pink light, they escaped. Finally.

*　　*　　*

The ground in the clearing began to rumble, and Blip glanced about as beings of all sorts took notice that something had changed.

"What's goin' on?" one of the creatures croaked.

"Bloody earthquake!" said another monstrous voice.

"I... I don't feel so great," a random Fomorian wheezed.

"Nor do I," answered another, "what is happening?"

"I think, my dear fellows, our revels now are ended," Blip said with some amusement and a mock salute and bow.

Indeed, the Fomorians, those fierce, horrid, and ancient beings who had so longed to rule this world again, began to fade away, like fog evaporating in the morning sun.

"No!" several of them cried out as one. "No! Help us, tenebrous king! Save us, Lord Balor!"

"I suspect that you are pleading to your dead god in vain," Blip taunted. "But do keep trying."

And one after another, they started to dissolve, to fade away in a dark fog that rose into the sky and dissipated. And their foes could only stare in wonder.

*   *   *

"This night can't get any crazier!" Moirin said. The dilemma of her loyalty resolved in the next instant.

Qwyzz and the boy scrambled out from the forest. And someone dressed up like a ridiculous superhero stepped up right behind the scowling Aeval and tapped her on the shoulder.

"You know," he said, "I'm not normally one to hit a lady, but you're a bloody supervillain, and we've all really had just about enough of you!"

He let fly a vicious punch right to her face. She fell back and hit the ground with a thud, her magical attack sputtering and shutting off like a tap. Moirin gasped, impressed with the man's courage. Jilly stumbled back, regaining her balance.

"How dare you!" Aeval hissed, picking herself up. "You insolent worm! You dare to strike one such as me? I have lived a thousand generations, and you are nothing before me! I will grind your bones to dust, I will—"

She doubled over, as if in pain. But the hapless hero hadn't hit her again. She lurched up, her eyes wide with shock.

Moirin covered her mouth with her hands.

"No!" Aeval screamed. "This, this cannot—"

She shook and convulsed. Her legs and arms no longer seemed under her control. She flailed about and a look of panic fell over her.

"Great ancestor?" Aileen whispered, reaching toward her.

"Aileen, wait!" Moirin again pulled Aileen back by her arm.

Aeval looked up at the girls with pleading eyes. "It cannot end, not like this!" A horrific cry escaped from her, unlike anything Moirin had ever heard, the sound of raw, primal terror.

Aileen screamed.

Moirin held Aileen close, watching in disbelief as Aeval began to dissolve in front of them, as if turning to dust. Aeval stared at her hands as they became transparent, and her body transformed into a dark mist.

"No!" she shrieked one final time as her form turned into grey fumes that wafted away on the wind, until nothing was left of her but a hollow cry that echoed in her wake.

Aileen fell to her knees. She sobbed in uncontrolled convulsions, striking the ground with her fists.

At once, Moirin sank to Aileen's side, arms wrapped around her, holding her, cradling her.

"She's gone," Aileen cried. "I cannae feel her inside anymore."

"I know. I can't either," Moirin said through her own tears.

"She's left us," Aileen sobbed. "She's left me. I'm all alone. I have no one."

Moirin hugged Aileen close as she cried and swayed back and forth. "You're not alone, love. Not ever. You have me. Always."

*   *   *

Jilly staggered back from Moirin and Aileen, motioning for Lluck and Carl to do the same. They started off into the clearing, which was now, well, clearing. Her arm ached, and she leaned against a tree to take a few deep breaths. As she glanced down at the wand in her hand, she remembered.

"Granny!"

She looked around in haste and panic. She darted into the trees, looking for any sign of her mentor.

"Granny! Where are you?"

She heard no answer, but a moment later, spied someone slumped against a tree.

"Granny!" she whispered.

She ran to the old woman and knelt beside her.

"Hello, dear," the venerable witch looked up and gave her a weak smile.

"Oh, thank goodness! And thank you so much! You saved my life, and we did it! We stopped Aeval, and I think Balor is gone, and the Fomorians are fading away! It's amazing!"

"That's wonderful, dear, and I'm not surprised. Not in the least. I always knew you and that strange lot of friends of yours could save the day if you really put your minds to it. You've proven yourself to me, and that makes what I have to do that much easier." She coughed.

"What do you mean, what you have to do?" Jilly's stomach tightened.

"Oh, that blast from Aeval was pure, dark Fomorian magic, not the kind of thing to toy around with. It would have killed you, but I couldn't let that happen. Not when we were so close. So, I made a decision." She coughed. "It was the right one."

"What are you talking about?" Jilly's eyes watered. "You're fine! Aren't you?"

Granny clutched at her breast and shook her head. "No dear.

I'm not. That blow was fatal, I'm afraid. It's only sheer willpower and bloody-mindedness that's kept me around this long! But I had to see, I had to know you were ready. And now I do."

"But," Jilly cried, "you can't go! I'm *not* ready, I can't do this without you!"

"Oh, you can," Granny put a gentle hand on Jilly's face. "And you will. You've already shown that you don't need me around to work magic. And you're only going to get better!" She coughed again, taking more time to recover, and steadied herself against the tree.

Jilly squeezed her hand. "I don't want you to go!"

Granny smiled. "But it's not up to us, is it, dear? Even the wisest and most powerful are still subject to fate. That's something your friend Qwyrk has learned today, too, I think. But I won't leave you completely. I can still stop by from time to time to check in on you, rather like the martial arts wizards in those science fiction films that are so popular. You haven't seen the last of me!"

Jilly smiled and wiped tears from her eyes.

"Don't cry child. I'm very old, and it's time for me to rest. You have my wand, you have my books, and you'll have my home when you turn eighteen. It's all been arranged. In the meantime, keep up your studies, but also, keep up with your art. Magic is all fine and dandy, but you need diversions. I've been quite partial to knitting and gardening over the years. It's good to keep one's mind sharp with new challenges."

She lapsed into another fit of coughing. Jilly's heart was breaking, despite Granny's hopeful words.

"I'm tired, so tired," Granny whispered. "I'm going to close my eyes in a minute, but I want you to do something."

Jilly nodded. "Of course, anything."

"There's a little girl out there with her mother. Her name is Ashanti, and she is bursting with potential power. When she's ready and when her mother approves, I want you to befriend her, take her under your wing. The two of you might one day have to save the world yourselves, so you'll need to be ready."

Jilly forced back a sob and nodded. "Of course, I'll go see her."

"Good." She took Jilly's hand. "Now, I'm going to rest. Let me remain here. My form will find its way to where it needs to go."

Jilly nodded again, a new wave of tears overcoming her. "Goodbye, Granny."

"Goodbye, dear one, but not a final farewell. Not for a while."

"I love you."

"And I love you, child."

Wiping away tears, Jilly squeezed her hand, kissed her on the forehead and stood up. She took one last look, and then turned and ran to the clearing, knowing she couldn't bear to watch.

*　　*　　*

Qwyrk groaned, reeling from the awful pain in her side. No, it was more like a burning sensation. Maybe? Human pain was odd and so different from what she'd experienced in her Shadow form. Just as unpleasant, but it hurt... more? She managed to sit up a little, but dizziness struck her. "Bollocks!" she swore. "Being human kind of sucks!"

"Qwyrk!"

She looked up to see Holly stumbling toward her. Holly fell to her knees, lifted Qwyrk up gently, and cradled her in her arms, kissing her head.

"Oh, my darling, my love!" Holly held Qwyrk and cried. Qwyrk's own tears rolled down her cheeks as she reached up to return Holly's embrace, but she found it all quite painful. She winced and closed her eyes.

"How do you feel?" Holly gazed at her with concern.

"Honestly, I've got Balor's blood all over me, which is disgusting, and I think I might have a broken rib or two. And maybe I have a really bad bruise," Qwyrk said. "That's a thing humans get, right?"

Holly laughed in between sniffing. "Well, if that's all it is, we'll have you patched up in no time!"

"No, no, I don't think you understand." Qwyrk grinned a little. "The pain is excruciating. I might even pass out, which I've never done before, but it seems like a thing I might do now? So, if I'm to recover properly, I'm going to need all of your care and attention. For days. Maybe even longer."

"And you'll have it! I shan't let you out of my sight." Holly half-laughed and half-cried, as she kissed Qwyrk's head again.

"Will you hand-feed me in bed, and give me massages and candle-lit bubble baths, and tell me I'm magnificent and gorgeous and brilliant?"

"All those things and more." Holly pulled her closer. "We'll even use one of your wretched bath bombs: 'Bewitched, Lathered, and Bewildered,' or whatever!" She hugged Qwyrk.

"I like that... ow!" Qwyrk blurted out. "Careful, I told you I'm in a delicate state at the moment. My condition could take a turn for the worse at any time. Requiring even more of your attention."

"Tell me something." Holly narrowed her eyes. "Are you going to do this every time you get your arse kicked in a fight from now on?

Because at the moment it's rather adorable, but I could see it being quite irritating if it becomes a regular thing."

"Wait, are you suggesting that me getting my arse kicked is a regular thing?"

"Well, you don't have the best track record, it must be said."

"I'm bold, and I take risks!"

"Which often end badly for you, case in point. You're not a tank anymore, love, so you'll have to modify your behavior just a bit. Maybe a tad more looking before leaping?"

"Fine, but I can still complain when I'm hurting, can't I? And maybe some other times, too?"

"Of course, darling, and I'll be here to listen to all of it." She leaned in and kissed Qwyrk, who decided she was more than willing to set aside her fishing for sympathy if it meant more Holly love and care.

Qwyrk sighed, looking at herself. "Damn it, I really do need a bath!"

"You and me both, darling!" Holly kissed her again.

CHAPTER TWENTY-FIVE

Jilly wandered into the still-hazy clearing. An odd mix of Templars, creatures that looked like Blip, Nighttime Nasties, and even some Darkfae, were all chatting with each other in mixed groups. It was one of the strangest things she'd ever seen, but nothing surprised her anymore.

In the distance, she saw Star Tao, trembling. Before she could react, she saw a bright, silvery light shoot forth from the top of his head, straight up into the sky, where it dissipated. Scáthach, presumably, had left him.

"Blimey," he said, "that was... intense."

"You did it!" She ran to him and embraced him. "You channeled again!"

"Yeah, and she really helped," he said. "Like, she gave Qwyrk and Holly the extra mystic boost they needed. Nice one!"

Jilly spied Dill and Chives in the distance, standing like watchful hawks near an African woman and a little girl.

"Look, I need to go chat with someone," she said, "but we'll talk about it soon, all right?"

"Yeah, no worries, cheers. I'm gonna bask in the moment."

"You do that! You've earned it."

She hurried over to Dill and Chives, with a smile and a greeting.

"Excellent to see you in good health, Ms. Pleeth," Dill said (or was it Chives?).

"You too," she said, delighted. "Everything's good here, then?"

"The enemies appear to have been vanquished and banished back to their realm," Chives (or was it Dill?) said in his typical, monotone voice. "We are simply overjoyed with the outcome."

"Uh... I can tell."

She turned her attention to the child. "Are you Ashanti?" The girl smiled and nodded. "My name is Jilly, and I was told to come meet you. I think we're going to be friends." She looked up at Adjua. "If that's all right with you."

To her relief, Adjua nodded and smiled. "Yes, when the time is right, you will be most welcome."

"Good, great, thank you. Oh, I'm Jilly, by the way." She extended her hand.

"Adjua," she shook Jilly's hand. "Qwyrk has spoken highly of you, so I know I can trust you."

Jilly's stomach tightened. "Have you seen them? Qwyrk and Holly? What happened?"

"They clearly have been successful in banishing Balor," Dill (Chives?) said, "but as we are all now just regaining our bearings, no one has yet searched for them."

Jilly looked around and spied the dark smoke rising from a raised outcropping in the distance.

"Look!" Ashanti exclaimed with glee, grabbing Jilly's hand and pointing to the smoke, which began to clear.

"What?" Jilly asked. "What is it?" She knelt down to Ashanti's level and looked in the direction her new friend indicated, seeing Holly holding Qwyrk and kissing her.

"Auntie Holly and Auntie Qwyrk are all right and they're in love!" Ashanti jumped up and down with excitement.

Jilly laughed, relieved. "Yeah, they are. It's brilliant isn't it?"

"Will they go and live together and be happy, now that the Balor monster is gone?"

Jilly put an arm around Ashanti. "Honestly? I think they will!"

"And can I go and see them?"

"Yeah, I think they'd like that. You and your mum both."

"Indeed, my darling." Adjua knelt and embraced her. "They've saved us all. We'll visit them often, I promise."

Ashanti squealed with delight.

*   *   *

Penelope stumbled up to the site of the smoking ruin. Thick, black, choking smoke clouded her view and stung her eyes. She batted away the fumes with her arms and strained to find the source. Her heart pounded, and she didn't dare to hope. As the smoke cleared a little, she caught sight of something. No, someone. She gasped. Lying amid the pile of ash and blackened rubbish was...

"Winston!" She rushed to him. His clothes were charred and in tatters and his face looked rather like he'd stuck his head up an unswept chimney. He sat up, appearing quite confused.

"Penelope?" he asked as she slid down beside him and put her hands on his shoulders.

"Yes, Winston, oh, my dear Winston, it's me. You were right! You were right about the spear, it worked."

"So that wasn't just my imagination. I really did communicate with you!"

She nodded. "Yes, you did. I heard every word in my head. Somehow."

"How utterly remarkable! This whole experience has been nothing short of extraordinary. Do you realize that we now have absolute proof of other orders of sentient beings, living among us and in extra-dimensional realities? Why, this changes everything! The entirety of human mythology may well have its basis in fact! This is perhaps the most extraordinary discovery of all time! Why, the academic papers alone that will be written are simply—"

"Winston?" She kissed him, which shocked her as much as it probably did him. "Just for once, shut up!"

*   *   *

Qwyrk staggered back down to the clearing, her arm over Holly's shoulder, supported ever so gently. Ahead of them she could see the entire array of their friends, plus quite a few others, including Templars, Nasties, jirry-jirries, and even Darkfae.

"Qwyrk! Holly!" Jilly bolted toward them.

"Mum!" Lluck rushed to Holly and wrapped his arms around her.

Qwyrk smiled as her young friend rushed up to hug her. Holly did the same for her son.

"Careful, love! I'm a bit fragile right now," Qwyrk cautioned.

Jilly gave her a light hug. "You're all right, you're both here, and it's amazing and... hang on," She let go and gave Qwyrk a surprised look. "Why are your ears round?"

Qwyrk sighed, just now realizing that her head covering had slipped off. "It's a long story, love. And we'll tell you all about it, I promise. But let's go see everyone else first?"

Jilly nodded and walked down with them, holding Qwyrk's hand. In the main clearing, their friends had gathered, exchanging a round of greetings, hugs, and salutations, as each tried to catch the other up on what had happened.

Qwyrk was relieved that no one else asked her about her ears. They all seemed content to know how Balor had fallen, and Qwyrk was more than happy to explain.

"Turns out would-be gods have nadgers as sensitive as any bloke!" she said with a grin. "After that, it was all down to the spectacular efforts of our dear Holly!"

"Oh please," Holly looked embarrassed. "It was teamwork, one hundred percent!"

"Of course it was, Beti," Vishala smiled, stepping up to give her daughter a hug. "You and Qwyrk have saved us all. Never have I been more proud of you!"

"Thank you, mother. That means the world to me."

Mango and Minty slunk up to Holly in their now-dented armor, and spent a good amount of time rubbing their faces on her calves.

Vishala stepped back and regarded her daughter with a look of suspicion. "Something seems, different about you. Was it Fayette? Did she do something to you?"

Holly frowned a little, and Qwyrk worried that she was being put in an awkward place. "It's a very long story, mother. I'll tell you all about it soon, but for now, I just need to rest. Qwyrk is hurt and I must see to her."

"Qwyzz can help me. He'll know what I need," Qwyrk interrupted with a white lie before Vishala could offer up her well-intentioned assistance.

"Very well." Vishala asked, putting a hand on Holly's face.

Qwyrk turned her attention away from those family matters, and her gaze fell on someone else, someone she'd threatened to pound into the dirt not long ago. Blip started toward her, but his expression didn't reveal his thoughts.

"So, you didn't betray us, then?" Qwyrk asked.

"Hell's belles, girl, no, I most certainly did not!" He crossed his arms, indignant.

"Then what the bloody hell were you doing?" Qwyrk burst out, which made her side hurt again, but she didn't care. Holly joined them and put a gentle, caring hand on Qwyrk's back.

"I was on a secret mission," he answered, "to infiltrate the suspected traitors' den and learn their plan. We discovered early on that we didn't have the power to stop it beforehand, but at least we found out where it would occur. So, I informed my colleagues, and thus they came. We knew it might well be a suicide mission, but we had to try."

He turned to Jilly. "You see, when I told you I was meeting with my fellows, that was not a lie, but it was not to plan a reunion, it was to train and prepare for this battle."

"So, you really were a spy," Qwyrk shook her head. "Bloody hell."

"I told you that I engage in espionage on occasion!" Blip looked both offended and smug.

"Yeah, all right, sorry about that. You and your lot did good tonight. No, not just good. You did brilliant."

"Thank you. And... I am dreadfully, terribly sorry," Blip said, his tone becoming solemn. "But I couldn't tell you. I couldn't tell anyone. There was a very good chance that they were following me in this world, so I had to keep up the ruse, no matter how much, um—"

"How much what?" Jilly asked.

"No matter how much it hurt me to do so! Do you think I enjoyed deceiving you, Ms. Pleeth? Pretending to threaten you? Allowing you to think I was some perfidious traitor? I despised it! And I hate myself for it. I probably always will. Especially for what it might make you think of me, and you, young man."

Jilly's cool demeanor started to warm, and Star Tao smiled a knowing, relaxed smile. "I never doubted. I knew you was up to something," he said with a nod. "I bow to your divine cleverness, my lord!"

"Blip..." Qwyrk said as she was about to apologize, trying not to let Star Tao turn this into a pseudo-spiritual experience, but a veritable beau monde of jirry-jirries (Qwyrk would later learn that this was, in fact, the correct term for a group of them) now approached.

"Splendid, simply smashing!" the bullfrog at the lead and wearing a red velvet Regency coat and sporting a waxed mustache declared. "Well done all around. A capitol outing, I'd say!"

"Um, thank you," Qwyrk managed. "And you are?"

"Oh, do forgive me!" he bowed with a circling of his wrist. "Percival Paxton Pritchard Periwinkle IV, at your service."

"Enchanted, I'm sure," Holly said. She leaned towards Qwyrk and in to whispered, "Goddess, he's exactly like Blip!"

"Yeah, there're hundreds of them, maybe thousands... lovely, eh?"

"We shall have to have a celebratory drink, dear Peri," Blip said, slapping him on the shoulder, "a fine brandy would be in order, methinks."

"I'm rather more partial to a good single malt scotch myself," Periwinkle answered.

"A jirry-jirry after my own heart," Holly beamed.

"I think a good Armagnac might be more appropriate under the circumstances," another announced as he strode up. He resembled a tree frog and addressed Holly and Qwyrk with a bow. "Thomas Tancred Torsby Tottenham Senior, simply charmed to make your acquaintance."

"And we yours." Holly gave him a slight curtsy and flashed a quick look at Qwyrk.

"Montague Marmaduke Montgomery Malmesbury the Younger, ever yours," another spoke up, this one resembling a badger. "And fine Champagne is the only appropriate libation for such a stupendous occasion, Bernard!"

Blip smiled. "I'm almost inclined to agree with you, Monty. This time, perhaps."

"Arthur Archibald Algernon Astor II honored," yet another—a porcupine—addressed Qwyrk and Holly. "But gentlemen, don't discount a well-aged Bordeaux."

"Wallace Ward Wilford Winklebottom, Esquire, a true pleasure." This one was another variety of frog. "Methinks a quality English gin would also be a libation worthy of such a mesmeric and enthralling occasion?"

"Gregory Gervais Gaston Grumblesby," a beaver announced.

"And quality cognac cannot be discounted as suitable for such conviviality."

"Goddess, we're going to be here all night, aren't we?" Holly whispered to Qwyrk.

"Afraid so, love."

*   *   *

Moirin and Aileen stumbled out of the woods arm-in-arm. Moirin saw all manner of strange folk lingering about and in the distance, caught sight of Jilly, Qwyrk, Holly, and the rest of those that she'd once hoped to be friends with. She was pretty certain they would all hate her now.

As they walked, she shuffled past a number of creatures, but she ignored them all, no matter how odd. All save for one who seemed to be blocking her path.

"Do you mind?" she asked, making sure to sound annoyed. "We've had a hell of a night, and I'm in no mood... wait a minute." She squinted. "I know you!"

In front of her was a young man with stringy hair, a skinny body bedecked in a tee-shirt and jeans, and an overall odd demeanor.

"Oliver, right?" she said. "We met after the Leeds gig last spring? What on earth are you doing here?"

He turned to walk away but paused and looked back at her with a knowing smirk. His eyes began to glow yellow. "Did ya ever hear about the time that a pile of Darkfae teamed up with Shadows, humans, Nasties, and faeries to defeat a common enemy? Yeah... that was me and me mates!" He winked at her and walked off.

"Are you bloody kidding me?" She stared after him with an incredulous gaze.

Aileen looked up. She didn't say a word, but her tear-streaked face spoke volumes.

"Come on, love," Moirin said. "Those folks over there? They're good people. We can trust them."

"But they'll never trust us," Aileen said in a hoarse voice.

"Probably. But maybe they'll surprise us?"

*　　*　　*

They were, in fact, surprised.

"Moirin!" Jilly ran up and threw her arms around her. Moirin still didn't know how to handle spontaneous displays of affection and decided they were best avoided.

"And you're Aileen," Jilly said with a smile. "Hi, I'm Jilly, by the way. I'm so glad you're here, both of you."

"Yeah well," Moirin said, "the alternative didn't seem too nice." She glanced at Aileen, who looked exhausted and withdrawn.

"We didn't abandon you, I promise!" Jilly insisted. "Qwyrk and Holly *did* go looking for you, but things got crazy, and they were stopped from getting to you, and then all this happened."

"Yeah, I see that now, thanks."

"Come on, then, you can meet everyone." Jilly motioned to her friends.

"No, I'd rather not. I think we—Aileen and me—we just need to be alone for a while."

Jilly gave her a sympathetic look and nod. "That's fine. Why don't I ask one of the Shadows to take you over to my teacher's house?" She looked sad as she said those words, though Moirin didn't know why. "You can stay there for the night, or as long as you want, actually. I mean, if you're both feeling all right, and everything?"

Moirin nodded. "I think so. We're just wiped out. Nothin' twenty hours of sleep wouldn't fix."

Jilly nodded again. "Wait here, if you want. I'll ask and come back for you in a bit." And off she went.

"Thanks," Moirin called after her.

"So," Aileen half-whispered, "I guess they don't want to kill us, then?"

"Unlike our own kind? No, I think it'll be fine." And for once, Moirin actually believed herself.

*   *   *

"Well, that's that, then, eh?" Horatio looked around with a satisfied smug. "We did it. Somehow."

"Indeed," Bogtrotter said. "I am impressed and will be offerin' you a promotion for yer services."

"Aw, that's brilliant, boss, cheers! But I just did what hadda be done, din't I?"

"Stop bein' humble. I know excellence when I see it, and that was excellent."

"I would blush, were I able."

"Aw, you two are so sweet." Qwyrk limped up to them, having overheard their exchange and managing to extricate herself from the endless parade of formal jirry-jirry introductions. "Maybe go get a room, or something?"

Holly followed close behind, and Qwyrk saw her suppress a laugh.

"For once, your sarcasm falls on deaf ears," Bogtrotter replied.

"This is a truly momentous occasion, and I have so decreed that there will be a celebration unlike any we have seen in centuries. The banquets and drinking will last for weeks. My servitors are already off making preparations even as we speak. In a gesture of goodwill, you are, of course, most welcome to attend at any time during the festivities."

"Tempting, but I'm pretty sure I'll have other things to do, like pull out my eyebrow hairs with hot tongs."

"You could go and do the dance. Just saying," Holly quipped.

"You're not helping."

"Suit yerselves." Bogtrotter shrugged. "But it will be a bash of some magnificence, and you'll regret missing it."

"I'm pretty sure I won't," Qwyrk sighed. "Anyway, I'm injured and have to get it seen to." The pain in her side came back again, and she winced, hugged herself.

"Doesn't seem like you," Bogtrotter said, looking rather confused. "And what's up with your ears?"

"Long story."

"Do I want to hear it?"

"Maybe someday?"

"Fair enough. We'll be buggerin' off, then."

"Cheers lads," Qwyrk said in a moment of genuine gratitude. "Really, I mean it, to both of you. You helped save everything."

"You are most welcome. All in a day's work," Bogtrotter said with a slight bow. "But now, I'm gonna need to rest and relax for a month or two." He turned to leave, with Horatio following close behind, who looked at Qwyrk and shrugged.

"Of course you will," Qwyrk said. "Be careful not to pull any muscles while you're chomping on cricket pies and chugging asp ale."

"I'll do my best."

"You two look after yourselves," Horatio said as Bogtrotter marched off into the trees. "You're my best investment, and I need you both hale and hearty for maximum profit."

"I'm touched and overwhelmed by your concern." Qwyrk faked a smile, but for once, felt glad for this little nuisance.

"Just protecting my assets."

"Yeah, well I'll be kicking your assets if you don't watch it."

"You wound me, madam."

"Not yet, but it's a definite possibility."

Horatio just grinned and hopped into the woods, following his boss.

Qwyrk laughed, despite her aching body telling her not to.

*   *   *

"Look who we found!"

Qwyrk turned to see Sir John and a band of Templars approaching, Qworum limping along with them, and his hands tightly bound behind his back. He wore an amulet of some sort around his neck.

"Why's he wearing a necklace?" Qwyrk asked.

"Oh that?" John motioned. "That's to make sure he doesn't flash away from us and cause more trouble.

Qwyrk said nothing, but walked up to them, not knowing what to feel, or if she should feel. She came face-to-face with him and just stared.

"What?" Qworum mocked. "The valiant, always-sarcastic Qwyrk has nothing to say. No taunts? No puerile jokes? Perhaps your ordeal has taken more from you than you realized. If so, that would be a mercy."

Ah, now she knew what to feel. Qwyrk laid a punch across his jaw, knowing it would hurt her more than him, but she didn't care. It was enough to send him sprawling to the ground, even as pain surged through her fist and up her arm.

He looked up at her with scorn, a trickle of blue green blood at one corner of his mouth. "Did that feel good?" he sneered.

"Actually," she said, "it felt bloody wonderful! I'd be happy to do it again any time."

"No need." Qwyzz stepped forward, looking far angrier than she'd ever seen him. "I can promise you all that this perfidious quisling will not see another free day for the rest of his miserable existence!"

"We'll see," Qworum taunted, as two Templars dragged him to his feet and pulled him back.

"What about the other one?" Qwyrk asked. "Qwyll? You found her too, right?"

John shook his head. "There was no one else."

Qwyrk swore. "That means she's still out there somewhere. And so is Qwota."

"It's not like she can do much harm now," Holly pointed out. "She'll be hunted. They both will."

"Maybe," Qwyrk conceded, "but I've learned never to be confident too soon. If they can, they'll be back eventually to cause more trouble. Maybe in a year, maybe a decade, but I highly doubt we've heard the last of either of them."

"Well, for now, let's just enjoy what we *have* done." Holly put a hand on her shoulder. Qwyrk placed a hand over hers. "Besides," she said with a wink, "that punch looked very satisfying."

"Oh, it was, love. It was."

*   *   *

A while later, the ragged band of victors gathered in a circle, while Templars, jirry-jirries, Darkfae, Nasties, and other assorted folk combed the landscape looking for any foes who might remain.

"So, that's it, we won, then?" Jilly asked.

"We did," Qwyrk said, clinging to Holly for support. "I'm still not sure how we pulled it off, but we did it... again!"

"I, um, I may be able to help with that question."

Qwyrk and the others turned to see a strange sight: a man dressed in tattered black clothing, looking for all the world as if he'd stuck his head up a chimney, being held up by the human woman who'd tipped them off about the spear.

"Penelope, right?" Qwyrk asked.

She nodded.

"And I am Winston Croaf," the man said. "Retired Professor of Applied Folklorics at Dales University. I fear this whole calamity may have been in large part my fault."

He proceeded to relay his entire experience to them, frequently having to be brought back onto topic by his gentlewoman companion.

"Fascinating!" Qwyzz exclaimed with a stroke of his beard. "So, the key was placed where a human would find it, because they needed a human to put it in the lock and serve as a host for Balor."

Winston nodded. "Presumably. I'm still not quite sure why they chose me. It might have been chance, or they might have been stalking me for some time, knowing of my interest in such old tales."

"Oh, I suspect it was deliberate," Qwyrk said. "Qworum and

that lot don't take any chances. And I'm pretty sure it was them you met when you went for your nighttime stroll. They probably examined you to make sure you were a suitable host, and then glamoured you so you'd forget about it."

"But merely possessing the key forged a psychic link with Balor," Qwyzz added, "allowing him to subtly influence you, to make you go to the monolith."

"Indeed." Winston nodded. "Quite a horrid affair."

"What was it like?" Jilly asked. "Being inside of him?"

"It was most peculiar. There was a part of me that still *was* me, but I felt like I kept getting shoved aside, almost sent to sleep. It was only when his attention was distracted that I dared risk trying to communicate with Penelope."

"And it worked." She beamed.

"Thank you, both of you," Qwyrk said. "We wouldn't have been able to do this without your help. Once again, humans save the day!"

"Yeah, we're pretty good at that." Jilly gently nudged her.

"What about the key?" Winston blurted out, as if only just now remembering it.

"Oh, not to worry, good sir," Qwyzz said with a dismissive wave of his hand. "The monolith seems to have been buried when the cave collapsed. My people will take the key, study it, and destroy it if we can. No matter what, Balor and his kin shall never be able to walk this Earth again!"

"Seems a shame to ruin something so nice," Winston mused. "But I suppose it's for the best. How was it even found, do you know?"

Qwyzz shrugged. "Somehow, some of our own determined to assist Balor must have discovered it, maybe even centuries ago, and learned its true purpose. Whether by accident or design, we may never know. But they couldn't use it, so they kept it hidden and bided their time. These past few days have been an important conjunction of stars, planets, and other celestial events, you see. Balor couldn't have been brought back earlier. But any delay and it might not have worked for another century or more. They had this one magical window, and we effectively slammed it on their fingers! Ha!"

Winston sagged little, and Penelope caught him. "I'm fine, my dear," he said. "I'm just a bit weary, that's all."

"A bit weary?" She looked at him with disbelief. "Winston Croaf, you've been through an ordeal the likes of which no other mortal ever has!"

"And fascinating it was!" He answered. "I shall be studying this for years!"

"I need to get him home," Penelope said to the rest of them with a shake of her head.

Qwyzz nodded. "We can see to it that you have swift passage, once we know where you're going."

"Knettles," she answered.

"You live in my town?" Jilly asked. "How nice! I'm sure we'll see you again, then."

"Professor Croaf?" Qwyrk interrupted, feeling nervous and guilty. "How, um, how much were you, you know, connected to Balor's form?"

"A bit. I mean, I could sense what he thought, and to some extent, what he felt."

"Oh. Right. Um, so... sorry about, you know, clocking you in the clackers. It was the only thing I could think of in the moment. Hope it didn't hurt you too much."

"I barely even remember, to be honest." He gave her a

reassuring smile, but Qwyrk wasn't sure she believed him. "In any case, Penelope's right. I'm quite depleted. A good bath and a spot of sherry are decidedly in order!"

"I'll see that you get home, both of you," Qwyzz assured. "In fact, I'll take you there myself. And I have quite the library, Professor Croaf, should you ever wish to peruse it during your research."

"Why, thank you, my good sir, I shall indeed take you up on that!" Winston's face lit up, despite his fatigue. "I must point out, the appearance of some of you is most curious, if you don't mind my saying." He looked at Qwyrk. "In fact, I'd almost be tempted to say that you're... elves?"

"Oh, bloody hell!" Qwyrk rolled her eyes.

*　　*　　*

Qwyzz returned promptly after conveying Winston and Penelope safely back to the mundanity of his Knettles home.

"Positively excellent, my friends!" he exclaimed with a hand clap. "Each and every one of you played a part in this evening's triumph. We could not have accomplished this task without such fabulous teamwork. Why it reminds me of the time that—"

"Qwyzz?" Qwyrk interrupted, charmed by his enthusiasm, but aching. "Not now, mate. We need you to patch some of us up."

"Oh yes, of course. Terribly sorry. I'll be off and at my home preparing remedies for you and Ms. Qwykk. Until soon, my friends!"

"And we shall attend him," Gargula announced, flitting overhead with Babewin. "Adieu for now, my friends... victory is ours!"

Qwyzz waved his hand, and with a sparkle of ruby lights and a faint whiff of port, they were gone.

"Qwypp, can you take the injured on over there?" Qwyrk asked. "Starting with our stubborn and utterly brilliant best mate here?" She smiled at Qwykk, who clung to Qwypp and Star Tao for support. Knowing how painful a Fachan's wounds were, Qwyrk was immensely proud of her. "What you did down there was really amazing, and ridiculously brave."

"It was pretty bloody impressive, it must be said," Star Tao noted with a smile.

Qwykk blushed. "I just wasn't gonna give up, was I? Everything was at stake, so we had to just tough it out."

"Tough it out we did, love." Qwypp held her gently. "And you were pretty bloody impressive, yourself, mate!" She beamed at Star Tao. "Channeling that ancient Celtic warrior goddess and whatnot."

"Yeah, cheers for that," Qwyrk added. "She gave us an edge and a burst of extra energy. It was exactly what we needed."

"That's brilliant!" He said, blushing but smiling from ear to ear. "I'm just glad to get me mojo back. I feel like there could be a whole new series of workshops spun out of this adventure. Like, 'Spears for Fears' or maybe, 'Receiving with Rainsticks.'"

"Oh joy," Qwyrk said to herself.

"Anyway, we need to get those wounds looked at," Qwypp said to Qwykk. "And then I'll come back and fetch *you*, Ms. Qwyrk! You look like you've seen better days."

"That I have, my dear." She held Holly and winced in pain again, struggling not to let it show.

"And then you're gonna tell me exactly what the hell happened to you!"

"It's a date," Qwyrk promised.

"And tell that little Horatio bastard cheers from us, yeah? He's all right. Bye for now, dears!" Qwypp, Qwykk, and Star Tao disappeared in a flash of pink lights.

"Well," Qwyrk sighed, "that's them sorted, then."

Adjua stepped forward, holding a very sleepy Ashanti in her arms. "If I may, I would like for us to go home now. My dearest is exhausted and needs to sleep."

"Of course," Holly said. "Gentlemen?" She looked to Dill and Chives.

"Indeed, ma'am, we would be happy to return Ms. Adjua and her daughter to their home. All seems to have been restored, and the world is again free from danger, so there is no risk in doing so." Dill (Chives?) tipped his bowler hat to them. "Good night to you all. It was a thrilling evening, and we are utterly delighted and giddy with the result. Until soon."

"And might you deliver my mother and our feline friends to a suitable tree, as well, so they can find their way home?" Holly added.

"Of course, ma'am."

"Are you certain, Beti?" Vishala took a step forward. "I am wary of leaving you alone right now."

"I'm fine, mother, and I need to be with Qwyrk and the others while Qwyzz administers his remedies. I'll see you tomorrow and we'll talk, I promise."

Vishala gave her a nod and a lingering glance, and Qwyrk thought she was going to come to them for a hug, but instead, she just gave them both a slight bow, and turned to leave with the others.

"Goodnight, Holly!" One little furry creature, Minty to be precise, rubbed against Holly's leg.

"Goodnight darling." Holly said, reaching down to stroke his sleek head, now un-helmeted.

"Shall I sing you a song from my musical to cheer you before our parting?"

"I'm actually quite cheerful at the moment, love! Tomorrow, perhaps?"

Minty said something, it may have been a grumble, but he nodded and slinked his way back to Mango and Vishala. A final wave from all of them and Adjua, and they were on their way.

"You have to tell her," Qwyrk whispered to Holly.

"I know," Holly nodded, looking after them with a mixture of sadness and dread. "But not yet. Tomorrow?"

"Tomorrow is another day," Qwyrk said with a nod.

"That's a remarkably pointless proverb, isn't it?"

"It does kind of state the obvious."

Lluck wandered up to them, looking a bit apprehensive. "Sorry, what are you doing tonight, mum?"

"I need to stay with Qwyrk, keep an eye on her."

Qwyrk was again flattered and grateful for the care and the attention. It still baffled her that she meant that much to someone else.

"Tomorrow, though," Holly continued, "I must stop by and talk to you. To both of you." She looked back and forth between Carl and her son. "Something rather remarkable has happened, and it's going to change things. Change them in a very big way."

"Change how?" Lluck looked confused. Carl looked no wiser.

"Let's leave it until tomorrow, shall we, darling? I think we're all rather exhausted right now."

Qwypp blinked back into view in a flash of pink lights and the vague scent of patchouli. "Our girl's gettin' some top medical treatment from old Qwyzz at the moment, so I think she'll be fine. At least once her powers come back."

"Brilliant, thank you," Qwyrk said, relieved.

"Your turn now, missy." Qwypp shot her a look.

"Actually, can you take Carl and Lluck home first, love? I can wait a bit longer."

"Yes, please go home, both of you," Holly pleaded. "We'll be fine, and I promise to check in tomorrow." She hugged them and stepped back.

Qwypp nodded and taking hold of their hands, whisked them back to Leeds.

Qwyrk looked to Jilly, the only other friend left, who returned her gaze with one of confusion and upset.

"Qwyrk, what happened? Why are your ears round?"

"Mine are too," Holly said, pulling back her hair to show Jilly.

Qwyrk sighed. "It's a long story, love."

"Well, can I come with you to Qwyzz's so you can tell me? I also need to make sure you're going to be all right, you know!"

Qwyrk smiled. "Of course you can. I'd be happy for the extra company, to be honest. The last twenty-four hours have been mental! Let's wait for Qwypp to get back, and then she can pop us all over there."

"Qwyrk..." Holly tugged at her coat sleeve.

"Yes, my love?" Fatigue took its toll on her, and she felt weak and wobbly. Was this really what being exhausted was like?

"Over there." Holly pointed to a figure standing at the edge of the wood, robed in red, a hooded veil drawn over her grey face. "Guess who? I suppose she wants to speak with us."

"Yeah, won't that be fun?" Qwyrk rolled her eyes.

"That's her. That's Fayette, isn't it?" Jilly asked. "I got a chill just looking at her. Do you need me to come along with you?"

"Thanks, but no. Stay here and wait for Qwypp. I have a feeling this is something we need to do ourselves. Don't worry, we'll be fine. If she was going to off us, she'd've done it already."

With that unconvincing assurance, Qwyrk and Holly left their young friend behind and limped toward the unknown, yet again. They approached Fayette, silent as usual.

"All right?" Qwyrk said, with a wave of her hand.

Fayette seemed to incline her head, just a bit.

"I guess that's all we're going to get," Qwyrk whispered to Holly. "So, that's that, apparently," she said to Fayette. "We won! Hurrah for us! Is there anything else we need to do? To say? To sing? To recite in an epic poem?"

"You still have that Amazon outfit you got from Bogtrotter, don't you?" Holly teased.

Qwyrk glared at her. "It all seems a bit anticlimactic, to be honest." She directed her attention back to the Wyrd one before them.

"All has unfolded as it was foreseen," Fayette said.

"Yeah, well, it would've been nice if you could've told us how it was going to bloody unfold," Qwyrk shot back. "Especially if it was meant to be."

"I both knew it and knew it not."

"Of course you did. Or didn't. Whatever. So, that's it, then? The world is saved, we're human now, and you'll just be off on your merry way?"

Fayette said nothing.

"Of course not. Can't imagine you being very merry, it must be said."

Fayette inclined in a bow to them. "Fare you well, Qwyrk of the Shadows, and Vishala the Younger of the Yakshi. Be content in the lives you have chosen, and follow always your Wyrd. Fight ye not against the fate to which you are bound."

"Honestly, I'd be happy to do no more fighting of any kind for a quite a while," Qwyrk said.

Fayette turned to leave.

"Wait, before you go, I want to know something," Holly said. "Why couldn't I remember any of it before? All those things you told me about my fate, my death? For fifteen years, I only caught snippets, in dreams and faded memories."

"How can one remember that which has not yet happened?"

"You know," Qwyrk said, "that's either really profound, or just kind of ridiculous."

Fayette said nothing. As usual.

"But my mother remembered," Holly objected.

"She is not you."

"I'm never going to fully understand this, am I?" Holly asked with a resigned sigh.

"I don't think you have to, love." Qwyrk took her hand. "It's enough that we won."

Holly squeezed her hand.

"Right," Qwyrk spoke up, "this has all been an absolute barrel of laughs, really, but I think we'll be off now. And, no offense, but I'll be quite happy never to see you again."

"That will depend upon how your Wyrd unfolds," Fayette answered.

"Uh, yeah. So how does it unfold, exactly, then?"

"You would not remember if I told you."

Qwyrk buried her face in her palm.

CHAPTER TWENTY-SIX

Qwyrk and Holly stood in front of the remaining four members of the Shadow council—still seated at their dull and lifeless semi-circular table—summarizing all of the peculiar and astonishing and annoying events that had unfolded over the past few days. Those events, they noted, were the culmination of decades (even centuries) of planning, scheming, secret warring, and other skullduggerous chicaneries on the part of the ancients, the innovators, the Shadow traitors, a few Fomorians and their descendants, and Goddess-knew-who else, with everyone trying to gain the upper hand while staying hidden and pretending to be a part of the magical status quo.

"So, Balor's gone, banished, bollocked, wiped out, sent away, thank you very much Holly and Qwyrk and everyone else and you're welcome, it was a pleasure... except it wasn't," Qwyrk rambled. "It was a nightmare of ginormous proportions that'll have repercussions for centuries, thanks to your inept and utterly clueless handling of the whole bloody thing, not to mention that half of you were actively trying to help that bastard come back."

"There were only two traitors," Qwote interrupted.

"Oh, I'm so sorry." Qwyrk held up her hands in a mock apology. "So, two out of six makes it all right, then? Is there a ratio of treason and plotting to idiotically innocent, past which you actually get off your arses and do something? Does it have to be three out of six? Four? You know what? I don't actually care. You lot can get stuffed, because I'm going to make sure this epic stupidity is made known to everyone in every corner of Symphinity and beyond. The bloody Nighttime Nasties will be joking and singing about it by the time we're done and maybe, just maybe, somebody with some actual ideas will step up and take over from you useless pile of pillocks."

"May I remind you that this council still wields authority over all these matters?" Qwote glared.

"Oh, you can 'remind' us all you like," Qwyrk threatened, "but that doesn't mean I'm going to listen. In fact, given how badly you've cocked this whole thing up, it might be time for all of you to get the thumping you deserve. Public opinion can be a damning thing, as you're about to find out."

"I would watch my tone, if I were you," Qwote warned.

"Oh, I don't think I'll do anything of the sort. See, we fixed your mess for you, we outed your traitors, and we did it all without your approval or guidance." Qwyrk flashed a wicked grin. "And the best part is, thanks to our brilliance in finding a way to actually do something about Balor, we're human now and you can't tell us what to do any more, not even the slightest little thing. So, Holly and I get to be together without your interference, and you can take your outdated segregation laws and shove them up your collective arses!

And after I tell everyone about this crap, they'll probably want to shove the whole idea up your arses, too."

A worried look fell over Qwote's face. "Qwyrk," he implored, his tone changing, "understand that the law against interbreeding was created with the best of intentions, to prevent this very thing, the re-emergence of the Fomorians."

"Yeah, and that worked out real well, didn't it? You're all a bunch of tossers, propping up outdated laws so you don't have to deal with any real issues, always hoping you can string things along for a century or two longer with no change, but guess what? Things *are* changing, and you're bloody well not going to like it."

"What she said and more," Holly chimed in. "You lot are literally everything that's wrong with our worlds and why they're falling into decay. Bored beings with centuries of time on their hands and no practical ideas at all about how to bring about good changes. Qwyrk and I never should have had to do what we did, but we did more this week than you have in years. You should be on your knees thanking us and offering us seats on your precious council."

"Yeah, I'll pass on that, but you're all a bloody disgrace," Qwyrk added. "You had actual traitors sitting here, literally right in front of you, and you couldn't even see them for what they were. So, it's my honest pleasure to tell the remaining lot of you to go shag yourselves. By the time we're through, you're going to be sorry you ignored this danger for so long."

"We could stop you," Qwote warned.

"Yeah, I thought you might say that," Qwyrk answered. "But see? Like I said, you can't touch us, now that we're human. Funny that."

"And there's nothing in the laws anywhere that says that the prohibition on Shadows harming humans only applies to those born as humans," Holly added. "Believe me, we checked. If you try to hurt us in any way, try to silence us, try to intimidate us, the full power of your own laws will come down on your heads like a hammer, and you'll likely spend many decades in your own prisons. But, please, do feel free to try to stop us. I'd so love to see what happens."

The council members fell silent for a short while, exchanging uncomfortable looks and low murmurs.

"Very well," Qwote said in a contrite voice. "You may go, and we will endeavor to work to amend certain laws and regulations. Perhaps it is time to reconsider some of these matters. But do not think in your smugness that you can simply overturn centuries of tradition and established precedent in a matter of days, or even months. If we move too quickly on this, it could damage the social order, and if you push too hard, there will be consequences."

"That's sounds like a threat, Qwote, old lad," Qwyrk shot back.

"Not a threat, merely advice. You are toying with the deep structure of an ancient society, one that has lasted precisely because of its unwillingness to change quickly. You've both seen this in your own long centuries of life. Would you undo that all, for the sake of your own grudges?"

"Not undo, simply, as you say, amend," Holly answered. "Change is essential to any kind of vital life, and for all your wrong-headedness, the threats we've faced together have shown just how vulnerable a fossilized culture can be." She took Qwyrk's hand to show them the ward no longer worked.

"We will take your words under advisement," Qwire said, sounding more chastened. "Now, I recommend that you leave, before the ill effects of our world take hold on you. As you clearly enjoy pointing out to us, you *are* mortal now, after all." Her tone was icy and the way she said "our world" was obviously meant to hurt them, to let them know they were no longer a part of it. It stung Qwyrk, but she'd never let them know it.

They turned to leave. "Should we flip them off again?" Qwyrk asked Holly in a hushed voice.

"It seems rather unnecessary at this point," Holly whispered. "I think we've given them enough of a telling-off for now, and I do need to visit my mother." She look back. "But I'll happily leave the decision up to you."

The members of the council rose and filed out of the entrance at the back of the chamber, all save one. Qwalm approached them, a repentant expression on his face.

"Qwyrk," he said in a quiet voice. "Before you leave, I just want to say..."

She regarded him with a skeptical glare.

"I'm... sorry, for being so rude, for acting childish, for doubting you. I let my own anger blind me, my own jealousy cloud my judgement, and I failed to see Qworum's treason, even as it stared me in the face. I think I knew for a long time that something was wrong, though I wouldn't allow myself to believe it. But you saw the real danger. The two of you saved us all. Thank you."

"Well, it's what we do," Qwyrk said. "While you lot are sitting here on your bums, we're out there, doing the detective work, gathering clues, fighting the fights, taking the punches. A little more faith in the work of those in the field would go a long way toward repairing trust, just saying."

"Perhaps in future, as we try new ways of doing things," he said, "the council might need your services again? Both of you, I mean. Having human allies with your knowledge and experience could prove invaluable. I should be very grateful for your help and would support using your assistance, wholeheartedly."

"Maybe?" she shrugged. "Let's just wait and see, shall we?"

"Best of luck to the two of you." He bowed slightly and turned to walk away.

"Qwalm?" Qwyrk called out after him. He turned to look back at them. "We'll keep it in mind. Oh, and you're still a twat. Just saying."

He turned and walked away without another word.

Qwyrk and Holly looked at each other and burst into uncontrolled laughter.

"Come on," Qwyrk said, taking Holly's hand again, "let's get out of here before we really *do* start going mental."

"It's a bit late for that, I'm afraid," Holly answered.

*   *   *

Holly sat for some time, regarding Vishala, as they made small talk over tea. Her mother's face was by turns stern, softening, pleasant, annoyed, and back to stern again, or was it still annoyed? But something shifted, and she seemed to know that Holly was struggling, in that way that mothers do. She looked straight at her daughter and spoke in a soothing voice.

"You seemed troubled, child. Tell me, what is wrong?"

Holly fidgeted, she glanced around the sitting room, she hoped one of the finicky felines would make a sudden appearance and distract them for a while: Mango with a sad and epic tale of starvation, or Minty premiering the latest hit from his upcoming musical, all so she could put off saying what she needed to say.

"Come, it will be better if you eat something first," Vishala added, bringing her attention back to the moment. "All things improve with food in the belly, as my grandmother used to say."

"Mother, please, I don't need to eat. I just need to talk. It may be the most important thing I've ever had to tell you, and that's saying something."

"My child, what is it? What troubles you?"

Holly took Vishala's hands. Her own were shaking.

"There's no way to say this that will make sense, so I'm just going to come out with it."

"What happened? Did things with Qwyrk not last? Oh, my darling, is that what you must tell me? Did she leave you after all that? Did she break your heart? Oh, I will have words with her!"

"Oh no, mother, that's all fine. We're fine. Sort of. I mean, that's part of what I need to tell you, because it concerns her, as well. She and I... we had to do something, in order to stop Balor."

"Do something? What something? What did you do?"

"We had to come up with a way to stop him, and we did, well, Qwyrk did, and I went along with it. We went back to Fayette."

"What?" Vishala recoiled. "You know that seeress is dangerous! Her words are tricks, she folds many meanings into them, truths so hidden that they may as well be lies. One can ponder their meanings for ages and still not understand."
"Yes, I know, but we had no other choice. She offered a way to fight Balor and the ancients, to win. We entered her pool, and we were judged to be worthy."

"Worthy? What do you mean?"

"It granted us what we needed to defeat Balor, but there was a price. Actually, the price was what we needed to defeat him."

"I do not understand. Beti, what are you saying? What is this price?"

Holly sighed. She could barely look her mother in the eye. "There was a prophecy. In order to destroy Balor and stop him from ever entering the mortal realm again, one needed be from magic but not of it. The only way we could do that was to give up our magical essences and become mortal, to literally no longer be 'of' magic. And so... we're not. Not anymore, I mean. We're human now."

"What do you mean, you are human now?"

Holly sighed again and pulled back her hair to reveal one of her ears.

Her mother squinted. "Beti, what is this? Is this some joke? A trick for Samhain?"

"No, mother. It's very real. And a rather complex story, I'm afraid. If you'll indulge me, I'll try to explain."

And explain she did, telling her mother as best she could about the strange events that had led her to this unexpected outcome, to this twist of fate. She left nothing out, she gave nothing a sugar coating, but told the elder Vishala the whole apocalyptic, horrid, and absurd story.

"I did what I did because I had to, Amma." Her voice wavered as she struggled not to cry. "We had no other choice. We were running out of time. We had to defeat Balor and stop the Fomorians from claiming the mortal world, probably even our world."

She took Vishala's hand across the table. "But more importantly, I did it for Qwyrk, and I'd do it again, a hundred times. I love her with all my heart, and I know it was the right thing to do. Whatever time we have left to us now is precious, and we want to share it together. I hope at the very least, you can understand that."

Vishala was silent for a while. She stood up and paced about the room. Holly said nothing else but had a sinking feeling that she'd broken her mother's heart. Waiting for her response was unbearable. Where were those cats? A jaunty dance number about a door being closed would be very welcome right about now.

Finally, the elder Vishala sat back down and gazed at Holly for a moment. "When the Erlking came to your father all those centuries ago and told him that he wanted you for his own, like some cheap trinket or a piece of property, your father was furious. He came to me and raged about how horrible and vile that creature was. He said you were his treasure, and he would never betray you for anything. He said the same of me and told me he loved us more than his own life and would die to protect us. There was a fire in his eyes, a light of hope and goodness and devotion." She placed a hand on Holly's cheek.

"I see that light in your eyes now, my dear daughter. If you truly love Qwyrk, then yes, you have made the right choice, the only choice you could make. And knowing how happy your father was with us before the end, how could I deny that same happiness to you by not giving you my understanding? My blessing? It seems that by the hand of destiny, you were meant for Qwyrk and she for you, even if that means giving up your life here and... leaving me." She paused and tears welled up in her eyes. "I am sad, very sad, but I am also glad for you. It seems you have found your suitor and your warrior at last. Your joy is mine, so go and be with her. Be happy in each other's love, and may Kubera bless you and be with you always." She leaned in and kissed Holly's forehead.

"Thank you, Amma, thank you ever so much." Holly's struggle to hold back tears failed. "Her love and your blessing mean the world to me." She wrapped her arms around her mother, who drew her into a tight hug and held her.

"I know, my child, I know."

And Holly knew she did.

"But..." Vishala's face became a bit more serious as she broke away and sat back to observe Holly, even if there was a hint of humor in her eyes. "Wherever you two live, I'm going to visit and make proper food for you! You have to keep up your strength, especially if you are no longer Fae! And Qwyrk is very irresponsible, running about and starting fights with ancient gods and their minions. It leaves you open to attack. You'll need me to keep an eye on things and make sure that you don't fall into danger again! You'll need to train extra hard. But most important, you'll need my food! She's so thin! And you are, too! Maybe now that she's no longer a Shadow, she will eat properly."

Holly laughed. "We'll be delighted to have you as our guest, anytime you like, and we'll eat every last bite." And this time, she really meant it.

* * *

Moirin sat on a park bench in North Leeds, checking her phone, trying to pass the time. She looked up every half-minute or so, but her attention kept being drawn back to the insipid small screen in her hand and all the useless crap that flooded it daily. She kind of liked it and sort of hated herself for that. But today, she had more on her mind, and she grew disillusioned.

"She's not coming," Moirin said with a disappointed sigh, scrolling and feeling rejected. "Probably had something better to do than—"

"Hey, sorry I'm late!"

Moirin looked up to see a smiling Aileen jogging up to her, looking lovely in a long grey coat and red scarf, her wild hair unbound. Moirin found herself... smiling back? An unusual reaction, to be sure.

"Hey! No problem," Moirin lied. "I'm just wasting my time on this little idiot box." She turned it off and put it away in her bag. "So."

"So," Aileen said as she sat down and they hugged, which Moirin found far less awkward than she feared. Aileen seemed her usual, cheerful self, even more so now that her links with Aeval had been severed for good.

"I've just been chattin' with Holly and her boy," Aileen said. "I felt like I owed her an apology for deckin' her back in Newcastle."

"That's good of you, but it wasn't really you."

"I know, but I still felt bad. She's a good lass. Anyway, it's all fine now."

"I'm glad. How, um, how are you doing with it all?" Moirin felt nervous about bringing up their ordeal. "It must be quite the adjustment after, you know, having all that banshee power running through you for a fair bit. I mean, in my case, it wasn't all that long."

"It's strange," Aileen said. "While it was happenin', I loved it. I felt strong for the first time in my life, and I couldn't imagine bein' without it. But now, I feel like I was a drug addict, or something, and I don't want it back. Not ever. My head's clearer than it's been in ages, and I'm not havin' bad dreams anymore."

"Me either. Seeing Aeval in my head was creepin' me out. I'm glad she's gone. Good riddance!"

"Aye, good riddance!"

"So... are you going home? To Scotland, I mean?"

"I don't have a home. Like I said, my mum died after I was born, and my dad's a useless arse of a drunk. It's why I left, and I'm not goin' back. I never want to see him again. So, I'll have to go somewhere else. How about you?"

"Well, I got kidnapped by kobolds as a baby and never knew my real parents. And the brother I adored? I volunteered to forget about him, and then found out he was dead after I finally remembered him. So, yeah, I'm just as much of a mess. We're quite a pair, eh? Two homeless ex-banshees."

"Well, I was gonna tell you. Holly wants to help us out. She told me she has piles of faery gold and wants us to get on our feet again."

"That's very kind of her, but she's already helped me. I feel guilty accepting more, though I must admit, I wouldn't say no to a bit of a boost. So, what will you do, then?"

Aileen looked down, as if nervous. "I was kind of hopin' that maybe, you know, we could stick together?" She looked up. "Bein' that we're former keening women now, and all that. Look out for each other and all. I mean, I'm... fond of ya, like I said. That much was true, anyway. And seein' as we don't have anyone else, maybe we could be there for each other?" She offered Moirin her hand.

Moirin smiled and took it. "You know what? I'd like that, really."

"You would?" Aileen's expression brightened.

"I would!" She squeezed Aileen's hand, and they gazed in silence at each other for a moment, before Moirin looked away, embarrassed. "So, um, we could pick a new place to live. We could stay up north, or move south, whatever. I have to get back to the band soon, but we could share a place together, have adventures. It could be right fun!"

"Yeah, I love that idea! We could decorate a flat all funky and stay up late at night with wine and dark chocolate and bitch about how much the world sucks!"

"Talk about how everything's crap!" Moirin mused.

"Complain about stupid people over ice cream and whisky!"

"I could write depressing song lyrics, and you could give me feedback."

"Make fun of those Fomorian tossers over chips and beer!"

"You're... really into food and alcohol, aren't you?"

"Oh, aye! Two of my favorite things!" Aileen beamed. "Honestly? I love it!"

Aileen laughed and leaned in to kiss Moirin's cheek.

Moirin blushed but laughed too, in spite of herself. "Somehow, Ai, I think this is gonna be great!"

*   *   *

Qwyrk stood at Sutton bank, as she had so many times in the past; something about the place always drew her back. She was happy to be out in the afternoon sun and not scaring the wits out of passersby for once, but thankfully, there were few people out, anyway. Feeling the cold weather was still a new sensation, and she was experimenting with wearing a long black wool coat to keep it at bay, which she had to admit, looked rather fetching. Maybe some of Holly's fashion sense had rubbed off on her after all.

"Hey you."

Qwyrk turned to see a smiling Holly walking up the dirt path toward her. She wore her own long purple coat and grey woolen scarf, one of Qwyrk's favorite looks.

"Well, it's about time." Qwyrk smiled and winked, kissing her as they embraced. "Ow! Careful! My side's still a bit sore. Broken ribs on the mend and all that. Even though Qwyzz patched me up, it's going to take a bit to heal."

"Sorry, darling." Holly stood back to look at her. "And don't worry, I haven't forgotten about that special care I'm going to give you."

Qwyrk laughed. "So, what happened? I need to know!"

"Oh, I thought I might keep you in a state of anticipation for as long as possible," Holly said. "I was actually thinking of not telling you until tomorrow."

"Yeah, pretty sure that's not true. Then again, there's a part of me that believes you," Qwyrk said. "So? How'd it go with your mum? Come on, I can't stand the suspense!"

"Remarkably well. I mean, I shouldn't be surprised. I suppose I'm just used to her reserved and stern manner, but sometimes I forget that underneath it, she has the biggest, warmest heart. She accepts the life we have and gives us her blessing. Oh, and she insists on making food for us at least once a week for the rest of our lives."

"Well, there are worse fates, I suppose," Qwyrk said, relieved. "I'm still not used to this whole 'hunger' thing, I must admit. Three times a day? Every day?"

"At least! But it does make eating very satisfying. You'll see. And her creations are positively mouth-watering when you're in that state. I promise!"

"It's a whole new world for me." Qwyrk shrugged.

"Well, I for one am enjoying sleeping with you—quite literally—for a change."

"Yeah, unconsciousness is really odd, too. It's like being knocked out every night, but not having a headache when you come to in the morning. It's sort of Reverie times ten. Still, waking up and seeing you there next to me is something I'm definitely enjoying."

"Likewise! And it's nice not to roll over and slam my face into your knee because you're sitting up, cross-legged." Holly grinned her sly grin.

"That only happened once!"

"I'm sure it was more than that."

"Anyway." Qwyrk said, ignoring her. "Did she say anything else?"

"Well, she didn't say so out loud, but I've a strong suspicion that she wants to throw us an enormous wedding at some point. Musicians, food, dancers, animals, hundreds of guests, the whole lot. The kind of celebration that goes on for days. I mean, if you're so inclined. It would be quite the grand affair."

"Oh! Um, well, yeah, I mean, I suppose we could, we should talk about that at some point. I mean, I'm not saying it's a bad idea, or anything, not at all. It sounds amazing, but maybe we could get ourselves settled first?"

Holly nodded. "That's my thought as well. I'll let her know not to get too busy with planning just yet. She'll be mildly offended, but she'll understand. And she'll just use the extra time to make it even more lavish."

"Good, that's good. Um, gosh, things move pretty quickly in this world, don't they?"

"I'm afraid so. It's something I've really learned to appreciate from Lluck and Carl. Carpe diem, and all that."

"I guess." Qwyrk looked out over the land below them. "I mean, I understand that, but it's so much to take in. I'm still processing all of it, and I kind of go back and forth about everything. One moment, it seems like this is the best thing I've ever done, and the next, I get overwhelmed, which is kind of where I am right now." She turned back to Holly. "I mean, what if we've really, massively cocked up things for ourselves?"

Holly ran a hand through Qwyrk's short hair and caressed her newly-rounded ear. "We haven't, love. I can't speak for you, but I feel a renewed sense of purpose, of being at peace with the grand scheme of things. I don't know if I could have borne the idea of watching Lluck grow old and die, while I remained pristine and eternal. It just doesn't feel natural, and it would have broken my heart. Yes, the clock is ticking for us now, but that's all right. Let's get on with it and live the best life together that we can. I'm excited to see what happens next, and I'm excited to experience it with you!"

Qwyrk sighed in relief. "You always know how to say the right thing, don't you?"

Holly shrugged. "Well, not *always*, but after nearly a year's experience of being a mum, I'm practically an expert."

She grinned. Qwyrk grinned. They burst out laughing.

"This life with you is going to be quite something, Ms. Vishala," Qwyrk said.

"I do believe you're right, Ms. Qwyrk," she answered, turning and wandering toward the edge of the outcropping to look out at the splendid view.

"It is gorgeous," she said, as Qwyrk strolled up behind her.

"Yeah, it's been my special place for a really long time," Qwyrk said. "If you'd like, it can be *our* special place from now on."

"I'd like that very much. We did have our first date here, after all."

Qwyrk wrapped her arms around Holly's waist from behind and rested her chin on her shoulder, leaning her head against Holly's.

"My dawn," Qwyrk said.

"My evening star," Holly answered.

"My springtime sunset," Qwyrk sighed.

"My warm winter hearth," Holly purred.

Holly hugged Qwyrk's arms, and they gazed out over the autumnal countryside for some time. For once, Qwyrk didn't worry about impending supernatural doom, and instead just savored the moment, and the thought of each new moment together still to come.

"So," Holly said after a lovely silence, "am I ever going to get to see the dance?"

"...Yeah, all right."

*   *   *

"Ms. Pleeth. Jilly." Blip sat on the edge of Jilly's bed, hands clasped. "As we both know full well, your thirteenth birthday is approaching, and as such, my commitment to you must, sadly, soon come to an end. You are becoming a young lady, among the finest I have ever known. And while I hope that I have played at least some small role in your development into said new and remarkable individual, the fact is that you are, I'm quite sorry to say, rapidly outgrowing your need for my presence, even more so than a typical young person might, owing to your talents for magic and the exceptional nature of the events you have endured thus far. And so..."

He paused and looked down. He brought a froggy finger up to his eye, as if to wipe a tear away. He took a deep breath.

"Oh, to blazes with formality!" He looked up at her again to reveal tear-rimmed eyes. "I shall miss you terribly! These past eighteen months have been among the most interesting, exciting, and thrilling I have experienced in an age, and I daresay I will not see their like again. I feel that I myself have grown into a better being than I was before, and your friendship has enriched me immeasurably. I must apologize again for my appalling behavior and duplicity. It was crucial to the mission, but I won't soon forgive myself."

He composed himself. "Now, sadly, I must needs depart, but frankly I do not wish to. And yet I must. 'Farewell! A word that must be, and hath been; a sound which makes us linger; yet—farewell!' Lord Byron wrote that last part, you know. I have discovered a renewed interest in the gothic over these past several months, thanks to that musical ensemble of which you are fond, the Mysterious Matrimony Marmosets."

"Oh, Mr. Blippingstone." Tears filled Jilly's eyes, and she wrapped her arms around him. "I'll miss you, too. Terribly. Do promise me that you'll stop by when you can? I'd be very happy for your company." She couldn't quite believe those words were tumbling out of her mouth. "You could keep me updated on what's going on out there. And maybe I could help you too."

"Of course, my dear, of course! The bonds we have forged shall not be broken by the mere sundering of the compact of master and student. No, we have transcended such a simple, even potentially insufficient, relationship. We have become intellectual colleagues, comrades in arms, and perhaps best of all..." He paused, momentarily choked up.

"Yes?"

"Friends, my dear. Good friends, I should hope."

Blip wrapped his arms around her and squeezed. Normally, his choke-hold, professional wrestling-style hugs were best avoided, but just this once, she made an exception, even if it killed her. And she was pretty sure it would all be fine. And it was.

"So," she said, grinning through her tears, "are you ever going tell me what happened between you and Father Christmas?"

"Absolutely, positively not."

* * *

Sunset on a clear day in Knettles was a perfect time to stand at the castle on the hill and look out over the river, the rail bridge, the trees, and all of the delights this little town offered up, regardless of the season.

"It's something I never get tired of," Jilly said to Qwyrk as they gazed at the pink and orange loveliness filling the sky. "Especially at this time of year."

"It's funny," Qwyrk answered, "I don't know how many sunsets I've seen over the centuries. Quite a lot, I'm sure. But it's odd. I don't think they had the impact on me that they should have. There was always going to be another one, so on any given day, it wasn't all that special. Same for most things, I suppose. But now, knowing that someday I'll run out of them, they feel a bit more—I don't know— real, somehow? I'm not sure that makes sense."

"I think it does. Things mean more when you know they won't be around forever, right?"

"That's it. And somehow, that's more satisfying, too. I can't really explain it better than that, but maybe in time, it'll be clearer for me."

"It's still hard for me to understand," Jilly said. "I mean, beyond the whole magic side of it, how did you manage to even go through with it?"

Qwyrk looked at her. "It wasn't easy, believe me. After I figured out that becoming human was our best plan, I nearly knocked myself out trying to come up with alternatives, but it was the only thing that had any chance of working. I gambled that it would meet the prophecy's requirement—a pretty big risk, I know—but I was right.

I kept remembering back at Hermitage, when Thomas the Rhymer told me a 'price had to be paid.' I didn't know what he meant then, but it seems pretty obvious now."

"And Holly?"

Qwyrk's gaze drifted back to the sky. "She joined me willingly. I tried to get her to change her mind, but she was having none of it. Before her, I can't even remember when someone would have made that kind of sacrifice for me. I don't think I've ever known anyone who would. I'm still not completely sure what to think about it, honestly."

"But, you're both human now. And that means—"

"It means we won't be here forever, just like all of you. At some point, we'll shuffle off this mortal coil and presumably go somewhere else, the Summerlands, I suppose. But don't be sad. I mean, we're not going anywhere for a good while. Qwyzz thinks that because we're from magic, we'll age quite slowly and live for another century or two, or even a fair bit longer. That's not so bad!"

"But you had to give up everything! Your immortality, your 'job,' your home, your life, all of it."

Qwyrk sighed. "I'm old, Jilly. I know I don't look it, but I am. Old and tired. I need a change, I need to feel something new, something different. Holly said it: the clock is ticking, but that's all right, and I'm okay with it. Now, every moment counts for me in a way it didn't before, that it never could. Everything seems more meaningful. Yeah, I'm mortal now, but I get to spend the rest of my life with the woman I love, and that's a blessing I never thought would happen."

Jilly laid her head on Qwyrk's shoulder. Qwyrk wrapped her arm around her young friend and hugged her. After a few moments, Jilly looked up.

"So, what will you do now that you're living in our world?"

"Well, Holly and I will find a home nearby, obviously."

"You're staying here?" Jilly asked, excited.

"Of course! Lluck's still in Leeds. She'd never abandon him after all this. And I've grown quite fond of the area and the people in it." She squeezed Jilly. "We'll probably shop around somewhere out in the country, find a nice a house where we can live quietly and stay out of people's way."

"Is that because you're two girls, and you need more privacy? I'm sorry. I wish things were better. Some people are really hateful and stupid."

"No, it's actually because we both still have loads of ties to magic. It's probably best if we have any issues, that we aren't living right in town."

"What kind of issues?"

"Well, I have some old enemies that might decide to look me up if word gets around about my new not-so-enchanted status. Wouldn't want them making trouble here."

"But what will you do if that happens?" Jilly sounded alarmed. "How will you protect yourselves? I mean, I'll help. I'll kick their arses if they come anywhere near you!"

"You're so sweet!" Qwyrk joked. "But just between you and me, Qwyzz is busy making some workarounds for us on the quiet, like giving me back teleportation abilities and giving both of us a good bit of resistance to Symphinity's magic and spell shock, so we can still pop over there from time to time. Holly can visit her mum, and I can keep an ear to the ground, a non-pointy ear, that is. Plus, she's got her mad fighting skills, and I'm still quite strong, far more than the average human. If Qwyzz just puts all that magic and power into some jewelry or some such that we can wear, we'll be fine, honest!"

Jilly smiled and raised an eyebrow. "Jewelry, eh? Like matching rings, maybe?"

"Yeah, all right, let's not rush things. Holly's mum can't wait for us to get married, but give us a chance to settle in a bit, and then we'll decide when to go that route, fair enough?"

"I suppose." Jilly mock-sulked.

"I promise you'll be the first to know when I do. But, let's not jump the gun, all right?"

"Fine," Jilly said with a roll of her eyes, but a smirk on her face. "You know, I think Star Tao's ordained in some New Age church or other. He'd be chuffed to perform the ceremony."

"Oh Goddess, can you imagine? Instead of wedding bells, it'd be like, wedding didgeridoos. Yeah, no thank you!"

They shared a laugh and looked back out over the river.

"So, what are you going to do now?" Jilly asked. "I mean, everyone's expected to 'do' something for money or some rubbish like that, aren't they? Justify their existence every day, and all that nonsense. Prove they deserve to keep on being around."

"Yeah, that's a bit of a crap philosophy, isn't it? Well, Holly has enough gold saved up to last at least three human lifetimes, so we're good there. And it's easy enough to convert that into human money. She does it all the time. The same folks that take care of that sort of thing can also get us IDs, passports, whatever. We'll be fully human-passing, and no one will ever know we weren't born here as mortals. And if anyone ever does find out, I'm sure there's a spell of forgetfulness that one of our mates can conjure up to make the problem go away."

"Your secret's safe with me!" Jilly promised.

"Plus, we both have all sorts of other skills," Qwyrk continued. "Holly can teach martial arts. She's also got quite the green thumb, so she's thinking about opening a nursery, or some such. And she's apparently quite keen on photography."

"Is she? I had no idea."

"I didn't either! The things you learn about your girlfriend after six months, eh? As for me, I don't know, maybe I'll open up my own private investigation service, focus on paranormal problems, give Dill and Chives a run for their money. A little healthy competition wouldn't hurt."

"Or maybe you could work for them? Be their 'human' contact, or something. You'd be perfect for it."

"Not a bad idea. They might even be able to help me find out what happened to my parents. I need to revisit that whole business again, how and why they just disappeared. In my vision of them in the water, they called to me. Gave me the words I needed to summon the spear. Maybe they're still out there, somewhere?"

Jilly squeezed Qwyrk. "I'll help with that, too, in any way I can."

Qwyrk returned her squeeze, but gently so as not to aggravate her ribs. "Thank you. Maybe this time will be different if we put our heads together, eh? You're quite the smart one, Jilly Pleeth!"

"Yeah, well, you're pretty bright, too. And we geniuses have to stick together, you know!"

"Too right! So, how about you, then? What's on the agenda now that all this end-of-the-world nonsense is finished?"

Jilly shrugged. "I'm going to keep studying magic. Even though Granny's gone, she promised to stay around in spirit form as long as it takes to get me up to speed."

"Yeah, that's a bit creepy, isn't it?"

"Honestly, nothing surprises me anymore. And anyway, I have my art, and I've still got years of school to get through. Oh, and Blip said he'd come round on occasion. Star Tao, too."

"I'm so sorry."

Jilly laughed. "I'm actually looking forward to it, even if Blip did pull that whole secret double agent thing on us."

"Yeah, we still need to have some words about that, him and me," Qwyrk said. "But overall, he's a good sort. I think having him about to watch your back from time to time could actually be a good thing. My back too, Goddess help me." Qwyrk shuddered.

"Heh. Anyway, maybe I'll eventually go to university in Leeds or York, or something, so I can stay here. I want to help Ashanti when she grows up. When her mum thinks she's ready, I mean."

"Taking up the mantle of magical protectors of the North, then? You'll be worthy successors to Granny. We'll be in good hands with you two on the job."

Jilly beamed and looked out again at the sunset over the rail bridge.

"Rrrr!" Qwyrk grunted.

"What is it? What's wrong?"

"Oh, nothing. It's just this whole 'hunger' thing; I'm still not used to it. It's like, one minute I'm going along fine, and then all of a sudden my belly is like, 'Feed me now, you bastard, aarrghghgh!' It's really strange having a body that I don't fully control anymore."

Jilly smiled. "I know exactly what you need: pies."

"Pies?"

"There's a brilliant place just back in town to sort you out. It's a shop with every kind of pie you could possibly want. I go there all the time. Come to think of it..." Jilly paused. "I had one with me and dropped it when I ran from de Soulis and then crashed into you, right down there." She pointed to the river bank. "So, thanks to the magical world and all its rubbish, my first meet-up with you meant I lost a perfectly good meal. You owe me one!"

Qwyrk shot her a look. "I do, do I?"

Jilly giggled. "Come on then, let's go stuff ourselves."

"In a minute," Qwyrk said, turning back to look at the lingering glow of the sunset. "This, right here. It's these experiences that I want to have every day and remember: with you, with Holly, the others. Let's just stay here for a bit? Share a moment together."

Jilly snuggled up next to her again. "Any time, big sis. Any time."

They stood for a while longer, reveling in the last of the pink sky, the chill of the autumn air, and best of all, the warmth and love of each other's friendship. The pies could wait.

ACKNOWLEDGEMENTS

This final trip (for now) into Qwyrk's wacky world was a joy to write, even in saying goodbye. Will some of these characters pop up in other stories? Time will tell...

There are always people behind the scenes who help when one is writing a book of any kind. Thanks to my agent, Maryann Karinch, for continuing to encourage this strange and silly series and for being eager to share it with the world. And thanks again to Armin Lear for providing a home for all four books. We did it!

Special thanks to my always-wonderful partner, Abigail Keyes, for taking a deep dive into these stories and making suggestions to improve almost every aspect of them. She also puts up with me reading them to her, with all the appropriate accents! And thanks again for her amazing editing skills, taking my drafts and correcting the many mistakes I tend to throw into them with abandon.

Thanks to readers past and present, and to reviewers and "blurbists," who have provided useful feedback and have made these books better than I could have made them on my own.

And of course, thanks to Freya, who continues to offer inspiration, guidance, and insight.

AUTHOR BIO

 **TIM RAYBORN** has written a rather ridiculous number of books over the past several years (about fifty!). He lived in England for quite some time and has a PhD from the University of Leeds, which he likes to pretend means that he knows what he's talking about. His generous output of written material covers such diverse topics as music, the arts, history, the strange and bizarre, fantasy and sci-fi, and general knowledge. He's already planning on writing more books, whether anyone wants him to or not.

He's also an internationally acclaimed musician. He plays dozens of unusual instruments that quite a few people have never heard of and often can't pronounce, including medieval instrument reconstructions and folk instruments from Northern Europe, the Balkans, and the Middle East.

He has appeared on over forty recordings, and his musical wanderings and tours have taken him across the US, all over Europe, to Canada and Australia, and to such romantic locations as Marrakech, Istanbul, Renaissance chateaux, medieval Italian hill towns, and high school gymnasiums.

He currently lives in Washington State, surrounded by many books and instruments, as well as with a sometimes-demanding cat. He is rather enthusiastic about good wines and cooking excellent food.

timrayborn.com
timrayborn.bandcamp.com
mastodon.social/@timrayborn
facebook.com/TimRaybornMusicandWriting
twitter.com/Tim_Rayborn

www.ingramcontent.com/pod-product-compliance
Lightning Source LLC
Chambersburg PA
CBHW060240030726
47493CB00024B/1404